# Fearless Magic

The Star-Crossed Series

Volume Three

Rachel Higginson

Fearless Magic
The Star-Crossed Series
By Rachel Higginson

Copyright@ Rachel Higginson 2012

This publication is protected under the US Copyright Act of 1976 and all other applicable international, federal, state and local laws, and all rights are reserved, including resale rights: you are not allowed to give, copy, scan, distribute or sell this book to anyone else.

Any trademarks, service marks, product names or named features are assumed to be the property of their respective owners, and are used only for reference. There is no implied endorsement if we use one of these terms.

Any people or places are strictly fictional and not based on anything else, fictional or non-fictional.

Editing services provided by Jennifer Nunez.

Printed in paperback December 2012 and available in Kindle and E-book format as of December 2012 through Amazon, Create Space and Barnes & Noble.

To Lori Peters, Sandy Wood and Victor Fordyce,
Thank you for your encouragement and instruction.

To Carolyn and your fine-toothed comb,
Thank you for your time and wisdom, but most
Importantly for your patience.

To Zach, you are the greatest man I've ever
Known. Thank you for your support, your sacrifice
And constant words of encouragement.

# Prologue

"Get it back!" The King grew frustrated, shouting at the prisoner. The King had forgotten his poise; he had forgotten the rest of the Kingdom that would bend at his every whim. His brow began to sweat and a purplish, blue vein bulged from his neck, signifying a dangerous spike in the temperature of the room. His angry and violent magic swirled around the prisoner, choking off his supply of oxygen.

"No," the boy, just seventeen, replied simply. His brow, too, was sweaty, his face beaten beyond recognition and his arms tied tightly behind his back, while one shoulder hung awkwardly lower than the other. The smallest smile played at the corner of his lips, infuriating the King beyond what his stubborn disobedience could have ever hoped to accomplish.

"This is not a game!" The King yelled into the face of the defiant prisoner.

The boy was exhausted, both physically and mentally. He had been tortured, beaten and abused repeatedly, but always just to the brink of death, never beyond. He longed for death, that sweet relief, the peaceful afterlife, the great beyond that would end his suffering and finally offer silent rest.

He stayed silent now, even as his King yelled at him, even as the guards beat him. He did not speak. He did not cry out. His bloodied body and broken bones the only friends he had left, the only reminders of the war that was being waged beyond this cell, this four-walled prison of insanity. And of why he would never give up.

"Enough," the King ordered quietly, and the guard took a step back, dropping the strong arm that was about to strike against the boy's face again. "This is dangerous, this game you play," the King stood towering over the slumping child, hundreds of years his inferior. The boy did not look at him. The boy could not look at him, his tired, broken head hung down to his chest, lolling with the effort to keep from slipping into unconsciousness.

"But worth it," the boy spat in a hoarse and pained whisper.

"Is it?" The King couldn't help but laugh, the child reminded him of another he had once tortured, a prisoner arrogant, confident, sure of his cause. But that old man had perished at his own hands and this child would follow the same fate. "Will it be worth it when we find her? When we take the magic from her instead?"

The boy grunted his contempt at the reference to the girl. He struggled to hold his head higher, to sit up straighter. How dare this evil tyrant refer to her.

"Ah, now I have your attention." The King's lips turned upwards in the snarl of an evil man. His eyes darkened and narrowed to ominous slits of suspicion. He had found the right words, the right incentive. "She is being hunted as we speak; it will not be long before we find her. Get the magic back from her and we will leave her alone. She can live out her life; she can be free from us. You have my promise. My word as King, I will pursue her no longer. Just get it back."

The sound that pierced the damp stone walls frightened even the King. The deep, authentic laughter mocked the King and his guards standing around. The small prison cell reverberated in the sound of a child not fooled by empty threats or wasted efforts.

And then suddenly, the laughter stopped, the boys head raised and he stared into the eyes of his King with the passion of a man living out eternity in the splendor of a victory already won. "You are the ones being hunted!" He screamed, shouting through the stone walls of his prison cell, reaching beyond the depths of the pit they had thrown him into, far into the recesses of the castle and reverberating the truth in every ear that could hear. "She will be the one to find you, not the other way around. Your reign is over, the countdown clock has begun. You are the hunted," he finished quietly, with stone cold resolve.

"Remind him that I am King," the King addressed his guards with cruel intention. "Remind him he has no magic, that his life has been left to my will and that I will treat it as
    such." He took off his black, leather, work-gloves with an air of disgust and dropped them at the feet of his prisoner.

He would get what he wanted; it was only a matter of time. He was the most powerful man in the universe and an insignificant child that had been abandoned and left without magic would not stand in his way for long. No, the child's resolve would weaken, his courage would dissipate and his faith in the lost girl would diminish. It was only a matter of time.

He left the prison cell, closing the door to the horrified screams of the boy and found that he was smiling. No, it would not be long. Not long at all.

----

The girl woke screaming into the darkness, her body drenched in cold sweat and her hands trembling from the nightmare. The pain had been too much. The searing, sickening pain that would not quit.

And the man that haunted her, his ominous eyes and determined grin. He would not give up. He would not stop.

But already the dream was fleeting, disappearing into the gray void between consciousness and the sleep state. She tried to grasp on to it, tried to keep the memory sharp, but it was too late. The images were not even memories anymore, just a fuzzy idea that reminded her she was alone.

Completely alone.

# Chapter One

"Where will you go?" Angelica asked quietly from the doorway. I felt her magic as she approached, but refused to turn around and greet her.

I focused on my backpack, packing what essentials I thought I would need and trying to keep the bag as light as possible. I had a long journey ahead of me and I couldn't be weighed down with those things that weren't absolute necessities.

But that wasn't why I refused to turn around and greet the old woman that offered me sanctuary after my grandfather had been murdered, my brother stolen for evil intentions and my friends captured in the name of a depraved justice. After innocent blood was shed and my life ripped into hopeless shreds of misery, she was the only one left to give me a place to stay and help my body heal.

I took a breath, a long inhale of oxygen, closing my eyes and clasping my trembling hands together to steady them. Those miserable thoughts had become my constant companions, the fuel that fed my purpose. But they were dangerous; the burning passion to find justice for those that I loved teetered too closely to the depths of despair that threatened to swallow me whole.

And, that was why I refused to look at the ancient woman standing in the doorway behind me, radiating with concern and emitting the faintest hint of a magic almost completely lost. She was a reminder of a different life, of the family that I held so dearly, destroyed. She was the talisman of a promised hope gone forever, a symbol of the deepest kind of betrayal.

"To see Silas, to find out what he knows." I shook my head quickly, banishing the thought train before the forbidden name, the source of my betrayal, resurfaced.

"And then what?" Angelica pressed, her voice shaky.

When I found Angelica, weeks earlier, half-buried in bloodied snow, and nearly torn to pieces, I thought I would be saying another goodbye. She was left for dead; the Titans had not even bothered to load her old and broken body onto the prison trucks. And, I was too weak from applying the mark of the Resistance on my neck to be of any use. But then, something happened.

Something I still couldn't explain.

The blue smoke appeared from nowhere. The magical wind from

India that fused with my magic months earlier was unexpectedly there, wrapping the near-death woman in its wispy, cobalt folds and lifting her off the ground. I watched on, stunned, but somehow unknowingly in control. When Angelica returned to the cold slush that covered the ground, she was healed.

She was weak, and she lost a significant amount of magic during the battle that night, but she returned from the brink of death by the power of the blue smoke.

"And then I will find my parents," I answered firmly, deciding my course of action exactly at the same time I voiced it aloud.

"Do you think he will know where they are?" Angelica took a careful step into the room, and then walked over to the window looking out towards a wooded area that spread out across the backyard. The trees were still bare, and the remnants of icicles still clung to the stark branches.

When Angelica was finally ready, she suggested we move into Amory's house. I agreed, feeling as though there weren't many other options. But now, with him gone, the house felt more like a ghost town, filled with lost memories and a side of my grandfather I never knew.

I was still recovering from the painful magical ceremony I conducted on myself the night of that fateful battle. I touched my fingers absentmindedly to the still sore imprint on the space of my neck where my jawbone and earlobe met. The imprint had not faded like the other members of the Resistance. Unlike theirs, mine still burned brightly in the sapphire blue that colored my magic.

"I don't know," I replied truthfully. "But it's a start." I turned to her, watching her silently as she stared out into the distance as if waiting patiently for someone to come home.

They weren't coming home.

"It's a place to go," I whispered more to myself than to her. She was nothing but gracious to me, nothing but hospitable in the wake of our shared tragedy. But she had always been kind, even before I betrayed her people.

"And do you know how to find Silas?" she inclined her head to me. The once vibrant violet eyes, now dulled to a deep purple that burned with heart-wrenching sorrow. I looked away, unable to bear both her pain and my own.

"I'll start at the ruins of Machu Picchu," I cleared my throat, trying to banish the pain that wanted so badly to resurface. I was following Avalon's directions, my lost twin, taken away to be sacrificed. Remembering his name alone was enough to send me over the cliffs of sanity into the abyss of anguish.

"And follow the magic...." Angelica whispered the directions more to herself than to me, as if remembering a conversation held in a different time, a different life. "I will watch after Sylvia." She came back to herself and back to the present.

"Thank you," I said simply, not allowing myself to dwell on my human guardian for a second longer than necessary. I swallowed the anxiety that warned me not to leave her alone, unprotected and vulnerable.

I had begged her to come with me, or at the very least to go somewhere else, somewhere where they couldn't find her, somewhere she would be safe. But she wouldn't listen to me.

Sylvia had been broken with grief at the news of Amory's death and Avalon's capture. She had changed. Something had snapped inside of her that warned me she could take care of herself. A dangerous anger had risen inside of her and I was afraid that she was waiting for them to come find her.

A wave of panic washed over me as I weighed the consequences of leaving her behind, but she insisted. She refused to slow me down on my journey or uproot her life in Omaha. We both knew that this part of my journey must be taken alone, but that did not make doing it any easier.

I was glad that Angelica offered to look after her. The happiness that my Aunt would not be completely alone felt foreign and disturbing. Only two weeks earlier, I almost burst with happiness and now the emotion was altogether banned from my body.

"Do you think they'll come after her?" I asked, my voice shaking in part from fear, the other part unadulterated anger.

"No," Angelica assured firmly, turning to look back out the window.

I knew she was lying, she was offering a false truth to comfort me during the task ahead. I took it, accepted it. I didn't have any other choice but to believe her. I let the lie wash over me and bath me in false comfort. Without it, I wouldn't be able to leave. I wouldn't be able to walk forward.

"I have something for you," Angelica confessed, coming out of deep thought. She left the room for a moment and returned with a stack of papers.

I moved my backpack off the bed and onto the floor, and we sat down together on the single bed that was the only piece of furniture in the room. Her hands were shaking as she shuffled the papers about; looking for the one she wanted to start with.

"This is just," she started, holding the papers up for me to inspect, "some legal documents for you to sign, and an ID, passport and a few credit cards. Amory gave these to me a few weeks ago and asked me to pass them along should anything.... should anything happen to him." A tear fell silently from the corner of her eye onto her wrinkled, ashen cheek.

"Thank you," I muttered, trying not to let her grief affect me. I had to be strong. I took the papers from her and looked at the ID and passport, both listing my age as twenty-one. I turned seventeen yesterday, but barely remembered that it was my birthday. Avalon's and mine if he was still alive. Trying to stay focused, I cleared my throat, "And what is the rest of this?"

"Bank papers mostly. Amory named you and your brother as the sole heirs to his estate. There is quite a bit in there, it should be plenty to travel with." She pulled a piece of paper from the bottom of the stack.

I sat back on the bed, stunned while staring at the balance to one of Amory's bank accounts. I rifled through the rest of the papers finding numerous accounts to banks all over the world, holding obscene amounts of money and stockholder slips to hundreds of different stocks on all of the big markets.

"What is all of this?" I asked, turning my attention to the different plastic cards that had my name imprinted on the bottom.

"Amory was a very wealthy man," Angelica said softly, as if having to call up courage just to say his name, or speak of his memory. "Most of us are wealthy, I should say, but Amory.... well, he had the advantage of longevity and a knack for investing well. You will not need to worry about money again, my dear. This one," she held up a black key card absent of writing or symbols, "will get you into the Swiss vault. That's where the paintings and artifacts are held. The rest, I think, are just different credit or debit cards. If you use a credit card, the balance is automatically paid at the end of the month, so there is no worrying about that."

I wanted to ask her what would happen if I exceeded the balance of the account, but couldn't even wrap my head around the amount of money at my disposal. I couldn't comprehend spending the total amount in ten lifetimes, let alone in the next few months.

I pulled out my wallet and slipped the cards into the empty slots that only ever housed the one credit card Aunt Syl gave me when I got my driver's license, then tucked my passport inside, as well. After replacing the wallet in my backpack and zipping it closed, there was nothing left to pack. I was ready to go.

"I can hold on to those for you, dear," Angelica took the loose papers back from me and straightened them. "Eden, if you should ever need a place to go, or an ear to listen, I will always be here for you. Always." She turned to me, reaching out for one of my hands with gnarled fingers that were cold to the touch. Her eyes flickered for a moment and I saw the sparkling violet that had once been the light in her eyes, but then it was gone and they settled back into the deep purple of mourning.

"Thank you," I replied with the deepest sincerity, and then braced myself for the conversation I had to have before I could go. "Angelica...." I faltered for a moment, "Angelica, I am truly sorry for.... for everything that happened. I wish that I could.... I hate that.... You were right...." I couldn't even finish a thought, let alone a sentence and then suddenly I was a broken child in front of the ancient woman that had seen a full cup of suffering in her lifetime.

I let the grief consume me, filling my lungs and then my soul with the breaths only breathed in moments of deep lamentations. I leaned over, resting my head in her lap. She ran her fingers through my hair, comforting me absently, while her own tears stained the back of my head.

"Eden, I don't blame you," she insisted firmly, but still I could not sit up and look at her. "No one blames you. And you shouldn't blame yourself either. What happened was a tragedy of the worst kind, but it was not your fault. That man," her voice broke from barely concealed rage, "that King has done this before and he will do it again. He has no regard for the sanctity of life or for his people. What you need to do now is not cry over circumstances that cannot be changed, but succeed. Go on, child, and win this war. The future of your people is left in your hands and you alone hold the keys to a Kingdom without the scars of this life. You can save us. You can vindicate your grandfather's death and restore the magic. But no more tears, no more wallowing in self-pity. Move forward; find the strength to carry on."

I sat up and looked at her. The tears stopped flowing and my cheeks started to dry. She was right. I must remember the importance of this mission.

"You're going to want to keep this covered though," she touched the glowing tattoo of the snake curled around and eating its own tail. It was the symbol of the Resistance, of the Rebellion that was reduced to this old woman and me.

"I did it wrong, didn't I?" I moved my fingers through my long, black, tangled curls, pulling them over my shoulder and into a side ponytail, covering the blue ink.

"Well, yes." she smiled, the hint of humor playing in her dark eyes. "I still don't understand how you were able to mark yourself. You must have been quite determined," she mused, referring to the painful process of administering the mark. Resistance inductees were always strapped down and unable to move so the process could be completed without them lashing out due to the severe pain the process caused. I was not like the other inductees; I did it to myself, all by myself.

"I was," I agreed. "I still am."

"Good." She kept her smile, but her eyes turned hard again. "Remember, if you need anything, I am only a phone call away."

"Thank you Angelica, thank you for everything," I whispered, genuinely.

"Be careful." She ignored my gratitude and walked me to the front door of Amory's house.

I nodded in response and walked through her door, across the porch and out into the warm sunlight of a cold February day. There was still snow on the ground at the beginning of February, but the days were getting warmer. Soon, Omaha would be embracing spring, a season I wouldn't experience. I was off to South America, off to find a lost colony of Shape-Shifters, off to search out my parents, and off to avenge the injustices not only my family suffered, but my people.

I was going to fulfill a promise I made and burn this Kingdom to the ground.

# Chapter Two

The old van rumbled to a stop in front of a faded, red sign declaring the entrance to the Inca Trail, the path that would lead to the ancient ruins of Machu Picchu. The trek would take four days of hiking, possibly longer, since it was wet season and already the sky had opened up, emptying its stores of water onto the earth.

The trail was technically closed for maintenance during the month of February, but I would be taking it anyway. I hoped that the entire Citadel would be emptier than usual, thanks to the consistent and torrential down-pours that plagued the Southern Hemisphere in the winter months.

I took my bag from the short Peruvian man who gave me a ride from Lima to here. An old friend of Angelica's, he had driven the thirty hours with me in a much-appreciated silence. I handed him a stack of Nuevo Sol, the local currency, and turned my back on him.

Walking forward, I could feel the faint call of magic in the distance. They were out there…. somewhere. I had no idea where, or how to find them, but I could feel the quiet calling of magic and the prickling of electricity igniting in my blood.

The path was well worn, and difficult to walk. The ancient stones were slippery in the relentless rain and the air thin with the altitude. But I was moved by the beauty of the Andes.

I had never seen a place so vividly and distinctly green. The deep tones of the trees blanketed the distant mountain sides in dark, flowing monochromatic colors that stood drastically against the stone of the towering mountains. And the lighter, softer greens of the mountain grass stood out starkly in the landscape as if the two greens were not the same color at all. God's brush strokes painted these mountains and valleys with the blessedness of variety, and I could feel my soul swell in awe of the creation surrounding me.

The sky had never felt so vast from this vantage point, even under the thick canopy that housed the trail I walked. The rivers and streams tumbled down the mountain side in blue ribbons of moving water, weaving in and out of the thick forests. The raw beauty of such an organic environment reminded me that I was only a small piece to the elegant and divine puzzle that was this life. As small as I was in the middle of this magnanimous mountainside, so was my life in the scope of eternity. Yet, somehow, I found that comforting.

I walked for hours, deep into the wilderness that paved the way to a once sacred escape for kings of old. Not long ago, I would have been terrified to take this journey alone. But now, there was no fear, and no anxiety, just purpose.

I was beyond childish fears of the dark or being alone. I had reached beyond the naive immaturity that keeps one afraid of the unknown. When my grandfather died, something broke inside of me. When they took my brother, the innocent part of my soul was murdered. When I watched my friends, my loved ones, even innocent people I didn't know, loaded into armored cars as prisoners, all of my fears stood before me. And when my heart was ripped in two by the cruelty of betrayal, I gave up on emotions and feelings all together.

Alone on the trail, I tried to stay focused on revenge, on those loved ones I would vindicate, but my thoughts wondered unforgivably. I thought of him, that name I would not let myself speak aloud or even think. I thought of the man that had made me so blissfully happy and then betrayed those that I loved in the name of a selfish conquest.

The tears fell from my eyes, hot with the stabbing pain of the memory of his treachery. He took everything from me, everything, and then left me a shattered, and broken ghost of myself.

I stopped to catch my breath at the top of a slippery, steep, stone stairway and grasped at the necklace I kept tucked underneath my rain jacket. The large, emerald stone of the engagement ring dug into my chest, a painful reminder of its existence, but one that I had come to treasure. As long as that ring stabbed at the place where my heart used to beat with desire for its giver, I would always be reminded of what he had done.

Now, alone on this trail, this journey to redemption, I would find others that were wronged by him and his bloodline. I would rebuild the army of the Rebellion and we would fight against him and what he stood for. And we would not stop until there was nothing left of the Kendrick bloodline, until every last one of them was dead and buried, and until this people felt their blood thicken with vindication and their magic pulse with true Immortality.

----

I was soaked to the bone when the ancient city for Incan Kings appeared in the distance. The rain did not let up for even a moment, but even through the fog and haze of the downfall, the ruins, nestled against the steep cliffs, stood as a beacon for my weary legs. I hiked the trail for days, fighting against the mud, the slippery stone and the overwhelming fatigue.

A few times, I set up the small pop-up tent that fit easily into my backpack and slipped into the exhausted, dreamless sleep of the well worn. I hadn't truly been able to sleep since before.... since before the battle and always I woke in pools of cold sweat, screaming and lashing out. The nightmares kept the wild animals away and my magic kept my blood warm in the frozen temperatures once the sun was set.

Nightmares plagued my sleep since Avalon was taken. Every time my eyes closed the haunting torment of my subconscious attacked and I was always thankful just to be awake, gasping for air and clutching my throat, but awake.

At first, I wondered if maybe they were Dream-walks, that I was being tortured in a subconscious sleep-world without my knowledge. But, always before, the Dream-walk had been done consciously, and I was always capable of remembering the details when I awoke. These nightmares were fuzzy and disorienting and always, the particulars slipped away before I could put them together.

I breathed in relief, finally making my way past the modern structures set up as gift shops and ticket booths and to the doorway leading into the age-old city. It was very early in the morning and there was not a soul around. I stepped carefully through the stone passageway and onto the rough, carefully shaped rock walkways that stood the test of time.

I was alone. At this height, and with the ancient city sprawling down the mountainside at my feet, I was never more alone. I walked the stone pathways and up the hundreds of stone steps to the highest point of the Incan citadel.

I stood next to a wide square stone that was taller than me and housed some kind of pyramid built onto the top of it and felt myself moved again. Machu Picchu was a religious experience, a moment in my life when my soul felt bigger than my body.

I stood with arms wide and chin tipped towards the sun rising in the east, over the pointed mountain peaks. I breathed the thin, crisp air finding a perspective bigger than me, bigger than my problems. I stayed like that for a while, drinking in the sacredness surrounding me.

The Shape-Shifter colony was close, the magic grew steadily

stronger the deeper into the mountains I hiked and now I could feel the direction it was located in, clearly. Pressed with urgency until this moment, I took in the height of an antiquated Citadel that still stood, despite the modern world, as a gateway to the past. The hundreds of buildings made from chiseled stone, stairs worn with age and use, and religious structures for archaic gods all but forgotten, shined as sobering reminders that kingdoms rise and fall. I was just a small piece in the tides of change that dictated the currents of life. I had a part to play, but if I failed, someone else would rise. Injustice would not always be victor of this life.

The magic began to grow stronger, my blood igniting with the warning signs of an approaching magic. I dropped my arms, and opened my eyes, but I would not move. Whoever was out there would come to me.

A flash of black between two stone columns caught my attention. I witnessed wild animals along the hike here, but the soft coat of an alpaca was nothing quite like the sleek black fur of a wild panther. I tilted my head, waiting for the man to turn back human.

"I was coming to you," I called out before the man made himself known. "You didn't have to meet me."

"You're confident that you could have found us?" he asked in his rich Jamaican accent, smugly assured that I would not have been able to.

Silas stepped from behind the stone archway, leading up to the sacred high place. His skin was as dark as the fur of his panther shape. He wore the same brown work pants and forest green sweater I saw him in the night we first met.

"I guess, we will never know," I replied, not willing to humble myself, but not wanting to insult him either.

"So, you have come then. It has gone badly," Silas stated, and his words felt like a harsh accusation.

"Yes, but you knew that it would," I answered. We stood awkwardly far apart from each other. I expected a warm greeting and a man thankful that I came to him, but he eyed me suspiciously from a distance as if I were a threat.

"Still, I had hoped things would go.... differently." He looked passed me, at the surrounding mountains. His gray eyes clouded with sorrow, and his shoulders slumped in defeat.

"So did I," I surprised myself with morbid sarcasm.

"The old man?" Silas asked, ignoring my poor attempt at dark humor.

"Dead," I declared simply and then cleared my throat quickly.

Silas took a step back as if I had slapped him before continuing, "And the boy?"

"Taken," I responded in the same way.

"And you?" His eyes flashed back to suspicion and then met me with new interest. "How is it that you are here?"

His question surprised me. "You are the one who told me to come," I lashed out angrily. How dare he give me cryptic instructions and then question my obedience.

"Did I tell you to take so many magics? You are radiating with stolen blood." His eyes turned from suspicion to hard distrust.

"Yes, I am. So, what?" I crossed my arms defensively. "Do you know what it was like when they came for my family? Were you there?" It was my turn to accuse, but I answered my own questions before he even opened his mouth to speak, "No, you were not. You were here, protected by your mountains and hidden from sight. My people were massacred. They were betrayed. My grandfather was murdered and my brother kidnapped. Do not question my stolen magics when I was fighting to save those that I loved most," my voice broke, and a hot tear fell free from the prison of my eye and slipped without permission down my rain soaked cheek.

"And so you take other's magic without remorse?" he asked, disbelieving.

"I have remorse!" I screamed at the old man, my voice echoing off the mountains in a chorus of anger.

"No," he accused quietly. "No, you are an evil thing now. Unrecognizable and evil," his voice dropped to a whisper, but I had no trouble hearing his accusations.

I knew that he was right.

"Will you help me?" I cut to the chase, unwilling to continue the hurtful small talk.

"No, we will not help you," he vowed simply and with finality. He turned from me; this conversation was over.

I watched him leave. I came here for nothing. He would not help me and I had nowhere else to go. Worst of all, I realized the last of my fears. I wasn't myself anymore. I wasn't a future Queen, or the next Oracle. I had slipped into an evil version of myself, the greatness that was once whispered with my name would stay a hushed murmur that floated away with the wind. I wasn't recognizable anymore; Silas had said it.

I was evil. There was no more good left.

## Chapter Three

I stood alone for a moment longer. Silas disappeared; I could not move from the weight of his words. He was right. There was no more goodness. The circumstances that happened the night I was betrayed bled me of my purity and virtue.

But still, I wanted goodness for this people.

"Wait," I shouted after Silas, although I was sure he was already gone. I pictured him shifting into a sleek, black panther and disappearing easily into the density of the mountain side. "Please, wait!" my voice broke with the panic of a desperate person. I would drown without guidance. I was too alone to find my way. Even if I was evil, I was still the only hope this people had and if I were left alone, I would never find the way.

I ran through a stone archway leading to worn, uneven steps made from the same rock. The magic was sharp in my blood, a boiling, electric storm that quickened my step and gave my legs courage. I ran after Silas, following his magic to the main courtyards of the ancient city.

"Silas!" I yelled, stopping at the base of the steps and letting my voice echo off the mountain peaks. "What if I am evil? So what?" I chided loudly at the emptiness. "I *have* to be evil. I have to forget the good, if I want to do this for real."

"And what is it that you want to do?" Silas stepped around a stone building, arms crossed, eyes narrowed.

"I want to end the Monarchy," I promised simply and with finality.

"To end it? All of it?" The old Shape-Shifter rocked back on his heels, suspicious eyes becoming amused, and I couldn't shake the feeling that whatever the topic between us would be, I would always be defending myself.

"Yes, all of it," I folded my arms defiantly, mimicking him and unwilling to back down again.

"And so you welcome evil in order to accomplish this goal?" his Caribbean accent was thick and melodic, but demanding.

"No, I do not welcome it. Of course not," I protested hoarsely, relieved that I felt the words to the core of my being. "But, what I have to do *is* evil. Whether or not I believe in the Monarchy or the King or whatever, taking a life is the worst kind of corruption. And if I truly want to finish.... this.... I have to be.... I need to be.... at least part of me, has to be evil," I paused for a moment, struggling to find the words to describe the thoughts that rattled around in my head unspoken since the night I lost my family. "I intend to massacre a bloodline. That is an evil thing. But also, my intentions are a part of me. And because of that, I am evil."

"Ah, I see," Silas stood unmoving, his gray eyes flickering with understanding, but not with forgiveness. "And right and wrong? Do you still see the difference?"

"Yes, but does it matter?" I wondered for a moment if I helped or hurt my cause. "I have only stolen magic until now; I have never taken a life. And, honestly, I never thought I would get to this point. I never thought I would devalue anyone enough to end his life, but here we are. You have my exact objectives. But, I will not go beyond the Kendrick household. Well, maybe Sebastian.... I haven't decided yet."

"Interesting," Silas mumbled quietly. "So, when the Monarchy is gone, when you have killed off all possible heirs, then what? Will you take the Crown? Anoint yourself and rule as the good Queen?"

"No," I answered quickly. The word "Queen" resuscitated my heart in a way that brought painful memories of promises made, of an easier way once daydreamed to save my people and then stabbed at my soul, screaming reminders that my future would never include a crown. "Never Queen," I cleared my throat, banishing the emotion before continuing, "I just want this finished, I just want to go back to the way things used to be. I don't care what you people do after the Monarchy is gone. Honestly, I don't even want to be the next Oracle. I just want normal."

"You don't want to be the next Oracle?" Silas mocked harshly, cutting through me. "There is no 'next' Oracle. Child you *are* the Oracle."

I stood there stunned, unable to open my mouth. I knew this day was coming, I was told enough times that I would be the next Oracle that the truth of the phrase sunk in. But always before, I pictured the realization of the moment differently. I imagined the Monarchy gone, Avalon at my side, my friends out of danger, and maybe a ceremony of some sort.

I did not pictured this, that in the wake of the worst tragedy I ever knew, alone on the top of a mountain, begging for help from a man who insisted on calling me evil, I would be told that I was the Oracle.

The whole scenario seemed surreal and not serious enough.

"That can't be true," I objected.

"And why shouldn't it be?" Silas asked, the hint of amusement back in his voice. "The only other surviving Oracle is dead; you remain the only one of our people left that has true Immortality and you possess the magic of every kind in our people. How can you doubt that what I say is true? It is in your blood. You are the Oracle, whether the Monarchy lives or dies, that will not change."

"What about Avalon?" I asked, dumbfounded. I was still trying to sort out my imagination from reality and was having trouble making sense of it.

"Your brother? What about him?" Silas asked, the smallest hint of impatience marking his expression.

"Well, if I am an Oracle, shouldn't he be one too? We have the same magic." I stated plainly, swallowing the rising lump trying to remind me that we used to have the same magic. Avalon no longer possessed any magic. I had it all.

"Sure, why not?" Silas laughed harshly, "but he is at the bottom of a Romanian prison. He will not keep his magic for long, and then you will share that title with the King you intend to destroy."

"No, that isn't true. Avalon doesn't have any magic to sacrifice, I have it all," I clarified, trusting Silas and then instantly regretting sharing so much with a man I hardly knew and that would not trust me the same in return.

"How can that be?" Silas asked skeptically, his gray eyes clouding and un-clouding with every hint of emotion he felt.

"He gave it to me the night of his capture. He had to; we both knew that he would be sacrificed for it. And now I have it, and because he is human, Lucan will not kill him until he has me," I dared Silas to contradict our theory. I had nothing to really go on, nothing to help me hope that my words were true, except, that they had to be true. If I lost Avalon, if the King murdered for nothing, I would never be able to live with myself. It would be the undoing of my sanity.

"Clever," Silas said plainly, not complimenting me in the least. "So, you see, you *are* the Oracle. There is no one else."

"Will you help me then?" I plead urgently. Maybe holding a new title would carry some weight with this stubborn man.

"Help you how?" he asked.

"Tell me what to do," I unfolded my arms and raised my hands, desperate for advice.

"I cannot tell you what to do," he laughed harshly. "You are beyond being told what to do. No one remains for you to take orders from. It is time for you to decide how to act and when."

"But I don't even know where to start." I dropped my arms to my sides heavily, already feeling defeated.

"Haven't you already started?" Silas smiled, mischievously, flashing perfectly white teeth that contrasted pleasantly with his midnight skin.

I sighed heavily in response. Tired of riddles, and in need of concrete answers, I was getting impatient.

"Do you know where my parents are?" I folded my arms again, suddenly exhausted.

"No," he shook his head. I opened my mouth to question him more but he continued before I could speak, "They were here. A few months ago they came to ask the same questions you ask me today."

"They were here?" I asked, disbelieving. They were for sure alive and they had been here, I could hardly believe the news. "Where did they go?"

"I do not know. They do not want to be found," Silas looked passed me, into the wild expanse of the mountains and I believed him. I knew I would have to work to find them.

"What did you tell them?" I pushed down the despair that threatened to end my quest and shouted in my ear to give up now. I would find them, whether they wanted to be found or not. And they would help me. I was their daughter.

I was the Oracle. They had no choice.

"I told them, what I have told you," he replied dryly.

"That you won't help me?" I rolled my eyes, a subconscious sign of rebellious youth, a left-over habit of a life that was ripped from me. "But you will help me, Silas, I know you will. This fight is too big for you not to be included. You keep me away from your people because you are afraid for them, because you want a better life for them. That is why I know, when the day comes, you will help me. You will have to help me. I am the last hope this whole Kingdom has and if you have any hope in the future, you better hold it in me." I stomped my foot involuntarily. Filled with the righteous passion I believed accompanied any mission against the purest form of evil and at the core of my argument, I knew that I was right.

He would help me.

"You believe you will succeed?" He tipped his chin up towards the rising sun and stared into the achromatic void of the expansive sky.

"I have no other choice," I promised.

We stood there silently for a few moments. Silas looked to the heavens as if they would guide his internal debate and I looked at him, waiting for him to answer me.

"Then yes, I will help you." His eyes moved from the brewing seasonal storm to mine with an intensity that might shake a more uncertain person. I stood still, held to the ground with firm resolve, believing in my cause with every fiber of my being and daring him not to join me. "When the time comes, I will help you."

I heard his words clearly. He said nothing about his colony. He alone promised to help, so we stood there silently, letting his words ring out in an oath to creation. We let the fulfillment of his promise be pushed to a later date, a different time and a different place, when the call to come to my aid would be of greater importance than the call to protect his people.

"Thank you," I whispered, grateful I accomplished what I set out to.

"Hmph," he grunted in reply.

"Where should I go from here?" I asked, tired of riddles and realizing Silas was not prone to giving straight. I was used to following someone else's directions and although Silas was right, I would have to learn to lead on my own; I still felt some guidance was necessary.

"I don't know where you should go from here," he answered. My blood began tingling with the childish irritation of a foreboding mysterious set of directions. "There are many places you could go. And any place you do go, you will be hunted."

The first of the morning tourists began to mill about the ancient Citadel and I felt the flare of Silas' magic ignite with the desperation to leave. I shared his urgency and took a step closer to him, silently begging him for a lead.

"You will need more than my help Eden, you must find the others. You must convince as many as you can to help you. Go there next," he finished quietly and I knew I was losing him; he would be gone in a second.

"Go where next?" I demanded quickly, trying to hide my

irritation.

"Find all those that can help you. Go to the Church of San Agustin, in the village of Urubamba. There you will find a priest; his name is Gabriel. He will be waiting for you." He put a strong hand on my arm and squeezed gently before turning on his heel and escaping through the growing crowd.

I followed him, through the excited travelers, undetected through the exit gate. I had no idea where I was going or how I would find the rest of the Shape-Shifter colonies, but I could claim at least one on my side. At least one that would help me fight, one that would stand with me.

Silas wasn't much.

But, he was the beginning. All I needed was one, just one and the rest would follow. I just needed one to start, one to light the flame and then set it free.

## Chapter Four

I lost Silas in the crowd. His magic disappeared completely. I pushed through the people pressing their way into the ancient ruins and ended up in the gift shop. Miniature models of the Machu Picchu and overpriced coffee table books depicting its magnificent beauty in scenic pictures, filled the still empty store. The tourists visited the shop at the end of their trip, so I had the place to myself for a few more minutes.

I glanced over the full shelves, brimming with nostalgic memorabilia hoping to find a map, or guide to more than just Machu Picchu, something that would tell me more about Urubamba. The lone store clerk stared at me with the smallest hint of disdain from behind her tall, glass counter, but I tried to ignore her all together.

Bells clanged together from across the store, signaling someone else had entered. My blood ignited with the recognition of Immortal magic. I snapped my head up, while simultaneously slouching lower than the bookshelves, separating myself from the other.

My forearms prickled with anticipation and my veins coursed with lightning that snapped and crackled beneath my skin. I more than recognized that the other was Immortal. I recognized exactly who the Immortal was.

My breath caught in my throat and my palms started sweating. I clenched and unclenched my fingers, finding the willpower to settle down my nerves. He walked closer to me, finding me easily through the stacks of picture books and Inca replicas.

I stood up to full height, realizing hiding was useless and not wanting to seem like a coward. I would meet him with confidence, with courage, and without being a sweaty mess. First, I just had to pull myself together in the two seconds it would take for him to be face to face with me.

I straightened my posture, tilting my chin and clearing my throat just in time for him to round the book shelf and stop short. A sharp ripple of electricity, that started at my neck and worked its way painfully down my back, reminded me of how desperately I hated this man. Yet, the urge to drain his magic and be on my way felt far away and I struggled to even find the venomous words tugging at the hateful part of my brain, begging to escape and slap him in the face.

"Hello, Eden," Talbott said carefully, his voice the cool, accented, methodical tone it always was.

"What do you want?" I asked, jumping straight to the point. I narrowed my eyes at him, daring him to try something.

"We need to talk," he lowered his voice, glancing furtively at the clerk who had yet to take her eyes off us.

"Ok. Talk," I demanded, crossing my arms across my chest and tapping my foot impatiently.

"Obviously, I'm not going to talk to you here," he laughed.

Talbott's eyes suddenly relaxed and twinkled with amusement. I grew irritated beyond what was healthy. This was a bad way to start off a rebellion, if the bad guys didn't even take me seriously.

"Are you laughing at me?" I whispered harshly. I pulled at his magic, not intending to take it right that moment, but needing to drive home the point that in a second I could drain his life's blood from him and leave him helpless and human.

"All right, I'm sorry." Talbott jerked his shoulder back as if he could reclaim the small, stolen increment of electricity. His chocolate brown eyes flashed helplessly, mourning the loss of what little magic I took and then his expression turned offended, like he thought me above taking *his* magic, like we were friends, as if he wasn't one of them, one of those that had my grandfather killed and kidnapped my brother.

I backed off; holding my hands up in surrender, but it was my turn to be amused. Now, he would take me seriously. It might not matter by the end of our conversation, I would probably take his magic anyway, but at least I could be civil for a now.

"Can I have it back?" Talbott worked at staying polite, but the panic in his eyes was unmistakeable.

"No, you can't," I hissed with firm resolve, as if I knew how but wouldn't. The truth was, I still had no idea how to return stolen magic once I took it and Talbott was not about to be the first recipient of the miracle should I figure out how to perform it.

"You know, you're surrounded, Eden," he sighed loudly, as if exasperated. "You are completely outnumbered and outmatched, so cut it out," he finished quietly, and his eyes narrowed into hard slits of reprimand.

"How many?" I looked through the windows of the small store, not believing there was any number of Immortals that would be able to stop me; it wouldn't matter how many he brought.

"Enough," Talbott said simply.

"I doubt that," I countered, growing more and more irritated. I moved past Talbott, searching out the guide or map that I came in here for in the first place.

"Listen, we need to talk. Eden, you need to take this seriously." Talbott put a gentle hand underneath my elbow. The small gesture was almost too much for me to bear and I wrenched my arm away with revulsion.

I wanted to scream at Talbott, to accuse him of all of the hateful things I knew he was a party to. But when I spun around on my heel, he took a step back flinching before I got the chance to open my mouth. The effect was rewarding. He was so big, so strong and so confident all of the time, that the knowledge that he stood in fear of little, old me was enough for right now.

"How did you find me anyway?" I inquired; suddenly interested in how exactly he came upon the very store I would be in. I wasn't followed from Lima, or up the mountainside and until he entered the store, Silas was the only other Immortal presence I felt. I was sure of that.

Instead of answering aloud, Talbott nodded in the direction of my neck and specifically stared at my chest. I reached my hand up subconsciously and my fingers fell on the necklace and engagement ring hidden beneath my windbreaker. When my fingers closed over the two stones, Talbott nodded his head ever so slightly, confirming my suspicions.

"We have our ways," he replied more loudly, covering his clue.

I recognized that he was speaking to whoever was with him, but he shed light on a very valuable piece of information that could get me into a lot of trouble. I was very confused suddenly, not knowing if I could really believe Talbott or if this was a show to gain my trust and then betray me later. I was bewildered and that put the situation out of my control. I was at the mercy of Talbott until I figured out what his real agenda was.

"Sure you do," I mumbled, still fingering the large magical stone that rested against my chest. "What is it that you want, Talbott?"

"I want to make a trade," he offered carefully, glancing around the room. "Do you mind if we go somewhere else to talk?"

"Yes, I do mind. How do I know this is not just a trick to get me out of a public place? And what kind of trade? What is this?" I tried to keep my voice calm and without emotion, but Talbott was bringing back a flood of feelings that I was not prepared to deal with.

"Listen, Eden, we have you outnumbered," Talbott declared with all the confidence I expected him to have, but then he lowered his voice so that I was forced to read his lips to fully understand what he was saying, "besides, you want this trade. You need this trade."

"Fine." I gave in, following him out the side door he came in through. "But just so you know, just so we are clear, I am probably going to have to kill you and all of your little friends at the end of this."

"Just relax a little, all right?" he mumbled. We walked through the metal door and out into the first sunshine I had seen my entire time in Peru.

I stopped, just on the other side of the door. We walked into an empty area, the plush vegetation of the mountain just a few feet away and a pathway to the front of the store to my left. I should have decided an escape route by taking in my surroundings and figuring out exactly how I would escape should I need to run.

But I couldn't think.

I couldn't move.

Jericho stood before me, hands tied behind his back and the softest smile playing at the corner of his lips. He was alone, waiting for us.

I wanted to run to him, to throw my arms around him and never let go, but I resisted. The rest of the Guard stood just beyond the trees, just far enough away to stay out of my sight, but there nonetheless. I couldn't let myself become vulnerable; I couldn't so willingly open myself up for attack. But it took everything inside of me to keep the distance between us.

Every ounce of willpower I owned.

"You're giving me Jericho?" I whispered, putting the pieces together. "For what?"

"For Avalon's magic," Talbot stated soberly; the weight of his offer hit me in the chest with full force. "Lucan has offered Jericho in exchange for your brother's magic. As soon as Avalon has his magic back, I am authorized to hand Jericho over to you and you will both be free to go. If you agree, Lucan will not bother you any longer; he will leave you alone, completely and forever. You have his word. If however, you refuse.... then, I'm afraid you will be escorted back to

Romania where you can discuss the terms of your agreement with Lucan face to face."

I turned my head, needing to breathe and working desperately not to be sick. I couldn't look at Jericho and betray him at the same time. I couldn't long to touch him; long to hear his voice and know that I would not be able to set him free.

The compromise sounded so easy, but it would be the death of this race and I wasn't capable of extinguishing an entire people.... my people. Instead of saving Jericho, I was going to sacrifice him. That alone rang out loud and clear how unfair this journey I was on would be. I would never have an easy decision again. Every thought, every move, every conclusion I made would have heavy and lasting consequences. And Jericho would be the first, the first to suffer from my direct decision to sacrifice his life for the greater good.

Lucan asked too much of even an enemy. He was truly the worst kind of evil. If I lost Jericho, I decided then and there that he should also lose someone he loved, someone he cared for. Not later, not in the long term, but soon.

It would be my next move.

"Never," I whispered hoarsely, my gaze turning to ice and my fingers trembling with an overwhelming hate that grasped at my heart and flooded my veins.

"I told you," Jericho said arrogantly to Talbott and my eyes flickered to his for the briefest moment. His hazel eyes burned with pride and the smile that played at his lips took full form. He was satisfied with me, proud that I would refuse the trade. He knew the stakes and his willingness to be martyred echoed painfully in the empty chambers of my heart.

"You'd better give me the engagement ring back," Talbott changed the subject without warning; caught off guard, I stepped back unsteadily. I was poised to fight, my body radiating with the need to protect Jericho. When Talbott moved on so flippantly my mind raced to catch up.

"What?" I shrieked, "Are you kidding me?"

"Well, Kir-"

"Do not speak his name in front of me, Talbott Angelo, unless you have a death wish," I threatened in a low voice and watched his lips curl into the faintest and most unexplainable smile.

"Excuse me, the Crown Prince is engaged to Seraphina.... again.

The ring is a family heirloom," he explained.

I felt the bile rise in my throat, not from jealousy, but from the obvious cliché of it. I shouldn't have expected anything less.

"Of course he is," I mumbled venomously. "He can't have it."

I expected a fight, but again Talbott moved on without even the smallest protest, "The necklace, will you destroy it?" His eyes turned serious, and he leveled his gaze at me, raising his eyebrows as if his question was the most important thing he asked yet.

"No," I replied confidently, "I want him to find me."

"He will not be able to do that, Eden. He is very ill, too sick to leave the palace," Talbott spoke softly again, pulling his hands behind his back.

"The King's Curse?" I asked nonchalantly, feeling indifferent, and almost disappointed that I wouldn't be the one to kill him.

Talbott cleared his throat, "No, not the Curse. Something else, something they can't explain."

"Will he die?" I asked flatly, with no emotion for my voice to betray.

"It looks that way," Talbott said, and his sad eyes revealed his attachment.

"Pity, I hoped to witness the end of him," I grumbled. "Actually, I hoped to be the one to end him." I looked out into the density of the surrounding mountainside and tried to find the Immortal Guard that was staying very carefully hidden. "Talbott, are you sure you're not the only one here?" I asked, gauging his reaction carefully.

"They're out there, Eden, they're just a little more afraid of you than I am." He smirked casually.

"Are we done here?" I asked abruptly, Jericho's presence was painful. I glanced up at him quickly, not able to read his expression.

Talbott took a step towards me, bringing his hands forward and ripping his watch from his wrist. With one swift movement, he threw the watch in front of him and stepped on it, crushing it beneath his hiking boot.

"Listen carefully, they have already started to move," Talbott whispered harshly and I was too stunned to react. "You have to destroy the necklace. If you don't they will track you wherever you go. They will find you again. Take Jericho and run. You have to run. And you'll have to knock me out. Ok, go!" Talbott reached out his hand, pressing something small and cold into my palm and then closed his eyes tightly, readying his body for the blow.

When I stood frozen, staring at him, still unable to move, he grew impatient.

"Eden, do it now! But please, don't take my magic. Please don't take my magic." He shut his eyes again and squished his face.

I glanced at Jericho who gave me a confident head nod and looked behind him, making sure the other Guard was not here yet.

I released my magic forcefully against Talbott, sending him soaring through the air and against a tall, sturdy tree twenty feet away. I was a vessel of rage and vengeance and Talbott became the tool, allowing the bottled cruelty to escape. I used my magic to insure that his head hit hard against the rough bark; I watched him fall limply to the ground, the blood from his head injury pooling around his unconscious body.

Jericho turned his back to me, wiggling his tied hands in a bondage I hadn't seen before. His hands were bound in what seemed like metal handcuffs, except this silver metal flickered iridescently in the sunlight and radiated with a foreign magic that I felt but did not know.

I looked down at my hand, and found a small, silver key that matched the metal of the handcuffs. I hurried forward, unlocking Jericho's restraints. The shackles fell to the ground with a soft clanking sound, vibrating gently against the wet, stone pathway. I picked them up, not wanting to waste something so intriguing and shoved them into my backpack.

Jericho's wrists, raw and chaffed from the handcuffs, bled onto his hands, the blood dripping from his fingertips. But now that the handcuffs were off, he breathed in such a sigh of relief that I nearly wept at the sight of his now slumping body.

"Are you all right?" I gasped, coming to his side and helping him stand upright.

"We have to go," he insisted urgently.

He was right. The wilderness, nestled against the mountainside, began to shiver, the thick greenery vibrating with heavy movement. Knowing the Guard was on their way, we had to leave now or face the unknown number of Titans with orders to kill us, or worse, take us back to Lucan. I was willing to face them alone, but I refused to let Jericho go back there and suffer any more.

I grabbed Jericho's hand; our magics met in a cataclysm of relief, an overwhelming feeling that if we could escape, something in this cursed world would be right again.

I pulled him behind me, around the building and into a full parking lot of tour buses and people. We rushed between vehicles and pushed through pressing crowds of tourists.

We must lose the Guard; we must escape. If I lost Jericho a second time, there would be no forgiveness, no reconciliation. He was my last hope, the saving grace that would rescue my soul from the pit of despair and hatred. If Jericho were by my side there was nothing I could not do. My road to redemption, to righting the wronged people I betrayed to a cruel prison, would begin. I would have saved my dear Jericho and not let him fall at the hands of a hateful tyrant.

At least I would save him from dying against his terms. Because even if we were running for our lives now, we both knew this was only the beginning of a war that would wage until goodness reigned once again. The next time Jericho's life would be in danger, it would be his doing, his decision.

We would meet evil together and fight against it with all that we had.

We just had to find a way to escape today.

## Chapter Five

"Through here," Jericho grunted, nodding his head between two tour buses parked closely together. "I have a plan, but you're going to have to destroy the necklace first," he instructed through labored breath.

I turned my head and looked at him. A weakened, exhausted man, just seconds free from imprisonment and he was already giving me orders. I wanted to find him obnoxious, but his innate ability to lead, the very quality that was synonymous with breathing for him could not be silenced, especially in our very life-threatening situation.

I pulled the necklace from underneath my rain jacket and held it in my hand, trying to find the willpower to throw it on the ground and stomp on it. My hand was poised above my head and my mind screamed at my heart to let go, to destroy the detestable talisman.

I looked at Jericho, his eyes intent with urgency, and something more, something much like hope. I empathized with his expectancy, his desire to see me free myself from the tangled web I was trapped in. But I couldn't.

My heart betrayed the knowledge that what was done to me was done by the worst kind of monster. My heart, that treacherous, unfeeling organ, I had thought stopped moving when there was no goodness left to beat with, suddenly spoke up and refused to destroy a manipulative gift that led the enemy straight to me.

I glanced desperately at Jericho, wanting him to take it from me and annihilate the stone and every memory associated with it, but it was up to me. He made no movement and I wouldn't have let him pry the black stone from my firm fingers anyway.

So instead of crushing the precious gem beneath my foot, I used my other talents. With the rock grasped firmly in my hands I absorbed the magic into my own bloodstream and whispered a quick prayer that whatever made the stone a tracking device would not stay active once I owned the magic.

I slipped the chain around my neck again and marveled at the now dull, black rock that would no longer shimmer or shine in any different color. Whatever supernatural beauty and mysterious quality the gem once held was gone, it was now just a black stone.

"Ok, the magic is gone, we can go now," I whispered to Jericho and watched his eyes flicker with obvious disappointment. "What's the plan?"

"Over there," Jericho pointed to a tour bus reloading its senior citizen passengers.

"How are you at suppressing your magic?" I asked, wondering if his plan would work.

"Not good," he said simply. "Can you just take mine and then give it back to me later?"

"Uh, no, that would not be a good idea," I mumbled. "Let's just go."

We walked carefully between the tour buses, watching our backs and taking our time around corners. A flare in my bloodstream warned that the Guard was getting closer, at least close enough that if I could feel their magic, they could feel mine.

We ran the last few feet to the tour bus, hand in hand and then pushed our way gently through the last of the boarding passengers and onto the bus. I pulled Jericho passed curious elderly tourists and to the very back of the bus where we had a few rows to ourselves.

I had no idea how we would explain ourselves to the humans should anyone demand answers, but I hoped my magic could get us through any real interrogations that would threaten our hiding place.

I suppressed my magic, making it vanish as best as I could. Jericho slumped down, below the tinted window and I followed suit realizing the dark tint would not stop the Titan Guard from recognizing us.

I was closest to the window and so even after Jericho lay completely down on the long row of empty seating, I could not stop myself from peeking through a corner of the window to find out if they had arrived yet.

They had.

Fifty Titan Guard walked slowly and in pairs from around the gift shop building and did their best to blend in among the other travelers. They scanned the crowd and talked back and forth through their wrist watches.

Our bus was still not moving and the sick, twisting feeling in my stomach warned that we were not even far enough away from this dangerous pursuit to have made any progress. One of the members of the Guard walked closer to our bus, his head perking up as if he had found something.

I looked down at Jericho, his head on my lap and his hands still trembling. His magic was going to give us away. They would find us. They would search us out. And they would not let the fear of a scene stop them from dragging our kicking and screaming bodies away from this place.

I needed to do something. I needed to cover Jericho's magic. I slid to the floor and crawled to the middle aisle, before standing up and walking, slouched over, to the front of the bus. I had only pushed magic on a few other humans, on my way to Romania, months before and I never really got the hang of it. But this was another life or death situation and I needed to act.

I stood behind the bus driver, resting my hand on the top of his head rest, pretending to look back at the elderly crowd as if I had an announcement. I brought my magic back slowly and steadily and when the popping electricity was flowing through my blood again, I released what little increments of magic I could and helped the driver decide that it was time to go now.

The short, large-mustached, Peruvian man jerked forward in his seat, stepping on the gas and shifting abruptly into movement. The elderly passengers swayed roughly with the sudden movement and cried out in protest at the lack of warning.

I ignored the angry complaints being shouted at me and kept my eyes on the now alerted Titan Guard all aware of exactly which bus Jericho and I were on. All at once, the Immortal army moved against the bus working its hardest to gain an departure speed, but not succeeding.

I closed my eyes, trying to concentrate through the protests and angry questioning. I was desperate to put distance between this bus and the closing Titan Guard and I needed to do it quickly.

I pushed my magic again, this time not at my bus driver, but at all of the bus drivers sitting idly behind their large steering wheels waiting for their passengers to finish their sight-seeing. I didn't know what I was doing, or even if my plan would work. But if I could create a gridlock, a parking lot of chaos, in which every driver felt it absolutely necessary to leave the parking lot that very moment; I could trap the Guard inside for the few minutes we urgently needed to put space between us and them.

My blood boiled with the anticipation of putting my thought to work, the magic electrifying my veins. I felt the magic move through the crowd of people, working its way into all of the different tour buses and against all of the bus drivers.

The seconds it took for my magic to finally find its targets and put my plan into action were the most excruciating moments. I waited with baited breath for one of the Guard to come crashing through the bus door and drag me away by the hair to meet my doom. I knew my plan was taking too long and that the seconds that felt like minutes only felt that way in my head, until I looked up at the angry elderly people and noticed they were all in slow motion.

I Time-Slowed Machu Picchu and didn't even notice. The Guard was moving at the slowest pace, their menacing figures moving like snails against my bus in a uniformed movement. I watched with amusement as everything around me came to a near stop, and move only in the slowest of increments.

My magic now had plenty of time to work out the details of my plan and find all the drivers. Finally, my bus reached the end of the parking lot and was ready to escape down the mountainside; at the same time I felt the power of the Time-Slow come to an end and the world begin to catch up to the normalcy of gravity and physics.

When the reality around me finally caught up to the rest of the world, the parking lot was full of buses jumping to go, running into each other and blocking the exits. Our bus, however, merged casually onto the highway that would take us down the mountain away from the temporarily trapped Titan Guard.

I walked to the back of the bus, through the still upset crowd and sat down gently next to Jericho, who had yet to lift his head off the seat.

I picked up his head and set it gently down on my lap, running my fingers through his greasy, matted hair and working my hardest not to wipe away the dirt, grim and filth that accumulated on him during his time in prison.

"Jericho, we need to keep moving, are you up for this?" I asked sweetly, wanting to get off the bus as soon as possible.

He grunted, sounding exhausted and frustrated, but he stood up and started walking towards the front of the bus. Jericho leaned heavily on each of the seats as he walked by and up the aisle towards the bus driver.

"We don't belong on this bus!" I exclaimed dramatically for no one's benefit except my own.

The Peruvian bus driver whipped his head around at the sound of shouting and just stared. I had no explanation for the man suddenly glaring down his nose at me with dark, irritated eyes.

"I'm sorry," I tried to explain further, "we need to get off your bus."

When the driver did not immediately pull to the side of the road, I realized that he might not speak English and was working the Spanish words together in my head when he abruptly pulled into a scenic overview type area and forcefully opened the door.

Jericho and I exited the bus with hateful glares and irritated threats behind us. We both searched frantically for the next step in our escape, but I could tell Jericho was waning. I needed to get him to a safe place as soon as possible, or I would be left dragging his unconscious body behind me.

"Are they close?" Jericho asked with a gravelly, strained voice.

"I can't feel them yet, can you?" I asked, wishing I developed stage two of this flight for our lives before we got off the bus.

"I can't ever feel them. That's a Titan trait," Jericho mumbled nonchalantly.

"Oh," I paused for a moment, taking in the new piece of information.

A couple on a motorcycle sped to a stop next to us, taking off their helmets and hanging them on the handlebars. They climbed off the bike and paused for a moment to enjoy the breath taking view of the Andes. They stood close to the bike, with their backs turned, the woman resting a casual hand on the black, leather seat.

"Can you drive a motorcycle?" I whispered to Jericho who nodded positively in return. "Are you up for it?" I tore my eyes from the vehicle I was planning on stealing and stared intently at Jericho. I was afraid for him, I was afraid he wouldn't make it any farther than the highway before slipping unconscious and driving us off the cliff. And I didn't know how to drive a motorcycle.

"Eden, I will keep us safe, I promise you that," he affirmed seriously and then walked casually in the direction of the twenty-year-old bike.

"Would you like me to take your picture?" I approached the couple carefully.

They turned at the sound of my voice and smiled blankly at me. They were not Hispanic, but obviously did not speak English. I didn't have time to figure out how to cross the language barrier, so I pulled my hands to my face and mimicked taking a picture and then pointed at them, smiling the biggest, fakest, and most helpful smile I could muster.

The pull of other magic tugged softly at my blood, alerting my senses that the Titan Guard was on the move. I waited, impatiently for the couple to find understanding and then dug deeper for more as the man walked excruciatingly slowly to me and handed over his camera. He pointed at the button to push and then walked back to his girlfriend at the edge of the cliff.

I snapped a couple quick pictures of the happy couple while Jericho moved into place. I looked at Jericho who was ready to hop on the bike and then swallowed my guilt before tossing the camera high into the air and just over the couple's heads.

They both instinctively turned to grab their flying camera before it fell over the cliff-side and into the unreachable abyss below. Instantly, I sprinted the distance between the bike and me and jumped on the back, throwing my arms around the running motorcycle and a waiting Jericho.

The minute I was on board, he pushed down on the throttle and we were speeding down the winding roads of the mountainside, leaving a bewildered and wronged innocent couple behind us.

We were free for now, moving away from danger at the fastest speed we could. I had not factored helmets into my plan, so my hair, loosened from its ponytail holder, whipped violently around my face. I kept my arms tight around Jericho's waist, feeling his labored breath and wildly beating heart.

I buried my head in his back, protecting my face from the whipping wind, closing my eyes against the danger of the hair-pinned turns and steep drop-offs just a few feet from us, but mostly thankful to be near Jericho. I could smell him, I could touch him, he was really here with me. I wasn't alone anymore.

"Where are we going?" Jericho shouted over his shoulder, taking his eyes off the road for only a moment, but my breath caught in my throat and I clutched him tighter.

"Urubamba, there is someone I have to see," I yelled back into his ear, the wind assaulting my face.

"Ok, I'll go passed it first, and then we'll head back towards it tomorrow," Jericho decided and I agreed with his foresight.

I laid my head down against his back and closed my eyes,

wondering about his deep knowledge of the Andes mountains.

We drove for hours like that, far from danger and far from Machu Picchu. I worried about Silas and his people with the Titan Guard so close to them. I led the Guard right to them, but I forced myself to trust that Silas could protect his own people. I couldn't go back for them and to check on them would be an insult to one of the only allies I had.

Towards dusk, Jericho drove the old motorcycle up the drive and to an old Monastery that was turned into a hotel. The building was a long white rectangle with a red Spanish roof and a large courtyard in the middle. The rooms lined the inner walls of the courtyard and all had bright blue doors that stood out vividly, even against the setting sun.

I checked us in at the front desk in a quaint lobby, and paid cash for one room with two twin beds. The concierge walked us to our room without saying anything and I wondered if it was because he did not speak English or because of the frantic way our eyes darted about the room and the hushed whispers and distrusting stares we used with him.

Either way, once our door was open and the key was in my hand, the young concierge left quickly, walking back to the lobby and leaving us alone.

Jericho stumbled through the door first, walking into the small room and breathing a heavy sigh of relief. I followed him in, closing and locking the blue door behind me. We were safe. For now, we were safe.

I turned around to take Jericho in, to allow myself to believe fully he was with me. He leaned against the opposite wall and I rested my back against the door and we stood there staring at each other, not a word whispered, not a sound uttered.

His hazel eyes smoldered with hope even while his shoulders slumped from exhaustion and his hands trembled at his sides. His lips turned upwards in the smallest of smiles and I couldn't take it anymore. I couldn't bear the separation.

I crossed the room in a moment, throwing my arms around his neck and pressing my body against his. His arms were around my waist in an instantaneous gut reaction that would not let me go, even if that was what I wanted.

But it wasn't.

I would never let go of Jericho again.

## Chapter Six

In our small, dimly lit motel room, I held on to Jericho as if he were the last grasp I had on sanity, as if he alone were keeping me afloat, saving me from drowning in a sea of desperation and fear. My magic clung to his in happy reunion, wrapping it in warmth and energy, reviving his fading spirit.

With his muscular arms around me and his face buried in my neck, I could not stop the storm of tears that had been imprisoned behind firm resolve. I was a sobbing, hysterical mess in his stronghold. I finally could not stop the crushing emotion; everything seeped out in a tormented tragedy of tears.

Jericho did not mimic my breakdown, but stood strong, holding me tightly to him, waiting out the tempest. He did not pull away or sigh in frustration, but stayed patient, the healing rock of comfort I needed most.

And in his hold, I mourned again the loss of my grandfather, the loss of my brother, the loss of my people, the loss of all hope and the loss of my great love. And when my tears dried, when there was nothing left to cry, nothing left to feel, he walked me to one of the single, narrow beds and sat down with me, pulling me close to him again and resting his tired head on top of mine.

"I can fix you," I suggested through a hoarse, raspy voice, wiping my nose with the sleeve of the jacket I had yet to take off.

"What?" he asked, lifting his head and meeting my eyes.

"I can fix you, heal you or whatever," I replied casually, as if it were the most normal thing in the world.

"I don't understand you." His brow furrowed with confusion and the smile returned to his lips.

"Here, I'll show you." I released the blue smoke that had healed Angelica before and made its appearance at unusual times.

The smoke swirled around our feet, testing Jericho with the smallest hint of trepidation before wrapping itself abundantly around his ankles. In moments Jericho was blanketed in the thick wind that doubled as young, Immortal ability-tester and healing-savior at my beck and call.

I tried not to find the look of utter fear on Jericho's face amusing, but his eyes bulged and his mouth dropped open in silent shock.

I felt the blue magic move against his energy and against his broken body. The smoke pulled the fatigue and trembling away from him, off his tired spirit and weary resolution. I pulled the oppression out of him and into the magical air, dissolving it completely.

When it felt as though I absorbed it all, and had completely taken the pain away, I sent the wind into the far corners of the room where I knew it would slowly fade before disappearing completely. I was happy to find Jericho's hands had stopped shaking, his wrists were no longer scarred or raw and his distant eyes looked more vivid, although they were staring at me with intense bewilderment.

"What?" I asked innocently, holding up my hands in question.

"What *was* that?" he demanded, in a confused whisper.

"Um, I'm not exactly sure...." I admitted honestly.

"You're not exactly sure?" Jericho accused, not believing me for a second.

"Well, I mean, technically, it's the Wind from the Cave of the Wind, but other than that, I mean, I don't really know...." I trailed off, wishing Jericho had been brought up to date before.... before....

"What do you mean it's the Wind from the Cave of the Wind?" He grew more animated and more excited with every second I wasted not filling him in completely. Clearly he felt better and I could not have been more thrilled that he was back to his old self.

"Ok, so during the whole Immortal Walk thing, you know that the wind completely beat the crap out of me, right?" When he nodded I continued, "Well, I thought I was going to die. Like, I literally thought that the wind was going to kill me, so I fought back. And I don't know how it happened, I mean, Amory didn't even know why or how it happened, but somehow my magic fused with the wind, or the wind fused with my magic because after I left the cave the wind followed me. And now I can control it. Oh, and also it heals people, as long as they're not dead," I finished quickly, mentally tabulating to make sure I had gotten in all of the important details.

"That's impossible," Jericho mumbled, shaking his head slowly.

"Yet, here we are." I smiled patiently, wanting to brush over this part of our reunion and get to the more important stuff.

"So the wind, and the cave and wait... what?" He blushed; embarrassed that it was taking him so long to figure it out.

"Oh, Jericho," I sighed, gently brushing my hand over his forehead and pushing his hair back. His dark brown locks had grown long in prison, giving him a rugged, wild look. I smiled at him, letting him know that I was teasing him, but he didn't smile back. He stared at me intently, as if wanting me to do something, to act in a way that was beyond my understanding for the moment. "When I was in India, the Wind didn't recognize me. Amory thought because my magic was new, different from anything the Cave witnessed before, that at first it treated me like an enemy. But something happened during our struggle; while the wind tried to kill me and I fought to save my own life, we bonded somehow. When I left the cave..." I flinched for a moment, remembering *him* on the other side of that journey, his turquoise eyes so worried about me, his hands there helping me stand, the feeling that he would have moved heaven and earth to keep me safe.

"Go on," Jericho prompted, sweetly slipping his hand over mine. He was consoling me now, the role of comforted and comforter kept flipping suddenly between us tonight and I wondered if that was how we would live out the rest of this fight together.

"When I left the cave, the wind came with me. I didn't really think anything of it until it reappeared in Omaha before the Winter Solstice dance and then Amory," I cleared my throat, finding the courage to continue speaking, "Amory had Avalon and I practicing with it, trying to figure out what it could do, and why it would stay with me. But we never figured it out. He asked Avalon and me to keep working with it, but there wasn't time before.... before he was taken." I hung my head in shame, the floods of sorrow threatening to sweep me up in them again.

Jericho lifted my chin with his thumb, gazing at me with compassion, and smiling encouragingly. I swallowed the grief, saving it for a different moment, but still leaned into him. I let his body envelope me; he wrapped his arms around me and pulled me with him down onto the pillow where we stayed snuggled together in a fortress of shared heartbreak.

"It wasn't until everyone had been taken that I learned it could heal people. I found Angelica the next morning, nearly dead and when I went to her side to see if I could help her, the smoke just kind of acted on its own. It healed her entirely, she's Ok now," I whispered, thankful that I was able to rescue one life. It wasn't enough, she wasn't enough to forgive the sacrifice of so many others, but she was a start.

She was one life I saved.

"Angelica's alive?" Jericho echoed, his voice full of relief, proud and thoughtful at the same time. "Thank, God," he kissed the top of my head and when I looked up at him, intrigued by the gesture he kissed my forehead as well. "You did good there, kiddo."

"It's not enough." I blinked back the tears, refusing to ruin our happy reunion by crying through the whole night.

"It's a start. We'll get them," he vowed confidently into my hair. "We'll get them all back."

I had so many questions for him, so many concerns and strategies I wanted to talk through, but now was not the time. We were exhausted and at the beginning of a journey that would take us to the gates of hell.

Tonight, I would simply be thankful that he was with me, that I was not alone and that hope was on the horizon. Tomorrow we could talk until we were sick about rescue plans, and schemes of destruction, but tonight we would rest in the security of each other's arms. Tonight, I would breathe in Jericho and relish in the warmth of another person, of another person that cared about this cause and about avenging the loss of my loved ones and destroying the bloodline that left us both survivors of an evil tyrant.

Tonight I would sleep in someone's arms, someone that cared about me.

We drifted to sleep, holding each other closely, breathing steady, even breaths and allowing our minds to be dreamless, the sweet sanctuary of the quietness of an empty slumber.

----

When I awoke the next morning, the sunlight was streaming through the window, warming my face and waking me gently. I stretched for a long time, realizing I was alone in bed and that Jericho had covered me with a warm blanket. I turned my head, looking for him and it was a moment before I recognized the sound of the shower.

I sat up in bed, unwilling to leave the comfort of the blankets just yet and pensive for the moment. I was content, satisfied that Jericho was with me and I felt safe for the first time in weeks in our small motel room. I wasn't happy, I wasn't sure if I would ever fully feel that emotion again, but I was content.

The feeling felt strange and foreign, like an alien emotion not native to my body. Just a few weeks ago I believed I couldn't experience a greater happiness or sense of security but when that was raked from me, I was sure my heart would never soar upwards again.

    I knew that it wasn't much, that the small ounce of contentment today was just for a moment. Jericho and I would get to work in a few minutes, the emotion would fade away, and I would refocus on our mission. I knew that contentment was not happiness, and that everything I felt was only false security; but for now, I relished in the shared company and safety of the morning.

    Jericho suddenly tumbled out of the bathroom in an almost too small white cotton towel, water dripping down his muscular chest and gasping for breath. He was panicked, fear written obviously across his face and I jumped to my feet ready for battle, or ready to run.

    "No, no, Eden, I'm sorry," Jericho sighed heavily, his face relaxing into a smile and his cheeks flushing with embarrassment. "It's just that, it's nothing really, I, just.... something scared me, sorry, but it was nothing. I mean, really, it's nothing," he exhaled heavily, running one hand through his wet hair, the other gripping firmly to the towel around his waist.

    "What happened?" I asked carefully, not entirely convinced Jericho would be scared of nothing.

    Jericho hung his head, his shoulders slumping self-consciously, and shaking from humiliated laughter at the same time. When he looked up at me from underneath his thick, dark lashes, his eyes twinkled with life that had been missing yesterday.

    "It was a snake," he mumbled, turning back towards the bathroom and craning his neck as if to find it inside.

    "A snake?" I asked with a flat voice.

    "Yes, a snake," he answered. He stood in the middle of the room, dripping wet, water droplets running across his tanned, defined chest and in the smallest white towel afraid of a snake. "It slithered over my foot while I was in the shower, it just scared me that's all," he finished weakly.

    "Obviously," I agreed, and then burst into uncontrollable laughter, my body shaking violently and gasping for breath at the same time.

    "Don't laugh!" Jericho demanded but couldn't stop himself from joining in. "At the time, it was very traumatic!"

    He only made me laugh harder, soon tears were streaming down my face, but not the sad kind, the kind that only appear when something is beyond rational and funny, the happy kind. I laughed for minutes, doubling over and grabbing my side. I wasn't concerned with the snake or even Jericho's embarrassment; I couldn't stop myself from the sweet relief of laughter.

"It's not that funny!" Jericho whined, tapping his toe impatiently against the red cement floor. "Eden!"

"I'm sorry, I'm really sorry," I struggled to get control of my emotions, standing up and wiping at my eyes. "You're right, it's not that funny," I agreed, still unable to stop the left over laughter from escaping.

"I'm not scared of snakes, really," Jericho said bravely, "it's just that, I wasn't expecting to have to share my shower with a slimy, green, awful serpent, that's all," he cringed while describing the snake and then shuddered from the memory.

"Right, you're not scared at all." I rolled my eyes, good-naturedly.

I walked over to the bathroom door, afraid to go in lest the snake really be something to be afraid of. Jericho stood closely behind me as if I was the one protecting him. He playfully pushed me forward with one hand strong on my back and I took the initiative to walk over to the shower and pull the white curtain back dramatically.

I shrieked a little, afraid of the intensity of the moment, but then sighed in relief finding the tiny green snake slithering around the basin of a white porcelain tub. The snake was no more than a few inches long and completely harmless.

"Jericho!" I scolded, "This is what you're afraid of? It's just a tiny little thing!"

"I told you, it just snuck up on me and scared me, that's all," he defended himself, while still refusing to leave the doorway of the bathroom. "But you better get rid of it, I might lose my towel if I try...." he mumbled weakly.

"Mmm.... hmm....," I agreed, glancing back at him. He looked savage, standing in the door way, hair wild, water droplets slowly drying. I found it hard to believe he was actually afraid of the little snake; but then he shuddered after just looking in the direction of the tub and I had to laugh all over again.

I reached my hand into the basin intending to pick the tiny serpent up by his tail, but failed to find the courage. He slithered around the bottom of the tub frantically, terrified and lost. I could suddenly relate to him, but had no desire to pick him up.

"I need something.... like a stick or something," I glanced around the room, trying to find the right snake-extracting tool. I stood up and put my hands on my hips, staring helplessly down at the snake.

"Or you could, oh, I don't know.... use your magic?" Jericho suggested sarcastically.

"Oh, right!" I replied, holding up my finger like it was the best idea I had ever heard.

"Some things never change," he mumbled, thoroughly amused with me.

"Says the big strong man cowering in the corner and wearing a hand towel," I laughed at him.

I used my magic, like Jericho suggested and lifted the wiggling reptile out of the tub, carrying him to the bathroom door where Jericho retreated safely behind the nearest bed.

"Excuse me, Tarzan," I joked, opening the door to the outside with magic as well and tossing the little guy out into the grass. "Better?" I turned around to smile at him. He had not moved from his post.

"Much, thank you," he smiled back, "you're not going to tell anyone about this, are you?"

"Your secret is safe with me," I promised.

"Thank you," he said graciously, and then walked around the bed, on his way back into the bathroom.

"Until I need to blackmail you, that is," I finished smugly as he walked by. He turned on me playfully, pinching my side and sending me jumping.

"So what's the plan today?" he asked from inside the bathroom, not bothering to shut the door.

I blushed, and fled to the bed that was around the corner and away from the changing Jericho.

"Silas suggested that I visit Gabriel, in Urubamba. Apparently he is a priest or something?" I questioned, hoping Jericho might have a better idea of who this guy was.

"I think I've heard of him before. I couldn't tell you anything specific, but Amory definitely mentioned him at some point," Jericho said thoughtfully through a muffled voice. He walked around the corner, his head tipped forward, drying his hair roughly with his towel.

"So, this should be interesting...." I stood up to take my turn in the bathroom.

Jericho stepped in front of me before I could make it very far. He had put his jeans on, they had been washed in the tub and dried with his magic, but he was still shirtless. His hair was messy and still damp and his eyes were hungry, meeting mine with ferocity.

"Eden, I just want you to know.... I just, I mean, I just need you to know that I am really happy you're all right," I started to say something in response, but he cut me off by grabbing my bicep and pulling me closer to him. "After we left.... and in those dungeons.... all I could do was imagine the worst and that the unthinkable had happened to you. So when they brought me here, and you were.... here, when you walked out of that building.... I just, I just couldn't have been happier to see you, or be with you now."

"I feel the same way," I whispered softly, finding it hard to move or speak under his intense gaze.

He stared at me a few moments longer as if deciding what to do with me. I stayed still in his arm, not sure what to expect but not willing to leave him either. He leaned his face forward as if he was going to kiss me on the lips, but I knew that I was in no danger. Jericho wasn't being intimate with me; we were both just thankful to be near one another and safe. Instead of my lips, he kissed me sweetly on the forehead, his lips hot against my skin.

I looked up at him, trying to convey every ounce of gratitude that I felt for him, trying to radiate how fearless I felt with him here to help me. Together we could conquer this; together we could win.

His eyes turned curious for just a moment before I closed the distance between us and slipped my arms around his waist, holding him tightly to me. He hugged me back, and our magics met again in friendly reunion. We were together, and I refused to lose Jericho again.

## Chapter Seven

"I can't take it anymore," Jericho blurted out loudly while walking through the busy marketplace.

We decided to leave the stolen motorcycle behind at the motel and walk to the church in Urubamba. The incessant rain seemed to stop now that we had entered into March and I was thankful for the sunshine and clear blue sky.

The small town was bustling with life. Small stands stood close to each other, vendors flowing seamlessly together in a current of stubborn haggling and angry transaction.

I looked up at him, surprised by his outburst. He turned his gaze on me, the sincerity of his hazel eyes unnerving, the flecks of green hidden in the pool of soft brown reflected his essence, flashing with intensity.

"How is Avalon? Is he Ok?" he groaned, as if he couldn't raise his voice without betraying his heartbreaking concern.

"I don't know." I hung my head, disappointedly. "I was hoping you could tell me." I crossed my arms and brought my eyes up to the heartbeat of the city again. The marketplace was a color palate of every shade of brown imaginable, from the muted brown of the cloths covering the splintered wooden stands, to the lighter browns and tans of the clothes of the people, to the deep, flawless brown of the vendors skin. The monochromatic color scheme, as if each shade represented an entirely different color all together, moved me.

"No, they kept us all separate. Once we reached the prison, I was completely isolated. I couldn't even hear another person...." Jericho's sentence trailed off into melancholy pensiveness, his eyes shifted and became distant and his fingers started to tremble again. I reached out and slipped my hand into his, reminding him that he was safe. He looked down at our interlocked fingers, staring at them for a moment idly before coming back to himself. "But shouldn't you know how he is? Can't you communicate with him?"

He moved his eyes to mine and even though he asked with the softest of tones, I couldn't help but feel like he was accusing me. I should be able to talk to Avalon; I should have never let him hand over his magic to me so quickly. We could have seen how things went once he got to Romania.... We could have waited to find out Lucan's exact plans for him....

"Eden? Eden, can't you communicate with Avalon?" Jericho asked again, and the small hint of panic played in the higher pitched questioning.

"No," I ripped my hand away from his, using it to cover my face and my shame. I willed myself not to breakdown, not to start crying again, and not to slip into the void of despair, the painful abyss that was so difficult to climb out of. I shook my head, whipping my long, thick, black waves around my shoulders and face.

We stopped walking and stood at a vendor that sold different wears made out of Alpaca fur. The different shades of soft fur made beautiful garments that I would love to take home with me. Pure white pillows, heavenly, cream colored slippers, and soft chocolate colored teddy bears begged to be bought. Every object was hand stitched and unique.

"So is he.... is he..... so is he dead?" Jericho demanded with a hoarse voice, barely audible.

"No, I don't think so." I cleared my throat, reaching desperately for strength. "After everyone was captured, after they took him.... he decided.... we decided that he would be safest without magic. He gave it all to me in hope that Lucan would not murder him if nothing was left, if he was just human. Our hope was that he would use Avalon as bait instead of sacrificing him for no reason. It seems to have worked. I mean, I think it has anyway. That's what Talbott was asking for; he wanted me to give Avalon back his magic."

"Clever," Jericho mumbled as if in macabre awe.

"But that doesn't mean that he's all right," I added quickly, "and there is absolutely no way for me to find out unless I go to Romania myself and break him out of that hell hole."

"That's not seriously your plan, is it?" Jericho reached for my hand, holding it firmly in his and started walking again. The concierge from the motel gave us directions to the church, I was too distracted to pay close attention, but Jericho seemed to know where he was going.

"At some point, Jericho, I am going to have to face that Citadel and get those people out of there, I owe them that much," I promised with sincerity.

"Um, no you don't have to face that fact. That is a death trap just waiting for you. Lucan already assumes that is your plan, especially if he is holding your magic-less brother and the only army he believes will stand with you. Plus, there is only a fifty-fifty chance your magic will even work down in those prisons. It would be a suicide mission and nothing more," he stated emphatically. Jericho was suddenly grumpy, his eyes were hard and his jaw tight.

"What do you mean fifty-fifty?" I asked, ignoring his warning.

"Well, the only Immortals that have access to their full magic down there are the Titans. So, in theory, because of who your dad is, you could be fine. But on the other hand, Amory was not fine. That was the only place they could ever keep him. So it might not matter that you're a fourth Titan, the other three parts might cancel it out. So it's not even like fifty-fifty, it's more like twenty-five-seventy-five...."

"But there is a chance," I said with confidence. That was all I needed.

"Listen, if that really is your plan, if you are really hell-bent on going there, aren't there a few things we need to do first?" Jericho, always the strategic leader, was right.

"Yes, you're right. I have to find my parents; that is my first goal. And I would like to build more of an army, so that I don't just end up at the Citadel flying solo. I need an actual plan of attack, a way to draw the Titan Guard away from the prisoners."

"Ok, those are good ideas. Those are really good ideas," Jericho sounded surprised as he calculated my thoughts. "So how much of a following would you say you have now? Like, rough numbers."

I cleared my throat, and couldn't stop the blush that flooded my cheeks and neck, "Well, there's you and me, and Angelica, and.... Silas," I finished weakly.

"How many people are living with Silas now?" Jericho asked with furrowed brow, I could tell he didn't like the numbers already and I hadn't even dropped the bomb yet.

"I am not exactly sure.... but it doesn't really matter. I'm not counting Silas's people because they won't be fighting. I am only counting Silas.... just Silas." Too embarrassed, I couldn't even look Jericho in the eye. If the situation was reversed and I was the one taken and Avalon left on the outside to rebuild the Rebellion, I was sure Avalon would have a thousand people behind him and probably more by now.

"Just Silas?" Jericho turned on me, horrified.

"He says that his people have suffered too much already, that he wouldn't ask them to fight and I agreed. Each person should have their own say and since none of them was there to volunteer I.... Listen, I was just thankful for Silas, Ok. I didn't know you would be waiting for me behind lucky door number two. I was just happy that someone was willing to help me," I huffed honestly and remembered those despairing moments of loneliness before Jericho unexpectedly became part of my journey.

"You're right, of course, you're right," Jericho admitted, and he sounded humble.

"Plus, I mean, I can't be sure about this, but that night at the farm, like not everyone was there, right? Where are Titus, Xander and Xavier?" I asked a question that was nagging at the back of my brain stem for weeks.

"You're right!" Jericho said again with enthusiasm. "They would have gone underground, almost immediately. I'm sure they wouldn't have been caught. And the teams in India and Morocco and.... South Africa!" He was excited, his step suddenly had a bounce to it and he gripped my hand with purpose. "We just have to find them."

"Right," I agreed, finding his spirit catching; that was a lot more people than I planned on. Things were looking up. "Do you have any idea where any of them might be?"

"Xander, Xavier and Titus were in Paris the day that everyone was taken. Avalon and I just got off a conference call when the Guard showed up. There is a safe-house inside the city that they would have gone to once they heard, assuming they heard about the attack while they were still in Paris. We'll start there since they weren't scheduled to move on for another week. I know where the team in India keeps its headquarters after our trip there last winter, assuming they haven't completely gone underground also; we should be able to connect with them too. Morrocco and South Africa will be a bit trickier, but maybe once we hook up with the other teams they will have a better idea where to look."

"Ok, good." I was in awe of how things were starting build momentum. Jericho meant the difference between hopelessness and real action. We had a plan, we had begun to move on it and I could feel the aggressive, vengeful, excitement rush through my blood like kindle to a flame. I could feel the fearlessness growing.

"But what about your parents?" Jericho asked, as if he were checking off a to-do list.

"I'm hoping Gabriel will have more answers," I mumbled, almost sarcastically. So far, they felt like a completely unattainable goal, but at the same time necessary to my cause. I wasn't even looking for them as abandoned daughter seeking long lost parents; I was simply a general of an army that needed every last soldier to take up their arms and fight. Their son would be sacrificed and their life choices essentially got us into this mess. Their obligation was to help and I was positive I would give them no other choice once I found them.

If I could find them.

"Me too," Jericho mumbled underneath his breath as we stopped in front of an old, crumbling church with chipped, ecru stucco and a rusted, ancient red door that I was not entirely sure would still open.

"Um, are you sure this is it?" I hesitated moving forward. When Silas said Gabriel was a priest, I assumed he meant to a real congregation, not the caretaker of an empty building threatening to send the entire street of people to meet Jesus literally at any moment, and not just emotionally.

"I followed the directions from the guy at the motel. This is where he sent us," he said defensively, with the smallest hint of skepticism.

"Ok, then...." I walked bravely forward, forgetting the rational fears tugging at my subconscious. I couldn't be afraid anymore; life had dealt me different cards. I must walk into the church unflinchingly, and out of it in the same way.

"After you," Jericho joked casually, while pulling on the iron door handle, tugging at it roughly and then stepping out of the way so that I could walk into the cold sanctuary first.

The house of worship was dark and cold, the only source of lighting came from two stained-glass windows high above the front door and the hundreds of glassed red candles that lay as an alter of prayers at the front of the church.

I walked courageously forward, down the center aisle, past backless hardly stable benches sitting low to the floor and filling the empty places between the holy water near the door and the life sized statue of Jesus, reaching out his scarred hands to the invisible congregation.

I cleared my throat loudly, hoping to alert Gabriel, or a nun, or anybody, that the small sanctuary had visitors. A bird moved in the high rafters of the ceiling, flapping its wings violently as if angry we had disrupted its worship.

I turned back to Jericho. He stood in the door frame, head bowed in silent prayer. His act of reverence moved me. With head still bent, he dipped one hand into the holy water's stone basin and crossed himself in the sign of the cross, the Catholic Church's act of obedience to God. When his eyes finally met mine, he cocked his head and shrugged his shoulder in an attempt to downplay his veneration, but a new seed of respect and awe began to grow roots at the base of my heart.

"So it is true, you have come to ask for my allegiance as well?" A thick Latino accent called to us from a doorway beyond the statue of Jesus.

I turned on my heel, not sure what to expect or how even to respond to the question. My eyes met a man that appeared to be in his late thirties, although the prickling in my blood, alerting me of his Immortal origins, reminded me that his appearance meant nothing when it came to his actual age and my human-upbringing perspective.

Gabriel had deeply tanned, brown skin, and black, glossy hair shaved close to his scalp that shined even in the dim lighting. He wore the traditional garb of the priesthood, the white square against his neck standing out starkly in the delicate candlelight. Around his neck he wore a burgundy rosary with large, worn beads that he fingered absentmindedly.

He could easily have passed for any of the myriad of Peruvian Catholic priests, if it weren't for his eyes. Eyes that glowed orange against the poor lighting, eyes that at first I thought merely reflected the candlelight, but I soon realized that they glowed brightly as if on fire. Eyes that flamed orange as if they themselves were the setting sun, orange as if they were the spark of light in the oppressive darkness that were the only things strong enough to burn the entire world to the ground.

Turning uncomfortable under my scrutinizing stare, Gabriel clenched his jaw. I took a step forward, a step towards him and his lips pressed disapprovingly together. He was afraid of me, afraid of what I was capable of.

But, he had no reason to be. In his stance of firm determination, I saw what I needed; I saw what I wanted. He had the look of a man hungry for a fight, desperate for blood. His priest costume was only that, only a distraction from the eyes that burned brightest when challenged, that glowed when blood was demanded and sacrifice expected.

"I'm Eden," I offered, narrowing my eyes in gut reaction to this man who embodied the will to fight.

"I know who you are," Gabriel replied confidently, "your parents were here three days ago."

# Chapter Eight

"They were here," I demanded, standing up straighter and crossing my arms in an over-dramatic huff, "three days ago?"

"Yes." Gabriel tapped three of his fingers sequentially against his thigh as if mentally calculating his claim. "Yes, yes, three days ago."

"And were they.... were they...." I didn't even know how to approach this conversation. "Were they looking for me?"

"No," the priest replied simply. His eyes flashed with the color of fire, the brightest orange for a moment before settling into a burning flame that would warm the coldest room. He took a step forward, so that he was fully inside the sanctuary, and with his step the candles surrounding the alter flared suddenly, just like his eyes, and then settled back into soft flames offering the silent prayers uttered at their lighting to the heavens.

"Well," I started, trying to brush off the wave of irritation that washed violently over me. "Well, then, what were they doing here?" I asked indignantly.

"They came for the same reason you have, to ask me to join your cause." Gabriel's thick, melodic and rich Peruvian accent was answered me with the smallest of smiles, a deep dimple coming to life on his right cheek.

"And what did you tell them?" I inquired casually, downplaying the hope rising inside of me.

"I told them I would think about it," he answered, cocking his head to the side and gazing at me as if sizing me up through his unique eyes.

"So, have you?" I cut to the chase, realizing it might not be so impossible to catch up with my parents if they were only three days ahead of me. If Gabriel could just give me a lead on where they were headed....

"Yes," he responded with the easiest simplicity and at the same time the deepest gravity.

"And....?" I fought against the urge to stomp my foot impatiently.

"I do not like your parents," he said candidly; his comment took me by surprise. "I feel that they have played the cowards, that their absence has been too long and that their return is much too slow and calculated."

I locked my teeth together, biting my bottom lip as if to forbid it from moving. My fingers dug deeply into the flesh of my crossed arms, reminding myself that I needed this man, and that he offered another link in the armor that had to be created if I were to get to the rest of those that needed rescuing. But, who did he think he was?

His eyes flickered and flashed from bright to dull, from burnt to vivid, in moments as if they actually were on fire, as if they glowed and burned like a real flame. He was watching me, gauging my reaction, taking in my careful smile and deciding what he would do with me. I fought against every innate urge that I possessed to open my reckless mouth and give him more than he for.

"Do you know her parents?" Jericho stepped forward, walking purposely to my side and speaking for the first time to Gabriel. "Do you know them enough to accuse them like this?"

"I know them well enough," Gabriel replied, quieting his voice and relaxing his shoulders, "I knew Amory better," his gaze became distant for just the smallest of seconds, a brief moment of silence offered to the dead in reverence and respect. "The point is, I am convinced that you are right, that your cause is just and necessary. But you have not come to ask the priest his moral theories on the obligation for every Immortal to stand for justice. You, as well as your parents, are asking if I will personally join this war. If I will fight hand to hand against this King that wishes you dead. That requires a different sort of man than one chosen for the cloth. So, my answer was and is 'no'"

"Maybe an ordinary man of the cloth, but Gabriel you are anything but ordinary," I said slowly with firm resolve and deep seeded sincerity. "And your people are not ordinary. This is an extraordinary calling, for those of us who will not sit idly by as our mothers and fathers, as our children, as our sisters and brothers.... are sacrificed for a King that would see us *all* murdered for his gain, for his benefit. And as a man of God, you must be the answer against the evil that threatens to snuff out every last innocent life." I tilted my head, so that my chin jutted forward, daring Gabriel to argue with me.

"Silas said you would not be easy to turn away," he admitted with eyes narrowed.

"No, you have it wrong. I *will* not be turned away. I'm asking for your help, but I expect you to give it to me. I expect you to care enough about this Kingdom that you cannot possibly have another answer for me."

"You are right about that, child. I do care about this Kingdom.... All right, I will help you. I will travel this road with you, wherever it leads," he declared finally and I had to clear my throat quickly to banish the emotional excitement I felt building inside of me.

"Thank you," I offered genuinely and could not stop myself from breaking into a smile.

I walked forward, reaching out my hand and shaking his firmly. His aggressive magic jolted against my hand as soon as our flesh met. I knew I had not made a mistake in coming here; he was exactly what we needed.

"You might have to learn to like my parents though," I said playfully. "They are next on our list of recruits. Do you know where they were headed by the way? I want to meet up with them to.... I *need* to meet up with them before we leave South America."

"I don't know where they were headed. They are easily lost and not easily found, a trick that has kept them alive through all of this time," he observed with an air of amusement in his voice that hinted at an attachment to them and I couldn't help but wonder if he really disliked them as much as he claimed to.

"What do you think, Jericho? What's our next move?" I turned to him, looking up into his eyes, hoping he had a Plan B stashed somewhere up in his alpha male brain.

"That depends. Do you want to continue to pursue your parents or try to hook up with Titus and those guys?" Jericho sat down on one of the unstable and small wooden benches, pressing his palms together and chewing on his bottom lip. Too big for the tiny bench, his knees were bent at awkward angles. The wobbly bench jerked unstably beneath him, knocking his hair from careful placement and across his dark eyebrow.

"I don't know!" I shrieked in frustration. "My gut feeling is to get to Paris before those guys move on, and that connecting with them should be our first priority before we continue, but I will hate myself if I miss the opportunity to get to my parents. I know they are a vital part of this mission and without them, I feel like everything is only.... half done.... At the same time, do we continue to recruit others or spend our time gathering the scattered Rebellion?" I hung my head, moving my arms from crossed defensively in front of me to around my waist, holding myself tightly as if I had to physically keep myself together.

"A warrior must always follow his initial reaction, child;

otherwise what good is instinct? What good would you be in battle without those gut feelings?" Gabriel offered from his strong post near the statue of Jesus. He stood in front of the church as if, even now, with just the three of us, he was preaching a well-prepared sermon. "Your parents intend on finding you as well, so why not serve both of your efforts and allow them to recruit while you gather those you already know will help you fight?"

"How do you know they will try to find me?" I asked skeptically, letting the logic in his plan sink in while still reluctant to agree to something so simple.

"Because that is what they told me," Gabriel replied with casual resoluteness I struggled to grow used to.

"They told you they wanted to find me?" I narrowed my eyes at him again, wondering when I would ever be able to take him seriously.

"Essentially, they told me they wanted me to join them so I could help them help you," he shrugged his shoulders and the dimple in his cheek reappeared.

"Oh," I said simply.

"So? We should go," Gabriel left the room without warning.

I turned to Jericho, bewildered by this man, "Did he say 'we?'"

"Yes, I think he did," Jericho was as confused as I was.

We stayed in silence, watching the shadowed door that led beyond the sanctuary, wondering if we were waiting for Gabriel or if that had been our dismissal. I turned toward the exit and then back again toward the door Gabriel disappeared through and then once again toward Jericho and then back again toward the full statue of Jesus.

"I think he's planning on coming with us," Jericho mumbled, even more surprised than I was.

"Good," I said confidently, staring at Gabriel who just reappeared in the sanctuary. He was still wearing his priest outfit, but had added a pair of darkly tinted, aviator sunglasses and a brown, leather messenger bag slung across his chest.

"Ready?" he asked, somehow looking less like a priest and more like a hit man, despite his attire.

"What about Silas? Maybe I should go back for him," I worried about how primitive and underdeveloped my plan was. I didn't actually have a fully realized agenda, it was more like a plan to just get as many people to say yes, and then find my parents and then.... what? Was I really planning on making this trip around the world twice, the first time to get a commitment, the second time to tell them I was ready....?

"Why?" Gabriel asked.

"So, someone doesn't have to come all the way back here when we're ready for him," I answered, hoping no one would catch on to how inexperienced at leading I was.

"I can just call him when you're ready," Gabriel shrugged and took a step forward.

"Really? How?" I was in awe, wondering if this was another Immortal power I was just now discovering.

"With a cell phone...." Gabriel said obviously, looking at me like I had lost my mind.

"Oh.... right.... a cell phone," I couldn't mask the confusion from my face, I looked at Jericho with a mixture of embarrassment and relief. Immortals felt so archaic to me, with their ancient Citadels and closed off culture, but in reality they blended in with the rest of humanity easily, using private planes, and modern technology like anyone would expect. Their universal wealth and affluence allowed them any extravagance and amenity. Still, something about Silas, hiding out in the remote parts of the Andes Mountains, didn't scream tech-savvy to me.

"You do know what a cell phone is, don't you?" Gabriel questioned, sounding a little concerned.

Jericho burst into laughter, unable to contain himself anymore. It was a deep, hearty laugh that made him double over and cry at the same time. It was a sound that seemed foreign coming from him, a movement that had been absent from his lungs for far too long.

"No, I mean, yes. I mean of course I do. It's just that sometimes I forget you guys operate in two worlds," I fumbled through my response, smiling with Jericho but not finding it *that* funny.

"I don't understand," Garbiel stated plainly.

"You don't have to," Jericho spoke up, finding his composure. "Just know, that Eden was raised human," he smiled from ear to ear, his dimples were there, his hazel eyes sparkling; I was reminded of who Jericho was before the hell we were forced into.

"But, I thought, doesn't every human use a cell phone?" Gabriel asked, still trying to make sense of me.

"That's beside the point," I mumbled, still embarrassed. "The real question is how are we going to get to Paris? I have plenty of money to book flights, but I guess I don't know the best airline to take."

"The best airline? The best airline is Air Gabriel of course," Gabriel grinned at me, finally moving on. "We'll take my plane, it will be easier."

"Sure, why not," I said, still smarting from the cell phone debacle. "Am I the only Immortal that doesn't own a private plane?" I asked sarcastically as we walked out of the church, leaving the still sanctuary behind us and following Gabriel through the crowded streets of Urubamba.

"Maybe," Jericho smiled at me, taking my hand and pulling me along so that we wouldn't get separated.

"Probably," I heard Gabriel mumble and had to laugh.

Things were certainly going to be more interesting with him along for the ride.

## Chapter Nine

I stepped out of the tiny airplane, thankful to be alive. I was sure that Gabriel's private plane would resemble something more like a luxury jet than a rinky-dink little thing that putted its way across the Atlantic Ocean, only kept alive by magic and a ridiculous amount of prayer from me.

I offered one last petition of thanksgiving, before stepping down from the rope latter Gabriel lowered for me. I looked around and breathed in the fresh French countryside. It was dusk, the sun was setting low in the West and the air was cool and crisp.

I wasn't exactly sure where we were, but Gabriel promised we would be safe once we landed. I wondered if there were places we could land that would make us not safe, but I kept my questions to myself over the long ride from Peru. I didn't want to shout them over the loud, sputtering engine, or lose focus and forget to reinforce Gabriel's magic with my own, jointly holding the antique, tiny plane in the air.

The ground was hard underneath my feet, too hard after spending so much time bouncing around in what felt like a metal coffin over a depthless black ocean beneath us. I reached out for the belly of the plane to steady myself, while my equilibrium adjusted to solid concrete.

"Where are we?" I asked with a croaky voice and frayed nerves.

"Saint-Louis," Gabriel answered, while checking his little-engine-that-could over inside and out.

"We're close to Switzerland and Germany here and a few hours from Paris," Jericho offered, jumping down from the cockpit and smiling at me. "It's beautiful, isn't it?" he observed, looking out at the rolling farmland. The twilighted sun glowed with orange, pink and soft shades of purple on the horizon, sending fields of drooping sunflowers to sleep, and bathing the golden petals in soft light. "It's not the right season for sunflowers. It must be magic."

"Yes, it is," I sighed, leaning against Jericho. He stood still, letting me rest against him while we waited for Gabriel to finish his inspection of the plane and push it, with the help of his magic, into a white barn with a wide door.

Jericho helped Gabriel shut the large double doors, pushing them simultaneously together and latching them with a heavy iron lock.

Gabriel brushed his hands together and then spun around on one heel, walking with purpose passed me and towards a dark house several yards away.

Jericho and I followed behind quietly. Maybe it was Gabriel's earlier comment, or the Titan kicking in, but I couldn't shake the feeling that here in France, we were in enemy territory. My blood prickled hot with the quick bursts of lightning, reminding me that I could not be as bold as I wanted. I had to be smart. I had to take things slowly if I wanted to accomplish my immense to-do list. I wasn't afraid of being caught, but not accomplishing my goals would leave me forever disappointed and guilty.

Gabriel searched quietly for a key buried in a flower bed to the right of a bright yellow door. The house itself was painted in soft yellow stucco that matched the setting sun perfectly. Flower pots dotted every window. They contained soil, but no flowers. A thick hedge that ran the length of the property boxed in the house on every side, except the back that opened to the barn and the fields of mystical sunflowers.

The house was perfectly still, and was obviously empty. Gabriel mumbled something about turning on the power and disappeared into the darkened house. Jericho and I waited patiently in the foyer for him to return.

"Is this Gabriel's house?" I asked, hoping we weren't breaking into some unsuspecting human's house with the promise to leave it better than we left. That plot felt too familiar to something Avalon would have come up with and I wasn't ready to deal with those emotions; I was too exhausted from the trip.

"It must be," Jericho replied and I reminded myself that although Jericho was usually an expert on all things Immortal, we were experiencing Gabriel for the first time together.

For a moment the lights flickered above our heads and then came to life completely in the rooms surrounding us. I heard a generator kick on and roar to life and felt heat begin to flow gently from air vents at my feet.

"Hungry?" Gabriel called from deeper inside the house. Jericho and I followed the sound of his voice.

The small kitchen had just room enough for the usual appliances set up in a perfect square and opened to a table for four on the opposite side of the room. I walked to the table and collapsed onto one of the solid wood kitchen chairs, sighing heavily and silently refusing to be put to work for dinner just because I was the only girl.

Gabriel moved about the kitchen swiftly, opening and closing all of the cabinets rapidly searching for something to eat. He pulled several cans out of the different cabinets, lining them up on the counter and then stepping back to frown at them.

Clearly displeased, he went back to work, staring deeper into the cabinets and returning this time with a box of unopened rice and another one of lemon cookies.

"Well, this isn't much," he muttered sadly, his trimmed eyebrows furrowed together in consternation as he stared at the mismatched food hoping they would cook themselves. "I don't know what we're going to do with this," Gabriel gave in, running one hand over his closely shaved head and tugging at the collar of his tight priestly white square with the other hand.

"Ok, well let's see what we have here." Jericho stood up with energy, walking over to the food as if it was the most exciting meal he had seen in a long time. "Canned corn, canned mushrooms, a can of gravy, green beans, pimento, rice and.... cookies. There's plenty here!" Jericho exclaimed, showing Gabriel politely to the table by putting a gentle but strong hand on his arm. "Have a seat; I've got this," he declared proudly. He left Gabriel and me to talk while he rummaged around in the kitchen looking for the tools he needed to accomplish his difficult task.

"What is your plan after we find those Immortals that are here?" Gabriel asked, his orange eyes pensive and serious, burning darkly at the moment, like a flame well into a long fire.

"To find more Immortals," I replied plainly and then thought better of my short answered sarcasm. "Jericho and I know of at least three more teams of Resistance members stationed elsewhere across Africa and Southeast Asia, so we are hoping to get to them." Gabriel nodded his acceptance of the plan, but continued to stare at me to imply he had more questions.

"And then what? What will you do when you've assembled this army?" he inquired of me seriously, his eyes flaring brightly at the use of the word, "army."

"Romania," I said simply. "There's a chance that my magic might work in the prisons and my first priority is to get to my brother. I have to save him before Lucan.... before Lucan gets impatient with me," I finished softly.

"And what about Lucan? What is your plan for him?" Gabriel sat across from me at the small table, his hands folded in his lap and his eyes ablaze with intensity.

"I will have to kill him," I whispered, the gravity of the words falling on me heavily. Of course I had to kill him, of course I had to end this, of course I wanted revenge, but it was not in my nature to want to take another life. I swallowed my fears and reservations, pushing them down and into a small place that I could ignore for a little while longer.

"Is he the one that finished Amory?" Gabriel sat forward, his jaw twitching with quiet rage at the mention of my grandfather's death.

"Yes," I answered.

"So, if he owns Amory's magic, how do you propose to kill him? I have heard you are good, I have heard rumors about the strength of your magic. But, if Lucan possesses all the greatness that was Amory Saint, how do you, child, expect to end his life?" Gabriel sat forward abruptly, pounding his fist on the wooden table, demanding an answer.

"He doesn't possess *all* of Amory's magic," I replied, sitting taller with pride and daring Gabriel to question my resolve again.

"What do you mean?" Jericho asked, turning from his place at the counter and walking over to stare at me directly.

"I was there when Amory.... when Amory died," I forced the words out, scolding myself internally for letting those words continue to be so difficult to say. They were the truth. I had to be comfortable saying them, and instead of sadness, I needed to turn my emotions into fuel for this fight. "While he was dying, he took my hand and gave me everything that Lucan didn't take or couldn't take. At the time, it seemed like Amory was more in control than Lucan."

"He did what?" Jericho asked, his arm falling limp at his side while holding a dirty wooden spoon.

"I want to say it was, at least, maybe half of his magic, maybe less, maybe more. I don't know. It's hard to tell. What I do know is that it was more magic than I have ever felt before, more than I've ever held. There was a lot of it, and as far as I could tell, Lucan didn't even notice that Amory was giving it to me." I almost laughed, remembering how full of electricity my veins felt after he was finished.

"That is amazing!" Gabriel exclaimed, rising out of his chair and slapping me in the arm.

"That is really good news, Eden!" Jericho echoed Gabriel's excitement.

"Amory is still dead," I reminded them, surprised by their enthusiasm.

"Yes, that is true, but now our quest doesn't feel quite so.... hopeless," Gabriel answered with the same energy.

"Well, come on guys, you didn't really think I was going to, what? You didn't think I was just taking you to Romania so we could all die, did you?" I asked, horrified that they thought so little of my leadership skills, but a little flattered they were still willing to follow me there.

"I did," Gabriel nodded his head quickly, "that's actually exactly what I thought."

"Yep, me too," Jericho patted me on the shoulder and walked back to the counter where he continued stirring his concoction on the stove.

"Guys, I'm not completely unprepared for this..." I muttered defensively. "Although, thanks for coming anyway?" I said more as a question than actual heart-felt gratitude.

"Well, a good cause and all," Jericho mumbled from his place at the stove.

"I mean, you did tell me I had a responsibility to mankind and that I would single handedly be the reason for the downfall of our race if I didn't join you," Gabriel agreed with Jericho and I burst into laughter. Apparently I was on a mission with two kamikaze-jokesters. "Well, then, Eden, you are the only one on this blue planet that will be able to kill the King," Gabriel turned serious.

"Well, Avalon, too, once we rescue him and I give him his magic back. We share everything, as far as magic goes, so he'll have access to Amory's magic as well," I explained confidently.

"So, your brother gave you his magic before he was taken away and now he is being held captive without it?" Gabriel asked, putting bits and pieces of conversations together.

Jericho walked over to the table, carrying three soup bowls in hand. He set the bowls on the table; the aroma drifted up and around us, making my stomach growl ferociously and warm my spirit with feelings of gratitude. Tonight we were safe, tonight we had a real, home cooked meal, and tonight we sat together, figuring out the future in allied camaraderie.

"Yes," I mumbled through a mouthful of deliciously, hot food.

"But, why...?" Gabriel asked, his spoon hovering over his food. "Jericho didn't you say that you were brought to Peru for a trade, Lucan wanted to trade you for Avalon's magic?"

Jericho nodded, his mouth full of food.

"If Lucan has Amory's magic and in turn his Immortality, why does he need Avalon's?" Gabriel continued his thought; I looked up at him, realizing this was a thought I should have been figuring out several days ago.

"For his son," Jericho said simply and then took another bite. "He's dying."

Gabriel was satisfied and began eating as well. I took another bite, but couldn't taste the food anymore. I made myself chew, I forced myself to swallow, but it was the last bite I could stomach. I lost my appetite and nearly my sanity.

The fierceness I felt to rescue Avalon was there, and the intense need to give him back his magic would never leave me. However, the sudden and unexpected feeling to protect Kiran blindsided me. I was paralyzed by a deep need to save him, to keep him from dying. The internal war between inevitable vengeance and a buried and what I had thought was a dead love fought violently inside of me and closed off my throat, staggered my breathing and tore apart my soul in inhumane ways.

Kiran was dying and I was suddenly determined to save him.

# Chapter Ten

"I'll clean up," I offered, noticing Gabriel's drooping expression and being grateful for Jericho's willingness to cook the meal in the first place. I was still in awe of how he could put all of those ingredients together and come out with something not only edible but delicious.

"Thank you, Eden," Gabriel said solemnly and for a moment I wasn't sure if he was talking about the dishes or something more.

He stood up slowly, placing a firm hand on Jericho's shoulder before leaving the kitchen into the darkness of the hallway.

"The bedrooms are upstairs, I will set linens out for you and towels in the bathroom," he called.

I stood up, my hands full of plates and walked to the sink searching out dish soap. Jericho followed with more dishes in hand and the left-overs we couldn't finish. He rummaged around silently for a few moments, finding something to store the food in.

"What's wrong?" he asked after the food was stored in the small refrigerator. He leaned against the counter, his hands supporting his weight on either side and waited patiently for my response.

I couldn't look at him. For a moment, I couldn't even talk. I worked at the dishes, scrubbing them clean and rinsing them carefully under the water. My hands started to shake, so I slowed down, focusing on the dishes, not wanting to break one.

"Eden, what is it?" Jericho asked. There was a sweetness to his voice, a careful concern that felt like security, that felt like.... home.

"It's just.... well, you know, it all feels like.... sometimes it feels like too much. Like too much for one person to handle...." I admitted, shutting off the water and turning around to face him. I let my wet hands fall against my tan fitted, cargo pants, staining them with soapy water, but not able to find the will to care.

Jericho looked at me, his hazel eyes marked with desperate concern. He opened his mouth as if to say something, but closed it again, walking over and pulling me into his arms instead. I sighed, letting myself melt into his chest and putting my arms around him as well.

"And it's more than Amory and Avalon and.... everyone else. It's that.... I don't know how to explain, it's too awful," I closed my eyes, wishing I could banish forever the feelings that reappeared uninvited. I wished I could crucify those unwanted emotions that crept their way silently and unnoticed back into my heart and made their home again inside that wretched, barely beating organ.

"You still have feelings for him?" Jericho asked, but it wasn't a question, it felt like a resonating accusation.

"No, how could I?" I argued with myself. "But at the same time the thought that he could die, or that he is dying, makes me want to.... truthfully, I want to vomit."

I thought Jericho would pull away from me, or slap me, or get angry with me or anything but laugh. But laugh he did, the silent kind of laughter that shakes one's body and brings a tear to one's eye. I looked up at him, confused by how entertained he was at my expense. His laughter subsided, but the amusement never left his twinkling eyes.

"Eden, it's all right. What you felt for Kiran was real, as hard as that may be to hear, it was real. It became even more real by the fact that you planned this future with him and when that was taken from you, you didn't even get a say, or have a choice. You were as much of a victim that night as I was, or Avalon or even Amory. Even if you want to kill him, that doesn't mean you want him dead. Feelings like that, they just don't disappear because you want them to. They're irrational to begin with, so telling them to go away usually makes them worse. Believe me," Jericho explained in such a way that I felt weight was lifted from my shoulders. I looked up at him, and he looked back at me, resting his forehead against mine for a brief moment before kissing it gently and releasing his embrace.

"But they will go away, won't they?" I asked in a small voice, leaning back against the counter.

"Yes, I believe they will," he nodded confidently, smiling in a way that made his dimple come to life and his eyes shine with assurance. "Besides, it's not fair that he should get to die of this unnamed disease. I want to be the one to kill him."

"I feel the same way," I echoed Jericho's light tone, finding a smile to give back to him.

"There is something you should know though," he turned serious for a moment, the light in his eyes dimming and his smile fading away. He cleared his throat before continuing, "It was Kiran's idea to send me with Talbott. Lucan originally wanted to send Lilly; he thought she was less of a threat and the most compelling bargaining chip, but Kiran insisted that I would be stronger leverage. Kiran demanded that his father send me instead of Lilly."

I stared at him with confusion, wanting to ask questions, but he held up his hand to stop me.

"Talbott told me on the way over that Kiran wanted you to be protected. He sent me to protect you. Hell, it was even his idea for Talbott to let me go no matter what you decided about Avalon and the magic. He still loves you Eden, he's still trying to protect you, even from his death bed," Jericho finished quietly, as if he was making a case for Kiran.

"Why are you telling me this? Why are sticking up for him?" I asked, horrified. My stomach started to churn violently again and I felt for sure, this time, I would be sick.

"I just want you to have all of the facts.... I just want you to know the whole story. Eden, I want nothing more for you than to forget about him, I want you to move on and I want to be the reason you are able to move on." Jericho took a step forward, his voice deep with sincerity and his eyes burning with intensity. I felt the blush rise to my cheeks at his honesty, but I couldn't turn away. I drank in his words, holding them tightly to my heart and letting the hope he shared fill me. "I love you, that has never changed. I am hoping that one day, not any day soon, I get that, but one day you will be able to love me in return. So I plan on doing everything in my power to help you move past Kiran and onto.... different things. It's not fair though, if you don't know the entire story, so I'm starting with that; I'm starting with the truth. I will *always* give you the truth, and it will always be the whole truth." he smiled gently at me, almost mischievously.

"Thank you. I appreciate the truth and I, and I want to move on too," I promised sincerely and then walked passed Jericho intending to go to bed; I was suddenly very tired.

I turned around at the doorway though, feeling that I owed Jericho the same honesty he gave to me, "And Jericho," I started, he lifted his head and turned to me, "I am happy you are going to try to.... well, I'm just happy you're going to try." I smiled at him and then turned into the dark, empty hallway, stumbling around until I found the staircase.

I climbed the stairs thoughtfully, a soft smile never leaving my lips. There was life after Kiran; there would be hope after the death of my first love. That's all Kiran was to me, a first love, and at the very least, I could have one more. I could fall in love again, I could dream again. And after all of this was over.... I could live again.

The townhouse looked dark and empty. We stood outside the white brick house that connected seamlessly with identical dwellings flowing down the crowded Paris street, and waited. Jericho knocked three times on the aged, black door and so far, we neither saw, nor heard any movement inside the house.

I was getting impatient. After a three hour train ride and three more hours wandering around the foreign city trying to find the right safe-house, we apparently came at a time when nobody was home.

I tapped my foot rapidly and crossed my arms as if angrily willing Titus to show his face. The lure of Paris was overwhelming and as I stood outside the door, with my back to the still icy waters of the Seine River, I painfully suppressed the tugging desire to explore the city.

I could see the top of the Eiffel Tower in the distance; we walked past Notre Dame on our quest to find this house. I dreamed about what it would be like to wander aimlessly through the Louvre and I could smell freshly baked bread from a little bakery just a block away.

"OK, enough of this," I grumbled, finally reaching my breaking point after a local walked by holding his elegantly unique pastry proudly in his hands as if taunting my stomach in the cruelest of ways.

I pushed past Gabriel and Jericho who stood politely on the stoop and reached out for the door handle. I heard Jericho start to protest, but before I could figure out what he was saying, I used my magic abruptly on the door, bursting it open. However, something happened when I forced the door to move.

With my hand still on the handle, the brass doorknob fought back violently, sending me flying across the checkered marble floor of the entry way and head first into the ivory wainscoted wall opposite the doorway. At the same time, three masked men jumped from every direction, holding weapons high above their heads, screaming at me. I screamed back, covering my face with my arms and expecting the worst.

"Well done, gentlemen," Jericho called, clapping his hands, clearly amused.

I pulled my hands away from my face, finding courage in Jericho's sarcasm. The men around me too, paused and lowered their arms slowly. Now that I had time to take them in, I could see that their weapons weren't so much of the dangerous variety and more of the pots, pans and cricket mallet variety. I sat up straightly, pushing myself against the wall, which was now marked with a head-sized hole through it.

"Eden?" one of the men exclaimed through a black ski mask, his voice muffled since the mask lacked an opening for a mouth.

"Xander?" I asked, realizing who the three men surrounding me probably were.

"Jericho?" another one of them asked, and then the three of them simultaneously removed their masks.

Xander, Xavier and Titus all stood around me, suddenly relieved. Titus reached out a strong hand to me, pulling me to my feet and then into a giant bear hug.

"Man, are we glad to see you!" He practically shouted in my ear.

"Yeah, you look like it," I mumbled sarcastically, but smiling all the same. "Didn't you recognize our magic?"

"Oh, sorry about that," Xavier apologized sincerely, staring at the hole my head had made. "We felt your magic, but you can't be too careful these days, and we wanted to make sure, you know, extra sure you weren't the bad guys." He pouted his lips, one hand absently stroking the gruff shadow of a beard he kept nicely trimmed and nodded his head as if to say they had obviously done a good job at being "extra sure."

"Well, you definitely did that; don't worry." I rubbed the top of my head where a nasty bump started to rise. I sent magic to heal the wound, but no amount of magic was going to be able to heal my bruised ego from being the victim of easy magic.

Everyone laughed, even Gabriel, and the tension in the room was lifted. Jericho shut the door and locked it and then we moved into an elegant sitting room just off the entryway.

"Man, it is so good to see you guys!" Xavier echoed Titus's sentiments, plopping down on a perfectly white, pristine couch and bouncing up and down with excitement. He tucked his chin-length, dark hair behind one ear and I marveled at how similar he and Xander looked. They weren't twins, but they were almost identical, facial hair and all. "We heard what happened, but Jericho, man, I didn't expect to see you here!"

"Yeah, it's good to see you guys too!" Jericho echoed equally as animated. Titus reached out his arm and patted him roughly on the back. The moment felt like they would all get up and hug each other, but instead the four boys sat or stood staring at one other bouncing up and down with nervous energy. "I'm glad you're all here and all Ok."

"Oh, we were never really in danger," Xavier continued. "I mean, nobody even knew we were here or knew anything about us. But man, when we heard what happened at the farm, that our worst nightmare came true, well, we just.... it was hard to stay here. It was hard to sit still...."

The room fell silent for a moment, nobody moving, nobody making a sound. We sat staring at each other, lost in the deepest moment of remembrance for the dead and the heart-wrenching frustration of waiting for vengeance. Collectively we knew it would come, but for now, at this moment, we were prisoners of patience.

"Jericho, dude, we heard you were captured, what are you doing here? What happened at the farm? We need to know it all." Xander broke the respectful silence.

"It's a long story," Jericho sighed, glancing at me with a curious expression. But then I felt it; I felt the stab of longing and regret that threatened to sweep me up again in the trauma of memory. The story, and Jericho would have to start from the beginning, would force me to be fragile, would demand that I give credence to the painful emotions and I wasn't ready for that again. I especially wasn't ready for these boys to witness it.

"Eden, why don't we go make some coffee and let these friends catch up for a moment," Gabriel offered wisely.

"That's a good idea," I breathed a sigh of relief. "Oh, wait do you know these guys?" I asked, realizing how rude I had been.

"Are you Gabriel?" Titus asked, walking over and extending his hand. When Gabriel nodded, he continued, "I've heard of you. I'm Titus Kelly and this is Xander and Xavier Akin."

"I've heard of you as well; it is good to meet you," Gabriel said in his abrupt way that was always taking me off guard, even if he was saying the most normal things, "It is good to be here."

He turned on his heel and walked out of the room while I struggled to catch up with him before I lost him in the enormity of the house.

Gabriel walked straight into a large all-white kitchen that was perfectly cleaned and mouth-droppingly immaculate. I found a seat at the kitchen island while Gabriel tinkered with the coffee pot.

"Well, this blows the stereotype that boys can't clean up after themselves, out of the water," I mumbled to myself, impressed that three boys living together could keep a kitchen this perfect.

Gabriel didn't respond, so I turned my attention to some picture frames on the island next to me. My mouth dropped open again after realizing who was in every single picture.

"Gabriel!" I shrieked, forcing him to turn around and pay attention to me, "This is my English teacher! This is Mr. Lambert!" I held up a picture, as if proving my point, both horrified and shocked that we would be inside a house possibly owned by the single man that hated my habit for tardiness most in the world.

"Ah, Charles Lambert? Yes, he's an old friend of Amory's. Well, and an old friend of mine, too, actually," Gabriel turned back around to focus his attention on the dripping coffee pot.

"Wait, so does that mean this is his house? That's he's part of the Rebellion?" I asked, not comprehending that it was even a possibility. I didn't think the worst of Mr. Lambert, but the thought that we would be fighting on the same side of this war was almost too bizarre to believe.

"Oh, yes, for a long time now," Gabriel replied, pouring me a cup of coffee and then one for himself.

"Eden is definitely going to have to change, though," Xander announced playfully, walking into the kitchen and putting both of his hands on my shoulders. "Because this might cut it when you're climbing mountains, but sorry, E, they won't even let you in a place like that, dressed like this." Xander squeezed my shoulders in his giant hands, making me cringe and laugh at the same time.

"Let me in? Where are we going?" I asked, trying to catch up with whatever plans the boys had made in the living room.

"To a party, of course," Xavier replied, a mischievous smile on his face.

"And what party would that be?" I questioned, reservations already sending alarms off in my blood.

"A birthday party," Titus answered seriously, walking over to the coffee pot and accepting a cup from Gabriel.

"Whose birthday party?" I pressed, growing irritated that they were making me ask so many questions to get to the bottom of this.

"Sebastian Cartier." Jericho was the last to enter the kitchen. He took a seat next to me, reaching out for the cup of coffee Gabriel was extending to him. "It's his birthday and the Immortal community is throwing an extra-large celebration in honor of him tonight. Rumor has it that somebody took his magic. Apparently, he's a little depressed about that," Jericho finished snidely, the same mischievous smile on his face as well.

"Then somebody better finish the job," I murmured with renewed interest.

The large kitchen buzzed with anxious energy. It felt good to reunite with this team. We were finally an assembled group with a concrete mission ahead of us. Sebastian Cartier was more than just an end to tie up; he was a wealth of information and if we could pull off kidnapping him, it would be a serious message sent to Lucan. The tables were finally turned on our relationship; I would be the one stalking him this time.

## Chapter Eleven

"I still don't understand why we couldn't have at least brought *some* explosives," Xander grumbled underneath his breath. "I mean, I'm not asking for a whole lot here, just one or two or maybe five.... small.... small-ish bombs."

"Xander, for the last time, we don't want to hurt any more Immortals than we have to. And we only want to *kill* two of them, Ok *maybe* three of them," I scolded sternly, while we walked down the long concrete tunnel leading to a secret Immortal club deep beneath the streets of Paris. "Plus, blowing up an underground club might have some serious effects up in the human world," I reminded him casually, "and by might, I mean it would, we're talking major sink hole in the middle of downtown Paris, that is so not Ok."

My brand new, extra tall stilletos clicked with every step I took, echoing off the rounded concrete walls. Low, reverberating club music grew steadily louder in the distance the closer we walked to the Immortal Prince's birthday party.

"I didn't say we had to use them, I was just suggesting they might be useful, you know just in case," Xander protested and I gave him a hard look not wanting to go over my reasoning again, for the hundredth time. "All right, all right, you're the boss-lady," he said with hands in the air surrendering.

"Avalon would have brought explosives," Xavier mumbled and when I turned my glare on him, he shrunk away to the back of our group, but not before the corners of his mouth turned up into a smile.

The excited buzzing of magic grew stronger, the farther into the tunnel we walked. I looked around at the boys, who had all cleaned up very nicely. All except Gabriel who opted to stay home instead of trading in his priestly wardrobe for something that would be more appropriate for a night club. Titus was less lumberjack looking after he shaved the red stubble that grew long during their "underground" phase. He looked muscular in a tighter fitting white dress shirt and loosened tie. Xander likewise, wore a collared white dress shirt, but underneath a gray suit coat with matching charcoal trousers. Xander changed up the color a bit with a black dress shirt and went a little classier with a well tailored, tan suit. He pulled his longer hair back into a loose ponytail.

They were all good looking guys, made even more attractive by their boyish excitement for the mission ahead of us; but the best looking among them all was obviously, or at least in my opinion, Jericho. He smartly slicked back his hair out of his eyes, since he had yet to trim it and his angular jaw jutted out strongly against the severe hair style. He borrowed one of Xander's perfectly fitting suits, a charcoal pinstriped number with matching vest, a black collared shirt and a silver tie tucked stylishly into his vest.

I looked up at him for a moment, in awe of his calmed nerves and flawless resolve. I slipped my hand into his, desperate to attach my anxious energy to his magic, hoping he could sooth my frayed energy and strengthen my shrinking courage.

"What if they notice me?" I asked aloud, biting my bottom lip and reminding myself of Amory's all-powerful magic that blended seamlessly with my blood.

"That's bound to happen," Jericho said hoarsely, looking down at me with a mischievous smile, and letting his eyes sweep over me.

I cleared my throat nervously, smoothing out the wrinkles in my short, fiery red evening dress that I picked up earlier. Titus took me out this afternoon to the Champs Elysees, the main street and shopping district in Paris, where I ran into a store, shouted in very broken French what I needed, and threw down one of my new credit cards without even trying the new dress on or looking at the total.

I gasped in horror when I clambered back into the taxi, precious dress in my possession and thousands of dollars poorer. Titus promised that I would not even notice the spent money and talked me down from my buyer's remorse ledge. I was grateful for him in that moment.

I was even more grateful for the store clerk that must have taken pity on my wild eyes and tragic appearance and outfitted me with one smoking hot cocktail dress. The top was tight, hugging my curves with silky red satin in the front and elegant black lace in the back. The neckline was high and felt modest, but the way the bodice hugged me suggested anything but propriety. The skirt ballooned out in silky, tiered, uneven ruffles that ended somewhere short of mid-thigh. A black satin sash tied in a bow, almost too big of a bow, around my waist pulled the look together.

I pulled my long, wavy black hair over my shoulder and pinned it carefully so that my unfading, shimmering, blue tattoo would stay hidden. I kept the necklace on the outside of my dress, the dead black stone dangling against the delicate satin and knocking the emerald engagement ring while I walked. The necklace was a reminder of my place in royal society, or lack thereof. After the look was pulled together, after the black heels were fastened and the matching crimson lipstick applied, I couldn't help but feel dangerous. I was on a mission tonight, and poor Sebastian didn't know what was about to hit him.

"All right, does everyone remember the plan? We enter separately and meet back at the bar in fifteen minutes," I reminded the boys. My heart pumped in rhythm to the fast bass line as music grew louder; we were almost there.

The guys nodded in reply and I laughed to myself. This was not their first mission, I was the newbie. There was absolutely no reason to remind them of anything. Titus quickened his pace, holding a wrapped birthday present awkwardly under his arm and took the lead.

The rest of us held back until Xander and Xavier felt that there was adequate space between Titus and them and then separated themselves from us as well. They each held a gift; I found it amusing to think about a time when someone would open all of these presents and find someone's random throw pillows and a cricket mallet that was almost used to smash my head in earlier in the day.

Jericho looked down at me, our hands already interlocked and smiled. "We will have to pull off looking like a couple," he said shyly.

"You have no objections from me," I replied coyly. The dress was making me feel a little vixen-like tonight. I let go of his hand, and slipped my arm through his, pulling at him gently so that when we approached the bouncers I was pretending to whisper something into his ear, although whispering at that point would have been pointless against the resonating house music echoing off the enclosed hallway. He blushed appropriately and I finished the act by bravely nibbling on his ear lobe.

"Gentlemen," Jericho purred suavely, reaching into his suit jacket and removing an elegant invitation with the royal seal stamped on the front. The invitation had been stolen earlier in the week by Titus, Xander and Xavier when they thought they were the only ones left of the Rebellion. At that point, explosives were definitely involved.

The bouncers inspected the invitation and then the two of us. Thuggish, burly and robust Titans, they wore menacing looks that sent a shiver down my back. I smiled constantly at them, my face feeling like it was turning to plaster, and leaning in to Jericho so that I was almost hiding behind him.

The two bouncers talked back and forth in hushed, fast tones and then one of them walked back inside of the club. We stood their awkwardly staring at the remaining bouncer while a line of other party-goers formed behind us.

The second bouncer returned after a few minutes and motioned for us to enter. We handed him our make-shift gifts and then walked past them into the crowded club. The electricity in my blood ignited in a lightning storm of warning as soon as we were past the guards. They recognized me, or us, or both of us; that much was clear.

Inside the club were hundreds of Immortals pressed together on a dance floor that took up the entire room, except for a bar and small seating area towards the back of the club. We walked in on a balcony overlooking the party, and as we mosied down the stairs, we watched the Titans move into place. They moved discreetly to block all of the exits, surrounding the room with tight security and sending Jericho and I a clear message that we were caught.

I swallowed the lump rising in my throat and clung to Jericho, trying to find the courage not to run from the room that very second. We expected this, I reminded myself, so far everything was going according to plan, everything except my nerves. I needed to look in control, to appear unconcerned; I had to at least act like I could take down the entire room with just one stomp of my magical foot.

"Remember what they did to your family," Jericho shouted in my ear, feeling my tension.

"Yes, you're right. Thank you," I yelled back, as we pushed through sweaty bodies, locked together in the rhythm of the dance floor.

Bubbles of every size floated through the room and popped on bare shoulders and hands raised high in the air. The chandeliers that hung from the ceiling were clear crystal and the candlelight that flickered on their ends, sent the reflections of the glass sparkling around the room like modern day disco balls. A DJ spun songs in a booth hovering over the dance floor, and extending from the balcony circling the room. Beautiful girls danced on pedestals, and Immortals of every kind, color and country celebrated together to the sounds of worldwide hits mixed into dance beats.

I looked around for Sebastian but the sea of people moving like violent waves around me swallowed me. I let Jericho pull me through the crowd, pushing people out of the way who barely noticed our efforts.

The bar was just as crowded as the dance floor, and the mix of hundreds of magics made it impossible to feel out Titus, Xander and Xavier. Jericho stood on his tip toes; trying to get a better view until eventually he saw something he must have recognized.

He pulled me again, through more impossibly small spaces and to the corner of the bar where Xander and Xavier waited for us. They ordered themselves drinks and were sipping them slowly, trying to look bored.

"Where's Titus?" I shouted at them, working hard to be heard over the music.

They shrugged their shoulders, and shook their heads. I turned around, hoping to find him in the flashing lights and crowded room, knowing it was impossible and hoping beyond hope that he was Ok. However, as soon as I thought the worst, he violently thrust his way through the edge of the dance floor, sweating and looking frightened., but most importantly, shimmering head to toe with glitter.

His shirt opened at the top, revealing his smooth chest, appeared as if some of his buttons had popped off. His tie was completely askew and looser than it was earlier and his reddish hair was tussled. His eyes turned from wild to relieved as soon as he found us and my instant reaction was that he had been detained by some Titans.

"Titus, why are you covered in glitter?" I exclaimed, using my fingers to try to brush it away from his exposed chest.

"There were these girls, and they were.... they were.... they were crazy!" He screamed, his eyes turning feral for a moment.

Even in the heat of the mission, that was the funniest thing any of us had heard in a long time. We burst into laughter, while Titus tried to pull his look back together and I tried to brush the glitter off his clothes.

"Whatever dude, just as long as you're Ok with carrying this thing out looking like Disco Barbie, it's cool with us," Xavier teased him and I tried to control my laughter while Titus stared down Xavier threateningly.

"Ok, well, we were right," I shouted, focusing their attention, "We're pretty sure they recognized me or Jericho or both of us and now that we are talking with you guys, I'm sure your cover is blown too. So let's focus, find Sebastian and get the hell out of here before

Titus gets kidnapped by girls who want to glitter him to death." I smiled, trying to keep the mood light.

"Same teams?" Xander shouted, gesturing among all of us.

"I say we all split up," I shouted back, "if anyone finds him, get him up on the balcony where we can see you and we'll all converge. I don't think any of us will be in trouble unless we try to leave. It's going to be messy no matter how we get out of here. And if you get into any trouble, shift," I said pointedly, looking at the three boys that were Shape-Shifters, "Or send up a sign," I turned to Jericho, "Which door is the best way to the surface?"

"That one." Titus pointed to the opposite entrance than the one we came through, the one behind the DJ booth. Then Titus, Xander and Xavier immediately split up, disappearing into the chaos surrounding us.

"I'm coming with you." Jericho demanded, "I don't want you to be alone in here."

"I'm not alone," I replied confidently, "and I'll be fine. Trust me. This will go faster anyway. Besides if I'm alone, I might distract the Guard long enough for you to find him." Jericho stared at me for a moment longer; I could see the internal debate he was having. I made sense from a tactical standpoint, but from an emotional one, not so much. "Go!" I shouted, pointing my finger and he reluctantly obeyed, walking backwards into the crowd before disappearing completely into the black hole of the dance floor.

I entered the swaying wall of people through a different gap and forced myself in and out of impossible spaces in search of Sebastian. I hoped I would be able to feel out his magic if I got close enough to him, but the bodies pressing against me in one solid movement of celebration with a mixed frenzy of electricity suggested otherwise.

It wasn't until I literally ran right into him that I realized he was looking for me as well. "Are you here to wish me a happy birthday?" he shouted over the roar of the party. I stood up straighter, trying to take a step back from him. Our bodies were firmly pressed together in the middle of the frenetic floor.

"Actually, I did," I shouted into his ear. I took a small step back, realizing that I was never going to be able to feel his magic, because he had none left; I had taken it. Now he stood before me a hollowed shadow of himself, with dull and lifeless eyes, in sunken black circles. He was ghostly white, and trembled while standing as if the effort to remain upright was tremendously tiring.

"Then you won't mind coming upstairs with me?" he asked with practiced politeness, his eyes menacing in their dark sockets.

"Not at all, as long as you don't mind leaving with me," I shouted, smiling at him with the same set of manners. I felt in control. Even if Titans surrounded the room, Sebastian was weak and helpless. And that was all that I needed to fuel my vengeance.

"Eden, if you finish what you started, I'll go anywhere with you and do anything you want," he yelled desperately, his voice gruff and strained.

"Then it's a deal," I agreed quietly, glancing up at the Titan lined balcony and wondering if, even with Sebastian's willingness to leave, our escape plan was suddenly good enough of an idea.

## Chapter Twelve

The crowd cleared a path for Sebastian; with every step he took, the people in his way took a step back. Immortals who were wildly enjoying themselves on the dance floor, solemnly and respectfully stepped out of the way for the once-Immortal Prince. They shrunk away from him as if he were poison and most of them couldn't even look up from the ground.

I felt the chill that followed him, the bad energy and the fear that if they touched him, they would become like him. I thought that would make me feel powerful, and I would find vanity in single-handedly ruining this man's life; instead I felt everything but pride. A treacherous pang of guilt crossed my heart and I too followed after Sebastian with eyes lowered to the floor, temporarily ashamed of how I humbled this royalty.

He walked proudly up the staircase, head held high, and chin jutted forward. I glanced back down at the dance floor. The music had quieted and those dancing were temporarily stilled. I spotted my team easily in the crowd and watched as they moved into position.

At the top of the stairs, Sebastian walked towards the DJ box and the door behind it. I half wondered if he was just going to walk out of the building with me trailing behind, but realized that was way too easy of an option.

Behind the DJ booth were two doors, one that led to the surface and one that led to a private office, filled with Titans waiting for me. Unfortunately, Sebastian chose door number two.

We walked into the office, and three Titans stepped in front of the door, to guard the exit. Although the room remained silent, the energy buzzing rampantly about the room was not. It screamed at me, calling me a traitor, demanding my blood to save their beloved Crown Prince; it cried hungrily to avenge what I did to Sebastian.

My blood ignited with electricity, every sense at its sharpest. I looked around at the olive-toned Titans, each man different but identical at the same time. These dark haired, unquestionably strong creatures held the keen look in their eyes of those trained and disciplined in the military style and they all, without exception wanted me dead.

Sebastian motioned to a mustard colored, velvet chair sitting in the middle of the room, across from a large, imposing, cherry wood desk. I took it, feigning unconcerned and crossed my legs to maintain the semblance of lady-like behavior. Sebastian walked around the desk; taking his seat in a high backed, brown leather chair with bronze detailing and wide, dark wooden armrests.

He didn't speak for a while. He moved papers around on his desk, stacking them neatly to the side and then rested his elbows heavily on the cleared space. He stared at me for a moment, and then his head drooped into his hands, covering his face and rubbing his eyes as if he was fighting to stay awake.

A knock at the door jolted Sebastian back to life; he sat up straighter, pushing himself forward in the chair. The door opened and in walked Bianca, Sebastian's mother and his father, Jean Cartier. Bianca's face, twisted into hatred, stared at me with enough contempt that I thought I would burst into flames. His father, too, looked at me with eyes that would kill me if they could.

"How dare you come here!" Bianca shrieked at me. She stayed near the door, clinging to her husband for support. "How dare you show your face here!"

"Mother, please," Sebastian sighed, "we have her now. Look, it's worked to our advantage."

"Yes, you're right," Bianca calmed down considerably, but her tone was marred with venom. "You will give Sebastian back his magic this moment, you little tart. Right now!" She finished loudly and so forcefully that Jean Cartier adjusted his hold on her to keep her from stumbling.

"Or what?" I asked, finding my confidence, and hiding the fact that I couldn't give back Sebastian's magic, even if I wanted to. "You can't hurt me, he can't hurt me," I motioned to her husband. "This Guard is not *enough* to hurt me. If I don't give Sebastian back his magic, then.... what?" I asked haughtily.

"Then I will rip your pretty little head off!" the Princess shouted, her long blonde hair tumbling over her shoulders and shaking with ferocity. Even with her face contorted into hatred, she was strikingly beautiful. Although her perfectly poised English accent emoted a violent rage, she still remained a Princess, even in a fit of fury.

"Mother, please calm down," Sebastian soothed with a replica of his mother's accent. He stood, walked over to the Princess and laid a gentle hand on her forearm. "We have to take her to Uncle Lucan, you know that."

Sebastian stood taller than his mother. He towered over her and came close to his father's height. She looked up at him and her expression immediately changed. She turned from an angry woman who promised my death to a loving, caring mother broken by her son's suffering. She reached a trembling hand to his face, caressing it gently; he bent down to kiss her on the forehead.

"Kiran is dying, and I am not. Eden is meant for him," Sebastian whispered compassionately. "I will take her to Lucan; he will know what to do, I promise. He will not let me suffer like this forever."

Bianca's eyes flickered with uncertainty. The frown lines around her mouth returned and I could tell that she did not believe Lucan would do anything for her son. Her eyes flashed to mine for a brief moment, but instead of hatred, for the briefest of seconds, I saw hope.

"All right, take her to my brother. Go now. I want our entire Guard to travel with you though." She looked up at her husband who nodded his agreement.

"Not all of the Guard, but very well, I will only leave a few." He smiled down at his mother and his father patted him on the shoulder. Apparently, the Grand Duke of Canesbury was a man of very few words. "We will leave immediately."

"I have a team of people with me, they will never let you take me," I spoke up, pretending to protest. I needed to include the other guys and get them to the surface. Once there, we could easily escape. Or at least, I was confident we could escape.

"They are already in our custody, you stupid girl," Jean Cartier announced, his French accent thick with hatred.

I shut my mouth, biting my lip to keep from spitting something sarcastic back, and then crossed my arms defiantly. I would play this game until I was safe, until I was back on the streets of Paris.

"Leave us," the Princess suddenly demanded. "I would like a word with her before you go." She leveled her clear blue eyes at me, and I squirmed uncomfortably in my chair. I wasn't afraid of her magic; I knew that I was stronger. I was however, a little uncomfortable with her callous determination.

"Darling, you can't be serious." Jean Cartier tensed his grip on her arm. "She is a monster; I will not tolerate you being alone with her, unprotected."

"She cannot hurt me anymore than she already has," Bianca whispered huskily to her husband and I looked away before my face betrayed the guilt rising inside of me.

    Jean Cartier tipped her chin up towards his mouth and kissed her sweetly before leaving the room without another word. She waved her hand at the Titans lining the walls of the office and they too filed out, although reluctantly. The last was Sebastian who stopped at the door and turned to me. He opened his mouth as if to say something, but instead took his mother's hand and kissed it, bowing respectfully before closing the door behind us and leaving the King's sister and I alone.

    She stood staring at me, her blue eyes turning to ice, and sending a chill down my spine. She wore an elegant silver ball gown with diamond detailing. A small, matching silver crown sat centered on top of her head where a giant ruby glinted and shined, reflecting the golden glow of the above light fixture. Her apparel reminded me that she was royalty, and I was not.

    "Is there a way to save him?" she asked coolly, her words and demeanor carefully controlled.

    "No," I answered quickly, but then thought of the leverage I had in Avalon and immediately retracted the word with my concrete sincerity, "Maybe. I haven't had reason to try.... yet," I finished, hoping to sound not only convincing but confident as well.

    "My son is a reason to try," Bianca appealed. Her eyes melted into sapphire orbs of sorrow.

    "So you say," I remarked slowly.

    "You were friends with him once; surely there is a shadow of goodness still left inside of you." She fell to her knees at my chair, gripping my hand between the two of hers before I could react and pull away.

    "I am not the one that has lost my moral compass," I accused harshly, hardly able to comprehend her pleading. "Your family destroyed mine; they have murdered or taken everyone I have ever loved! How dare you ask me to spare your son, when here he stands *with* you. I cannot have the indulgence of being surrounded by my family!" I half shouted at her, pushing her away and moving to the far corner of the room.

    I wanted to hate her in the same way that she hated me. I wanted to laugh and mock her attempt to convince me to save Sebastian, but I couldn't. The sickening, guilty waves of an undeserved compassion washed over me and I fought with wavering resolve to say no to this woman.

"You will not help him?" she asked quietly, her eyes daring to meet mine one more time.

I jutted my chin forward and crossed my arms defiantly, "He has already requested my help. I will give him what he asked for."

"He is my son," she begged desperately, her voice breaking and tears falling from her blue eyes turning them into clear pools of mourning.

"And he is my enemy," I vowed menacingly.

She turned her back on me and her shoulders shook with the weight only a mother could bear. I swallowed the lump in my throat and walked out of the room. I was at war. I reminded myself and continued to remind myself that I was at war with forces of dark evil. Bianca could look as heartbroken as her callous heart would allow her to perform, but she was my enemy. Her son was my enemy. Every single member of that godforsaken royal family was my enemy and if I wanted to give this Kingdom any hope of freedom, I was going to have to break every last one of them, starting with Sebastian.

Outside the office door, the Titan escort waited for me. Sebastian leaned against the wall of the DJ booth, looking tired and bored. When the door closed behind me, we moved as one unit in silence through the other door. Surrounded on every side, Sebastian walked next to me.

After a few yards through another concrete tunnel we reached an iron staircase that wound in small circles up several floors to the surface, to downtown Paris. The staircase shook and swayed with the weight of our mobilized battalion and I clung to the railing, not trusting anyone's magic but my own.

We stopped several times for Sebastian to catch his breath and rest. The climb was significant but not for an Immortal. For Sebastian, I wondered if it would go faster if one of his bodyguards would just carry him. But I kept my mouth shut.

Finally, we reached the door at the top of the staircase, leading into the lobby of an expensive apartment complex. White marble surfaced the floors and a luxurious sitting area decorated a small alcove next to four elevators leading to the upstairs rooms.

Titus, Xavier, Xander and Jericho sat crushed together on one couch, looking terribly uncomfortable and sinfully mischievous at the same time. They appeared to be unharmed and I could tell from their anxious energy they were just waiting for me to get there before the fun could begin.

"Well, gentlemen," Xavier stood up and stretched his arms widely, as soon as I walked into the lobby; even completely surrounded by guards and unfairly outnumbered, he was confident of our plan. "It's been fun, like super fun," he laughed, very sarcastically, "but it's probably time we get going."

The other boys on the couch smiled at his brazenness and stood up as well. The attitude was catching and I found myself grinning, walking over to them with an air of premature victory.

"You don't really think we're just going to let you go, do you?" a confused, brutish Titan asked gravely.

"You can do whatever you want, but we're going to go. Uh, yeah, we're going to go," Xavier continued with a hard edge to his voice.

The temperature of the room jolted into latent hostility and every Immortal stood to battle-ready attention. The magic buzzing about was wild and frenetic, angry and vengeful, from every side of the argument. We were trained and vetted fighters, disciplined for battle and well-prepared for moments like this. I was as prepared as any Titan in the room to lose my life fighting for the side I served.

"You are not going anywhere," growled an imposing Titan standing a few feet from me.

"I told you, E; we should have brought the explosives," Xander grumbled underneath his breath in good humor.

"Listen to me carefully, before you decide to blow each other up," Sebastian stepped forward, commanding the attention of the room; he was immediately given it, even from my team. "Not one of you will harm these prisoners. I am going to leave with them now, that is my choice and you can do nothing about it. If any one of you tries to harm them, especially Eden, I promise that you will die. Everyone else that has crossed her has, and I swear to you, that you will be next. Do not make that mistake tonight."

"What will we tell the Duke and Duchess?" a weary, skeptical Titan asked bravely.

"You will tell them that their son is dead and that the prisoners escaped," Sebastian sighed wearily. "And if you do not let us go peacefully then it will be the truth anyway, only I will not be the only one that dies tonight. Is that clear?"

Sebastian's guard backed away from us slowly. It was obvious that none of them truly believed his every word. Instead, his instructions confused them; not many royal family members chose willingly to walk away with the Resistance, commanding their guard to stay put. Jericho, Titus, Xander, Xavier and I moved as one solidified wall towards the door that led to the outside and into the busy, crowded Paris streets.

"Eden, they have been warned. If they move against us, do what you must," Sebastian said gruffly, walking without concern, past the five us that moved so carefully and out the door.

I stood up from a slightly crouched, protective stance a little befuddled. "Follow him," I commanded to my team and they were through the door in moments.

I was the last to leave, wanting to give my team ample time to melt into the crowds and nightlife of the City of Lights.

Now that I was alone in the room with the team of fifteen Titans, they eyed me with less caution. They stepped towards me, hungry with violent greed and opportunistic eyes. I made a good catch, if they could take me down; no doubt the King would reward them gratuitously.

"Be careful now," I warned, readying my magic with a flare of electricity.

"You're not so scary, all on your own." One Titan stepped forward from the rest, his forehead marked with a long, jagged scar and his large, beastly hands poised for a fight.

I stood up, a little annoyed and waited for his attack. Immediately, he sent a wave as strong, but not debilitating of magic at me that I stopped with a simple hand movement. My blood pumped with the electricity of the last Oracle. Did he really think that would be enough to trouble me?

He sent another burst of magic and then his fellow Guard joined in. I stopped as many as I could with my own magic, but eventually I got bored with their arrogance. I stomped my foot on the floor, sending a ripple of magic shattering the expensive marbled floor and knocking all fifteen of them off balance.

I picked up the first Titan with magic, holding him precariously in the air before tossing him through the plate glass window in the front of the lobby. I could feel his magic surge to heal his body and I knew that it would only be seconds before he was back though the broken window causing more trouble.

Another Titan converged on me, hoping to have better results, and I held my hand out to him, blasting a lightning bolt of blue electricity into his gut. He tumbled across the broken marble, unconscious and groaning.

The first Titan returned back into room, and this time he hit me in the back with a harsh blast of magic that forced me forward and into the arms of his waiting team. I struggled against them, but their brutish arms pinned me down.

It was time to move on, I needed to end the fight and send a clear message. The Titan with the scar stood in front of me, his face happy with triumph and his eyes alight with greedy satisfaction. I decided to teach him a valuable lesson.

I picked him up again, shaking him violently in the air. I drained his magic without even moving a finger; the other Titans in the room felt it drain slowly from his blood. When nothing was left, I tossed his unconscious body to the corner of the room with a little bit of an over-dramatic flair and wiggled free from the now loose grasp, barely containing me.

"Wise decision boys," I congratulated the Titans, walking away from the now open-mouthed Titans and feeling like I needed to have the last word. Then I was gone through the door and disappeared into the night.

The outcome of this mission proved easier than I anticipated. The outcome resulted far more favorably than I had hoped, and as I hurried to catch up with my team and our newly acquired prisoner I was filled with expectancy. I moved fearlessly through the streets. We had acquired a significant piece of this puzzle, and I was one more step closer to reaching Avalon. I would get what I could out of the suicidal Sebastian and grant him his wish. Then I would move on to the next step, to the next portion of this wearing journey. I would forget all about the original intruder and how he betrayed me alongside his cousin and caused the downfall of my family and the necessity to kill him in the first place.

It would be that simple.

# Chapter Thirteen

I walked slowly down the townhouse-lined street. Paris finally quieted well into the night, the streets darkened, and the City of Lights went to bed. The river flowed quietly to my left and I used magic to direct me back to the safe-house.

I would be the last to arrive, the last one to make it back, as long as everyone executed his task safely, and as long as everything went according to plan. I expected more of a fight, more of a struggle to get away, and without one I instantly believed every member of my team would be safe.

Now that the black door was in front of me, I found my breathing labored and the familiar stabbing fears that warned something could have gone wrong. I had offered to be the last to arrive so that I could sweep the streets for other magics, and that I could, with absolute certainty, walk into the safe-house and know that it was not compromised.

I stopped in front of the stone-step stoop and swallowed. I stared up at the door wondering if I would ever be capable of unabashed bravery. My thoughts flickered to Avalon, and the moments before we walked into the hotel in Geneva so many months ago. He was never afraid, even though it was nothing more than what we were told it would be. Moments before we entered the room Avalon was convinced it was a trap. Yet, he barreled through the door ready for anything.

I cowered in front of what appeared to be safety, still terrified of the unknown. I searched deeply for the courage to move, for the resolve to banish the fear. At times, when my Titan skills took over, I was so sure of every move, confident that I could do anything. Now, in isolation and without adrenaline, I was frozen by nameless fears.

They swirled about inside my head, creating doubt and whispering foundation-less threats. I closed my eyes, fighting them; fighting the belief that I was destined to lose everyone I loved. What happened up until now was a tragedy, an evil phenomenon that would not repeat itself. Blinded and deceived before, my eyes were wide open now and I would not lose another loved one.

Not again.

It was there that the courage, the fire of vengeance, would supply my magic, and the spirit to be fearless. I just had to remember it.

I sprang up the stairs and through the door in seconds. Heads snapped to attention and the surge of adrenaline could be felt throughout the room. Titus, Xavier and Jericho stood over Sebastian who slept on the couch, not even moved by my entrance. Gabriel and Xander stumbled from the kitchen, clearly exhausted, but still up, waiting for my return.

"Finally," Jericho breathed and I watched his body relax. I should have simply been grateful to see everyone; I should have stopped and breathed in the relief the rest of them felt, but I was worked up now. I remembered what happened to Amory and where Avalon was now and alleviation would not satisfy me.

"Move," I commanded, walking past the team and to Sebastian's sleeping body. I stared at him, watching him breathe evenly in the peaceful nothing of sleep and I couldn't take it anymore. I picked him up with my magic, violently shaking him, startling him from his dream world. When he looked down at me with dead eyes that could barely be bothered to open, I lost my temper entirely and threw him across the room. He crashed into a decorative side table and smashed a delicate antique vase before sliding to the floor in a heap of helplessness.

He moved slowly, struggling to pick himself up out of the expensive wreckage and sat back on his hands, smiling at me.

"You've come to fulfill your promise so soon?" he said smugly, and then leaned to the side and coughed blood in speckled stains across the checkered marbled floor.

"You would like that, wouldn't you?" I asked, shivering with anger.

"Eden," Jericho was at my side, laying a gentle hand on my forearm and whispering soothingly into my ear. "Maybe you should get some rest? The rest of us have worked out shifts to watch him, it's been a long several days for you, maybe you could try to sleep, hmmm....?"

I flinched at Jericho's reasoning, not wanting to listen, not wanting to hear him. I tore my eyes away from Sebastian, away from his lifeless, bruised and sunken brown eyes and focused reluctantly on Jericho. His light brown eyes speckles with green sparkled with life, with concern and with the energy of magic.

"It's all right, Eden; get some sleep. He'll still be here in the morning," Jericho continued.

"Let her finish," Sebastian shouted with surprising force.

My gaze flew to his and the hatred renewed.

"You are not a Prince here, inside these walls you are our prisoner and you will act as such," Jericho shouted back and Sebastian fell silent. His eyes drooped again and his demeanor lost the moment-long spark of something desired.

"I'll take you upstairs," Jericho's voice was soothing again and he gripped my elbow inside of his hand.

I let him. Somewhere, deep inside, I knew that he was right, I knew that I needed to sleep and that whatever the end result would be with Sebastian tonight, whatever it was, I would regret in the morning.

Suddenly I was exhausted. I tried to remember the last time I got a full night's sleep, but I couldn't. Even before I set out on this.... this.... journey, I wasn't able to sleep. I leaned heavily against Jericho and let him guide me upstairs.

The townhouse was gigantic. Upstairs were numerous bedrooms, all fully prepared for house guests and plenty of bathrooms to let the house get full without any visitor feeling inconvenienced. Jericho led me to a bedroom with a full bed, and private bathroom. My backpack and clothes from earlier that day lay on a small chair sitting next to a white, decorative, writing desk.

The bed, covered with a plush, navy blue, paisley comforter and at least ten pillows with the same design, reminded me of home, of my bed back in Omaha, with at least an equal number of pillows. I almost burst into tears at the sight of it.

"Is this Ok?" Jericho asked, gesturing towards the bedroom.

"It's perfect," I gushed and then turned into him, throwing my arms around his neck. He, likewise, wrapped his arms tightly around my waist, absorbing me into him. I fought the tears that banged against the floodgates of my eyes, and in the end won.

'It's been a long day," Jericho whispered softly in my ear, pulling away just a little.

"It's been a long couple of days," I mumbled sarcastically. "Thank you for intervening down there." I pulled back and looked into his eyes.

I felt something then, something that moved at my heart like a crash cart against a heart attack victim, violent and reviving. I could trust Jericho, not just with protecting me from others, but from myself as well. He didn't just want what was best for the Resistance or my brother, he wanted what was best for me, but he never forced that on me. He let me decide and gently offered his help every step of the way. The trust was there, I couldn't do anything to stop it.

Moments ago, I believed I would never trust another person for as long as I lived. Yet, I couldn't help but trust him; the decision was made before I even realized what was happening. He forced my soul back into innocent belief, not by empty words or false promises but by consistent action that never failed. He was safe.

"Of course," he answered. "You'd better get some rest. Tomorrow we can figure out what to do with...." and he moved his thumb back and forth toward the stairs, motioning downstairs.

I looked back at the bed again, excited about the idea of getting in to it and then back at Jericho. I didn't want to be alone tonight. As much as I craved the idea of falling asleep, I was still afraid of being completely alone. Jericho had yet to pull away, had yet to even look away, but I couldn't ask him to stay.

Whatever would come out of our time together, whatever feelings or relationship that either of us anticipated, needed to happen naturally. And I wasn't ready for Jericho. I wasn't ready for everything a relationship demanded. Trust was a step, but Jericho deserved more than what I could give him right now. If anything my chest remained an empty cavity where a heart used to beat, one day there might be more, but it was definitely not tonight.

Still my blood quickened at our closeness and some animal instinct took over, silencing my better judgment. I leaned forward on my tiptoes and kissed him on the cheek. My lips lingered for several seconds longer than what would have been natural, but even if my emotions weren't ready, it didn't mean my body wasn't crying out for my heart to move.

I tried to walk away from him. I tried to leave his arms, his safe embrace and walk all the way into the room, but I was fighting an internal war and everything inside of me, except my heart fought against letting go.

My lips moved, without my permission from his cheek to his lips, and there they stayed for moments too long. I kissed him with a passion I did not know was waiting and with fervor that should have been buried. His lips moved against mine with equal feeling and for a few seconds the world melted away; my problems, this journey disappeared and all that remained was the two of us.

Our magics met with slow consideration, mine reluctant to move and his waiting as if always in that position. But when they finally touched each other, when our auras finally found the other, it was as if it should have always been this way. It was as if this was how the world was meant to turn.

I pushed my body against his with more force so that his embrace would cover me completely. My weight shifted towards him still, I couldn't bear any separation between us, no matter how small, and the boards underneath my feet let out a loud squeak of protest. The sound was deafening in the silence of the hallway and I immediately pulled away from Jericho, shrinking back into the shell of solitude I had come to accept.

"Goodnight," I half laughed at Jericho, touching my fingertips to my lips. I promised myself there was life after Kiran, but maybe, after that kiss, I could actually believe it was true.

"Goodnight," Jericho replied, confused and disconcerted.

I stepped away from him, courageous enough to brave the isolation of my bedroom now. I shut the door behind me, waving a silent goodbye to Jericho who still stood outside the doorway as if lost about what to do next.

I stripped on the way to the bathroom and left a trail of dress-up clothes behind me. I searched out the gratuitous amenities I would need for the night in the well equipped guest bathroom and once my teeth were brushed I dove under the still cold covers, enveloping myself in the thick blankets and burrowing into the numerous pillows with thoughts of home and Aunt Syl and how simple life used to be.

My eyes closed before they even adjusted to the darkness and I drifted to sleep only moments later. Inside the quiet of the bedroom, everything held the possibility of turning out for the better.

----

"My patience is wearing thin, child," the King said coolly, calmly, as if he were telling a lie, as if he possessed all of the patience in the world. "Your time is running out and yet you do nothing about it."

"Let it," the teenage boy grunted. His mouth tasted of iron, and his vision was unfixably blurry.

"That would be so easy for you, wouldn't it?" the King replied, his eyes flashing with an anger only nobility was capable of. The spoiled anger stirred from a man used to getting everything he wanted as soon as he wanted it. "Oh, if only I would let you die, if only your meaningless life were to be snuffed out with just the motion of my finger, how wonderful things would turn out for you," he mocked, with vitriolic tones. "But you do not understand!" his voice suddenly turned to screaming, "I will make her pay! I will treat her ten thousand times worse than what you have suffered and I will enjoy it!"

"Then find her," the boy coughed blood as the words tumbled from his mouth, but still the smile was there, still, the arrogant resonance the King detested so much would not leave his voice.

"Do not make the mistake of thinking I will not be able to. If I cannot find her, surely she will come to me, surely she will try to save you," the King looked at his prisoner with a ravenous hunger, as if he were a piece of delectable meat to be devoured.

The boy recognized the look in the King's eyes and tipped his head back towards the heavens. His dark his prison, offered no sunlight, no light to move with the day. He lived in perpetual night and with a simple motion of the King's finger, his night would turn to nightmare.

He stared at the dripping stone ceiling and cried inwardly for strength. He could not see the heavens or even remember them clearly enough to picture them, but he cried out to them for courage. He needed just one more night of faith, just one more minute of bravery and once he was through, he could die. He begged his silent God to take him, to make this the last night he would suffer, but gritted his teeth and dug his fingers into the arms of his chair in preparation for what was to come.

If God did not call him to Him tonight, surely she would be there in the morning. Surely she would come for him instead. Surely, she would fulfill her promise and save him.

----

My eyes shot open and my trembling fingers clawed at the soft, feather pillows surrounding me. I reached out in the darkness for the boy in the dream but he was already fading, he was already disappearing back into the gray void of the dream world.

My hands clasped quickly over my mouth as if to stop it from screaming the cries of a tortured soul. My face drenched in sweat and my hair matted against my skin, I tried quickly to remember the dream, to remember the boy's face but it was already gone. The dream held no meaning now as my eyes adjusted to the dark and my shoulders stopped shivering violently.

Everything was Ok; everything was how it should be.

"Bad dream?" an amused English accent inquired from a corner chair.

"Who's supposed to be guarding you?" I demanded, pulling the comforter up to my neck.

"Poor lad, fell asleep," Sebastian answered with mock concern.

"So you've come to kill me?" I asked, confidence lacking.

"Oh, I think we've all learned that valuable lesson. The all-powerful Eden, that cannot be killed," he ridiculed, as if I were a circus act.

"And yet, here you are," I replied, wishing I had worn pajamas to bed, or at least something other than underwear.

"And here you are," Sebastian stayed in his chair, his fingertips pressed together, and his face completely hidden in the night. "Believe me, I have felt my fair share of internal objections with how things have gone for me, but there are things you need to know about the Monarchy. There are certain.... things you need to know about Kiran, and before you go off destroying my family, you are going to listen to me. You are going to hear everything I have to say."

"You cannot be serious," I rolled my eyes, reminding myself that I was the boss, not him.

"I am completely serious," Sebastian promised, and if I hadn't been dressed to nearly nude I would have walked out on him, "And in exchange I will give you specific directions to get to Kiran. He is dying; you could kill him easily and I know where he is."

I couldn't argue with that, so I pulled the comforter closer and I listened. I would listen to everything Sebastian had to say.

## Chapter Fourteen

"The first thing you need to understand is that Avalon is barely alive," Sebastian declared coolly from the corner chair. His face came into focus once my eyes adjusted to the darkness, but I struggled to look at him without feeling unwarranted pangs of sympathy.

"I figured," I mumbled, pulling the warm covers over my mouth and doing my best not to feel the heart-wrenching pain that accompanied Sebastian's words.

"Eden, I don't know what you're planning, but if your plans include rescuing your brother then you are going to have to do it sooner rather than later." Sebastian was so serious that I wanted to believe he actually cared about Avalon. I wanted to believe him, but I couldn't even entertain the idea.

"Thanks for the advice," I spat, venomously.

"You're welcome," he countered. "And another thing, if you want to get to Kiran, now is the time. He's practically dead already, and if you want responsibility for the death of the Monarchy then you shouldn't hesitate."

"Is there anything else, Sebastian? How about the King? How would you suggest we go about murdering him?" I was fed up with his attitude, how dare he come into my safe-house and order me around.

"I have several thoughts on that, if you're really interested, actually," he mumbled, looking out the window at the moonlit-bathed street. "Also, your neck is glowing."

I tugged at my hair angrily, pulling it over my shoulder, and combing it with my fingers to cover up the small serpentine tattoo. "What are you doing? What kind of game are you playing here?" I demanded, finally unable to keep up the charade of taking his advice seriously.

"I'm trying to help you," he hissed, as if it were obvious.

"Ok, let's be real here. Sebastian, you don't have to pretend anymore, you're our prisoner, I'm going to probably kill you either way, so it's not necessary for you to lie to me anymore." I was over playing games with these people, my new policy was upfront honesty and I was bound and determined to expect it from everybody.

"I understand that we are not playing games, Eden. Look at me! Do I look like I'm playing games anymore?" he snarled, his voice raised and his sunken eyes hard.

"Then, what is this? Why are you trying to help me?" I wanted to believe him; I wanted to listen to his advice. He possessed intricate knowledge of the palaces and where the royal family would be. I couldn't, though. I couldn't, in good conscience, remember how he was used against my family and me and believe him now. His loyalty remained with his uncle and cousin.

"I can't do this any longer, I can't.... Listen, I'm not sure what is good and what is evil anymore. I thought Lucan had my best interest in mind, but now.... now, I'm not so sure," he finished quietly, the hard edge in his voice dominating every sentence.

"So, at Kingsley, I mean, in Omaha, they sent you.... to spy on me?" I asked, not as boldly as I would have liked, but those memories were still agonizing.

"No, they didn't send me to spy on *you*. They sent me there to watch you and spy on Kiran. Lucan had his mind made up about you the moment he laid eyes on you, the minute you walked into that Romanian courtroom. I was there for Kiran, to find out how deeply his feelings for you really were. I think you know what I discovered."

"That he was a lying, manipulating bastard?" I grumbled, barely able to stomach a conversation about him.

"Hardly," Sebastian snorted.

"Are you kidding me? Don't defend the cousin that got you into this mess," I accused, raising my eyebrows at his pathetic loyalties.

"No, Eden, let's not fool ourselves. You're the one who took my magic…. you and you alone. I cannot even pretend that it was my cousin, just like I cannot pretend that Lucan didn't know something like this would happen to me. I can't quibble in the gray areas of this life you live, I'm going to be honest with you and I expect you to be honest with me as well."

"All right, fine, that's what I'm trying to do," I admitted reluctantly, but exasperatedly. "I took your magic, but you forced my hand. You were on the wrong side of that argument. You still are."

"I can agree to that," he replied. "But be honest with yourself; Kiran thought he was doing what was best for you."

"Be honest with myself? I *am* being honest with myself. He should have known better! How is destroying my entire family, helping me? He took everything from me. Do I need to remind you of what happened that night?" I growled, knowing full well if Sebastian wanted me to recount the details of the night, I couldn't.

"I clearly remember what happened that night. But don't fool yourself; whatever the faults of his plan were, Kiran did what he did for *you*. And now he is dying, wishing he would have done things differently, but dying all the same," Sebastian explained icily.

"Enough. I don't want to hear about Kiran; if you have something to say that I need to hear, then say it. Otherwise go back downstairs so I can get some sleep," I whispered fiercely, I was tired of talking in circles with Sebastian and the memories of his cousin opened a wound in my heart that hemorrhaged inside of me.

"He is in England; in the London palace should you want to have a deeper discussion on ending the Monarchy. At some point Eden, you must come to terms with taking a life. If you want to finish what you've started, then stop dancing around the issue and arrive at the conclusion that murder is inevitable," Sebastian insisted softly as if regretting every word he said, but knowing they were necessary. When I didn't say anything, he continued, "I expect you are searching for your parents?"

"No, they are on their own mission. At some point it will be necessary for us to meet, but as of right now, I have other things to do." I wondered why I was discussing my plans with Sebastian, but I wasn't able to stop the words from falling out of my mouth.

"All right, I can live with that. What is your plan for Romania though? How do you intend on rescuing your brother?" Sebastian asked, calmly. He sat up straighter and crossed one of his legs over the other as if he were the important adviser I had called for.

"Sebastian, do you really expect me to discuss our plans with you?" I jeered, half appalled, half amused.

"No, I guess not," he sighed, running his fingers through his chestnut colored hair. "There is a wedding date set," he continued, looking back to the window. "If he doesn't die beforehand, they will be wed the first of May."

"Of course, Lucan will want a living, healthy heir," I let the conversation happen, forcing myself to believe this was important information that could further my cause.

"Yes, of course he does, but the engagement, the wedding, all of it was Kiran's idea," Sebastian explained, and for some reason his words felt like punches in the stomach.

"Well, good for him," I remarked forcefully, demanding that the words come out of my mouth and that they sound sincere.

"He went to Seraphina that same night, and took her back to London with him." He spoke slowly and calculatedly, each word feeling like a new and painful kind of torture against my heart.

"Why are you doing this Sebastian? What is it that you want to say?" I demanded, my voice breaking and my spirit not able to hold his words any longer.

"It should have been you, Eden. You should be the one waiting for a wedding.... you should be the one by his bedside. You could have changed everything as Queen, and you could have done it peacefully. But now, you have broken the best man I have ever known and started the beginnings of a civil war that will kill more Immortals than help them. How dare you be so selfish," his words were poison and I sat back against the headboard as if he slapped me.

"How dare you! How dare you be so.... be so.... wrong!" I half shouted at him, "Lucan has his precious Immortality, I would never have been Queen. And don't think for one minute that he was going to let me marry his son and peacefully change his Kingdom. His one goal has been to destroy my family from the start and he is nearly there."

"You can say that about Lucan, but what about Kiran!" He stood up from his chair, staring down at me contemptuously. The sky outside of the window had started to lighten; soft beams of light crossed his face, darkening the shadows under his eyes. "Kiran would have helped you destroy his father, he would have helped you change the Kingdom, he would have done *anything* for you."

"No," I countered, "he would have done anything for himself and for his own selfish gain. I was merely a catalyst for his Immortality. Nothing more," I relaxed into my pillows, realizing that I was right. As disgusting as Sebastian's argument was, it was the same one I was having with myself. Talking through it aloud with Sebastian, helped me remember what I needed to do.

"And yet, you still love him," Sebastian said softly, sinking weakly back into the chair.

"Maybe," I couldn't argue that point if I truly wanted to. "But soon, I will love only a memory of the King that never was."

"How can you say-" Sebastian started, as my bedroom door thrust open.

Xavier and Jericho came flying through the door, but stopped short finding Sebastian sitting in the corner of my room. I clung to the covers even tighter, pulling them close to my neck and cursing myself for not throwing at least a t-shirt on before bed.

"Oh, Ok, just you know, making sure everything is Ok," Xavier gave a lighthearted thumbs-up while panting heavily.

Jericho slapped him on the back of the head before turning to me, "Eden, are you all right?"

"Yes," I sighed, "Except that I am never going to get a good night's sleep again, so I don't even know why I try!" I shrieked, letting my face fall into the folds of the blankets.

"Well, you can sleep on the plane; we need to go.... now!" Jericho demanded when neither Sebastian, nor I moved.

"Why?" I asked, my blood flaring with electricity.

"The Titans are on the move, apparently they didn't take Sebastian very seriously," Xavier said sarcastically, almost laughingly. "What?" he asked defensively after Jericho shot him a warning look. "Fine, I'll go tell the others," his head dropped and he sulked out of the room, more offended that no one found him funny than of getting kicked out.

"We really need to get going," Jericho pleaded with his eyes for me to move, but I was too embarrassed to explain my clothing situation. "We need to get out of here and decide what our next step is."

"I've already decided that," I answered confidently. Sebastian stood up slowly, and walked to the corner of my bed. Jericho mimicked his movement and stood on the other side of the bed, watching him carefully. "Xavier and Titus will go track down the other teams, and Gabriel, Xander, you and I will take our good friend Sebastian here across the Channel and to the London palace. We are too close to ignore how sick Kiran is right now. Sebastian's right, if we want to strike, now's the time."

"Sebastian's right? About what?" Jericho hollered, turning on our prisoner with disdain.

"That your bloody target is on his death bed and if you want to take credit for his death, then you need to get to him now. Otherwise, Lucan will explain his death away as just another victim of the King's Curse and the Kingdom will accept it and believe it's more reason for his father to maintain his tyranny," Sebastian answered plainly, his English accent clicking crisply with every consonant.

"But we still need to get to the other teams as quickly as possible. I think we can get away with just sending Titus and Xavier, don't you?" I held Jericho's attention, hoping by including him in the decision making process he would feel more in control and ignore the advice I was taking from Sebastian.

"I don't like it," Jericho mumbled. "I don't like the idea of you going to the palace. Why don't you go with Titus, and I'll take Xander and meet back up with you later?"

"Absolutely not, I'm not leaving you. That is out of the question," I countered adamantly, refusing to lose him again. The other guys were important, but if I lost Jericho, or if something happened to him.... I would lose myself.

"Ok, then you and I will head to Morocco and leave the rest of the guys to London," Jericho offered, clearly wanting to keep me as far from the royal family as possible.

"That will mean nothing to your people, Eden," Sebastian rejoined the conversation, his voice full of a force and fight that had been missing since the loss of his magic. "If some nameless Immortal kills him, so what? But, if you kill him, his former fiancée, the granddaughter of the last Oracle, and the leader of the Rebellion were to kill him, that sends a message. That could be the activator you need to gain the people's respect."

"Whatever, Sebastian," I sighed, trying my best to maintain a healthy level of suspicion with him, even though his advice was sounding rather dependable. "The point is, of course I want to be the one to kill him, but also, I'm sorry to say this, but I just don't trust anyone else, Ok? We're going to London and that's the end of the story. I'm the," I looked at Sebastian, reluctantly quoting him, "I'm the leader of the Rebellion and all...."

"Fine, all right, you're right of course," Jericho agreed, slowly as if talking himself into it.

Both boys continued to stand still at the end of my bed, the silence growing awkward and the need to be on the move becoming greater. Jericho tilted his head towards the door as if to ask me what I was waiting on.

"Ok, I need to get dressed," I finally admitted, "I am not wearing anything under here so you're both going to need to leave. Like, now." I held tightly to the comforter with one hand while pointing towards the door with the other.

"So you're not wearing anything right now?" Sebastian asked, and Jericho's cheeks flamed red.

When I shook my head negatively, Jericho suddenly couldn't look at me in the eye, finding the paisley print on the comforter very interesting.

"Well, if I would have known that, I wouldn't have stayed so far away all night," Sebastian mumbled, an impish grin lighting up his face.

"Jericho!" I shrieked.

"All right, it's time to go," Jericho said firmly, grabbing Sebastian by the arm and tugging him out of the room.

I slammed the door behind them with magic, locking it forcefully and then flopped my head back against my pillows. We were on the run again, only this time I was more afraid of our destination than being caught.

I was officially on my way to kill Kiran. The only thing that terrified me more than taking an actual life was coming face to face with the man I once imagined spending forever with. Death bed or not, I would still have to meet him.... be near him.... face him before I could finish what some unknown disease had started. And I wasn't entirely sure if I was prepared for that.

## Chapter Fifteen

I walked downstairs, in my traveling outfit: jeans and a long-sleeved, white, fitted t-shirt. The boys stood anxiously at the door, waiting for me.

"Ready?" Jericho asked calmly, but his eyes darted around the room nervously.

"She'd better be," Xavier mumbled, "we never waited for Avalon."

"Xavier, I swear, I'm going to kill you before this is over," I threatened softly, almost seriously.

"All right, do you guys know what you're doing and where you're going?" Jericho addressed Xavier and Titus who nodded.

Xavier turned to Xander looking at him anxiously, silent thoughts communicated easily between the two brothers. Xavier bounced apprehensively on his heels and Xander let out almost a wince, like a hurt puppy before pulling his brother into a tight bear hug.

Moved by their interaction and the sharp pains of longing for my own brother reminded me that it was not fair to separate the two of them. If something happened while they were apart, they would never forgive themselves. I knew that to be the hardest truth.

"I change my mind," I blurted out, startling everyone. "Titus, you come with us, Xavier and Xander, you guys stay together."

"Eden, it's fine." Xander stood up straight, releasing his hold on his brother. "We'll be fine."

"I know you will," I promised, but without losing my resolve, "but if you aren't.... if things go differently than we want them to, you should have each other. Trust me, whatever you face, you would rather do it together," I finished sadly.

Xavier and Xander nodded appreciatively and the climate was suddenly very somber.

"Besides, I can't really stand either one of you," I mumbled, lightening the mood.

"Let's go then," Jericho reached out a hand, shaking each of the brother's firmly.

Titus, even with his shorter stature and burliness, didn't let others watching deter him from pulling them both in for a quick, but manly hug. Xander and Xavier towered over him, but seemed scrawny next to his lumberjack-like frame.

I realized then, that I was still separating brothers. In the year that the four of these guys had been together and the weeks that recently separated them and made them unsure of the future, circumstances bonded them just as closely as blood ever could. Only this time I didn't feel sympathy; it didn't break my heart to send them different ways. This time I felt encouraged; they were just as determined to get Avalon back as I was.

When the goodbyes were said, and the door opened, we walked out boldly into the crisp, spring, Paris morning and went opposite ways. Xander and Xavier headed back to St. Louis and the small plane that belonged to Gabriel.

Jericho hailed two taxis for the rest of us. Gabriel and Titus climbed into the first one and Sebastian, Jericho and I, the second. Sebastian sat in the middle of Jericho and I, idly playing with the hem of his navy blue dress shirt, while Jericho in perfect French instructed the driver where to go. We would be taking the Chunnel from Paris to London. Thankful that claustrophobia wasn't on my long list of fears; I imagined how an almost three hour tunnel ride in very close quarters could become unbearable quickly.

"Jericho, promise me I will get to come back here as a tourist," I remarked breathily, staring out the window as Paris passed by me in a flash.

"I promise," he answered, very amused.

"Under different circumstances, I would have been glad to give you the tour," Sebastian mumbled coldly.

"Under different circumstances *I* could have given her the tour," Jericho grunted.

"Under different circumstances she would have left you behind in Omaha like the peasant you are," Sebastian countered.

I sat up straighter, wishing I were the one sitting in the middle.

"Really, a peasant?" Jericho whipped his head around to face Sebastian, with a look of pure fury in his eyes.

"All right, that's enough of that," I said casually, sliding across Sebastian in the cramped cab and wiggling between the two of them forcing Sebastian to scoot over and take my place.

"Yes, a peasant," Sebastian repeated, under his breath.

I let out an exasperated sigh, hoping the rest of the trip wouldn't be like this.

"How did you know the Titans were looking for me all night?"

Sebastian asked quietly. He was addressing Jericho, but refused to turn his head, because either he was too tired or because he couldn't stand Jericho as much as Jericho couldn't stand him. I wasn't quite sure.

"You mean, besides what common sense told me?" Jericho grumbled sardonically. "Not, every Titan is loyal to your Crown."

"So, it's true then," Sebastian sighed, "Eden and Avalon are the real subjects of the oath."

"There hasn't been enough time to truly test that theory," Jericho maintained his cold tone, and I was surprised he hadn't just jumped on a positive answer; I hoped that he would have come to that concrete conclusion by now. I certainly wanted to believe I was the real heir to the throne and that was the reason Titans were dying when they crossed me.

"Sure, there hasn't, meanwhile any Titan that has gone up against Eden and Avalon are dead, whilst your traitors walk around perfectly unharmed," Sebastian turned his head towards Jericho, his sunken eyes turning to steel.

"For now, only time will tell. Besides, not *every* Titan that's stood up to Eden and Avalon has died. Kiran's bodyguard still lives," Jericho explained quietly.

"I suppose," Sebastian admitted, and then in the same calm voice, "I know that man up there, he is part of my father's Guard." Sebastian pointed to a cafe not far from where the cab sat in the middle of crowded traffic. A man stood next to a small table, watching us with barely veiled hatred. "They've found you."

"Damn it," Jericho cursed underneath his breath. "Sebastian, will they make a scene?"

"Truthfully, I don't know," Sebastian replied. He sounded sincere, but I doubted every emotion and feeling I read from him.

Jericho instructed the driver in French and the taxi attempted to defensively-drive its way through the stopped traffic surrounding us. We were on the Champs Elysees, probably the busiest thoroughfare in Paris. The man, that Sebastian pointed out stood in front of a sidewalk cafe with wrought-iron chairs and tables, watched us carefully. His eyes did not leave mine, not even when he lifted his wrist to his mouth and spoke quickly into the cuff of his navy blue pea coat.

Jericho was on the cell phone with Gabriel, instructing them to continue on to the Chunnel station. It wasn't just that he was confident we would come out of the fight unharmed, he also couldn't risk losing

Titus or Gabriel. If we failed, at least they could go on.

I stared back at the stoic Titan. I wasn't afraid of him, or of the backup he called. I wasn't even afraid of the audience we would have, should there be an altercation. If he wanted to fight, I was more than willing. What I was most afraid of was losing Sebastian, and the vital intelligence I needed to break into the London palace.

"Sebastian, I am going to destroy your father's Guard, is that clear?" I asked without taking my eyes from the Titan now only a few yards away.

"Yes," Sebastian answered coldly.

"Are you going to stay with us, or am I going to have to hunt you down again?"

"I'll stay with you," he mumbled, unconvincingly.

"Seriously, I don't care what you do. I just want to be prepared, either way." I sat forward in the cramped cab, readying myself for the fight.

"Eden, I gave you my word. I will not leave you until you have fulfilled yours," he said quietly, somberly.

"All right, let's go then. Jericho, let's just get this over with," I demanded, tapping the cab driver on the shoulder and throwing a chunk of Euros at him.

"Here? Now? Wouldn't you rather wait?" Jericho asked with one hand on the door handle, the other on my knee. Excited and anxious for battle, his magical current pulsed rapidly in his palm, and I caught his energy, my electricity flaring with blood lust.

"A busy train station will be worse. Besides, I don't want to have to wait for them to make the first move. Let's go." I gently shoved Jericho's shoulder and he was out the door. Grabbing Sebastian's hand, I pulled him along, following Jericho from the cab.

"So, how do you want to do this?" I demanded, taking a few more steps forward so I was only a few feet from my enemy.

"Um, I, um, well, you should come with me." My fearlessness caught the nameless Titan off guard flustering him. I started to enjoy myself.

"No, that's not what I meant. I mean, do you, like, want to fight here? Or go somewhere a little more private?" I half smiled, hoping everything stayed this easy.

More Titans walked around the corner, filling in the background and every possibly escape route. Maybe twelve Titans, and what felt like more than that, surrounded the three of us just waiting for things to go badly.

They were going to go badly, I felt like I should just make that announcement.

"How about we go somewhere a little more private?" The first Titan grinned, his sinister lips curled back revealing perfectly straight, white teeth.

"Ok, wait, before we do this.... thing...." I started, wanting to debate every option. "If I go peacefully with you, where will you take us? Like, exact location, where are we going?" I narrowed my eyes at him, thinking through the easiest way to get inside the London palace.

"To the King of course," the Titan snorted.

"No, you're not listening," I accused, and he stood up straighter, offended by my complaint. "Exactly where would that be? Like, um.... which palace?" I danced around the exact verbiage I was tempted to use. I wanted to find out more information than I gave away.

"Well, I suppose, the Paris palace, until the King decides to move you to Romania." The Titan thought it out, his fingers twitching impatiently.

"Ah," I sighed, "well, that won't do."

"Won't it?" The Titan laughed with the same accent Talbott shared, thick with amusement.

"No, it won't," I said boldly, readying my body and igniting the magic dauntlessly in my blood.

The Titans moved as one body to enclose our space, to trap me inside of their unified army. My magic was pulsed violently through my blood, electricity palpable underneath my skin. The energy was boiling, and popping and my fingers trembled underneath the strength of power.

All of my senses came into painfully sharp focus, and my blood burst with magic both mine and stolen. I struggled to get used to the energy force I must now work with, the separate magics combining powerfully together in the melting pot that was my blood. Inside both of my hands, I held white orbs of magic waiting to be released. The amount of power I was held back overwhelmed me and I knew that if I didn't release the energy soon I would cause much more destruction than anything I could have planned.

"This was a terrible idea on your part," I mumbled sympathetically to the lead Titan who chose that exact moment to move forward and try to grab me.

With a feral scream and my blood seconds away from its breaking point, I reached one hand out toward the approaching Titan, released my magic and sent a lightning bolt of bottled fury.

He instantly fell to the ground, popping and sizzling underneath the weight and destructive power of my disposable magic. I rolled my head around in a circle, the joints in my neck cracking, readying for the next victim.

The Titan on the ground recovered slowly, his magic obviously not as strong as mine. But I left it intact for now. Another Titan moved tentatively from the crowd and I called on the same power, sending another bolt of magic through the crowd of Titans, disrupting restaurant tables and carelessly tearing the awning overhang that shaded the now scattering café customers.

Despite the haphazard movements of my electricity, it met its mark and that Titan, too, fell to the ground, writhing in agony. The still standing Titans shifted uneasily back and forth on their toes, trying to decide what to do next.

"Who's next?" I asked calmly. "Come on, seriously," I finished quietly, demanding a challenger.

"Eden, we need to go," Jericho whispered in my ear, reminding me of our mission and the gathering crowd of onlookers.

The humans near enough to feel involved in our altercation stared up at the sky, trying to make sense of what they would inevitably find to be unexplainable. The crowd around us gathered quickly and I understood it was impossible to continue this way. I glanced back at Sebastian, who stood; shoulders slumped, looking bored and unimpressed.

I was tempted to give him back his magic, just so I could take it again.

"All right, gentleman, I really need to get going, so here's what we're going to do," I spoke softly enough that I wouldn't draw human attention, but with enough confidence that the Titans surrounding us gave me their undivided attention. "I'm going to walk through this crowd and you are going to let me. You are not going to follow me and you are not going to try to continue this conversation. If you do, you will force me to take something from you that you would prefer to hang onto. But, please don't mistake me, I will take it from you without hesitation. It's better if you just let us go, k?" I finished sweetly, pulling on a few of the magics that were closest to me. It was almost too easy, almost too simple to prove my point. The Titans that felt their magic start to diminish acted out, panicked and afraid.

    I stopped pulling, leaving them sighing breaths of relief and clutching at their throats. I motioned to Jericho and Sebastian and then walked through the crowd, moving forward and never looking back. I didn't want to make any more enemies; and the truth was I knew that if I wanted to take over this Kingdom I would have to eventually gain the Titans trust. But right now was not the time. Right now, I had a Prince to assassinate.

# Chapter Sixteen

"Who's going to stay with the prisoner during the mission?" Titus asked, as soon as Jericho and I walked through the door of a London flat, our new safe-house, owned by someone in the Resistance I had never heard of before.

"You all are," I announced, catching them completely off guard. "I'm doing this alone."

"Excuse me?" Jericho stopped short, turning on his heel to face me.

"I'm doing this alone," I repeated confidently, staring Jericho in the eyes, until I couldn't stand the intensity of his hazel-eyed, silent accusations.

"No, you're not," he countered.

I walked passed him, finding the kitchen and the refrigerator. The last three hours were intense. Although we made it to the Chunnel safely and were under the impression that we were not followed, we couldn't be positive. The three of us had spent the entire two and a half hour ride in silent pensiveness and now that we were on the other side of the English Channel, fears and jitters heightened.

Paris had felt very much like enemy territory. The City of Lights was the home of the Cartiers, the Grand Duke and Duchess of Canesbury, the King's sister, the next heir to the throne should the Crown Prince meet an untimely death. *And* Sebastian should get his stolen magic back. Paris was their home, and definitely enemy territory.

But London?

London was the lair of the best. And I didn't just want to infiltrate that den of iniquity, I intended to cut the beast's head off and hold it up high for the entire Kingdom to witness. Or at least figuratively, that's what I wanted to do.

I searched the small refrigerator for something to drink and when I realized there was nothing but water, I gave in and grabbed two, ice cold bottles. I tossed one to Sebastian, giving into my guilty conscience for just a moment.

"This is not up for discussion," I declared, gasping for breath and wiping the corners of my mouth with my sleeve, after taking the lid off the bottle and drinking its entire contents in seconds. "I've thought about it. The mission is risky enough, but besides that, I'm the only one that can shut off the magic. I'm the only one they won't feel coming."

"We can figure that out, that's just a detail," Jericho argued, not at all convinced by my reasoning.

"It's just a detail, but a big detail, and after what happened in Paris, security will be heightened. It's just too much of a hassle. I'll just go in really quick, finish the job, and be out in no time," I reasoned, lightly. I had already made up my mind; Jericho was not going to dissuade me.

"No, absolutely not, it's out of the question," Jericho, turned around, running his hands through his hair and sighing exasperatedly.

"You can argue with me, but we all know that it's the only way into the palace. The Titans are going to sense any out of place magic. Sebastian, tell them I'm right." I turned towards Sebastian who found the closest chair to the door and slumped down into it, his head in his hands, staring at the floor. I wasn't even sure if he was still awake.

"Come on, E, nothing he says will make any difference," Titus laughed. "But, Jericho, she has a point. If I or you or even Gabriel tries to get in there, they will feel it. They will know something's wrong. But she just might be able to get all the way inside without setting off any alarms. *If* she can get all the way in without blowing something up. Can you, Eden? Can you suppress it that long without exploding something the minute your magic turns back on?" Titus turned to me when Jericho ignored him.

"Yes, of course I can," I panicked inwardly though, deciding I'd better practice before I followed through with my plan. Amory's magic was so strong, so consuming that I wasn't sure if I had the willpower to suppress it. Or like Titus said, make it all the way inside without blowing something up. "I'll practice though, just to be sure."

"Good idea," Titus agreed. "Hey, remember when you used to break stuff all the time? Before you knew about being an Immortal and all that?"

"Uh, yeah, I remember," I mumbled, rolling my eyes at the memory, and then cringing because I suddenly hated the idea that people were watching me during those trying times.

"That was the best surveillance," Titus joked, his blue eyes twinkling with the mischief.

"For you maybe," I couldn't help but laugh too.

"Jericho, I think Eden is right," Gabriel offered his opinion for the first time. "Two of us could be close, just in case anything was to go wrong, but with only one person on the palace grounds, it will be easier for her to move around undetected. If she can really suppress her magic, like she claims, than it is our only option if we want to get all the way to the Prince," he finished thoughtfully.

"She is right," Sebastian lifted his head, eying me seriously. "The grounds are a full five acres before you even reach the palace, there is no way you could all make it all that way undetected. Your only option is Eden."

"Of course, it is." Jericho turned around slowly to face me again and I saw the concern in his eyes, his face wrinkled with worry, my heart sunk. "Our only option is always Eden."

"I'll be Ok, I promise," I walked over to Jericho, unable to bear the distance. "And I'll be fast; I'll be in and out before you can miss me."

"If only that were true," Jericho sighed.

"This is the way we're doing it, Jericho; I need you on board. I need your support." I reached out for his hand, and he gave it to me easily.

"You have my support; you'll always have my support. I don't like this, but of course, you are right and so go alone, I guess. Go do your super-hero thing...." Jericho smiled sadly down at me, and his expression was so caring, so filled with longing that I almost gave into him even though he wasn't fighting me.

"Ok, good." I cleared my throat, tearing my eyes away from Jericho's and stabilizing my resolve.

"Sebastian, rumor has it that underground tunnels lead to a pool house. Are they true?" Jericho turned from me, asking our prisoner for directions to kill his cousin with the first hint of respect I had heard in his voice.

"Yes, they're true, and they do lead to the pool house on the north side of the property. Kiran and I used to play in them when we were younger, so unless something drastic happened in the last five years then they should still be open. I can draw you a map of the grounds, Eden. Once you're on the greens, you'll still have to get inside the house, and to Kiran's room," Sebastian explained quietly.

"I should be clear right now, Eden," Jericho interrupted, "I know that we use the word, 'palace,' but really it's an extremely large house in the countryside just outside of London. It's not like what you saw in

India. It just happens to be one of the larger, nicer estates in the country."

"Ah, ok." I had to mentally adjust my thinking. I pictured a medieval stone castle, dark and gloomy with lots of secret passageways and echoing hallways that would be easy to hide in. I pictured Romania. Now, I would be breaking into a house, with narrow hallways and smaller spaces. "So are there security cameras?"

"Of course," Sebastian snapped and then shook his head as if to come back to himself, "I apologize, there will be security cameras, but the palace is not a fortress, it is not like Romania. Give me some paper, I'll draw you a map."

Silence prevailed for a few minutes while the rest of us searched the apartment casually, looking for a paper and pen. Gabriel found what we needed in a desk in the sitting room and brought it over to Sebastian who immediately began drawing a rough sketch of the grounds.

"Here is where the tunnel will come out." he drew a building labeled pool house and a treed area with an arrow pointing outwards from it toward a large box labeled main house. His sketch was basic and crude, but obvious enough so that I could understand the lay of the land.

A large main house sat in the middle of ten acres of land. Five different swimming pools dotted the property, but only the largest pool had a house connected to it. From Sebastian's drawing I could tell a thick wooded area and a tall, secured, stone wall surrounded the entire property.

"It might be easier," Sebastian continued, "if you could get to Kiran's room from the outside, instead of breaking into the house." He sat back on his chair, biting his thumbnail; the simple gesture reminded me of Avalon, sending an agonizing chill down my back.

"Where is his room?" I asked, wishing I hadn't missed the P.E. rock climbing trip so I could do my Eternal Walk in India, after all.

Sebastian pointed to a box on the south side of the house with a large balcony drawn around it. He explained that it might be possible to scale the outside of the house using the vined lattice that adorned the backside of the mansion. I could climb the lattice and shimmy my way over the balcony, quietly take out Talbott, or whoever was in there with him, finish the job, and leave the same way; no one would know the difference.

The plan actually sounded like it could work.

"It sounds way too easy," I mumbled, finding my own thumbnail to chew on.

"I was thinking the same thing," Gabriel offered, less than comforting.

"Sebastian, if this is some sort of trick, I swear to God, I will kill you myself," Jericho growled, from behind me. He ran his fingers through his hair and then started pacing the length of the kitchen nervously.

"Well, obviously, the Guard doesn't anticipate someone without magic wanting to break into the palace and that is why it will be easy. If Eden can turn off her magic then she can move around the grounds undetected, theoretically, anyway. That's why it sounds easy, this is not a trick," he insisted sadly, slumping down further in his chair, his sunken eyes turning black with misery.

"My magic will not be a problem," I promised everyone in the room, including myself. "Are you sure he will be in this room, though?" I asked, pointing to the rough map on the arm of Sebastian's chair.

"That is his room, but whether his is there for sure, I cannot say." Sebastian looked up at me, with desperation. He was giving me directions to murder his cousin, his best friend, and his Crown Prince and I almost broke for him. Kiran was my enemy, and Sebastian too, for that matter, but I couldn't separate my compassion for a human life from my desire for revenge.

"How many Guards will be there with him?" I asked, trying to put together as much intel about this mission as I could.

"The grounds will be covered with Guard, and the house as well, but as far as in his room, last time I visited there, it was just Kiran and one other Guard, usually Talbott. There will be a nurse as well, but as far as magical ability, she won't be anything you need to worry about." Sebastian looked to the side, towards a window on the far side of the apartment. My eyes followed his and I stared out at the busy London street, wishing I was meeting all of these beautiful cities under completely different circumstances.

"Will Lucan be there?" I asked. My fears subsided at the mention of his name and the angry vengeance that swallowed my soul, swelled inside of me, reminding me of my purpose.

"No, he is in...." Sebastian cleared his throat nervously,

"Romania."

"Of course," I whispered, almost going blind with rage at the idea he was with my brother. I knew that Lucan was torturing and assaulting Avalon daily, but those were the kind of facts that would always claw at my heart and make panic and hysteria nag at my neck.

"I don't like this," Jericho interrupted loudly. "Something just doesn't feel right."

"Do we have another choice?" I turned to him, asking genuinely. "Is there another option? Another way to get to him? Is there another alternative besides killing him?" I asked, looking to each man in the room individually, but I was met with silence, even from Jericho. "Seriously, if there is another way I am wide open to suggestions, but we all know that there isn't. We all know that this is our only option and our only opportunity."

I looked at Jericho, hoping that above everyone else, I had convinced him. He looked back at me, pain etched in his hazel eyes. I wanted to say more, to comfort him, to promise that I would be all right, but I couldn't find the right words, or the false hope that even I didn't believe in. He stared at me a moment longer and then left the room, mumbling something about needing a shower.

"Man, there is nothing to eat here!" Titus exclaimed, breaking the tension in the room.

"Are you hungry, Eden?" Gabriel asked, his voice and thick accent soothing against my frayed nerves.

"Actually, yes, I am," I lied, deciding I needed to have as much energy for tonight as possible.

"Titus, do you know a good place to get some food to bring back?" Gabriel asked, his fingers never leaving his rosary, and Titus nodded, lighting up at the mere mention of sustenance. "All right, then, let's go get some. Will you be Ok, Eden?"

"Yes, of course, that's a great idea," I assured them.

"We'll be back in a few minutes. If you try anything, if you even look at her wrong, I will break your scrawny, mortal arm off, got it?" Titus threatened Sebastian on his way out the door.

Sebastian rolled his eyes, but shook his head yes anyway. After the door closed behind Gabriel and Titus, I walked to a couch across from Sebastian's chair and sat down; silently suppressing my magic, making sure it would disappear without complication.

"How is it that it comes so naturally to you and I feel like the definition of death?" Sebastian asked almost playfully.

"What comes naturally? My Magic? How can you even tell?" Amory's magic did not give me the fight that I thought it would. I could easily turn it off, but turning it back on was a different story. The strong magical forces came back more aggressively than I expected. I could handle the jolt of electricity now because there were only seconds between the magic turning off and turning on, but I was nervous for later tonight when there would be an hour or more of buildup.

"Even without my own magic, yours rather suffocates everything else in the room. No wonder, poor Jericho is so in love with you," Sebastian sighed, never taking his eyes off me.

"That's none of your business," I said casually, trying to play off Sebastian's words, but wondering what his game plan was here. I knew that he was saying things to me, trying to get a reaction, trying to provoke an emotional response, but so far, I couldn't figure it out.

"You're probably right," he laughed, "I just feel bad for the chap. Do you think that when you finish with him, and you've taken your smothering magic away that he will end up like poor Kiran? Will he on his death bed, wonder what he could have done differently to keep you by his side?"

"How dare you!" I stood up, wanting nothing more than to slap him. "Do not talk about me like I am some fickle woman with time to spare and love to throw away. You know better!"

"Forgive me," he answered quietly, but sarcastically, "I do know better, don't I?"

I walked to the window breathing deeply and fighting off the rage. I focused on tonight, on my mission and the work it would take to pull it off and pushed Sebastian's words from my mind. I couldn't let him get to me now; I couldn't let him distract me from my goal. I wasn't the reason Kiran was dying. He was.... at least for now.

But tonight, I would take all of the credit for his death. And then Sebastian could blame me all he wanted. The whole damned Kingdom could blame me.

## Chapter Seventeen

We walked silently to the mouth of the tunnel, hidden well behind a boulder and thick silver birch tree. Jericho held my hand tightly, he remained silent the entire walk from the car where Gabriel waited patiently for him to return.

"So, this is it," I whispered, more afraid of letting go of Jericho's hand than anything I faced so far.

"Eden, you don't have to do this, we can find another way. Or you could just let whatever he is dying of kill him, the result is the same and the Kingdom will not know the difference," Jericho reasoned, speaking quietly but confidently.

"They might not know the difference, but there would *be* a difference. We both know that, Jericho. Besides, this is something I want to do. I have to face him, I have to.... to.... I have to remember what he did to my brother and how he betrayed me. I must find vengeance or I will never be able to face his father," I confessed slowly, finally understanding my own need to see this mission through.

"Come here." He pulled me into a hug, burying his face in my thick, black hair I had piled on top of my head. "If you need anything, I'm just a phone call away," he whispered.

"I know," I replied softly, my voice thick with emotion. "One day, we will be able to leave each other for short amounts of time and it won't feel like we are saying goodbye forever."

"One day," he agreed hoarsely and then stepped back so that he could look into my eyes. "Eden, hurry back to me." He kissed me on the forehead and then hugged me closely one more time before turning his back on me completely and walking away.

I was alone now, without even magic to keep me company. The dense canopy of the thick, dark forest blocked out any light that the cloudy sky could have produced.

I reached into my backpack and pulled out the large flashlight that Titus picked up for me this afternoon, flicked it on and headed into the cave. I said a quick, silent prayer asking for strength.

The cave narrowed into a tubular tunnel, with rounded sides and rough, uneven ground. Each foot step echoed in the darkness, and the glow from the flashlight only shone a few feet in front of me. I tried to run, to reach my destination as quickly as possible, but the broken terrain and constricted space made it impossible.

I cursed, frustrated by fear and uncertainty. I heard all kinds of sounds and hated that I couldn't distinguish real from imaginary. I tried to talk myself into courage, I tried to convince myself that the far off echoes of rocks skidding against concrete and the splashes of water were rats or foxes or any other rodent interested in dark tunnels and isolation. I reminded myself that I would feel the flare of magic, I would sense another Immortal, but my imagination was working on overtime and my anxiety already heightened.

I picked up my pace, putting confidence in years of yoga without any knowledge of magic. I used to be athletic and had to try at it. I hiked mountains recently; I walked the city of Paris. I could do this.

Eventually, I found the other side of the tunnel, coming into the soft, eerie glow of the moonlight next to a white brick house with one wall made completely out of glass. My blood flared instantly once I was out of the tunnel, the sixth sense of magic alarming me that enemies surrounded me.

I paused for a moment, hugging the cool brick and taking in my surroundings. There were five acres of land between the main house and me. I could see the house in the distance but without magic it was hard to determine the best route. Titans walked the ground tirelessly; back and forth all around me, making sure every inch of the palace was secured.

I had to move, if I stayed where I was, they would find me. The Guards would stumble upon me during a routine check of the area. I steadied my quickened breathing and took careful steps forward; passed the pool house and into the midnight shade of a water shed not far from the pool.

I would have to make progress slowly the entire way. I did my best to remain noiseless but I knew my hearing was handicapped without magic. The Titans however, did not share the same disability.

After the shed, there was a small landscaped area of trimmed bushes and after another Titan sweep of the area, I moved to them. I slowly started to notice a pattern of how the guards walked and moved across the grounds. So far, there were at least ten groups of four Titans and they moved back and forth across the property, starting at the main house and zigzagging to the end of the acreage opposite the two teams surrounding them.

My small movements and calculated steps could work, as long as

I stayed quiet, motionless when they were near and banished any trace of untamed magic. I moved again from the brush to another outer building standing next to a large jacuzzi tub. The water boiled and bubbled, reflecting brilliantly in the moonlight and the building that hid my shadow made loud pumping noises.

I stood up from my small, crouched position ready to move on, when I suddenly froze by the sound of two guards that were just on the other side of the building. One of them was relieving himself against the building while the other one stood guard.

I shrunk back down into a ball of camouflage and held my breath not wanting to make even a blade of grass shudder unnaturally.

"They say the Prince won't live through the weekend," one of the Guards commented quietly. My ears instantly perked up, I quickly pushed myself closer to the stone, wanting to blend in as effortlessly as I could with the darkened wall.

"And then what?" the other one asked.

"Well, we don't really need him anymore, do we? The King has all the power he needs to live forever, an heir isn't necessary," he answered, almost amused.

"But the old man died, didn't he? Eventually, the King's luck will run out and then this Kingdom will be leaderless again," the other one mumbled carefully, as if afraid someone would hear him.

"Well, we could always turn to you know who! I hear rumors that she is supposed to be the one with a crown on her head anyway," the other one whispered and my heart started beating wildly at the accusation.

"Shh, if someone hears you, you'll find out what the inside of that Romanian prison is like," the other one warned. "But do you think it's true? Do you think she's the reason the Prince is dying now?"

"I don't know what to think," the first one said seriously. I heard the zipper of pants and then the two men turned and their voices disappeared into the still night.

I followed stealthily after them, moving from hiding spot to hiding spot until the latticed vines stood ominously in front of me. I crouched, hidden in the bushes that lined the back of the house and directly underneath the balcony Sebastian had drawn accurately on his map, without any idea how I was going to climb the wall without being seen.

I reached into my pocket and pulled out the cell phone I borrowed from Titus. Texting as quickly as I could, I sent a message to Jericho asking for a reason to have all of the Titans run toward the front of the property. I threw in a suggestion about an explosion and then instantly regretted sending Xander, the explosives expert, to a different continent.

I received Jericho's response in no time and whispered another silent prayer that the plan would actually work. I waited in the dark for what seemed like an hour, but after glancing at my wrist watch realized it had only been fifteen minutes.

My magic was getting harder to suppress the more anxious I became and since the grounds were already buzzing with magical energy, I knew I didn't have much more time. I had to keep the magic shut off until the exact moment I would kill Kiran, otherwise the Guards in the hall would get inside the room before I was ready.

I worked on breathing calmly when the midnight sky suddenly glowed with a distant light disturbing the peaceful night and an explosion so loud, my ears started ringing.

Angry shouting could be heard all across the acreage and I sunk lower to the ground as the Guard policing the back of the property all rushed to the front in a mobilized effort to secure the Crown Prince.

I couldn't hesitate another moment. As soon as the last trailing Guard was around the corner, I shimmied my way up the lattice, carefully slipping my feet into the tiny squares housing the wild vines.

At the top of the lattice, I stretched as high as I could to reach the floor of the balcony and pulled myself up with muscles I didn't realize I possessed. On the outer balcony ledge, I scrambled to my feet, throwing my chest over the top of the tall, thick stone railing and tumbled to the ground on the other side.

I immediately crawled to the corner of the balcony, hiding myself in the shadows and pulling my knees to my chest. I buried my face in my knees, willing myself invisible in the darkness.

I heard the balcony doors open and someone step outside looking for anything out of the ordinary.

"Mimi, I'm going to go see what is going on, will you be all right alone?" Talbott's thick, accented voice asked from the balcony only a few feet away from me.

"Yes, I'll be fine. You need to go see," Sebastian's sister replied from inside the room.

"There are Guards right outside the door if you need any help," I heard Talbott assure her.

He left the balcony door open and from inside the room I could hear him exit through the other side.

This was too easy.

I stood up, brushing the dirt and dust off my black, monotone, cat-burglar outfit. I walked carefully to the balcony door, passed some lavish outdoor furniture and into Kiran's room.

The night breeze rustled behind me, sending the wind into the room and moving the covers gently that lay across a sleeping Kiran.

"Eden," he gasped suddenly, lost in the depths of his painful coma. I froze in place, not sure what to do. He reached out in unconsciousness; his eyes tightly shut and sweat tricking down from his brow. I paused for a few seconds longer, making sure he was still asleep and the utterance of my name was only a coincidence.

My magic was suddenly very hard to control, and I swallowed the lump in my throat that had unexplainably begun to rise. In the back of my mind, I remembered that Amelia was still in the room, that she was probably watching me, moments away from screaming out for help. But all I could do was stare at the dying, unconscious figure of Kiran, peacefully unaware of what I had come to do and remind myself to breathe.

I was slammed with emotions that I had not accounted for. I was prepared for rage, and hatred and vengeance, but not for love and desire, and most certainly not for longing.

I took quiet, careful steps to his bedside, breathing in the familiar scent of him and wanting more than anything in the world to brush back his blonde tussles that had fallen across his forehead.

A floor board creaked from across the room and I heard a gasp. I turned quickly to Amelia, remembering my purpose, remembering my cause. I brought a single finger to my lips, warning her silently not to say anything else or make another sound.

I thought she would be afraid, I thought I would startle her, I assumed I would frighten her. But when my eyes met hers I was greeted with a smile. She rushed to my side, throwing her arms around my waist and hugging me tightly.

"I knew you would come, I knew you would," she whispered excitedly. "He was so close to death, so ready to give up, but you have come to save him."

"Amelia?" I questioned, confused by her presence. "What are you doing here?"

"I am Kiran's nurse, I have been by his bedside for weeks now," she answered plainly, still happy to see me.

"Do you know that I made your brother a promise about you?" I whispered, still confused. Surely, Sebastian wouldn't suggest that I come if he knew his sister would be here. I swore to him that I would kill her if anything happened to Avalon. And something did happen to Avalon. But as she stood in front of me I could find no strength to hurt her. There was nothing inside of me that wanted to take anything from the sweet, innocent child and I worried about what kind of bad guy I really was.

"Sebastian told me what you said, but I don't believe you. You are too good." She slipped her small hand into mine and her big, brown eyes searched mine for confirmation that she was right. "So you've come to heal him?" She asked, her doe eyes large and insisting.

"No, no, no. Amelia, I'm sorry, you have it wrong," I insisted, wishing with everything I had that I didn't like this girl so much.

"No, I don't have it wrong," she implored, "I told Talbott you wouldn't let him die like this, but he didn't believe me. And see? Here you are, right before it is too late."

"Amelia, listen to me," I tried to reason, hardly noticing that my magic had started to escape in a desperate attempt to find Kiran's. I was disoriented and frustrated and I had lost control of the magic that so desperately wanted to find its soul mate.

"You have to hurry though, he needs you, Eden; he will die without you." She pushed me closer to him, so that I was touching his bedside and hovering over his unconscious body. My fingers, absentmindedly, clutched the black stone necklace, pulling it out from underneath my shirt.

My heart began to hemorrhage again, the hurt and pain, the agony and despair began to flow like a river from my broken heart. My magic was completely out of my control by now, the unfeeling, emotionless entity searching out Kiran's waning electricity in sweet reunion as if it was waiting for this moment since we parted ways. My life's blood, without thoughts of vengeance or unconcerned with deserved hatred betrayed me silently and I was powerless to stop it.

"I haven't come to save him, Amelia," I said firmly, hot tears unforgivably tumbling down my cheeks. "I've come to kill him."

She took a step back from me, appalled at the very thought. I couldn't take my eyes from her, she stared at me accusingly, silently screaming at me for betraying the man I once loved as if our love were the only thing in the world.

I froze in place, unable to think, unable to breath. Kiran's cold, weak hand slipped without warning into mine and I struggled to remain standing.

"It doesn't matter why you've come," he whispered with a strained, husky voice, "You're here. That is all I need."

# Chapter Eighteen

"Don't touch me," I growled, the hot tears flowing faster, but still I did not pull my fingers from his.

He opened his eyes, with their aqua brilliance as bright as ever, and held mine. The glow of the moonlight bathed his bedside in soft light through the open balcony doors. His touch paralyzed me. He gazed at me with ferocity, with deep sorrow and intense longing. I stopped breathing. I stopped living. I stood next to him a prisoner, captivated by an irrational and hateful love.

A sharp knock on the door jerked me from my trance and I stumbled backwards, my hand leaving his and my eyes finally finding reprieve from his gaze. The banging on the door brought my blood back to life igniting the warning bolts that Titans on the other side of the door waited hungrily to drag me away and crucify me.

"Amelia!" one shouted through the golden trimmed door. "Amelia, is everything all right in there?"

She looked at me, panicked. She so desperately wanted me to save her cousin that she couldn't bear to have me taken away, but I threatened to kill him myself. She stayed, bound in place, glancing back and forth between Kiran and me.

"Amelia," Kiran whispered with a stronger voice, "assure them that everything is fine, and that you need Talbott." When she did not move, his eyes grew hard and he struggled to sit up in his bed. "Amelia, now," he commanded and she obeyed.

I moved, stealthily to the high corner of Kiran's bed, hidden behind a long, dark curtain. Amelia straightened her dress and then opened the door just a crack. She promised the Guard that everything was fine, that Kiran was awake and that he needed Talbott and no one else.

The Guard, shocked by her news, did not question her instructions. He left immediately to fulfill her request and she shut the door behind him, locking the handle and leaning back heavily against it.

"So you've come to kill me?" Kiran asked, his voice stronger yet.

I moved from behind the curtain to face him. He was visibly better in the seconds it had taken for Amelia to get rid of the Guard. His eyes were shining, his face less pale and he was sitting up strongly in bed.

"I came to finish the job, I was under the impression that you were dying," I stated flatly. A paranoid feeling nagged at my neck that this was a trap.

"Ironic, that if you would have stayed away you would have succeeded," Kiran smiled at me, his lips were dry and cracked, but his old mischievousness was still there.

"I will still succeed," I threatened, taking a step towards him against my will. I wanted him dead, I wanted to witness the end of him, but I couldn't escape his gravitational pull. His magic stayed wrapped in mine; it suffocated my willpower and drowned my purpose.

"It would be easier for us if one of us were dead. It would be easier to keep living, to keep breathing," he reached out to me again, and I folded my arms defiantly, physically pinning my hands to my chest, unwilling to lose all self-control.

"It *will* be easier when you're dead, easier to accomplish my goals. I will be one step closer to finding vengeance for my family," I promised, my eyes finding his with firm resolve.

"Then do it," he tipped his chin upwards in equal defiance. "Kill me."

"Why are you so anxious to die?" I asked, fighting to reign in my magic, fighting to keep control.

"Anxious to die? Eden, I am already dead!" He whispered passionately. "There is nothing left for me but to love you and since I cannot do that, I am nothing. I am the walking dead. Until you are by my side again, I am hollow."

"No, that is not true!" I tried to keep my voice quiet, but I was outraged and I was tired of being lied to. "You could have had that, you could have had me by your side and you chose to destroy everything that we were. If anyone is dead, it is me! I lost everyone I loved, including you!" I shouted in a hoarse voice, finally face to face with the demon that haunted me.

"Eden," Kiran's voice broke and he stood up from his bed taking slow steps towards me. "If I could have seen the outcome of that night, I never would have let any of it happen. I would have warned Amory, I would have fought by your side, I would have done anything in my power to protect you from that tragic night."

He walked closer to me; he was shirtless in the midnight moon, the light illuminating his muscular chest. Pain etched his face, and passion filled his dark eyes. I stepped backwards from him; I was afraid of him, and the ghosts of our love that were persistent even now. My heels bumped against the wall of his room and I was paralyzed in place, desperately wanting to touch him again, and desperately wanting to end everything right this very moment.

"See how we are meant for each other?" he asked sweetly, taking the final step to close the distance between us. "I was at death's door without you, Love. Your magic makes me breathe, your presence makes living possible. Do not take it from me again, I beg of you. Let us forget what has been said, forget what has been done and live as the stars have meant for us to live." He reached for the necklace resting against my chest and rubbed at the black stone delicately.

I trembled in his proximity; his electric pulse radiated from him and our magics wrapped in a feral, raw reunion. His other hand reached out, brushing my fingertips gently and I shivered, fighting with everything I had.

"I need you," he whispered desperately, tipping his lips to mine. "I will live my life in repentance, in agonizing penance if I have to. I will do anything you ask, anything, but do not leave me again. Please, my love, I cannot survive without you."

I closed my eyes, struggling to think, to speak, to move and suddenly his mouth was against mine as if I had no warning. He pulled me to him, one arm holding me tightly around the waist and the other hand tangling itself in my hair. I felt like a rag doll in his arms, moving against my will, but unwilling to stop him.

Our magics entwined themselves together like strands of unbreakable rope, soaring in palpable energy, flashing brilliantly in the darkness of the room. His magic was black next to my blue and together they cracked and sizzled with fierce electricity.

This was home. No matter what happened, no matter how much pain I went through, no matter how much loss I suffered, I would always be home in Kiran's arms. My magic would always search for his, my electricity always be most alive captive in his and my soul only complete when connected with his.

And it was then, when I let him in, when I couldn't escape him any longer or run from the feelings that were so reluctantly but obviously there, that I hated him more because of it.

A sudden knocking at the door interrupted our intimate moment. I came back to myself, stronger and in control. Amelia gasped and Kiran reluctantly removed his lips from mine.

"It's Talbott, you'd better let him in," I said confidently, maneuvering away from Kiran's hold and breathing deeply.

Amelia opened the door just wide enough for Talbott to enter. He walked in the room immediately on alert. He felt my magic, he recognized my presence and his protective instinct took over. On palace grounds, he looked much more the military style than he had in Peru. His chestnut brown hair was slicked back, out of his face and his pants and polo, respectable but practical.

"Eden, so glad you could join us," Talbott growled; he was a wiser man than Kiran.

"Thank you," I replied with mock enthusiasm. "We were just noticing how well Kiran was doing since I've arrived. It must be my magic, don't you think?"

Kiran turned back to me; his eyes had lost something, something I couldn't define. But in its place was the realization that reuniting our love would not be as easy as he hoped.

"We've thought that all along," Talbott said carefully, moving around the huge king-sized bed, closer to us. Amelia stayed where she was, across the room. And Kiran too, stayed where he was, close to me.

"Eden, don't do this," Kiran whispered, his voice panicked with recognition that his trance over me was gone. "Stay with me," he begged.

"No," I answered flatly, my hands landing defiantly on my hips. "I am not some weak girl you can woo with charming words and a sweet kiss. Do you remember that you are the sole reason my grandfather is dead? Or that my brother is being tortured in *your* father's prison as we speak? Will you fix those things for me, Kiran? If I stay, will you fix them?" I demanded sarcastically, venom dripping with every syllable.

"Yes, I will, I promise I will." He was not playing my game, he was genuine and desperate and I knew that he would do anything, absolutely anything to keep me. And because of that I needed escape. My resolve was strong now, but my magic was still not my own and I had to sever the tie between us or I would never finish my revenge.

"You will rescue my brother?" I asked carefully setting the trap. He nodded enthusiastically, taking a step closer to me as if he could not keep himself from me. "That's a start, I suppose.... But what about Amory, Kiran? How will you bring him back from the grave? And everyone else that has been murdered by your betrayal or sent to prison and held there at your father's amusement? How will you fix those things?"

"I don't know, but Eden I will live my life trying to make those things right, I swear to you." His voice broke again, but his strength had almost completely returned. His magical current was powerful next to mine and I could physically see how much he healed in the few minutes we were together.

"You can live your life however you please, Kiran. I want nothing to do with it." I met his gaze with confidence.

"Amelia, get the other Guards," Talbott ordered. He stepped forward, ready for battle.

"Relax, Talbott. I've changed my mind," I started but Amelia had already slipped through the door. "I will not kill Kiran tonight. I'm going to fix him. I will completely heal him so that when I leave, he will not be affected by our lost magic. His poor, weak, pathetic energy will be able to go on living even unconnected to mine."

"I don't want to be fixed," Kiran shouted. "I want you!"

"You cannot have me! I am not something to hold and possess, I am a force to be reckoned with!" I screamed at him, unconcerned with staying hidden any longer. I released the healing winds on him violently, the power almost swept him away and wrapped itself around him, severing our connection and healed whatever brokenness remained.

Talbott stepped forward, but did not attempt to touch Kiran. I could feel his body healing, his magic relaxing its grip against mine and I was suddenly shaken with the effort to remain standing. Eventually, the winds subsided, the blue mist scattering to the corners of the room and I relaxed, panting and trembling from the effort.

"There, you won't suffer without me anymore," I gasped.

Kiran sat down unsteadily on the bed, looking stronger than ever, but visibly shaken. "Maybe physically I won't. But, Eden, I will suffer without you, and you will suffer without me. My magic might be able to survive on its own now, but I cannot survive without you. Whatever has happened between us, we are meant to be together. You can run from me, from us, but you are lying to yourself if you believe differently."

"Believe what you want." I smiled indifferently, recovering from the efforts to heal him. "I'm sure your fiancée will be happy you'll make it to her wedding day."

I watched Kiran swallow and his eyes shift towards Talbott as if he were more than angry at him. The door to the room suddenly burst open and filled quickly with Titans ready to fight.

"Yes, a wedding, my father's idea," he lied, holding up his hands to stay the Titan Guard. "You can have until then to change your mind. I will wait for you until that day, but I will not be able to stop the ceremony, if you wait too long. Do not be mistaken, Beloved, I will forever love you. And you are only wasting time until you are with me again."

"The next time I am with you, Kiran, I will not forget why I have come," I promised menacingly.

The Titan Guard moved as one unit forward, some pulling at my magic, others firing lightning bolts of electricity at me. I turned my back on them, understanding I would not be able to win this fight and sprinted through the balcony door, across the patio and over the stone railing.

I jumped without fear, allowing the magic full reign of my senses. I fell in a crumpled heap against the cold, wet grass. Surging the magic quickly to heal my body before I was up again and running. Guards all around me were more spread out down on the ground and I landed in front of them without warning.

I used magic, sending a few flying backwards and into anything I could find. I stole magic from them when possible, but now a hundred Guards descended on me and I was more concerned with fleeing than sticking around to see if I could win against that many.

I reached the tunnel next to the pool house and turned around for a split second to destroy the entrance, exploding the concrete walls into heavy debris. With full use of my magic, sprinting the awkward tunnel created no problem now and with a fast dial of the cell phone in my pocket, I shouted instructions to Jericho expecting them to be waiting for me on the opposite side.

My plan backfired. Honestly, I knew that it always would. I was never going there to kill him. I always intended to heal him. I was weak. I was dishonest with myself and I let my naivety blind me.

But no more, the next time we met, I would not be caught off guard and struggling to breathe. I would be standing over his dead body.

## Chapter Nineteen

"Drive! Go!" I shouted as soon as I was inside the car; Gabriel took off before the door even closed. We had borrowed a small but incredibly fast Mini Cooper from the owner of the flat and as I struggled to right myself in the tiny backseat, the questions started to come.

"Is he dead?" Jericho asked with a raised voice, magic surging protectively around the car.

"What happened?" Gabriel inquired more calmly, while he weaved in and out of traffic expertly. I glanced at him skeptically, still picturing him more as a hit man than clergyman in his traditional priestly clothing.

"I don't know what happened!" I shouted back. My tone and manner were both uncalled for, but I was frustrated and angry with myself. I slammed my back against the leather seat and glared out the window. "He's not dead. In fact, somehow, instead of killing him, I may have.... I may have healed him...." I trailed off quietly, refusing to look either man in the face.

"You may have what?" Jericho turned on me. His expression confirmed complete confusion and disbelief.

"The Prince is still alive? And healthy?" Gabriel questioned. He glanced back at me in the darkened car, his orange eyes flared with anger as if they were on fire.

"Like I said, I don't know what happened," I said softly, frustration getting the best of me. I didn't want to explain my actions to them, I didn't want to admit aloud that I couldn't kill him, and worst of all I couldn't even bear to watch him suffer.

"I need to know exactly what happened," Jericho said coolly.

"Ok, it wasn't as easy as we thought it was going to be. First of all," I lied, but pushed through the guilt, "there were Titans everywhere and Talbott was inside the room with him and Amelia was there. And I didn't expect her to be there. And I made a promise to Sebastian that I would kill her and then I was confused and then my magic, the blue magic, the, the wind-magic healed him and I couldn't stop it and then I had to just run and that's basically, the whole story," I rambled on and on, not making cohesive sentences or even convincing lies. I was a mess.

"Eden, relax, everything will be all right. We will find another opportunity," Gabriel said soothingly and his words helped bring me back from edge of breakdown.

"We have to; we have to find another opportunity. I can't go on living with him also.... living," I growled, pushing the blame of tonight's failure onto Kiran.

"Eden, have you ever killed a man before?" Gabriel asked, and his question felt unwarranted and unnecessary.

"No, not completely," I admitted.

Nothing more was said the entire way home. I could feel Jericho's concern, his radiating protective spirit, but something more triggered his quietude. He was jealous. His hope for the fall of the Crown Prince went deeper than starting the Monarchy over. He hoped for the death of the despised bond that tied Kiran and I together. I wondered for a moment if he knew how hard it would be for me.

"When will we need to leave?" I asked as Gabriel parked in the underground parking lot hidden from the street and connected to the London flat.

"Eden, you tell us," Jericho snapped. "You're the one running this show."

"Damn it Jericho, what the hell is your problem?" I half shouted, scrambling out of the car after him.

"My problem is that.... that...." Instead of finishing his sentence, he grunted and threw his hands up in the air. "I was just hoping for a different outcome tonight. We all were."

"Yes, we all were, including me." I couldn't take Jericho's attitude right now. Too many other emotions competed for my attention. "If I could, I would take this whole godforsaken night back. Believe me." If I hadn't insisted on coming here, if I hadn't been so eager to be the one to kill Kiran, he would in all likelihood be dead by now. I couldn't say that out loud, but the thought alone made me sick to my stomach, both because I wanted him completely out of my life and because a small part of me, a very small part of me, was thankful he wasn't.

"And it's more than about tonight," Jericho continued, turning on me in the stairwell up to the flat. "If you are going to be the leader of this Rebellion, you have to act like it. You can't just make decisions like breaking into the London palace alone and then let someone else decide when we're leaving and where we're going next. You can't just pick and choose what suits you best whenever you want to! You have to be a leader all of the time or none of the time, and you have to make up your mind!"

"Oh really, is that what I'm doing?" I was beyond angry by now. "This might come as a surprise to you, but this.... this whole, good guy, bad guy, covert ops, James Bond crap is all new to me. I wasn't trained or taught how to travel the world covertly, how to fly jets or even how to speak f-ing French fluently. No, I was hidden away, and left in the dark, and now I'm trying the best that I can, so excuse me for not knowing what the hell I'm doing!"

We were to the apartment door. Gabriel stood back, wary of approaching either of us. I had had enough, tonight was more than I could handle and Jericho was making everything worse. I forced open the apartment door with magic and stomped angrily passed Titus and Sebastian sitting on the couch, watching TV calmly.

I found a bedroom and slammed the door shut, deciding I might never come out again.

"Things didn't go as you hoped they would?" I heard Sebastian ask and I forced myself to suppress a scream.

I threw myself onto the soft double bed and pulled a pillow over my head, closing my eyes, muffling the sound, and letting out the sobbing hysteria caused by coming face to face with Kiran.

Nobody bothered me, nobody tried to knock on the door to see if I was Ok and that was how I preferred it. Eventually, I found sleep. I found the dark abyss of unconsciousness and hoped for the rest that had been beyond my reach for too long.

----

I woke up screaming sometime near morning. I clutched at my throat; I was drenched in sweat and my pillows and blankets had all been tossed on the floor. I couldn't stop the screaming, I couldn't make my mouth close. The dream felt so real, the man, the blood, the torture.

But the images diminished, and began to disappear the more awake I became. I was freezing cold but still dripping with sweat, my long hair loosed and sticky against my face. I grasped at the dream, to bring it into my consciousness but the pictures and scenes darkened and blurred. Nothing substantial remained of them.

Jericho came bursting through my door, in athletic shorts and disoriented. He was rubbed at his eyes but his magic was full force and when he took in the sight of me, alone and in my pajamas he relaxed a little.

"Are you Ok?" he asked softly, walking over to the bed.

"Yes, I think I am, sorry if I woke you," I mumbled, finding an askew pillow and putting it over my bare legs.

"Was it a bad dream?" He sat down next to me, pulling me into a side hug. I still wanted to be mad at him, but his comfort soothed my frayed nerves; forgiveness was not even in question.

"I think so, I can't really remember anything about it though," I admitted.

"Hmmm....." Jericho sighed, resting his head against mine.

"Anyway," I mumbled, snuggling closer to his warm body, wanting desperately to apologize for my actions the night before. But even more, with the sunlight pushing past the curtains and lighting the room with the softest and newest of lights, I wanted to apologize for the twisted and distorted feelings I still felt for Kiran. As meaningless as they were and as hard as I planned on fighting to destroy them completely, it didn't seem right that Jericho had to suffer because of them.

"Listen, I want to apologize for last night," he said sweetly, beating me to it.

"No, don't worry about it. I think we were all.... disappointed," I grumbled, playing off his sincerity because I felt like he owned the right to be mad.

"Eden, it doesn't matter how I felt, I should never have raised my voice to you and I'm sorry. Sometimes, I just, I just expect you to, you know, be able to do anything. But killing someone is a whole different thing, I get that. And I'm sorry I expected such evil out of you." He lifted my chin so that he could look directly into my eyes and I felt the weight of his words immediately. He was a good man…. a really good man. He certainly deserved better than me.

"I forgive you," I whispered hoarsely, remembering the kindergarten manners I learned as a child. I smiled at him and he smiled back, his magic soaring, searching for mine but it would not budge. It remembered Kiran. It sensed the strong hold Kiran's magic held over mine and it would not move.

I stood up, awkwardly moving away from Jericho, praying he wouldn't notice, but I knew that was impossible.

"Jericho, I know that I'm supposed to be in charge and everything, but.... Ok, let's be honest, I have no idea what I'm doing!" I confessed, picking a blanket up from off the ground and wrapping it tightly around myself. "Please help me, please, please, please, please...." I begged, clasping my hands together and sitting heavily down next to him again.

"Of course I will. I was always going to help you. Last night, I was just acting like a jerk," he conceded honestly.

"Oh, good, that's really good!" I threw my arms around his neck, the blanket falling off my shoulders. "So what's our next move then?"

"Well, Xander and Xavier called last night after you went to bed. They found the Morocco team and moved on to India, so if you're up for it, they would like us to meet them there. They said they've found something very interesting that we need to come see for ourselves," Jericho finished by rolling his eyes and I had to laugh at the camaraderie between this team.

"Sounds like a good next step." I nodded my head once, deciding that we needed to move on and India was just as good of a place as any. I decided last night that it was time to get Avalon; that I couldn't wait any longer. He needed me. I certainly lacked the number of people I had hoped to bring with me, but I also didn't want to risk any more lives than was necessary.

After we met up with the teams in India, I would speak to Jericho about heading back to Romania as soon as possible. I knew he was as anxious to get Avalon, as well as the others, free from their awful prison and the longer we waited the worse it would be for them.

"Eden, what do you want to do with Sebastian? Are we going to continue to drag him around with us?" Jericho asked carefully and I realized that was exactly what I was planning on doing.

"We'll take him to India with us, for sure. He is too helpful right now to completely just throw away. Plus, Jericho, we might still be able to use him as leverage."

"I guess that's true," Jericho agreed, "It's just that, I really, really don't like him."

"Ugh, me either!" I echoed his sentiment, enthusiastically, "But you know what? I think I've thought up another use for him!"

"What is it?" Jericho asked dryly, not believing there was anything Sebastian could do that wouldn't irritate him.

"I need to figure out how to give another person's magic back. I mean I've tried before, but nothing has worked. I'm going to practice with Sebastian until I get my magic to cooperate," I explained, proud of the idea and realizing the necessity for it.

"I remember what happened to Oscar though; you might end up killing him in the process...." Jericho mumbled. He wasn't trying to be rude, but the memory of Oscar flying across the steel barn back in Omaha was a painful one and not an action I would like to repeat on Avalon once we were face to face.

But Sebastian was a different story.

"You're not worried about killing him?" Jericho asked, almost amused.

"Actually, that might solve a couple of my problems!" I laughed, glad that Jericho and I worked things out. I was happy that we were on our way out of England and away from the Prince, and satisfied that I found a solution to working on giving someone's magic back.

The night before had been the darkest moments of hopelessness. I had trembled, and cried and shrunken in fear. But now, in the clear light of day and with a new plan ahead of me, I could face this day, this mission.... this fateful purpose of mine again with courage. I could be fearless again.

## Chapter Twenty

"How are we getting to India?" I asked casually, emerging from my bedroom, showered, dressed and ready for another long flight.

The guys milled around the door, all ready to leave and waiting patiently on me. I didn't want to believe I was the fussy girl that took her time getting ready and made everyone wait. This whole trip had been a series of wet ponytails and only eye liner, but every time we were getting ready to leave I was the last one ready. I blamed my long hair and conditioner; I doubted any of these boys conditioned.

"Well, we were thinking...." Titus began, looking at Jericho for encouragement to continue. "We were thinking we could take Amory- I mean your jet. The Cessna Amory kept in storage here?"

"The what? What jet?" I asked, not understanding what Titus was talking about.

"Your grandfather kept a Cessna here, can we use it?" Titus said slowly, as if that would help me understand.

"Titus, I don't understand the words you are saying, what is a Ces.... what is that? And since when do I own a jet?" I finished, wishing there was *An Immortal's Guide to Posh Living and Civil Warfare* I could pick up at the nearest bookshop.

"It's a private jet that your grandfather owned and now we assume it belongs to you, and Titus wants to use it to get to.... wherever we are going," Sebastian interrupted, clearly growing impatient with the banter.

"Oh, Ok, well then sure, we can use it." The fact that I now owned a private jet was going to come in very handy, especially today.

"Yes!" Titus hollered, fist-bumping Gabriel who didn't really understand what he was doing. "Can I pilot?"

"Do you know how?" I asked, skeptically.

"Um, of course I do. Don't you?" He rolled his eyes at me, and then bounced through the door like a kid ready to open presents Christmas morning.

Gabriel pushed Sebastian through the door after Titus, shaking his head in amused awe.

"He can drive, can't he?" I asked Jericho while he locked up the flat.

"Yes, he can *fly*, but Avalon never let anyone fly the jets but him. I think he's excited for the opportunity to put his skills to use." Jericho smiled dryly, mimicking Gabriel's headshake.

"Should I have said no?" I was suddenly nervous, I didn't know if I could take another plane ride like the one that got us over the Atlantic from Peru.

"And squash that spirit? Are you kidding me?" Jericho laughed again, which only made me more nervous. "Relax, he's a great pilot, I promise."

Jericho dropped his arm across my shoulder playfully and we walked down the staircase together.

"Are you all right after last night?" he asked casually, not referring to any of the details of the failed mission specifically.

"No, not really," I answered honestly, "but I will be."

I looked up at Jericho, his spirited hazel eyes, twinkling with life and I felt safe. I loved Jericho; I had for a while. I didn't love him like I loved Kiran, but soon I would put that detestable emotion to death and move on. Once Kiran was out of the picture it would be easy to forget how he moved me, how he entranced my every thought and how my magic was bound to his so effortlessly. I just needed to put that love to death first, and then I could move on.

The drive to the isolated airstrip outside the city was quiet. Crammed together in the Mini Cooper, nobody wanted to breathe, let alone make a sound; there just wasn't room for it.

I was disappointed to leave another foreign city without even visiting a single museum. London was worse than Paris, I didn't even lay eyes on a single landmark, or hardly notice the culture at all. Either we were holed up in our safe-house or working covert opts on an isolated ten acres of land housing a mansion that seemed more modern and unique than traditional and English.

The jet impressed with its luxurious esthetic that my grandfather provided. He always seemed elegant with expensive taste, but aside from the tweed suits he wore to school, I didn't know much about his style. Until my inheritance, I rather lacked any of my own.

So, with Amory gone and my new ownership of a fancy, private jet, I figured this would be a great place to start. I was a jet owner. A Cessna owner, whatever that meant. This would be my style.

I half wondered if I should be more worried about Titus, but he seemed to take off appropriately and once we were in the air, I didn't feel like the turbulence was out of the ordinary. I relaxed into my plush, leather chair and sighed. There was life outside of a miserably unsuccessful mission.

Titus and Gabriel closed the door to the cockpit and Jericho and I sat across the aisle from each other and across a table from Sebastian. Jericho's eyes drooped and his head rested against the back of his chair. I didn't know if he was entirely asleep, but he would be soon.

"So, I ran into your sister last night," I mentioned casually, gauging Sebastian's response. I still couldn't figure out if he had purposefully sent me in there with knowledge of his sister on the grounds, especially after my promise to him before anything actually happened to Avalon.

"Did you tell her I said, 'Hello?'" he mumbled darkly.

"Sebastian," I commanded louder, demanding his attention. "Did you know she would be there?"

"Not for certain, but I knew there was a chance," he admitted, playing idly with the hem of his shirt, he had yet to change from his birthday party. I made a silent note to myself that in India I would find him clean clothes.

"And you still thought it best for me to go? Do you remember the promise I made to you before Lucan took Avalon?" I asked, hardly believing that he would betray his little sister. Maybe that was the depth of his depravity; I couldn't be surprised by the Kendrick bloodline and their absolute disrespect for all things living, anymore.

"I remember," he agreed.

"Then you knew there was a chance that I would not only strip Amelia of her magic, but also kill her?" I crossed my arms in defiant disbelief.

"I knew there was a chance, but did you? Did you take her magic and kill her?" he questioned casually.

"No, but I could have!" I insisted. "I mean, I was there to murder your cousin; Amelia would have just been a detail at the end of the night, a loose end to tie up." I swallowed my guilt and revulsion, trying to hammer in my point.

"So, did you do that? Did you murder Kiran?" Sebastian asked, still an air of humor in his weak and whispery voice. His accent, crisp and British as Kiran's, but unlike Kiran, he got straight to the point and never tried to gloss over anything with flowery promises and pretty words.

"Well, no," I admitted softly, walking right into the trap Sebastian set.

"So, Amelia wasn't in real danger then, was she?" His dead eyes found mine and he sat across from me accusing me of something I could not define. I saw his point, I heard his argument, but to risk his own sister's life was unfathomable to me, while I forced all my efforts and energy into saving my brother.

"You should make it easier for them to win," Sebastian mumbled sarcastically.

"Do you know what? That's enough out of you." I narrowed my eyes at him, not liking the tone of his voice.

"Whatever," he sighed.

"No, don't do that," I sat up straighter in my chair, commanding a discussion from Sebastian, I didn't care how tired he was. "What are you trying to say? Spit it out."

"I'm just making the observation that you are not exactly playing this game on a level playing field. And if you want to win this war you've declared, you'd better step up and contend at the level your enemies are competing at," Sebastian mimicked my narrowed eyes, silently daring me to disagree.

"Step up? Are you kidding me? I just broke into their fortress! Into the Prince's bedroom! There were like hundreds of Titans and I got out of there completely unharmed." I sat forward in my chair, completely willing to arm wrestle my way to a win if I needed to.

"But instead of killing the Prince, you healed him and instead of finding out anything useful you gave them vital information about you and your damned healing smoke, so I'm not exactly sure what you intended to glean from your first espionage experience, but I don't think you won that altercation." Sebastian looked out the window and I suppressed the urge to slap him.

"Did you know that would happen? Is that why you advised me to go? So I could heal your beloved cousin?" I swallowed the rage, the blind hatred that urged me to push Sebastian out of the airplane.

"How could I have known that you were capable of healing people?" He turned back to face me, the smallest spark of life, lighting his face.

"Fine, but all of your people believe that he was dying because of the detachment of our magics. So whether or not you knew I could heal him completely is irrelevant. Did you believe my magic alone would heal him? At least give him more time?" I asked directly, putting the pieces together.

"That was part of it, yes. I wanted him to have more time." Sebastian looked down at the table, his chestnut hair, falling limply across his forehead.

"And what was the other part?" I asked carefully. I didn't know exactly what he would say, but still, a sweeping feeling of nausea washed over me at the anticipation of his words.

"Because he loves you." He looked up at me again; he was strong-willed despite his weak state. "Eden, he has regretted that dreadful night since the moment it happened and I thought, that if you saw him, if you saw him.... dying that you would rethink this war of yours and sort things out peacefully."

"Did you really think that was a possibility? That I would just walk into his bedroom, forget about my brother or my people, fall at his side all weepy and emotional and turn my back on this Kingdom? That was your game plan?" I stared at him bewildered. How weak in love did he think I was?

"I had hoped," he whispered.

"Please tell me that you have some semblance of loyalty for your family, that if Amelia was the one in prison, tortured daily and on the brink of death, that you would do everything in your power to save her! You have to love, at least her, enough to fight for her!" I accused and his dull eyes flashed with hatred.

"Of course, I would," he snapped. "I would use any means necessary."

"Exactly," I agreed.

"Then use Kiran, for the love of God, don't you see that he is your means?" When I shook my head in disgust, he continued, "If you went to Kiran, if you fixed things with him, he would convince his father to release Avalon. If you and Kiran wed, then Kiran would share your magic, your children would have that connection and Lucan would be pacified. Avalon would be free."

His argument sounded too inviting, he was giving me the exact words I longed to hear. Sebastian offered an easy way out, with my brother on one side and the man that I loved on the other. Only it would never be that simple. And my grandfather would never have vindication.

"That is a great scenario, Sebastian. Really, if I were to take your advice, everyone would get a happily ever after. Except of course, the rest of the Resistance rotting right alongside Avalon in prison, or the

Shape-Shifters, or the Titans for that matter; your Kingdom is still oppressed by racism and tyranny and everyone is still dying! Don't you see that this is more than Avalon, or even vengeance, this is about freedom. This is about restoring Immortality to every Immortal."

"You're a regular revolutionary," he muttered, looking back at the window and refusing to meet my eye.

"Sebastian, I am only unique in my Immortality because there is one of me, and my parents got a little bit lucky with their genealogy. But what I have, this power, this longevity of life, it could be available to this whole Kingdom if Lucan would let it. If he would open up marriage and allow the Shape-Shifters complete freedom, we could all live like this." I argued, confidently.

"Lucan will never do that," Sebastian promised and I believed him.

"And that is why his bloodline has to die," I countered.

"So you are not just worried about Avalon?" He asked, carefully.

"That is my goal, right now. Of course, I'm worried about him. But he and I both knew that when they took him that night, there was a chance we would never see each other again. And this cause was worth both Amory and Avalon fighting for, and worth dying for. And now I have inherited not only their willingness to sacrifice everything for freedom, but their passion as well."

Sebastian listened to my words, but didn't respond. I too fell silent, letting the reality of my claims sink in. Until this moment, I focused on revenge and rescuing Avalon, but I had to accept that my mission was bigger than my brother. I didn't have access to our open communication any more, but I knew without a doubt that he was willing to die for his people, even if I was going to do everything in my power to stop that from happening.

Somewhere along the way, I started to believe in something more than revenge, and found a purpose. Not that long ago, I was confused about which side of the aisle I stood and when they killed Amory and took Avalon, I thought they decided for me. But now I held my own beliefs, my own vision for this Kingdom and that alone was enough to lessen the hold on me that Kiran still owned.

# Chapter Twenty-One

We landed eight hours later at the same airstrip I used during my Eternal Walk. Jericho explained to me that Amory had several private hangars all around the world, and so storing a jet was no problem. I tried to comprehend what several hangars around the world meant, but wondered if I would ever get the hang of this literal jet-set lifestyle.

I almost expected the silent stewards to greet us at the end of the tarmac, and was a little disappointed when they didn't. I missed those women. We never spoke a word to one another, but I craved their calming presence and attentiveness. Most of all, I craved their femininity. I started to resent being the only girl. After India, our next stop would be Romania; I needed get to Lilly. Even Roxie would be an improvement, for that matter.

The moment we landed in India, something started to stir inside of me, the blue smoke was home and I felt that deep within. My magic perked up and my senses heightened. India held an eternal calling, a shared language with my magic.

I fingered Kiran's pendant and engagement ring, still hanging from my neck. They burned against my skin as if blasphemously out of place. I cleared my throat and shook my head, reminding myself that I stripped them of their power. I stole the magic from the necklace and I emptied the engagement ring of any significance. Still they lay hot against my skin, foreigners in a land where I felt native.

Despite the necklace, I sighed with contentment. India was the right step to take. I could leave London and my failure behind and breath in the humid air, listen to the jungle calling and cleanse myself from disappointment here.

"Do you know where we're going?" I called out to Jericho and Titus.

"Kind of...." Titus answered. The two of them were commandeering a vehicle for the trip. Titus insisted on individual motorcycles since before we landed, and Jericho was adamant that we needed something sturdier.

"Great," I mumbled, rolling my eyes. "Gabriel, aren't you hot? Don't you want to change?"

Gabriel hung back with me, tasked with guarding Sebastian. He still wore his priestly outfit, but the heat forced him to tug at his collar. He turned to me with a stern glare, the bright orange flare of his eyes, dimmed behind dark, aviator sunglasses.

"What a funny question you ask a man of God," he commented without answering my question. "I have taken my vows for life."

"No, I meant, your outfit. I am not asking you to give up the priesthood!" I shrieked, realizing we had serious communication issues.

"Hmmm...." he sighed and then walked away to see if he could help Titus and Jericho decide what to do.

"You do a fantastic good job of assembling the best of the best, don't you?" Sebastian asked, snidely.

"Don't start!" I threatened, grabbing a hold of his arm and pulling him along towards the other guys.

In the end, Jericho found an old, eight passenger, white van whose sides were completely rusted out and one of the back windows was broken and replaced with cardboard and duct tape. Not a lot of options existed for shopping around at an airstrip in the middle of nowhere.

Jericho volunteered to drive, when the rest of the men remained silent. Titus couldn't even look at the van without grimacing in disgust. Gabriel sat in the front seat with Jericho and I had to use magic to get the sliding back door opened.

The van smelled like rotten fish and none of the windows would open. The ripped seats, with exposed springs, made dangerous barriers between spaces. And to make it even worse, when Jericho finally started the engine, it roared and grumbled at an ear-splitting volume.

Sebastian gave me a sarcastic thumbs-up, and then lulled his head against the back of his seat, closing his eyes and crossing his arms. I decided to do the same. The flight was long, and I didn't sleep the entire way.

The burning sun was setting over India, as we drove the familiar road deeper into the jungle. The sky glowed brightly behind us in orange and soft pinks, but ahead of us laid the dark anonymity of dense trees and dangerous animals.

I remembered the road being rough the first time I traveled this way and physically tensed at the thought of traversing those roads in the death-trap I now bounced around in. I sunk lower in my seat, nestling my head against the rotten smelling upholstery and closed my eyes. I was happy to be in India, but even more happy to grow my team. In a day, we would be on our way to Romania. We would be on our way to Avalon.

----

The setting sun streamed brilliantly through the open window, high above the boy's head. He lifted his chin as if to touch it, as if he only needed to feel the warmth of that one beam and all would be right.

His hands, bleeding and raw, stayed tied, tightly behind his back; his ankles looked as though the skin was brutally torn away to the bone. He half laughed at the idea of restraints at all, he was too weak to move, let alone escape this new dungeon.

Outside his room he heard footsteps, the smart clicking of a stately walk, and knew what the next few moments would be like. He wanted to be afraid; he wanted to cringe in anticipation. He wanted to feel something, to feel anything, even fear.

But no emotions came, no sense of warning, no prickling in the neck. Not even his blood stirred. He was an empty shell, hollowed and beaten beyond recognition.

The old, wooden door opened, creaking at its hinges, pushing the loose straw that lay indiscriminately across the floor, towards the wall. In walked his captor, his tyrant, his King. He towered over the boy, his crooked crown glinting in the sunlight. The blessed light now tainted with evil and glaring in his eyes.

The King stood staring down at the boy, a sinister smile twisting his lips and his hard, blue eyes satisfied with victory. The boy's stomach lurched and the fear that he had been desperate for only moments before came now in waves of panic. His numb, tingling hands began to tremble against their restraints and he vowed to himself that if something had happened to her, he would murder the Immortal King himself, magic or no.

"Cheer up, dear boy," the King commanded, "the cavalry has arrived."

"What have you done with her," the boy growled. Even bound and weak, he was still menacing and dangerous.

"I haven't done anything with her.... yet," the King smirked. "But she has come!" He clasped his hands together in pure certainty, sure of his impending win. "She has finally realized that she cannot win, and she has come to make the trade. Your freedom for hers."

"She has told you this?" the boy asked, not believing even a breath that was exhaled from the oppressor.

"Why else would she be here?" the King snapped, stomping his foot and demanding his prisoner's answer.

"I wouldn't know," the boy stared at the ground, refusing the King's demand for attention. "But I highly doubt it's to rescue me. More likely, it has something to do with killing you," he scoffed through a strained voice that struggled to reach above a whisper.

"Hmmm.... you're probably right," the King agreed, more easily than the boy trusted. "At any rate, we know she is here, and we know exactly how to bait her out. Guards!" the King commanded, and the door opened immediately.

Three, strong, imposing men walked through the door, ominous simpers mimicked across every face. They glowered at the prisoner, hoping their King called them in for one reason alone.

"Make sure he looks nice and pretty for our guests," the King ordered, before turning on his heel and leaving the room.

----

I shot up in the darkness, bumping my head against a hard surface and grasping at everything around me. I took a moment to realize the ear-splitting screams piercing my ears, were coming from my mouth and clasped my hands firmly across my lips to silence them. My body trembled, drenched in sweat and stiff from sitting in the car too long.

I tried to hold still, to put the pieces together, but they were fleeing. This dream was more vivid, more cohesive than any of the others. There was more to it than fear, more to it than pain. There were moments of information, but they were slipping away before I could put them together.

I pounded my palm against my head, demanding that my brain work. I surged the electricity through my blood in weak attempts at forcing magic to make my mind obey. But the majority of my memories were gone, lost in the subconscious world I still shared with Avalon.

Avalon.

He was here.

In India.

The details of the dream fled and I would never nail down the specifics. But this nightmare was different from all the rest, this nightmare left an impression. In the moments where my mind drifted, where the subconscious took hold, I was back with Avalon, seeing through his eyes, feeling through his senses. And the only explanation for the new vividness had to be that we were closer together. He *had* to be here.

I looked around, wondering why someone hadn't asked me to keep quiet and realized we weren't moving. The van was parked, surrounded by exotic, Indian forestry and the sounds of the wild jungle calling out to each other in the darkness.

I looked around frantically, for a moment believing they abandoned me. The tingling sensation that alerted my blood that I was near Immortals prickled underneath my skin. I stepped out of the van, breathing in deeply the fresh, night air and spotted a campfire a little ways from where the van sat.

I stumbled through the darkness, too excited to bother with magic, toward the campfire, toward the gathered Resistance. The farther the dream flew from consciousness, the more sure I became that Avalon was here. He had no magic left, and the memories of nights awakened, screaming and clawing out in the darkness made my heart stop beating for fear of what he was suffering through. But I could still feel him, his blood, as weak and powerless as it was, still pumped in unison with mine. Not completely severed, our connection still searched each other out in moments of terrible struggle. He was my twin... my brother. And I could still feel him near.

I walked out of the deep vegetation into a circle of Immortals, laughing and talking quietly around a large fire. Jericho sat across the camp, conferring seriously with Gabriel and his reunited team members. I recognized none of the rest of the faces, representing a more global community than I expected.

The tight circle of the gathered Rebellion buzzed with excited electricity. Wrapped in an invisible cloud of collective magic, they pulsated with the same purpose and drive. We were in this together. I didn't know them, and they didn't know me; some of them, might not even know each other. But we moved as one entity, with the same goal, the same dream and because of that, we could sit together in happy union for tonight, not knowing what the morning would bring.

And not afraid of the unknown.

I took a breath, inhaling the smoky campfire and drawing the attention of the group, interrupting their excited chatter with my magical presence. Quieting down and growing still they looked to me. I was supposed to be their leader, they were the ones following me and yet I came to petition them for advice.

I stared at them for a moment, wishing I possessed Avalon's strengths, wishing I could just call the Titan part of me forward and demand that it take control of the crowd. Instead, fear and uncertainty governed my emotions and even in front of people who stood with me, side by side, I couldn't find the courage to request a response.

"Avalon's here," I blurted loudly, surprising most of them with information I should not rationally know.

"He's what?" Jericho stood up.

"He's here, he's in India," Most of the Rebellion knew about the telepathic connection Avalon and I shared. Before the tragic night at the farm, Amory trusted our secret with those that shared the mark of the Resistance. However, I was still sure that Lucan and his Guard were clueless to the open communication Avalon and I shared before he gave up his magic. With Sebastian sitting in the group tonight, I couldn't risk going into too many details and suddenly regretted my proclamation.

"How do you know?" A beautiful Indian girl asked, her long, shiny black hair pulled over her shoulder in a waist-length braid. With flawless skin, her perfect lips perpetuated a smile that she could not control and probably wasn't even conscious of. She was absolutely stunning, made even more exquisite by soft, pink eyes that shimmered in the darkness, almost glowing against the black backdrop of the jungle.

"I know, I just do. I know this sounds crazy and it's not something I can really explain.... But I know that he is here in the core of my being," I said with a stronger voice than I had started with.

"Do you know where he is?" A Korean man asked, clean-cut, with short hair, and narrow lips. His deep green eyes, like the color of grass at night, bore into mine, hungry for information. He sat forward, ready for my answers, while holding the hand of a woman of a similar ethnicity. She had short black hair too, sleek and shining and high cheek bones that turned her smile into light. Her eyes were like Gabriel's, orange and glowing, but deeper, more burnt orange, like the color of leaves changing in the fall, than fire.

"No, not exactly. With Lucan, but that's all I know." I shrugged my shoulders, wishing I had introduced myself, before I dumped my mysterious intelligence on these people. They were having a good time before I showed up.

"Well, Lucan is in the summer palace, we have been watching them for a week now," A college-aged blonde woman explained; she sat in between the Asian couple and the Indian woman. I decided they had to be the India Team; they held the spirit of resilient camaraderie that Avalon shared with his team.

"Why are they here?" I asked, wondering what in the world Lucan would want with my brother in India.

"Well, that's why I called Jericho," Xander stood up next to Jericho who had yet to sit back down after hearing the news that he was in the same country as Avalon. "Lucan always comes this time of year to oversee the Eternal Walks. However, from what we've, or rather Te and his team observed, the Walks are not working." He gestured to the Asian man sitting with whom I assumed to be his wife, judging by the bulging diamond on her ring finger.

"Yes," Te took over, "from what we've gathered, there doesn't seem to be any magic in the Caves, or at least what magic is there has refused to cooperate with Lucan. There is a whole batch of candidates for the Walk and not one of them has been able to conjure the magic."

"Oh, my gosh!" I shrieked, and the gathered Resistance collectively sat back, surprised by my outburst. "That is incredible!" I realized at that moment that the Caves would only answer to me from now on. My magic moved inside my blood, and not the electricity I could call my life's-blood, but the blue smoke, the healing magic I wrestled with inside those very Caves just months ago.

"Yes, it is," Te agreed with me, stoically.

"What are you thinking, E?" Titus asked from across the fire.

"The plan is this," I stated, making it sound simple, "We check out the Caves, first thing in the morning, and then rescue my brother right after, and then.... we get the hell out of here?" They sat in stunned silence, still just looking at me, but I was confident of my plan.

India was turning out to be a fantastic decision.

## Chapter Twenty-Two

I woke up the next morning before the sun, too excited to stay still for long. Near my brother and hours from being with him, I could hardly contain my nervous energy. The rest of the group lay sleeping in tents scattered around the jungle clearing.

I sat up and stretched, almost kicking my tent mate in the head. Somehow, during the night, I had twisted all the way around so that my feet were now in Grace's face and my sleeping bag all the way unzipped.

Grace Lewis, the blonde, college-aged girl, on the India team and very familiar with the jungle. Originally from Canesbury where Jericho went to school, came to India to work with the poor in Calcutta. Amory recruited her for the Resistance almost a year ago, placing her on the a team with Te Che and his wife Pan, Naima Desai, the beautiful Indian girl, and Sunny Magar, an Indian man, who appeared to be middle-aged, but was probably much older, with specks of gray salting his thick, curly black hair and navy blue eyes, standing out against his freckled, dark, brown skin.

The India team had been watching the palace since they heard about Amory's death, waiting for word from anyone who still might be in the Rebellion. They met Avalon's team during the surveillance opts for my Eternal Walk and were very thankful to see Xander and Xavier when they arrived.

The Morocco Team was the same way, diligent about their tasks, even though essentially, the Rebellion seemed dead. They held out hope, waiting for someone to arrive and tell them what to do next. Although, the Morroco Team was very spirited, from what I observed last night, and I was sure that if Xander and Xavier had not shown up, they would have taken matters quickly into their own hands.

They were a small team made up of mostly Americans, who were in Morocco teaching English as a second language. Nobody on the team was married yet, but by the way they interacted with each other, I got the impression they were already paired off.

Caden Halstead, the team leader, was a tall, skinny guy, with shaggy, dirty blonde hair and freckles from head to toe. He was very close with the second in command Kya Hasting. Kya, skinny and tall too, had long, wavy, auburn hair and pale skin. The team was rounded out with another American, Lucy Barello, a curvy, dark haired knockout with a prominent beauty mark on her neck that made her seem more voluptuous, pin up girl than Rebellion spy; and Bex Costello, the only non-American on the team. He was from Spain and Lucy's parents were from Spain, so as a couple they made a lot of sense. Bex was dark haired as well, and had a gritty, down-to-earth vibe about him that balanced Lucy.

The jungle grew quiet through the night, and into the early morning hours; even the wildlife found sleep. We stayed up late into the night, discussing our options and figuring out a plan of attack. Over the lengthy planning, I got the chance to meet everyone and through the course of discussion, I was able to get a feel for the personalities.

The Resistance differed from the students at Kingsley, with no concern for the Monarchy and without prejudice or reserve. I was more comfortable here, in the wilderness, surrounded by people that wanted what I did, but still something kept me from them. Something I couldn't define separated me from them. It felt like I should know what it was, but I didn't. I couldn't define the feeling and so I stayed close to Jericho and let his easy-going ability cover my awkwardness.

Grace lay sleeping next to me and so I decided to slip out of the tent and spend some time alone in the fresh air. I walked as quietly as I could to the campfire, but didn't stand there for more than a minute before I heard a zipper open and another person exit their tent.

The sun was still rising and underneath the thick canopy of trees, the jungle was still very dark. I strengthened the fire with my magic, taking a step closer to its warmth before inclining my head to greet Sebastian.

Sebastian watched us for a while last night. Sitting silently apart from us, but never really separate. He watched me mainly, his dull, lifeless eyes focused on my every move and I grew increasingly uncomfortable until finally he fell asleep. I didn't know what I was going to do with him. I promised to take his life, and end his misery, but I wondered if I really had it in me.

"Trying to sneak out?" I asked, half joking.

"And go where?" He grunted, joining me at the fire.

"The palace, to warn your uncle," I accused seriously, wondering if it were even possible for him to find his way out of the jungle and to a real road in his state.

"If I were going to escape, it would not be to my uncle...." He mumbled in response, and I half turned to him, my heart breaking for him the millionth time without my permission.

"Hey, are you up to trying something?" I asked, and then realized I should never have given him the chance to say no.

"What?" He asked, turning to me.

"I want to try to give you your magic back. Are you up for that?" I smiled sweetly at him, trying to charm him into agreeing with me. I doubted he had any idea how unsafe this was for him, and I decided that since he had a death wish anyway, I would leave the potentially dangerous details out.

"Why would you give me my magic back?" He questioned, honestly, but there was the tiniest spark of life behind his golden brown eyes. It thrilled me to see his interest.

"Ok, moment of truth?" I asked, and he nodded, "I don't know how to give magic back. I mean, I can take it no problem.... trust me. But I have yet to give it back to anyone. And I have got to be able to give it back to Avalon, I mean, like it's the first thing I need to be able to do. So, I'm thinking if I can figure it out with you, than it's like a win-win!" I did my best to sell the idea, but his expression went from hopeful to skeptical in a second.

"So, you don't know what you're doing?"

"No, I have absolutely no idea. But come on, it will be fun!" I turned completely to him and reached out my hands, shaking them impatiently when he didn't immediately grab on to them.

He looked at me, tilting his head sideways and I briefly recalled that I needed to find him new clothes. He reached out his hands to mine and grasped them with weak resolve. His magical current was there, suffocating, but there. It perked up at our connection, calling out to itself, hidden deep in the mixture of magics melded together in my blood.

I had absorbed a lot more magics since the last time I tried to give Oscar his back and so when Sebastian's magic didn't come immediately forward, I wasn't worried. I closed my eyes, concentrating on the little imprint he had left in his blood and the knowledge I remembered about him from times we made contact prior to him losing his magic.

Slowly I pulled it forward, through the myriad of others, and to the surface, where it now popped and sizzled with anxious anticipation. I didn't want to send him flying through the jungle as I had with Oscar and so I stayed relaxed, refusing to get frustrated. The more relaxed I was able to stay, the less my magic jumped all over his in order to hold it prisoner.

Taking an Immortal's magic felt like physically pulling it from them, using my magic against theirs in a tug of war like scenario, only a scenario where I always won. My natural reaction then, was to push the magic back into the other person, physically make them take it back. However, from my experience with Oscar I knew it wasn't going to work and so I stayed still, waiting patiently for an idea to come, to form inside my mind, or intuition to manifest suddenly and whisper what to do.

Sebastian, feeling awkward by my statue-like approach, squirmed a little, but I felt him stand up straighter and I hoped that was a sign that he could feel his magic. I rolled my head around, keeping my eyes tightly shut and wiggling my fingers. This would work; I would wait until it worked. I would figure this out.

His magic grew more frantic, the longer I waited, sizzling just under my skin and begging to be returned home. I willed the magic out of me, using the Psychic part of my brain I was learning how to use, but nothing happened. I used the Witch part of my blood to will it into Sebastian's body, but still nothing happened. I reminded myself to remain relaxed, but the tension between us increased and I knew I wouldn't be able to stand there much longer, while I held his magic captive just out of reach.

The sun began to poke through holes in the dense canopy above and tents started to open all around us. Zippers pulled and canvas ruffled, but once outside the tents nobody said anything. Other than the soft sounds of waking for the day, the jungle remained quiet and I held my concentration.

I gripped Sebastian's hands tighter, demanding my blood to obey, but nothing happened. His magic was wild inside of me, rushing through my body, pounding on my veins to be released, to be returned home, while my own magic raced alongside, demanding to bury it once again.

The pressure built inside of my head as well, while I heaped on the scathing disappointment and discouragement that nobody offered but my mind's eye. But nothing was as bad as the fear, the fear that I would hold onto Avalon's magic forever, that our true, complete connection was cut off entirely, and that he would not know his

Immortal life again, and I would know nothing but.

I decided to push the magic out, that had to be my only option. I hoped it just went too fast with Oscar. Maybe I could try slowly this time. How else could magic move between two souls; there was no other way. I tentatively pushed magic from my palms to his, waiting carefully for a reaction, or sign that he received at least some of it.

He shook my hands, as if asking for more and I believed that maybe it had worked. I pushed some more magic out, his escaping with my own and it found Sebastian's palms fiercely.

The magic came out so forcefully, despite my fragile intentions, that I threw Sebastian straight up into the air twenty feet. I gasped in horror and stared after him in terrified paralysis. He waved his arms wildly on his way down. My heart sunk and my stomach lurched; I feared that I killed him. I sent him to his death and not only was responsible for my first kill, but also gave Sebastian exactly what he wanted.

Strong hands on my back, pushed me away, and Jericho and Gabriel stepped in my place literally catching Sebastian right before he landed head first on the ground. The members of the Resistance broke out in clapping, relieved that Sebastian had not died and I felt, for not the first time, that I was a side-show at a circus, only around to provide tonight's entertainment.

Jericho and Gabriel stood Sebastian upright and helped him find his balance. He stared at me with a mixture of contempt and fear. I knew that I needed to apologize to him, especially if I ever expected him to let me try that again, but I couldn't make myself say the words. I argued with myself that we needed his memories of the palace to make our mission successful and there was no way I would get them without saying I'm sorry, but I needed a few minutes.

I had never been more frustrated in my life. I was usually able to conquer whatever I set out for my mind to do and the returned magic dilemma was currently the bane of my existence. In less than four hours, I was going to need desperately to hand Avalon's magic over to him without hesitation and in only moments.

We would never have another opportunity like this. With Avalon out of the Romanian prisons and Lucan without his Royal family, this was my one shot to be able to swoop in, storm the castle, grab the prisoner and get the hell out of Dodge.

So, I hoped Sebastian was ready for round two, because I stood up, brushed off his shoulder and held my hands out to him again.

"You've got to be joking me," he grunted, keeping his distance.

"No, come on, let's go!" I demanded, stomping my foot impatiently.

"Eden, maybe you could wait, and try again later?" Jericho offered carefully.

"Later? When later? On the way to the Caves? Or inside the palace? Or maybe right before I rescue Avalon, because my brother has been through a whole hell of a lot more than this guy and I can't risk blowing him up...." I trailed off, an idea coming to mind.

"You're right, but we will still be able to get Avalon out of there, even if you can't give him his magic back right away," Jericho reasoned calmly.

"Yes we can! Xander, get your explosives!" I turned on my heel, shouting orders. I needed to even the playing field like Sebastian suggested, I needed to raise the stakes to their level. They destroyed my Farm.

I would blow their Summer Palace to tiny, little pieces that even magic wouldn't be able to put back together.

## Chapter Twenty-Three

I walked carefully to the cave entrance. The last time I was here I was trapped inside, and even if I controlled the magic today, I still wasn't eager to relive those memories. Gabriel stood by my side, arms folded, aviator sunglasses on and hands moving expertly around his crimson rosary.

"Did you do an Eternal Walk?" I asked casually.

"Of course," he replied, waiting for me decide what to do. "For a different King."

I brushed my hands across an ancient stone pillar, feeling the gritty rock beneath my fingers. The blue smoke already surrounded my feet in soft, smoky swirls, blowing gently with the breeze. The healing magic was ecstatic to be home, and made its appearance as soon as my feet were on the stone patio leading into the caves.

It was just Gabriel and I now. Naima waited for us back at the car, which was at least an hour's walk. Bex Costello stayed with Sebastian at camp and Jericho led the rest of the group left to lay the ground work at the palace.

Our goal was to surround the palace at equal distances and when I arrived, I would take Gabriel straight to Avalon, while the rest of the team descended on the palace from every direction, strategically placing explosives to avoid killing Avalon. As soon as Gabriel and I had Avalon in our custody, the palace would go "boom."

If everything went as planned, we would be able to make an escape easily through the confusion and wreckage. It was simple. I just wanted to meet the Caves one more time, before I left India, probably for good.

"The explosions can't significantly hurt Immortals, right?" I asked Gabriel, going over the plan again and deciding there was still time to change course if I didn't feel comfortable.

"Not significantly, no. Everyone affected will be able to recover," he replied seriously and I knew I could trust Gabriel. Not because I knew him so well, or felt he would never lie to me. I *knew* he would never lie to me; he would never lie to anybody. "Everyone, except Avalon and if there are any other humans in the palace."

"Will there be? What about the stewards?" I panicked at the thought of martyring those beautiful women. I wouldn't go through with it if there were a chance they would be in the compound.

"They are not allowed to stay inside the palace and from Te's observations, all of the Walks have been suspended for now," Gabriel never lost his matter of fact tone, but now I found it very comforting.

"Ok, so let's do this." I sighed, finding the courage to move forward.

We walked silently into the Caves, our footsteps echoing off the cavernous walls. I breathed a sigh of relief when I didn't immediately feel an invisible barrier blockade me inside.

The Caves felt empty, hollowed and lifeless. During my Walk, I immediately felt the power radiate inside these stone walls, but now I walked their solitary enclosures and felt nothing. No pulsing magic, no electric force from the earth manifested itself into colorful winds. The empty rooms and natural hollows imparted nothing except the mere beauty of creation.

The blue magic flitted around my feet, rushing across the rock floor, in swirling patterns and playful wisps. Glad to be home and happy to be reunited with its origins, the blue smoke displayed no desire to return here for good, made no effort to struggle with me again and be freed from my bodily prison.

Gabriel stayed silent, quietly observing the phenomenon; I appreciated his company even more for it. I could find no words to explain what happened here, and had no explanation to offer for the consequences and the smoke that I carried with me.

I didn't know what I was looking for, or what I thought I would find once inside the empty caverns; but whatever I was looking for wasn't here. There was nothing left of the magic from the earth and I felt foolish exploring the Caves for something that was already at my disposal.

We walked further into the Caves, nearing the outside and suddenly there was something to feel. The hair on my neck stood up straight; my blood began to prickle with the warnings of other magic close by. We were not alone and no longer safe.

Gabriel tilted his head and the joints in his neck cracked. I knew he was not Titan and could not feel the other magic's presence, but he was a wise warrior despite his vows to the church.

"This was a mistake," I whispered.

"There are no mistakes, Eden, just different outcomes to our flawed expectations," Gabriel recited with confidence.

I stood up, distracted by his wisdom so when Lucan, and thirty

Titans, walked around the corner he found Gabriel readied in a battle stance and me, completely unprepared and confused. But Gabriel was right, I shouldn't be worried about messing up, I should be focused on how to turn our unfolding events into opportunity.

"Eden, what a pleasant surprise," Lucan practically sang. He glowed with victory, happy to have caught me off guard and almost alone. The blue magic that was scattered across the floor, gathered to me quickly, disappearing completely at the sound of Lucan's voice. He stared after it, his expression suddenly hard and angry.

"I heard you broke the Caves, so we came to see if there was anything we could do. Is there like a generator box around that I can take a look at, or power cord that needs to be plugged back in?" I asked sarcastically, narrowing my eyes and folding my arms.

"How clever...." Lucan sighed, looking me over with hungry interest. "And Gabriel, I had so hoped you were dead. Amory recruited you after all, did he?"

"No," Gabriel said simply, relaxing his stance a little and feigning unconcern.

"Eden, then? Really?" He looked back at me, his ice, blue eyes twinkling with amusement. "From what I've heard, she hardly lives up to her brother's potential. She probably doesn't even understand what a find you are. Or were, in this case...." He smiled cynically, pure evil marking his expression.

"I am often underestimated," Gabriel responded, and the hardness in his tone caused my attention to turn to him. His orange eyes fueled by hatred shimmered with rage, as if they were on fire. I struggled to tear my eyes away from him, absolutely certain they held a power of their own.

"Just curious, how long have you known we were in India? Or was this an accident?" I asked innocently, hoping to belittle the hateful King as much as I could. I shared Gabriel's detest. I was afraid at first and then caught off guard, but the longer I stood in Lucan's presence the more deeply I felt vengeful rage.

"We watched you land yesterday; maybe you were unaware that your grandfather's hangar is adjacent to my own," Lucan explained smugly.

"And so you just hang out at the airport?" I asked, letting my teenage sarcasm get the best of me.

"At least your grandfather understood respect," Lucan snapped, his eyes hardening to stone.

"And look what happened to him," I growled, taking a step forward at the mention of my grandfather.

At my reaction Lucan smiled, a contorted grin of satisfaction that made my stomach churn violently. "Yes, look at what happened to him," he repeated in a cruel, victorious whisper. "Kiran!" He called suddenly, and my heart stopped beating.

The room grew silent; not even a Guard dared to fidget. I stood, paralyzed by the realization of why Lucan would know what went on at the airstrip yesterday, someone had been there to pick up Kiran. I shouted to myself to hold it together, to remember how I was able to walk away the other night and that I was stronger than him, stronger than whatever hold he thought he had over me.

Kiran entered the Caves, dressed in tan, linen pants and a blue, plaid, button up shirt with the sleeves rolled up. He was perfection as always, but only his eyes caused some hesitation, I had moved beyond being impressed by looks alone. He walked to his father, standing next to him and directly across from me. The real distance between us was probably five feet, but it felt both canyons apart and suffocatingly close at the same time.

He stared at me, his mouth unmoving, his body unflinching, but I fought the desperation to find his gaze. I would lose myself in the ocean of his eyes and I could not allow myself to misplace my focus. So instead I stared at his father, my grandfather's murderer, and the orchestrator of oppression for my people.

"Impressive recovery," I mused, keeping my eyes from him, even while addressing him. "Already up and about, hmm?"

"Yes, I am," he answered softly. I could feel his intense gaze on my face, pulling my eyes toward his with gravitational forces rivaling the sun.

"Don't we have you to thank for that, Eden?" Lucan asked with a pleased, vicious voice.

"Ok, what's the plan here?" I shook my head, forcing my attention back to Lucan, "Like, do you want to just meet us back at the palace, or.... what?" I was really getting a kick out of treating this so trivially and it helped that I knew it was driving Lucan mad.

"We would be more than happy to arrange the transportation." He smiled with practiced benevolence at me before snapping his fingers and turning on his heel.

The Titan Guards surrounded Gabriel and me, pushing us forward and out the other side of the cave. The elephants were dressed in their traditional Cave Walk costumes and I couldn't help but dread another long ride on one of the mammoth beasts.

"Seriously, we drove here," I whined, hoping by some unrealistic miracle my complaints would be heard, "you fly jets, why don't you make yourselves some roads, for like, cars?"

"Eden can ride with my son," Lucan demanded, ignoring my protests and I couldn't stop my eyes from rolling and a long sigh from escaping my lips.

I grumbled the entire way to the top of the elephant, refusing to use magic on the principle that riding an elephant, as exotic as it was, was really uncomfortable. The basket on top of the large mammal was big enough for at least two people, so I knew I would not be confined next to Kiran, but this was a brave risk Lucan was taking. Wasn't he worried I would just kill his son?

Lucan's elephant moved next to ours and I couldn't contain my curiosity, "Aren't you afraid this will be the last time you see him alive?" I shouted to Lucan, gesturing at his son.

"If you touch him, harm him in any way, I will kill your brother tonight. And then tomorrow morning I will execute every single one of your friends at dawn. Do not play games with me, child," Lucan said seriously and I kept my mouth shut. At the moment, he held the upper hand, I couldn't argue with that.

With Lucan's threats hanging heavily in the air, he did not even bother to board a Titan with us. I sat across from Kiran, bouncing roughly with the uneven and slow steps of our elephant transportation moving up the mountainside. He stayed silent for a long time, his back to the elephant's head and still stared, his gaze burning a hole through my soul.

"I'm glad we have a moment to ourselves," Kiran said after minutes of silence, as if our togetherness was the most normal thing in the world, as if I wasn't his prisoner. "I wanted to say thank you, for healing me." His inflection was genuine, but I yawned in response, I had nothing to say to him.

"Eden," he began again, and the way he said my name, forced my eyes to his. He held my attention completely, I was transfixed by his turquoise eyes, shining in the bright sunlight; he was hopeful but reserved. I kept my mouth closed and my magic under control, but still his gaze held me. "If you would like, I could have them bring.... I could send for Lilly, if you wanted. I mean, if you wanted, I would get her for you, I know how much she means to you."

I narrowed my eyes, and tried to swallow the bile rising in my throat. Why had I never been disgusted by how spoiled he was? Was I supposed to fawn over how generous and self-sacrificing he was being? How sweet of him to fetch my captured best friend for me and let her be a prisoner with me in a palace instead of the dark, horrifying dungeon he was keeping her in presently.

"That's all right, I think I'll just get her myself," I whispered hoarsely, venom dripping with every word.

He smiled at me, a patronizing smile that let me know how little he believed in me as leader of the Resistance. Although, I didn't think my recent captivity was doing my case any favors.

"She's Ok, if you're worried about her. I mean, I know she is fine. Talbott has been finding any reason to get to Romania, so I know he is making sure they treat her fairly and that she is well taken care of," Kiran babbled and my hardened eyes turned incredulous; what was he trying to accomplish?

"How's the wedding planning?" I asked, changing the subject to something as far from us as possible.

His eyes shifted uncomfortably, and he cleared his throat nervously before answering, "Good, I mean, I think good. I've only been a part of them the last twenty-four hours or so. Well, you know that...." He laughed nervously.

"Right...." I sighed, removing my eyes from his and searching the jungle for a distraction. Naima would know by now that something had gone wrong and would hopefully figure out what. I trusted the individuals of the Rebellion far more than I trusted myself in these kinds of matters and I believed they would adjust their plan and assume we were captured.

Not a whole lot changed as far as the chain of events would go. In fact, an escort into the palace made things much easier. Once inside, I would just continue with the mission according to plan and hope that was what everyone else would be expecting.

"Your aunt is all right, too," Kiran spoke up again, more nervously than before. I snapped my head back to face him, my mouth falling open from shock, "I mean, don't worry, we don't have her or anything, it's just that, my father put a small detail on her, just in case you went home. She's fine; she isn't in any danger or anything...." I shook my head in disgust, and he cleared his throat nervously again, "She is with Angelica and my father will not cross Angelica. She practically raised him.... Besides, entangling a human is messy business.... I just thought you would want to know that she is fine; I didn't know if you talked to her recently. I'm sure you're worried about her and I didn't want you to-"

"I get it," I snapped, cutting off his nervous rambling.

"I'm sorry, I just don't know how to be with you like this, without our magics...." he trailed off, and I realized that I was keeping control of my magic the entire ride. In his room, in London, I had not been able to even pretend to keep my magic from the magnetic pull of his, but today, in the daylight and having had the shock of seeing him for the first time wear off, I was able to hold myself together.

"You'll figure it out," I mumbled, turning my attention back to the jungle and the palace walls interrupting the exotic vegetation and centuries old trees.

"I don't want to figure it out." He leaned forward, across the distance that was separating us and whispered passionately to me.

We were entering the palace grounds, and the gates the elephants walked through. The gate was only wide enough for one elephant to pass through at a time. Gabriel was held prisoner on an elephant in front of mine, with two other Titans keeping their eyes secured on him.

"Eden, my offer still stands," Kiran continued, "please reconsider saving our Kingdom a different way. If you were my wife, if we stood together, we could make a difference, any difference that you want to make. I would be on your side."

He reached for my hand, grasping it in his as he appealed his case and my magic was suddenly pulsating under my skin at his unexpected touch. His eyes smoldered, turning from turquoise to deep blue and I felt his magic sigh in relief at our connection.

"Sounds lovely," I found my sarcasm, and a plan formed decisively in my mind, "but I think you've made those promises to me before and I would rather not go down that road ever again."

I ripped my hand from his and stood up abruptly. My necklace tumbled from underneath my shirt and his face lit up with pride and victorious possession. I couldn't take it anymore; I couldn't stand to be in his presence. So, I took in my surroundings quickly and threw myself over the side of the elephant. We were just inside the palace walls; Lucan's elephant was the first one through and on its way to the stables. I shouted at Gabriel to follow suit and he did, jumping over the side of his elephant and landing gracefully on the ground.

Before I could think about it, I sent magic, zapping the feet of all of the elephants still carrying the angry Titans, sending them reeling in fear. They bridled up, like angry horses, sending the Guards and Kiran in every direction and jamming the entrance from more entering.

I forced more fevered energy into the melee and fueled the confusion. The Titans struggled to gain control of their animals and protect Kiran at the same time. The elephant gridlock, loud and dangerous, drew the attention of the palace Guards who waited for their King's arrival.

Gabriel pulled on my arm and we were off, sprinting across the palace grounds and into a hotbed of Titan activity. I learned a little bit about the palace over my stay in December, but not nearly enough to know where the prisons were or the best way to get there.

"Do you know where they would keep Avalon?" I shouted at Gabriel, while we ducked from some Titan fire, sliding through an arched doorway and using our magic to keep from slipping on the slick marbled floor.

"Of course," he shouted back. "If you've lived as long as I have, then you have seen the inside of a few prison cells." He looked back at me with a smile on his face, his eyes alit with intense surety and I couldn't help but smile back. "That was quick thinking, Eden, I am very impressed!" He half laughed at me, while we dodged more Titans, and turned down another long hallway.

"I just hope it works!" I mumbled.

Gabriel reached into his pocket and pulled out his cell phone. I smiled, still finding the technology severely out of place, hidden in the long folds of his robes. He dialed while we moved and shouted instructions to whoever was on the other end. At least the rest of the team would know how to act now.

We were inside the palace.

We just needed to get to Avalon now, and then get out before the whole place went up in flames.

# Chapter Twenty-Four

I followed Gabriel as he turned again and again. He seemed to know his way around the palace expertly. I trusted his direction, his innate ability, but I knew that even without him I would have found Avalon. There was not a part inside of me that was not conscience of his nearness.

Titans were everywhere, around corners, at the end of hallways; they pursued us with every step. I used magic as fast and as fiercely as I could. Gabriel was a skilled warrior, his priestly robes flowed out from behind him as we ran, and magic lead the way from his fingertips.

"How quickly can you take someone's magic?" he questioned loudly over his shoulder.

"Pretty fast," I yelled back, throwing out more magic and missing a Titan by just an inch. I hit the marble wall instead with shocking force, sending shrapnel soaring and debris littering the hallway. I picked up the same debris with my magic in a whirlwind of energy and buried the Titan in a heavy heap of rubble. It wouldn't keep him for long, but it would buy us some time.

"When we get to Avalon, I have no doubt his cell will be Guarded by at least a dozen guards," he continued to yell over his shoulder, while dialing a number on his cell phone simultaneously. "It would be best if you took all of their magic at once and immediately. That would be our best chance for survival."

"Sure," I replied confidently, inwardly freaking the hell out. A dozen Guards? At once? Immediately? Who was he kidding?

"Eden, I'm serious!" he shouted back, "If you cannot do it, we will never leave that prison cell."

"I'll try," I promised back, and then amended my words, "I'll do my best."

"Then do it now!" he ordered and we rounded one last corner, finally entering the dungeon part of the palace.

Fifteen Titan Guards stood, ready and waiting for us in front of a long, dark hallway with wooden doors, evenly spaced, lining the right side of the corridor. I skidded to a stop, a little off balance, waving my arms and trying to stand tall. Gabriel stepped behind me waiting for my magic to take over. The Guards however were not thrown off and immediately started to use their magic either against us or with objects against us. I dodged out of the way, by diving back behind the wall, landing on Gabriel who had the same idea.

"I thought you were going to take their magic!" he questioned me. The sound of the walls crashing around us was incredibly noisy and I struggled to hear anything.

"It's just not that easy!" I defended myself, throwing my hands over my head to protect myself from falling or flying debris.

"Make it that easy!" He shook my shoulders, forcing me to pay attention, his orange eyes flashing with unhurried intensity.

I leaned my head back against what was left of the destroyed wall and concentrated. I had to pull their magic, all fifteen of their magics. But I didn't have to be facing them. So I focused on the violent energy circulating around the room and began to draw it to myself. I couldn't count the individual magic I was stealing, so I continued feeling out the rest of the room, searching for more.

When I was confident that I was draining the room sufficiently, I stood up and nodded to Gabriel. We walked around the corner this time to find weakened Titans struggling to hold on to their power. All fifteen of them had taken a knee, begging me with their eyes to stop. They knew what was coming, they knew the fate that awaited them and that whatever whispered rumors they heard were true.

I wanted to have compassion on them, to find the bits of humanity that still resided in my soul and remember mercy, but my eyes flickered to the first, locked door behind the weakening Guards and I remembered Avalon. I couldn't be kind to men who would willingly torture my brother and turn their heads from tyranny.

I stomped my foot in anger, taking the last remnants of magic from the room and rendering the men unconscious with one collective blow. I tried to stand up straighter, to revel in momentary victory, but I was suddenly tired. Fifteen magics at once turned into the opposite of strength. I was suddenly weak, and frail. My body buzzed with the frantic energy of the newly acquired magic. All of a sudden, I felt as I did before I knew I was magical, before I knew what to do with my energy. I was too inundated with electricity to function. I needed release and hoped Avalon's prison cell would be room enough to expel the excess energy.

I stumbled backwards, and Gabriel was there to catch me, "Are you all right?" he asked, pushing me forward, without waiting for a response.

"I'm fine, open the door," I commanded, sending a powerful burst of magic down the long hallway. The back wall exploded into a million pieces, breaking a hole into an atrium of sorts. I felt better, not completely myself, but put together enough that I wasn't afraid of hurting Avalon.

Gabriel forced the prison door open with his shoulder and then tumbled through to the other side with me on his heels. I stopped short however, finding my brother in front of me and barely alive.

He sat in a wooden chair, with his hands tied behind his back and his ankles bound to the legs of the chair. His head drooped forward and I couldn't tell if he was conscious or not. His shoulder length hair was blood-soaked and matted to his head. His body trembled in agonized weakness, his chest heaving unevenly with the effort to breath. His green-ink tattoos stood off his pallid skin in stark contrast, their intricate lines raised from his body as if God created his veins in the shapes of Avalon's choosing.

"Avalon?" I asked carefully, quietly. The sight of so much suffering made me ill.

He lifted his head so that I could just see one swollen, black and blue eye, dripping with blood and making his face nearly unrecognizable. His one shoulder still sagged, like it had the night he was taken from the farm and his clothes were soaked with dried blood.

The stench of the room was almost unbearable, but even worse was Avalon. He was broken and beaten and I could hardly bare to look at him, let alone believe that I let this happen to him for weeks and had done nothing tangible to help him.

I ran to him, kneeling at his feet, afraid to touch him. Carefully, I lifted my hands to his face, cradling his swollen head and matted hair gently, afraid that I would break him completely with the smallest of movements.

Tears flowed freely from my eyes; my spirit broke at the sight of him. How could anyone allow such cruelty? I knew that Lucan was evil; I watched how he had easily taken my grandfather's life.

But this was different. This was torture and suffering at a level I could not comprehend.

I thought of Sebastian, my own prisoner, how I felt guilty for not offering a change of clothes. Yet he was fed, accommodated and treated with respect. This was inhumane. Lucan truly was a monster.

My magic moved aggressively next to my brother, longing for

him, longing to be divided again between us. But I couldn't even fathom attempting that inevitable failure with him in this state. First, I was determined to heal him. Then, I could conquer trying to give him his magic back.

"I knew you would come," he whispered through ragged, broken breaths, but I hushed him, knowing I could fix at least the physical damage.

I sent the blue smoke out with purpose, wrapping Avalon in its wispy tufts and turning everything in the room to blue. I felt the healing magic work at his scarred appendages and wounded body. It wove its way around his legs, healing the skin on his ankles and then to his wrists that were raw, to his shoulder that was dislocated and to his back that was etched in scars from countless unanswered questions or small signs of rebellion. His face slowly began to reform into the shape I remembered, and the swelling, gradually began to decrease.

The smoke helped him sit up straighter, feel his muscles again, and find purpose again. I heard the sickening, crunching of bones and saw the inflamed areas of his face, squirt with abused liquid. He was coming to himself again in the gentlest way possible, but still the healing process was agonizing.

"So that's what it does," he laughed in short bursts of strained whispers, finding the smoke amusing. Only Avalon.

Gabriel ripped off the restraints from his wrists and then the shackles from his ankles with his magic and Avalon stood up a strong and determined man. His eyes remained tired, but I knew that was only because he didn't have his magic back. That would change as soon as I could get him out of here.

"We have to go, we have to leave now!" I whispered fiercely, pulling on his hand.

"Of course," he agreed and Gabriel walked from the room first, surveying our escape route and nodding his head. We followed Gabriel, the hallways feeling empty. Something was wrong, I could feel it, but I didn't have time to analyze now. I had to get Avalon as far from the palace as I could, and my magic still wasn't under control. I pretended to be all right, but my magic buzzed uncomfortably underneath my skin and I was dizzy with the effort to keep it contained.

Gabriel was on his phone again, texting frantically the instructions to set the bombs off. From his confidence, I had to believe that the explosives were set and we were just waiting for the scattered teams to push ignite.

I grasped Avalon's hand, pulling him with me as we ran through the solitary hallways waiting for the inevitable fight. I couldn't help but feel the nagging sensation at the back of my neck that something was wrong, there should be Titans, there should be explosions. Everything felt like slow motion and my heart was pounding wildly against my chest in suspense.

We exited a hallway into another corridor, but it was at least one I remembered. We were not far from the doors, not far from exiting the palace, we were almost there. Gabriel slowed his run however, and I felt the room fill with magic that was not mine. Magic that I recognized, magic that I wanted so desperately to forget.

Kiran walked through the opposite side of the corridor, surrounded by Guards on every side. I expected a hundred different emotions to play out on his face, but relief was not one of them. He walked purposely towards me, stopping just short and smiling.

"You're Ok," he whispered, making the moment surprisingly awkward.

"I'm fine," I grunted, battle ready and wondering if I was physically able to absorb anymore magic today. My intuition told me I wasn't, but my urgency to leave this palace with my brother was bound and determined.

"Give me Avalon and you'll be able to escape," Kiran insisted, taking a step forward and holding out his hand expectantly.

"No!" I replied adamantly, "There is no way in hell I would leave him here with you. I'm taking him with me!" I shoved Avalon forcefully behind me as if I were a shield of protection.

"You will never get out of here with him like this. You've healed him, now give him to me. I won't let my father torture him anymore," Kiran promised, his tone turning to stern.

"No! I don't think you get it, I'm taking him with me!" I half shouted, frustrated with the roadblock and my untimely weakness.

"My father is waiting on the other side of those doors with two-hundred Titan Guards. You cannot fight them alone; now give me your brother so that you can escape. Eden, I give you my word, now that I am healthy, I will not let anything happen to him."

"Your word means nothing to me!" I screamed at full volume, tired of playing games.

"Eden, he's right," Avalon interrupted, letting go of my hand and walking to my side. "I am just going to slow you down."

"We have a plan Avalon.... we just need to get out of here, like now." I didn't want to explain to Avalon that the palace was loaded with explosives and about ready to implode in front of Kiran, but if he didn't start moving with me now, I would have to.

"Eden, he will be safe with me." Kiran took a step forward, holding my eyes and begging me to believe him.

"We have to go," Gabriel said seriously, glancing between his phone and the exit.

"I don't believe you," I answered Kiran, grasping Avalon's hand again and pushing past Kiran.

"Let her go," Kiran demanded of his Guard, and they moved out of the way.

Gabriel led the way through the arched palace doors, into the afternoon sunlight and a courtyard filled with Titan Guards. He slowed to a stop, stepping in front of me, and me in front of Avalon.

"I am very curious to know how you did that," Lucan walked forward from the center of his Guards, gesturing to Avalon. "The same way you healed my son, I suppose."

"Something like that," I growled.

"Is that the reason my Caves no longer work?" he pressed. I tilted my chin in defiance, wondering if he understood what happened any more than I did. "I hate to see you rush off so soon, Eden. We were just about to offer you a room," Lucan snickered, his lips curving into a cruel smile.

"How thoughtful of you...." I mumbled surveying the courtyard for a way out.

I heard the palace doors open, Kiran and his Guards filled in the places behind us, completing the circle of our enemies. Gabriel tilted his head impatiently and I felt his anxiety. The bombs would be going off any second; I needed to get Avalon out of here before we were caught up in the explosions. There was no way Avalon could survive.

My arm jerked sporadically, the electric build-up was getting out of control. There was a high-pitched ringing sound in my ears and my vision narrowed into a tunnel. I was seconds from passing out, there was no time left to wait, I had to act now.

I sent a forceful burst of magic forward, creating an explosion of my own and sending ten Guards soaring from the impact. I felt a little better, but it hadn't been enough to calm my frayed nerves. I rushed forward, Gabriel and Avalon on my heels, expelling as much magic as I could in short bursts, but nothing was helping. The buzzing grew more frantic, my blood was unbearably hot, and my hearing hardly recovered.

Titans surrounded us on every side, there was nowhere to go, no way out, but I was relentless. I made it this far, there would be no stopping my escape. Rationally, it shouldn't have even made sense that the other side of the palace walls were safety, the Titans would have pursued us to the ends of the earth.

It felt like progress though and so I continued fighting and pushing my way towards the exit. I wasn't unscathed, my head was bleeding and I was filthy from the fighting and debris of the palace, but I couldn't feel pain, I couldn't feel anything but the panicked magic pulsing through my veins.

And then the explosions started, from the back of the palace making their way towards us in rapid succession before anyone could turn their head and understand what the sound was or where it started from. The courtyard suddenly filled with blinding light and ear-splitting roars.

I turned back to Avalon, his fingers slipping from my hold as we were propelled in opposite directions. He was sucked back into the inferno and I was flying through the air towards the stone walls that surrounded the palace grounds. I felt my throat burn from the screaming, but I couldn't hear anything other than the palace being ripped apart from the inside.

In that moment, I knew I had lost my brother; that he would find his sweet freedom in the middle of a bomb I might as well have placed there and ignited myself. Everything happened in slow motion, I seemed to be in the air forever, even through the hysteria and danger, the magic inside of me still fought to take my consciousness, but I refused to take my eyes off my brother.

I was losing awareness, but some small part of me realized I wasn't imagining the slow motion, someone had Time-Slowed the events. As Avalon fell through the air, into the roaring inferno, Kiran was suddenly there, tackling his body mid-air to the ground and shielding Avalon from the danger around him.

I felt the momentary realization that Kiran saved my brother's life but then I was lost to the frenzied magic and sent into violent unconsciousness.

## Chapter Twenty-Five

I woke up, drenched in sweat and shivering at the same time. I was sweating, because I was simply too hot to stay dry, but shivering from the magic still frantic in my blood.

Sore and shaken I sat up slowly; when I could take in my surroundings, I reluctantly remembered the palace and losing Avalon. I let my face fall into my hands.

I sat on a hard, single bed with unkempt sheets and no pillows in a small bedroom; I clearly had a fitful sleep. Just a sliver of light from the bottom of a boarded up window lit the dim room. The room smelled like mold and dust, and the only other pieces of furniture in the room were a petite, beat up writing table and rickety, chair occupied by Jericho.

I looked up at him, my hands still over my mouth, trying to breathe regularly and stay the tears that threatened to flood my vision. I failed before, I made mistakes, but waking up to safety without Avalon was the hardest loss to swallow.

"Do you at least know if he survived?" I asked, with a hoarse voice. My throat burned, and my head pounded; I was a complete mess.

"Yes, we watched him board the plane with Lucan. He was walking by himself, he looked healthy," Jericho whispered, somberly.

"A plane?" I asked without inflection.

"The Royal Family has removed itself from India," he said, the smallest hint of amusement in his harsh tone. "We suspect they will head to Romania. They can hide behind those walls and trust in the magic of the earth there to protect them." He looked down at the writing desk, finding a splinter of wood to pick at.

"How could I have failed so miserably?" I exhaled into my hands, dropping my face into them again, wishing I could hide forever.

"You didn't fail," Jericho sat up straighter, his voice stern and commanding. "You destroyed a palace, and healed your brother which probably saved his life. Gabriel said Kiran promised to keep Avalon safe. Things are better. We made progress."

"Where is Gabriel?" I asked, not believing a word of encouragement Jericho offered. I was a terrible leader. "Is he all right?"

"Yes, he is. He is resilient," Jericho smiled gently, looking back at the piece of wood his fingers were fidgeting with absentmindedly. "He's hardly left your room. You have him to thank for surviving. He pulled you out of there, fought off dozens of Guards.... He's...." Jericho trailed off in awe of the wise priest.

"Often underestimated, I'm told," I finished his sentence, smiling sadly and thankful for Gabriel despite the consuming bitterness I felt for another failed mission.

"Where are we?" I looked around the room again, not recognizing any part of it. "How long was I out?"

"A safe-house, we are still in India. It didn't seem necessary to move until we knew you would be Ok and the King is gone, there is not real danger here anymore." I nodded my approval, waiting for Jericho to tell me how long I was unconscious. "Eden, you've been out for two days. And you've been thrashing about, shaking violently and expelling random magic in your sleep. Are you all right? What's wrong?" Jericho's brow furrowed and he leaned back in his chair ready for my response. He was incredibly handsome, his longer hair falling across his forehead and his eyes smoldering with concern. I breathed a sigh of relief that I could count on him with every single detail of my life. Somehow when I was near him, I could find hope again. I could believe that everything would be all right.

"I don't know what's wrong with me. Did Gabriel debrief you?" I asked and Jericho nodded, "It happened after I took the Guards in front of Avalon's cell. Something feels off, I feel like.... I don't know how to explain it, I feel like before I knew what my magic was, when I tried to suppress it and it would build up and explode everywhere. Only this time, expelling the magic doesn't do anything, it's still too excited.... too.... panicked."

"Do you think the Guards had the King's Curse, like before?" Jericho asked, moving from across the room to sit next to me on the bed. He held open his arm and I snuggled next to him, content in my nook.

"No, this is nothing like the King's Curse. Good lord, I think I would just choose to die if I ever went through that again!" I half laughed, trying to make a joke out of what I knew to be the honest truth. "No, this is.... I think this is just my body adjusting to so much magic. Honestly, it feels like too much. I don't know, maybe there is a limit to how much magic a person should take, and maybe I've reached it. Or maybe it was just too much, too quick; I don't know."

"Maybe," Jericho mumbled thoughtfully.

"I'll be fine, I just need to get used to it, Ok?" I looked up at him, hoping to reassure him with my confidence and then stood up to stretch, trying to prove that I was already feeling better.

"Something else happened during the mission that we need to talk about," Jericho said carefully.

I instantly tensed up, terrified that we lost somebody, "What? What happened?"

"I think it's good news, it has just been somewhat of a struggle since you've been unconscious. During the mission, while we were setting up the explosives, Xander and Xavier ran into, literally, they ran right into Talbott. He was on his way back from the airstrip, we think. He was alone on a motorcycle and Xander had the advantage. If it weren't for their explosives, though, I don't think they would have been able to capture him. Although, capturing him was the easy part. Now.... I mean, we're holding him here, but he is somewhat of a difficult prisoner."

"That's great news!" I exclaimed, finally feeling like I had a tiny piece of the upper hand.

"Well, we thought so too, at first," Jericho continued, his brow furrowing again with intensity, "Except that he's actually, not that easy to keep locked up. I don't know how much longer we can hold him. As of right now we have to have at least five guys with him at all times, but we don't have enough people to keep everyone fresh and rested. He doesn't seem to get tired. Honestly, he's one of the toughest Titans I have ever come across."

"Well, I'm sure he wasn't picked to be Kiran's body guard for nothing. Did you use those handcuffs he had on you?" I asked, putting my hands on my hips and pacing back and forth across the small space.

"Yes, yes, but he's.... he's really resourceful," Jericho admitted.

"I better go see him, yeah?" I asked, wondering if I could handle confrontation. I felt fragile and frail and I hated every moment of it.

"Well, yes, probably. But are you sure you're up for it?" Concern still was written obviously across his face.

"No, but if nothing else, I can use him for target practice." I smiled and Jericho laughed. My heart literally felt ripped in two with Avalon fresh in my memory, but Jericho made things easier. And I couldn't sit around and cry about it, I had to move on, to try again and next time I would not fail.

"He's downstairs when you're ready. I thought you might want to get cleaned up first, though?" he asked gently, and I nodded enthusiastically. I was filthy and afraid that I smelled bad. "There is a fresh pair of clothes and shower in the bathroom. You won't have hot water, but at least you can wash up."

"Thank you, a cold shower actually sounds amazing!" I gushed, letting Jericho open the door and point the way to the bathroom.

Outside the bedroom I could hear voices downstairs. Listening to the soft chatter and bits of laughter of other people committed to the same cause felt like salve to my wounded heart. This house was healing in a way; these people provided the soothing medication I needed to move forward. The Rebellion was still alive, still a force to be reckoned with and with their help we could conquer the oppression. We could not only set Avalon free, but an entire race of Immortals.

I took my time in the shower, washing the blood out of my hair and using a razor that someone miraculously left behind. I didn't know whose it was and that was kind of gross, but my legs appreciated the grooming.

I dried off with a thin towel and changed into the clothes left on the sink. The short sleeved, gray shirt was a little tight and the black, linen pants a little big. I pulled the drawstring as tightly as I could, but still they hung low on my waist, leaving two inches of skin between my shirt and my pants. It wasn't a look I would normally rock, but looking down at my discarded, filthy clothes, I decided I didn't have a choice.

I pulled my long hair over my shoulder and combed through it with my fingers. This impossible mess of tangles desperately needed a trim, but working with what I had, I braided it, using magic to loosen the especially tough areas.

I stared at myself in the mirror for a moment. I hardly took time to look at myself since this entire debacle started and now I barely recognized myself. I felt decades older and was positive I looked it. My black eyes seemed impossibly darker, more like a midnight storm than the onyx stone I once compared them to. I could swear I saw the beginning of wrinkles on my tanned face. I had always been happy with my appearance, self-confident enough to know that I wasn't ugly, but now I couldn't even decide. The face in the mirror felt like a stranger, and I didn't even know how to begin to get to know her again.

I breathed a frustrated sigh and then left the bathroom. I knew there were more important things to worry about than meditating on self-revelation or vanity.

I bounced down the stairs, feeling more energized after the shower, although magic still buzzed uncomfortably underneath my skin. The bottom of the stairs opened up into a living room area, where Naima and Grace talked quietly together on a couch. They were close friends, it was easy to see and I longed for Lilly for the millionth time.

They looked up at me, smiling graciously; an idea suddenly hit me. "Where are they keeping Talbott?" I asked and Naima pointed towards a door to my left.

Jericho stepped through the door at the sound of my voice, shutting it quickly behind him. He tilted his chin, for me to join him, putting his hand on my shoulder when I reached him.

"Are you sure you're up for this?" he asked.

"Yes, of course," I answered, firmly.

"Ok, let's get this over with then. He's been a bit feisty today." Jericho opened the door and then leaned into my ear, "You smell good."

I walked through the door laughing, but quickly stifled it when I met Talbott face to face. The magical hand-cuffs that were supposed to diminish magical power bound his hands, and he sat in a chair that was tied to his legs, much like Avalon had been. But he flailed his body and the chair wildly in a stuttered circle. He was furious, rage written across his angular face and I didn't know what do with him in that moment.

"Talbott, settle down!" I scolded loudly, hoping he was willing to listen to my reason.

"Eden, you'd better let me go!" he growled, jumping his chair a foot towards me. The room wasn't very big to begin with, but even I flinched at Talbott's behavior. I was unprepared to take any more magics on and I really hoped he wasn't going to push me into taking his. I sent his chair backwards with magic, setting it forcefully down on the ground and shaking it a little to grab his attention.

"Calm down!" I demanded, "I am here to help you, but if you're going to act like a maniac about it, then I'm just going to leave and you can continue with your escape planning. It really seems to be working out for you." I rolled my eyes and hoped he would see how ridiculous he was behaving. I suddenly understood why Jericho said we didn't have enough people to contain him.

He resentfully settled down, but still bristled at his captors. He was clearly not used to being the one in the prisoner's uniform, so to speak.

"Now, I think I have a plan that will get you back to Kiran and get me something that I want in exchange, all right? Assuming that's what you want?" I bribed carefully, watching as he stayed unpacified.

"Yes, I need to get back. There are people counting on me," he agreed, but I couldn't help notice he left Kiran's name out.

"I want Avalon, I want to trade you for Avalon," I said simply and Talbott rolled his eyes at the idea.

"You might as well just kill me now then. Lucan will never give you Avalon." he snapped, frustrated with me and irritated with his restraints. This side of Talbott proved very entertaining.

"Well, let's just try anyway. Maybe Lucan has changed his mind," I suggested, playing it cool, despite the exhaustion that was sweeping over me from fighting with the frenzied magic. "Does somebody have a cell phone? I am assuming you have a number to call that will get you in contact with Lucan?" When Talbott didn't answer, I sent him flying backwards in his chair until he slammed into the back wall, "Do you want to go home or not?" I shouted, my nerves getting the best of me.

"I have a direct line to Kiran," he admitted.

"Fine, that will work. Someone give him a phone," Te, Caden, Gabriel, Xavier and Bex were charged with guarding Talbott for now and all of them reached into their pockets digging for their phones. I started to believe, I was the only one who left my cell phone at home. I made a mental note to take it with me next time I decided to travel around the world.

"Can I see you outside for a moment?" Jericho asked, pulling on my arm and opening the door.

"Get on the phone with Kiran and find out if Lucan will make the trade," I commanded before letting Jericho close the door on us.

"I trust you, Eden. But I need to know what the plan is. Lucan is never going to trade Talbott for Avalon, he would rather kill Talbott himself," Jericho whispered, in hushed, curious tones.

"I know that," I agreed, "but I have to get to what I want, without making it seem like I'm getting.... what I want," I explained cryptically. "Listen, I know that Talbott has this thing about protecting Lilly, but if I start with Lilly, I'll never get her. I am trying to get *them* to offer her to us."

"You watch too many movies," Jericho smiled at me, opening the door and allowing me through first.

"You can't have Avalon," Talbott said as soon as I walked through the door. Gabriel stood next to him, holding his phone to Talbott's ear.

I stared at him for a minute, chewing on my thumbnail, pretending to think it over. "Then I want Ryder Thompson."

Talbott repeated my demand into the phone, listened for a minute and then shook his head "no."

I cleared my throat and tried again, "Then I want the Immortals that don't have any magic, Ebanks Camera, Oscar Rodriguez, Jett Fisher and Ronan Hannigan."

Talbott spoke into the phone, repeating my request almost word for word. This time he listened longer, before shaking his head "no" again.

"All right, Talbott, ask them who I *can* have then? Seriously, what is your life worth? If they don't come up with an answer soon you can let them know that I will kill you, without hesitation or remorse." I folded my arms, staring defiantly at Talbott, mentally willing him to figure out my plan on his own.

He repeated my words into the phone and then without hesitation, without waiting for a response on the other end he said with confidence, "You can have Lilly."

I rocked back on my heels, trying not to smile. I couldn't believe it was that easy, "Fine."

"He said he will only do the exchange if you come alone, completely by yourself," when I rolled my eyes, he continued, "he will send only one person to do the exchange, but he wants to be assured that it will be you and only you."

"I can't trust him, how do I know he will really only send one person?" I asked skeptically.

"You don't," Talbott answered simply, "but if you don't agree, or bring someone with you, the deal's off."

"Fine," I relented, thrilled that I was at least able to save Lilly through this whole mess. I couldn't stop the smile from coming so I turned to leave the room, trusting that Jericho could finish figuring out the details. "But tell him, if he sends Kiran, I will kill him on sight. I will literally rip his head off and send it back to him in a box."

# Chapter Twenty-Six

I left the room, remembering I made a promise to myself. Grace and Naima still chatted quietly on the couch, so I approached carefully.

"Where is Sebastian?" I asked, smiling at them.

"He is in that room over there," Naima answered, her head bobbing a little while she talked. "Eden? Are you alright? Gabriel explained how horrific the mission went and I am worried that maybe you need to rest for a bit longer." Her pink eyes darkened with worry, their jewel-like tones shimmering against the white of her pupils.

"Thank you, but I'm fine, really. I just realized that Sebastian hasn't had a change of clothes for more than a week now and I want to make sure he is treated fairly, that's all," I explained and Grace immediately stood up.

"There are extra clothes in the back bedroom, I will get him some," she offered politely and then disappeared down a hallway.

I smiled one more time at Naima and then went to find Sebastian. I knocked softly on the door, expecting him to be asleep, but was surprised to find Titus inside, laughing with him.

"Am I interrupting something?" I asked, noticing how relaxed Sebastian looked.

"No, sorry, I was just um, guarding Sebastian," Titus stood up, unnecessarily coming to attention. It dawned on me that Titus and Sebastian were becoming friends. I knew that I should be more worried about that, but I was having a hard time believing Sebastian would ever be a threat again, I couldn't really blame Titus for thinking the same thoughts.

"It's all right; I just need to talk to him for a second, that's all." I smiled at Titus, waving at him to sit back down. "Sebastian, do you know that we have Talbott in the other room?"

"I think the whole city knows," he laughed, rolling his eyes.

"Well, I've decided to trade him for one of their prisoners," I explained, gauging his reaction. When nothing in his face changed, I continued, "Lucan agreed to the exchange, but only if I meet his man alone, like completely alone." I paused for a moment, letting my words sink in.

"Lucan agreed to the exchange?" he asked, skeptically.

"Yes, but like I said he wants me to go alone. I need to know if this is a trap. Either way, I don't mind going alone, I'm certainly not afraid of anything that Lucan would send, and I would feel a large number of Titans miles away, but I want to know what I'm getting into."

Sebastian sat thoughtfully for a moment before answering, "If Lucan agreed to the exchange, then I have to believe he will hold to the terms of the agreement."

The door opened behind me and Grace walked through, carrying fresh clothes for Sebastian. "Jericho asked if he could speak with you when you get a free moment," she mentioned sweetly to me, handing the clothes over.

"Thank you," I said, "tell him I'll be there in a second."

She left the room and I turned back to Sebastian, tossing the clothes on his lap.

"What's this?" he asked, his face involuntarily lighting up.

"I thought you might want to shower and change, sorry I've been neglectful about it," I smiled at him, genuinely apologetic I let him suffer even this small amount. My heart broke again for Avalon, remembering him in that prison cell, beaten and bloodied. I was desperate to figure out a way to rescue him, a foolproof plan this time, one that could guarantee success.

"That's Ok," Sebastian waved off my apology, "I think *you've* only showered and changed like once this whole time." Titus let out short barking laughter that I shot down quickly with an annoyed glance. Sebastian stood up, holding his clothes to his chest, "Eden, this is very unlike Lucan to even entertain the idea of a prisoner exchange."

"So you *do* think it's a trap?" I asked, narrowing my eyes at him.

"No, I don't. I am just saying, this doesn't really sound like *him*." Sebastian shrugged his shoulders and then left the room, leaving Titus and I alone.

"What are you guys now? BFF's?" I joked and Titus rolled his eyes

"He's actually, kind of cool." He shrugged and then changed his story, "I mean, not cool, but he's, he's just not that bad, I mean, for a prisoner he's all right?"

"Not that bad?" It was my turn to roll my eyes. Sebastian was like a terminally ill, but naughty pet. Everyone hated him when I first brought him home, but now people were growing attached to him.

Eventually, he was going to have to be put down; I just hoped it didn't upset too many people when that finally happened.

I left the room in search of Jericho and found him in the kitchen, dishing up a bowl of hot soup. He turned around when I entered the room and gestured to a splintered, old table to the right of the stove. He set the bowl of steaming stew in front of me and then returned to a large, cast iron pot that simmered with the delicious spices only India had to offer.

"So, we're taking advice from prisoners now?" Jericho sat down across from me and stared at me from over his steaming bowl of Indian stew. I felt like a small child about to be scolded.

"I just wanted to know what I was getting into. Sebastian has offered his help in return for mine and I needed to know if I could trust the terms of Lucan's arrangement or not, that's all," I explained, blowing on a hot, soupy potato before devouring it. The stew was scrumptious, abundantly flavorful, and a little spicy and it helped that I couldn't even remember the last time I sat down to eat a meal.

"And do you think that you can?" Jericho asked, narrowing his eyes intensely at me from where he sat.

"Honestly, I still don't know. However, I'm willing to risk it. As I told Sebastian, if he has a trap waiting for me, I'll be able to feel it from miles away. If he is sincere, then I will have Lilly back." I shrugged as if the task was as simple as the words.

"I don't like it," he mumbled, staring down at his soup.

"Do you ever like it when I'm in possible danger?" I smiled at him, and his tanned cheeks blushed with embarrassment.

"Eden, I'm serious; this could so easily be a trap," Jericho reached out his hand, took mine and held it gently; his thumb moved back and forth across my palm and I couldn't help but stop eating to give him my full attention.

"You're right, it could be. But, we can't keep Talbott here much longer, you said so yourself. At least this way, we get something out of it." I gazed into his eyes, getting lost in their soulfulness. "Besides, because it's Lilly, I know I can trust Talbott to behave until the exchange. He wants her out of there as badly as I do."

"You really think Kiran's personal Titan bodyguard is in love with a Shape-Shifter?" Jericho questioned skeptically, laughing a little at the idea.

"Yes, I do," but I couldn't help but laugh too, "Jericho, this is a new age we are ushering in. When we win this war, they can finally be together!" I squealed, excited for Lilly and the idea that her feelings for Talbott had never gone away.

"As long as Talbott doesn't die first, fighting for the wrong side," Jericho mumbled, killing the moment.

I sighed, realizing he was right. "Anyway, where am I doing this whole prisoner exchange?"

"Morocco, there is an isolated air strip in the middle of the Sahara that our two sides have used before for situations like this," Jericho explained, turning his attention back to his soup.

"Well, the good news is, I was kind of disappointed that I missed the sight-seeing when we went to London instead." I smiled, trying to shake off the growing nerves and buzzing magic.

"Well, good." Jericho wasn't quite sure how to respond to my nonchalance. "The advantage the desert brings, is, that you'll be able make a circle of the area and have a visual of what you're up against before you land."

"A circle of the area? Did we forget that I can't fly a plane?" I asked, realizing my plan might be dead in its tracks.

"I've thought of that, and if you really trust Talbott, then I suppose you can let him pilot. He should know how. Or you can trust your magic, but somehow I don't think you'll agree to that." Jericho looked up at me from underneath thick, dark eyelashes and for a moment I wanted to forget the whole trip and never leave his side again. Then, I remembered Lilly and knew that I had to do everything in my power to get her out of there.

"Ok, but how will I get out of there, after the exchange?" I asked, trying to think the whole plan through.

"Lilly can fly you home, as long as she isn't incapacitated for some reason. Otherwise, you really will have to use your magic. Or, I can go with you; that would solve all of your problems." His expression flickered with hope. I knew he was serious, and trying to hide behind sarcasm, and I found it endearing for some reason. I stared at him for a moment, finding his eyes and letting them hold me. There was nothing special about our conversation or anything that he was saying, but something about his concern for me, and willingness to support me in whatever I decided, helped me take another step away from Kiran, helped to loosen his hold the smallest amount and fall that much more for Jericho.

"Does everyone know how to fly a plane, except me?" I asked, feeling myself flirting for the first time in a very long time.

"Um, yeah, I think so," he laughed. "Part of it is magic though, and the other part is this global lifestyle we live.... Eden, there's something else I need to talk to you about."

"Sure," I smiled, my charming smile, hoping Jericho felt like he could talk to me about anything.

"Something else happened while you were out of it," he started nervously and I sat up straighter, prepared for whatever news was coming. "Angelica called Silas, who called Gabriel.... Your parents are in Omaha. They want you to go back, they're waiting for you."

I sat in stunned silence for a few minutes, staring past Jericho at a spot on the wall I wasn't really seeing. I had been thinking about going back to Omaha. I wondered if we, or at least I, needed a place to regroup and figure out our next step, strategically. I was exhausted from the constant traveling, and I was desperately homesick for Aunt Syl, after Kiran mentioned her so callously on the elephant. Intuition was guiding me to check on her.

However, my parents waiting for me was an entirely different story. I started this whole thing by looking for them, but now that the time was here, I couldn't decide if I was emotionally ready. I supposed I didn't have a choice, and I would have a couple days to prepare, but this life I was living was non-stop, physically and emotionally.

"Ok," I sighed, searching for the strength to sound confident. "I have been thinking about going home anyway."

"We don't have to go if you don't want to. We can go to South Africa or even straight to Romania, if you want. It's up to you." Jericho reached out both hands this time, taking mine in a comforting gesture.

"No, it's all right. It's time, I suppose. I'm only seventeen, it's probably time I met my birth parents," I tried to joke, but it came out flat and overly sarcastic. "You go to South Africa, get the last team and then we'll rendezvous in Omaha. Now that Avalon is healed, we can at least create a plan of attack, I can't fail like that again," I referred to losing Avalon, knowing that if I tried again and failed, Avalon would not survive. "The farm is flattened, but there is enough room at Amory's for everyone to stay. Aunt Syl will have the key. As soon as I get Lilly, we will head straight back."

"That is very decisive of you," Jericho teased. "You're turning into quite the leader, Eden."

"It's only taken me this long to learn how to make a decision on my own, just think what another ten years might accomplish," I laughed, but Jericho was right. Decisions were getting easier, tough choices were becoming a part of my daily routine. I was getting the hang of leading. I was letting go of Kiran, daily. I was reclaiming bits and pieces of my attachment to him and I was even releasing my desire for vengeance in honor of the collective goal.

Still, I knew that Avalon would have made a better leader. I was not blind to my weaknesses. All I could do was focus on the task at hand, and so far, this looked like the most promising mission yet.

To get Lilly back.

# Chapter Twenty-Seven

"Talbott, if anything happens to her, I will hunt you down myself, is that clear?" Jericho threatened with every intention of following through.

"Jericho, I understand. I've told you a million times, nothing is going to happen to her. This is not a trap." Talbott put a strong hand on Jericho's shoulder as if comforting him father to son.

I turned my head to keep from laughing at the look of shock that flashed across Jericho's face. Talbott was considerably calmed down since we put the plans for the prisoner exchange into motion. I knew he was looking forward to being in control of something again, and from past experiences, I knew how hard it was for him to be away from Kiran, but I wanted to believe that it was something more. Lilly's safety appeared to be enough leverage to incentivize Talbott and I wondered if one day, she would be enough to bring Talbott to our side.

"All right, you should go. Get this over with and then get out of there, yeah?" Jericho turned to me, pulling me into a hug. His magic buzzed around mine in excited nearness, but mine was reserved, afraid to attach itself to more magics.

"Yeah," I whispered into his chest, not wanting to let go, despite the uncomfortable closeness of his magic. The relentless electricity driving my rapid circulation left me drained and completely exhausted, but Jericho was my rock. His presence alone provided perfect comfort and when we touched, I couldn't help but feel hope deep in my bones that everything was going to be Ok.

He kissed the top of my head, and then my cheek as if he couldn't help himself. I reluctantly let go of him and joined Talbott in the Cessna that even he marveled at. Talbott closed the door behind us and I followed him into the tiny cockpit. Not that it would have made any difference if I was sitting with him or not, because there was absolutely no way for me to be sure he was going where he was supposed to; but I felt like my presence would at least pressure him to stay accountable.

"Now you're sure you know how to fly this thing?" I asked, hesitantly letting go of irrational fears, like him crashing my grandfather's plane into the side of a mountain.

"Yes, Eden, of course." He turned and grinned at me. His deep chocolate eyes were twinkling with the same excitement that Titus had when he flew. I inwardly sighed, boys and their toys.

I leaned back in my chair, and tried to get comfortable. The nine-hour trip to the Sahara would allow Talbott and I a lot of time to get to know each other.

"I'm sorry we had to tie you up before," I offered an apology in the awkward silence once we were in the air.

He looked at me, unsure what to say, or how to react, but I just smiled. Talbott and I had our differences from the very start, but I knew that if there wasn't a civil war in between us right now, we could have learned to get along.

"I accept your apology," he replied chivalrously, after the initial stupor wore off. "Besides, you are not technically to blame. From what I gather, you were not conscious."

"True, but still, I'm the.... leader and all that," I struggled getting the words out, knowing they would fall flat in my mouth. Talbott would never really see me as the leader of the Rebellion. I could hardly take myself seriously when I thought about it and someone like Talbott, with military training and on the winning side, certainly wouldn't be able to say those words without laughing.

"Yes, but maybe your brother would have and that is the kind of leader they are used to," Talbott argued wisely, changing my mind about him. "You are not only trying to transform my side of the war, but your side as well, I think."

"Talbott, I'm not a revolutionary, I just want revenge for what happened to my family," I mumbled, embarrassed by his view of me.

"You want more than that," he said seriously and I knew that he was right. I had started to believe in more than just revenge, but at times, it was just easier to dwell on retribution.

"So, if something were to happen to you, like you crashed the plane into the ocean or something and we both died, is there a stand in for you? Like, someone to replace you?" I pried, trying to lighten the mood with some morbid humor.

"Of course, Kiran has nearly an army of personal Guards. If something happened to me, there would be hundreds more to choose from. However, it would take more than a plane crash into the ocean to kill me." He tilted his head, weighing the idea thoughtfully. His thick, flowing accent made his words run together like cursive.

I found Titan magic easier to be around than Witch or Medium magic. Titan magic, less electric and more fluid, was based more in movement and the actual action of thought processes than blood and brain. Witch or Medium magic created action. It was as if Titan magic *was* action, so it didn't pop or sizzle, it didn't get frenzied or invasive, it just stayed calm and relaxed, already prepared for battle and five steps ahead of everyone else.

Because of Talbott's *relaxed* magic, my magic calmed considerably in his presence. His magic stayed completely separate from mine and I finally found the breathing room to relax a little.

Even still, my energy was panicked, my blood burst with too much electricity and I was exhausted from the effort of holding it inside. I hoped this trip would give me the rest I needed to recover before I got back to Omaha. Shape-Shifter magic was not as aggressive as the rest either, but it was more so than Titan, especially right before a shift. I hoped that Lilly wasn't going to need to shift anytime soon.

"I am so excited to see Lilly!" I exclaimed, forgetting that Talbott and I were enemies. "This had better go as planned, Talbott, or I'm going to be very mad." I turned serious, shaking my finger at him.

"Eden, this is not a trap. There will not be Titans waiting for you, you have my word," he was serious enough that I believed him. "When we land, I mean, before you take off again, if it's not too much trouble.... What I am trying to say is, if there are a few extra minutes, would you mind if I spoke to Lilly alone? Just for a few minutes, I won't be long, I can assure you," Talbott stumbled through an adorable request, and I found myself cheering for their relationship even though I knew beyond a shadow of a doubt that it not only made absolutely no sense, it would also never work.

"If you do something for me, you can have all the time in the world," I bargained, deciding I should play this cool.

"Within reason, something comparable, then yes, I will do something for you," Talbott agreed.

"I would like you to pass a message along to Amelia Cartier," I said with confidence, knowing it would be something that Talbott was not expecting.

"Amelia Cartier?" Talbott echoed, completely caught off guard.

"Yes, I want you to tell her that her brother is fine, that he is even happy and that he will have his magic back soon," I confessed softly, believing my words to the core of my being.

"You want me to give that message to Amelia Cartier?" Talbott clarified, unbelieving.

"Yes, and to absolutely no one else, not even your... Prince. And tell her she can't tell anyone either," I added amendments trying to cover my tracks uselessly. I was seriously the worst Rebellion leader in the history of rebellions.

"Sebastian told me you were going to kill him?" Talbott questioned not only my sincerity but also my motives.

"And he's probably right." I rolled my eyes, and folded my arms, remembering our ridiculous arrangement.

"Then why would you have me tell his little sister that he's Ok?" he pressed, more confused than ever.

"Because," I shrieked, fed up with this whole situation, "because if it were my brother I would want to know that he was all right, I would want to believe that everything was going to work out, even if it wasn't true. I would want to believe it every single minute until somebody could tell me differently, that's why. So do we have a deal or not?" I raised my voice unnecessarily high and tears fell hot down my cheeks.

I wiped at them with the sleeve of my shirt, turning away from Talbott to stare out the window at a blue, cloudless sky. Talbott remained quiet for a long time, and the cockpit grew awkward and tense. I pulled myself together, but remained adamant that our deal would stay the same, only I hadn't found the courage to demand that of Talbott yet.

"All right, Eden. I will tell her," Talbott agreed after several more minutes of silence. "And Eden?" I turned back to him. His voice lost the serious military style of speaking and grew soft, almost sensitive. "Your brother *is* Ok."

I didn't respond. I knew he was offering me false hope, that he had no idea how Avalon was really doing or what was happening to him. But, he had taken my emotion, my cry for help and turned it into a comforting response. His generosity dazed me.

We were still enemies, still fighting on opposite sides of the war, but those words were an offer of hope, an enticement to continue the mission and they came from Talbott of all people.

He had matured over the last few months, and became a man I hardly recognized. He embodied authority, and was infinitely more mature than Kiran, but now he could add compassion and intuition to his long list of skills. This new side of him made me root for Lilly and him even more. I didn't know how it would work out, how it could possibly end with them together, but sometimes relationships don't make sense or fit into natural order, sometimes are were written in the stars.

I shook my head, finding my thought path dangerous. That was true for Lilly and Talbott but nobody else. As Jericho said, Talbott was probably going to die at the end of this thing anyway.

We spent the rest of the trip in silence. I eventually dozed off and when I awoke, we were circling an endless desert, aiming for what felt like a miniscule airstrip surrounded by sand for miles and miles. The sun was setting low in the west, casting long shadows across the golden sand dunes.

I had never been to the desert before, the vastness of the sand amazed me. It felt very much like the ocean when you stood with your feet just touching the tide, and looked out to never-ending water. The sand flowed outwards in the same way, touching the horizon in every direction.

Landing on the small airstrip was frightening. I tried to comprehend being this far away from anything or anyone and couldn't. I was more than just days from civilization; I was a lifetime. Being stranded this far from help would be a death sentence, that much I knew.

I breathed deeply as Talbott shut the engine off, remembering that I was magic, that I would survive, even if the plan were literally to abandon me to the wild nature of the endless sand dunes. I rolled my head around my neck, and dug for courage deep within. I needed to be the first one off the plane to establish authority. It wouldn't say much about my leadership skills if I just let Talbott exit the plane alone, while I cowered in the cockpit.

I cleared my throat and stood up, smoothing out my black, linen pants and reaching for a turquoise scarf with gold detailing, that Naima gave to me in India. It was a beautiful piece of fabric, but I bristled at the idea of coming off flashy. Still, the wind blew violently across the sand, picking it up and scattering a million specks at a time, and so I wrapped the scarf around my neck, pulling it over my mouth for protection.

I walked from the cockpit with feigned confidence, waiting silently for Talbott to open the door and let down the staircase. At the bottom of the stairs, I stood for a moment and took in the most beautiful and exotic Moroccan styled tent. Black and ivory paneled fabric sprawled across the desert wasteland, glowing from the inside with candled lanterns and welcoming any traveler like a picture perfect mirage that only existed in fairy tales.

The closer we walked, the more extravagant the tent became. I thought, from a distance, that it could have actually been a couple tents huddled together, but now that I was, closer I saw that it was one long tent, with three different rooms. The entrance was wide, with a paneled canopy billowing in the evening breeze. The floor was golden silk, protecting our feet from the sand that would infiltrate everything if it could. Delicious scents wafted from inside, as if the most intricate meal had been prepared for our arrival.

"Um, are you sure this is the right tent?" I asked Talbott, wondering if the idea of a prisoner exchange had gotten lost in translation somehow.

"Yes, Eden, you are exactly where you should be." Kiran appeared in the entrance of the tent, turquoise eyes smoldering and Lilly at his arm.

## Chapter Twenty-Eight

"What is this?" I demanded, stomping my foot in the sand. "I thought I warned you what would happen if he came!" I turned to Talbott, frustrated with him. When he didn't respond I whirled back around to Kiran, "I warned your father that if you came, I would kill you. So now you can blame him for your untimely death," I finished matter-of-factly, Kiran's magic already frantically searching out mine, sending shivers of electricity down my back. It was almost too much, his aggressive magic was suddenly suffocating mine, making it hard to breathe.

"I have no one to blame but myself," Kiran took a step forward, extending his hand as if I would take it. "Talbott never spoke with my father; I made all of the arrangements for tonight's exchange. Actually, he knows nothing about Talbott, or Lilly, or any of this." His signature smirk was back and the appearance of his smug grin made me regret saving his life the most. "Eden, please join me; otherwise, I will have to take your friend back to Romania with me."

"No, I don't want to," I snapped, crossing my arms with immature rebelliousness.

"Don't be a child, I only want to talk for a few minutes and then you can decide what to do," he appealed.

I looked at Lilly and I knew Kiran had already won. I would do anything to take her home with me. She didn't look as though she was tortured like Avalon, but she was intolerably thin, and the dark circles underneath her eyes suggested severe trauma. At that moment, a few minutes with Kiran seemed insignificant compared to the reward.

"Fine, a few minutes, and then we're leaving," I tilted my chin defiantly.

"Eden, our deal?" Talbott whispered and I nodded.

"Lilly, Talbott will help you on to the plane, I'll be there in just a few minutes," I instructed, trying to assert my authority again.

She looked up to Kiran who nodded his permission. As soon as she got the Ok to leave, she rushed forward, throwing her arms around my neck and hugging me tightly. I was so thrown off guard by Kiran that I had forgotten how relieved I was to see her alive. I hugged her back, my eyes filling with tears that threatened to ruin any semblance of strength I still had.

Kiran cleared his throat impatiently, and I reluctantly let go of her, reminding myself that she was free now, and we would have unlimited time to catch up.

Talbott took her arm, helping her walk across the sand. It was obvious she was weak from her stint in prison whether she was tortured or not. They disappeared onto the plane; there was no more time to stall. I turned back to Kiran who extended his hand to me again. I stomped passed him, eying his hand with revulsion and hating the idea that we were utterly alone.

The inside of the tent was exquisitely plush. I was right about the different rooms inside the tent. On one end was a dining room, with wide, heavy, burgundy, floor pillows surrounding a low table laden with exotic delicacies creating the delicious scent I could smell from across the sand. Steam still rose from the silver platters, making my stomach growl angrily. I threw my hands across my waist, silencing the hungry protests. The dining room reminded me too much of the night Kiran and I were engaged, and then un-engaged only hours later.

A sitting room occupied the middle of the tent. Here the ceiling was highest and the lanterns the brightest. Low, deeply reclining couches lined the back wall and a small coffee table of sorts sat in the middle, holding steaming carafes and dainty, hand-painted, teacups.

On the far end of the tent, a sheer, ivory curtain created a glow with the soft light of dimmed lanterns. Curiosity got the better of me, so I walked over to the curtain, lifted it back and peeked behind it.

A king-size bed was the only piece of furniture in the room. It held dozens of bright, colorful pillows with delicate embroidery and a silk, jeweled, golden comforter that lay across with one corner pulled down as if ready for someone to crawl inside and go to bed. I couldn't hide my surprise at seeing the bed and cleared my throat nervously.

"Just in case you were tired," Kiran explained, his voice gravely but mischievous. He had walked over with me, so when I turned around to scoff at the idea, I bumped into him.

"Ok, let's focus, and just get this over with before I decide to kill you anyway." I fidgeted with my hair, wishing I had agreed to anything else but being alone with him.

"The exchange isn't over yet, Eden. My Guard has your friend alone on a plane that he is perfectly capable of commandeering. Which one of them do you think could win, if Talbott decided to take off with her right now? Or do you think she would even protest?" Kiran asked, his eyes flashing with something I couldn't define.

"He wouldn't dare!" I shrieked, realizing too late that he tricked me. Kiran raised his eyebrows at me and gestured to a seat next to him on the couch in front of the tea carafes. "Ugh, it's official; I am the worst leader ever!" I crossed my arms and paced the room frustrated.

"Yes, you are," Kiran agreed and I spun on my heel to face him. "You should give it up, surely there is a different way to save your people...." his voice trailed off and he patted the seat next to him.

I cleared my throat, focusing my magic, trying to find control again and walked to the seat. I stared at it for a moment, preparing myself for the close vicinity of Kiran's magic and then plopped down on the too soft couch.

I sat for a moment, facing the bedroom. I could see the outline of the bed through the sheer curtain. The silken curtain moved gently, swaying in the night air that the open entrance could not keep out. The breeze distracted me and enhanced the beauty of the thin divider. I forced my magic to shut the tent entrance violently, blocking out the breeze and any other beautiful part of the Moroccan night.

I looked up at Kiran, satisfied with my action, but then I looked back at the bedroom and realized what that must have looked like. I stood up suddenly, not sure how to explain.

"Trade places with me," I demanded, walking to the other side of him so that I could face the dining room instead of the bedroom. I cleared my throat for a second time, and attempted to focus completely on Kiran. I tried to cover my sporadic behavior, but there was nothing left for me. This was another epic failure.

"Is everything all right?" Kiran asked, both concerned and amused.

"Yes, everything's fine. What is this about, Kiran?" I sat up straight and talked evenly, desperately searching for my composure.

"I think you should reconsider my offer," he began, offering me a cup of hot tea that I refused. "I am not trying to tell you what to do by any means, but you said so yourself that you are a terrible leader. If you traded places with your brother, he could go back to leading the Rebellion and you could rest in the knowledge that you saved him."

His words hung heavily in the air. I knew what Kiran really wanted, that his grand scheme was much more devious than philanthropic, but still they rung true and I searched for reasons why I shouldn't agree.

"Ok, let's talk this out," I allowed, deciding I should have all of my facts. "If I were to say yes, if I were to go with you tonight, how would I know that Avalon would be let go, that you wouldn't just kill him immediately?"

"You have my word," Kiran promised passionately, but then he saw the mistrust in my eyes and continued, "I brought you Lilly tonight and I saved your brother's life in India. I have good intentions, you can trust me."

"No, I can't." I rolled my eyes, "Besides, you had to save Avalon's life in India; he is your only leverage. And, I still haven't left with Lilly, so we'll see how this plays out." My magic was growing increasingly more difficult to handle; it had turned into an electrical storm in my veins, like furious lightning assaulting my blood. "Anyway, let's move passed whether or not I can actually believe you would let Avalon go, what happens after that? Like to me? Are you going to sacrifice me? Take my magic? What happens next?"

"No, I'm not going to kill you!" Kiran defended himself, appalled by the idea. "If you gave yourself over to me willingly, there would be a wedding of course, but in the future. It would be necessary to marry me; that would be a concrete part of the deal, my father would demand it. However, if it seemed to be your idea, then you would have some control over when that date was. It obviously couldn't be decades in the future, but you could buy yourself at least a year, I'm sure."

"Ok, let me see if I completely understand this. I turn myself in; you may or may not let my brother go free. Then we get married.... in, at the very most a year and then let me guess, in a few more months, probably nine to be exact, I produce a healthy, little heir to the throne and everyone lives happily ever after?" I narrowed my eyes, completely disgusted by the idea.

"Eden, I am trying to offer you an alternative to your brother's ultimate death and the imprisonment of your friends!" Kiran implored, frustrated with me.

"Marrying you is not an alternative! It's just a different form of the death penalty!" I whined, desperate for him to understand.

"I didn't say that it wasn't," he snapped, a flash of dark blue changing the color of his eyes, "but saving your brother is what you want. That's all I'm saying. India was a dismal failure for you. You will not break into the Romanian Citadel and even if you do, your magic is useless in those prisons. I am asking you to consider a different alternative for your brother."

"You promised to keep him safe," I accused venomously. I never believed his words before, but with the dispiriting picture he painted, I was grasping at straws.

"And I am doing my best, but my father is a desperate man and he will not be satisfied forever."

My hands began to tremble and I wiped a small trickle of sweat that had formed on my forehead. I dropped my head into my hands, trying to find the reasons to say no to him, to believe in another way.

"Please," Kiran whispered, leaning in closer to me, his magic suffocating and raw, "please, go with me. Choose the easy way, save your brother."

I shook my head, the consequences of my answer breaking my heart. By choosing to defy Kiran's offer I was risking my brother's life more than I ever had and I was forced to come to terms with that. I couldn't say if I would ever be able to break into the Romanian dungeons and save Avalon, but I would spend every day trying. I would put faith in the Resistance, in Jericho and in myself and not let the sweet manipulations of the son of a tyrant persuade me.

"No, there is no way in hell I will go with you, are you kidding me?" I sat up straight, finding my courage and almost laughing at him. "We're done here, I can't even believe you."

"That is the wrong decision, Eden. Please do not make me take you by force." Kiran stood up, menacingly.

"Don't push me, Kiran," I stood up too, trying to make myself equally as threatening.

"Look at you, you are clearly not well, now is not the time to say no to me," he reasoned, his voice full of frustration.

"Give it up!" I exhaled, sending a magical wave against him, mostly by accident. He stumbled backwards, before catching himself. He glared at me for a moment, deciding I started something. I turned to leave, alternatively determining I was in no shape to fight him.

Kiran sent his magic firmly against the tent folds; blocking my way with a magical force field I didn't even know anyone was capable of producing. I spun around, ready to fight, despite the pulsating electricity that was ringing in my ears from the spike in magical temperature of the room. I threw my magic at him, finally giving the built-up energy some release.

He blocked my blow with his own magic and our electricity stayed locked together for a few minutes before escaping to opposite sides and burning holes through the tent flaps. I sent another burst of magic with the other hand, picking up the tea table and smashing it against Kiran's side.

It hardly fazed him, sending me stumbling backwards with a blast of his magic. I was off balance, my feet were tangled in the silk floor and soft sand, and before I could recover Kiran sent another beam of magic, lifting me off the ground and pushing me backward another few feet.

"Do you really think that by forcing me to go with you, against my will that I will somehow madly fall back in love with you?" I shouted, through dangerous bursts of magic and flying furniture.

"Of course not!" He answered, his voice thick with disgust and for a moment the fighting stopped and something changed in his eyes. It wasn't desire he fought with but hatred. "This isn't about winning you back, Love. This is the nature of the war you declared."

I tried to return his blows, but my magic was slow and frantic, hardly cooperating and barely reacting to my commands. Kiran hit me with another firm blast of electricity that threw me in the air, crashing through the sheer curtain and landing me heavily on the bed.

I was dizzy and disoriented, frustrated with my magic and refused to believe that I had lost. Kiran walked over to me, standing next to the bed, towering above me, his wicked grin curving his lips and all I wanted to do was slap him.

I was certain I only had a few moments before I would lose consciousness to the fitful magic ruining my life and so I needed to act quickly. I refused to be taken prisoner; I refused to believe that the only way to save my brother was to become Kiran's bride and hand over my magic to a Kingdom I was fighting to destroy.

Kiran stared down at me, his face satisfied with victory but his eyes hungry for mine again. The tension between us was pulsating violently and our magics had collided ferociously into each other, a consequence of the struggle between us.

I cursed under my breath and then did the only thing I knew how to do that would sufficiently distract him. I reached up to him, clutching at the collar of his shirt, and pulled him down to me on the bed.

My mouth crashed into his, my lips moving against his mouth in desperate distraction. He gave in to me immediately, sighing sweetly with our connection. His hands wrapped around my waist, holding my body to him as if he would never let another inch come between us again. The magic around us became a palpable color field of energy and the entire tent buzzed with fevered electricity.

I stayed in his arms, convincing myself this was part of the plan. His mouth had never tasted so sweet and his lips had never kissed me this way before. My heart pounded wildly against my chest, threatening to rip a hole and break free, forever binding itself to Kiran's.

His hands slipped underneath my shirt, pressing me ever closer to him. His skin was hot against mine, leaving burn marks on my lower back. I had a plan and I was desperate to remember it, to escape not only his hold, but this fearful desert and find safety at home.

Our magics intertwined in obstinate union, but I was determined to be stronger than a masochistic electrical field with a hard to break habit. This was not my life anymore. I would save my brother on my own terms and owe nothing to Kiran, and one day soon, I would feel nothing more for him.

With my hands holding his face to mine, I let the magic build inside of me, unnoticed by the frenetic aura of our passionate kiss. I pressed my palms tightly against his face and then I released the vastness of my magic against him.

The bed crashed to the ground, splintering into hundreds of pieces from the force of my magic. Kiran lay in the center of it all, unconscious and covered in debris. I struggled to climb out of the mess, resenting the smirk that still marked his sleeping face.

I ran through the tent, not even bothering with the entrance, I just forced myself through the side folds. I sprinted across the desert expanse between the now ragged tent and the plane. I could feel my swollen lips, my hair was a wild tangled mess, and my clothing disheveled, but thankfully, I wouldn't have to explain any of that to Talbott.

"Get off my plane!" I shouted at him as soon as I was up the steps.

He and Lilly were sitting across the aisle from each other in the leather passenger's seats, but they were leaning in and talking quietly and I couldn't help but feel like I was interrupting an intimate moment.

"Get off!" I yelled again, pointing with a straight arm towards the exit. "Kiran needs you and I need you to get out!"

I found the right words, with one last glance at Lilly; Talbott disappeared from the plane and into the dark, desert void.

"We have to go, Lilly! Like, right now!" I was still frantic, using magic to close the door behind Talbott and then I joined her in the cockpit where she was already working the equipment to start the plane.

I rocked back and forth, completely wrecked from everything that just happened. I chewed on my thumbnail, trying to make sense of Kiran and his crazy ideas and then of my own reactions and feelings.

I had meant to distract Kiran, not get lost in a kiss that made my heart pound with the very memory of it. I shook my head, thankful that Lilly was safe and that she was capable of getting us into the air, away from Morocco, away from Kiran and away from compromising decisions that I could never entertain again.

# Chapter Twenty-Nine

"Eden, are you Ok?" Lilly approached conversation carefully after several minutes of silence.

The plane was in the air and on its way back to Omaha. Lilly worked the dials and maneuvered around the cockpit like an expert while shooting me furtive glances and crinkling her nose in concern.

Wrapped in misery, I felt weak and foolish. My fingers touched my lips that still burned with the memory of Kiran and I couldn't stop beating myself up for losing myself in the tension of the fight. The inner turmoil reached a feverish-pitch that threatened my sanity all together.

It wasn't that I was fighting to keep myself from Kiran. Not a piece inside of me wanted to be with him again, to stand by his side or call myself his bride. Our kiss felt more like goodbye than the continuance of any significant emotion.

I fought the original attraction that brought us together in the first place. From the very first time I saw Kiran, I couldn't keep myself from him or him from me. Our relationship possessed something magnetic, something gravitational that pulled us together without choice or real objection. This force beyond our control guided our paths into a catastrophic collision of tragic fate that would haunt us both for the rest of eternity.

This same battle I fought since the beginning of all this, would be stronger this time. This time, I wouldn't allow him to convince me I felt differently or to blind my common sense and moral obligation with his obtrusive magic that called so sweetly and manipulatively to mine. This time I would win.

"Ugh! I should be asking you that!" I huffed, forcing myself from a miserable brewing session.

"What happened back there?" She ignored my dramatics and looked at me with her trademark sensitivity.

"I don't even know," I grumbled into my hands, too ashamed to look at her. "He wants me to give myself up in return for Avalon. If I turn myself over, then they will let Avalon go, and leave everyone else alone...." I trailed off, trying to figure out the reasons I didn't just agree to the terms in Morocco.

"You're not seriously considering it, are you?" Lilly gasped, her red curls bouncing with enthusiasm.

"Well, no, not seriously...." I admitted, sinking lower into my seat and hoping to disappear until this whole thing was over.

"Eden, you will not solve anything by doing that! You cannot possibly believe that handing your magic over to Kiran will be a better solution than Avalon without magic. They would kill you or worse yet make you marry Kiran. And then you would have all of eternity to watch as Lucan destroys us!" Prison impassioned Lilly; there was a fire in her green eyes that I had never seen. She was right.

"So what do you suggest I do?" I asked, more whiny than sincere.

"Eden, keep doing what you're doing! It's working! I know that it doesn't feel like it, but even in the prisons the Guards are scared to say your name. I've only heard about some of the stuff that's happened, but from what Talbott says, you seem to be doing a good job. You got me out! And that is the greatest thing to happen to me, since.... since probably the last time you got me out!" We both laughed at the harsh reality of our lives. I was so glad she was with me that the events with Kiran started to fade into memories and I breathed easier, trying to accept her words.

"I don't know if I actually get the credit for breaking you out though...." I teased, and when she turned to me confused, I added, "I'm pretty sure that was all Talbott."

"I doubt that..." she mumbled, her cheeks flaming red.

"Lilly, seriously, I'm pretty sure it was his idea! Plus, Kiran told me he would find any excuse to visit you in Romania, so...." I purposely left out the part about him wanting alone time on the plane, simply because I didn't know if that was really him or Kiran's idea of leverage.

"Oh, no. No, it's nothing like that." Her blush spread across her porcelain face, down her neck and suddenly she was fidgeting with the dials. "I mean, yes, he did visit me once or twice, but I think it was just to find out more information about you. I mean, because we're so close. Lucan probably sent him down to pump me for information or whatever."

"Yeah, I'm sure that's what happened...." I laughed.

"Eden, seriously.... if it seemed like I like him or whatever, it's just because I knew he was kind of willing to help me. I was just trying to get out of there alive, that's all...." she confessed quietly and my heart broke for her.

"Was it awful?" I asked in a whisper.

She was silent for a minute, tears filling her forest green eyes and her chin quivering gently from the memory. She breathed out slowly as if to control her emotions and then conceded with a raspy voice, "Yes.... but it wasn't as bad as it could have been." She sat up straighter, finding strength for her voice. "I know Talbott helped me, even when he wasn't there, this time was.... this time was easier than the last time."

"I'm so sorry, Lilly," I insisted, holding the weight of believing her imprisonment was entirely my fault.

"Eden, don't be sorry!" she gushed, turning the full intensity of her expression on me. "I asked for this life! I'm the one that signed up to fight. I knew this would be part of it, and if more is asked of me than a few weeks in prison, I will gladly give it all."

"But you won't have to," I promised. Even if Lilly was willing to martyr her life for this cause, I wasn't willing to let her. She had been committed even longer than I to fighting for freedom, but I was in charge now and if anyone was going to die it was going to be me. Still, the bleakness of the fight reminded me that more than one innocent life would end before this was over.

She was silent for a few moments, not wanting to argue with me and I didn't blame her. I couldn't promise that she wouldn't lose her life over this and if I was perfectly honest with myself, I didn't want to try to stop her. She had just as much right to fight for our people as I did, if not more.

She was the oppressed, the exiled. She stared prejudice and extinction in the face and demanded they move for her.

"Were you able to find anything out about your parents while you were there?" I asked timidly, breaking the silence. I didn't want to bring up anything painful for her, but I sincerely hoped she at least got to see them while there.

"Yes, once. Talbott arranged a short meeting with them individually. They are kept isolated, just like everyone else, but somehow he got me a visit." She sighed with relief, but her jaw tightened with firm resolve as if cementing her purpose forever stronger.

"Are they Ok?" I asked, knowing that even if they were physically fine, they could never really be Ok inside those prison walls.

"They are.... they are alive." Lilly cleared her throat and shook her head gently to rid the crushing emotion. Her vibrant curls, bounced with the movement, falling across her face and catching the lone tear that escaped down her cheek.

"Oh, what a mess we're in!" I sighed, frustrated with the whole Kingdom. "Will it ever get better?"

"It has to," she insisted. "Things cannot be this difficult forever, we won't survive it."

"Doesn't he feel it? Doesn't Lucan understand how his family has destroyed this kingdom?" I was suddenly disgusted with the bloodline that brought destruction upon its own people. "Or do you think he has ever thought of our people as his Kingdom? Has he ever even looked beyond the plight for his own Immortality?"

"I don't know...." Lilly thought seriously for a few moments, mulling over the answers that we could really only ever speculate. "You know, that's why my parents sent me to Kingsley. They knew there was a risk and that in essence they were gambling with my life. But they trusted Amory. They wanted me to have a real education, to make something of myself and in our communities; I mean.... in the Shape-Shifter communities.... I would never have had a chance."

"Really? Because I thought you were well off and stuff. I mean, don't the Shape-Shifter families still have money?" I had never talked to Lilly about her family's money before, but she lived in her own apartment when I came to Kingsley, so they had to have something.

"There is money, of course. But, most Shape-Shifters live as part of the human world and go to human schools. There are only a few isolated Shape-Shifter communities where they have been fortunate enough to stay together, but circumstances are usually so uncertain that they neglect formal education. My parents believed in a better way for me; they wanted me to live as an active citizen of the Kingdom I belong to and for them it was worth prison. How can it be anything less for me?" Her voice was full of the passionate fire that revolutionizes tyranny and in that moment my pledge strengthened.

These people needed saving; this was a Kingdom that faced extinction and a greedy, power-hungry King that would stop at nothing until he was the last Immortal walking this earth. My fight wasn't with Kiran, who acted ignorantly from selfish conceit. This hostility was against his father, who hunted my family, murdered my grandfather and would gladly tie my brother onto the altar of sacrifice for blood sport and entertainment.

"Do you think one day we will look back at all of this and laugh?"

Lilly asked, her mood turning hopeful.

"Not laugh, but yes, one day, we will sit together and remember how we changed things. We will remember the way things used to be, and teach our children to be better than us. The generations that follow will remember with us. In that day, we will all be free," I vowed, my soul swelling with the hopeful song of revolution.

We fell silent, each to our own thoughts of the future, and in those quiet reflections, I remembered Kiran and our kiss. The memory was distant and fading, my heart had stilled and my mind stalled its racing.

This war wasn't about scorned love or heart-wrenching betrayal. In fact, it wasn't about me at all. It was about a people on the cliff of extinction and deep-seated prejudice that kept our magic separated and small.

These weren't small complaints or short-lived mistakes. This war.... this Rebellion was the difference between survival and death.

When I weighed the eternal consequences Kiran was an insignificant speed bump in the road for the betterment of this Kingdom. It was easier to dismiss him than to forget about our kiss or feelings that resurfaced or stayed buried.

There were more important things in my life than teenage romance.

# Chapter Thirty

The taxi dropped us off in front of Aunt Syl's house close to midnight. The house was completely dark and seemingly empty. I wondered if Aunt Syl was at the hospital, and the thought alone sent me into a deeper depression.

Still, it felt good to be home. Omaha was beautiful at the beginning of April. The trees were finding life again, the buds just beginning to open and the grass turning from brown back to green; the entire city smelled like flowers and rain. I walked slowly to the front door, feeling like I had been gone for years, and not just a few short months.

I knew the house was being watched; Kiran said so, but I couldn't be afraid anymore. I wasn't hiding, and my mission wasn't a secret. If Lucan wanted to watch my aunt work emergency surgery at the hospital and me open the refrigerator and devour everything in it, then he was more than welcomed to.

I opened the door with magic, stumbling inside and holding it open for Lilly. I was so grateful that she was back; I finally had someone I could open up to and would take equally as long to get ready.

We talked almost the entire flight home. We continued to discuss our hopes for the Kingdom, and what it would be like if we actually became in charge one day. I told her about Jericho and how something had started to blossom between us. She opened up about the prisons and how truly awful it was for her. Between us, every topic was exhausted.

It was odd to watch her fly a plane. Although she wasn't hurt in any way, she was incredibly thin after her captivity, and extremely exhausted. I was surprised she was able to keep up with my conversation. By the time we landed in Omaha, I thought surely she would have slipped into a coma.

I didn't have many nice things to say about Talbott, but if fatigue was her only ailment then I could forgive him some of his faults. She held to her position that she was only using him for security, which apparently worked, because he ensured that she was cared for from day one of her captivity and visited her with every chance he got.

She admitted his attention made no sense, and tried to pretend indifference, but she appreciated his generosity and was thankful he was around to take care of her as much as he was. She was too sweet to hold anything like opposite sides of the war, or he was my mortal enemy's personal bodyguard, against him and I had to laugh at that. She tried to tell me that Kiran was actually encouraging Talbott to visit her, but I brushed it off, assuming the facts of the story were coming from Talbott. Kiran was playing the same song, more manipulations, more lies.

She didn't know how anyone else was doing. The first time she survived prison, she actually stayed with the other prisoners. This time, Lucan ordered them to all remain separate, so what was happening to everyone else was a mystery. That information was the hardest to accept, no one else had a Talbott to look after them. My memory instantly reminded me of what Avalon looked like when we found him and I couldn't help but worry that everyone else was suffering the same fate.

I knew that Jericho set up camp at Amory's house, or thanks to my inheritance.... my house. But I needed my own room, my own bed. And, I needed Aunt Syl.

I dropped my backpack on the floor in the entryway, deciding that I was home and didn't have to worry about putting my things away just yet. Nobody knew we were here. I thought about calling Jericho just to let him know that we were safe and that everything was fine, but I couldn't find the strength. He wouldn't be in Omaha yet anyway. If everything went according to plan, he would arrive with the South Africa team and everyone else, tomorrow night.

By the time I closed and locked the front door, Lilly had kicked off her shoes and said goodnight to the world. She collapsed onto the couch and covered herself with a blanket. I got the feeling she wasn't planning on moving for a very long time.

I wandered into the kitchen, hoping for something to eat. I didn't really have an appetite, but my stomach hurt and I was hoping food would satisfy it. I rummaged through the kitchen, but on her own Aunt Syl wasn't much for well-balanced, homemade meals. There were a few cartons of stale fried rice, and an expired gallon of milk, but that was it.

I closed the refrigerator door again and leaned back against it. Now that I was home, I didn't really know what to do. It felt good to be here, relaxing and de-stressing, but still, my life had been so crazy the last several weeks. I was constantly moving from one thing to the next, flying across the world and fighting bad guys, that now the normalcy of home was disconcerting.

I checked on Lilly to see if she wanted a glass of water, but she was already asleep. She lay curled up in a ball, her breathing deep and heavy and her red, curly hair, shining even in the darkness, even after all that she went through.

The garage door opened in the kitchen and I turned to greet Aunt Syl, so thankful to see her. She stood in the doorway, half in shock. Her dirty, blonde hair pulled into a ponytail she was dressed in her work scrubs. Tears had already begun to spill from her eyes and her shoulders were shaking with the gentle sobbing of the truly relieved.

"I saw the light on, but I couldn't even hope that it was you," she whispered and I moved across the kitchen as a lost child would to the mother that found her.

She opened her arms and I knocked the wind out of her, crashing into her and throwing my arms around her waist. I couldn't stop the tears then, she didn't try to pull away or even stop crying herself. Together we stood, hugging one another, finding solace in each other's sadness.

"I've been so worried about you, and Angelica hadn't heard anything. I just, I just wondered if I would ever see you again," she sobbed into my hair.

"Ugh," I grunted, wiping at my nose with the back of my sleeve. "I felt the same way; I just had to come home."

"I'm so glad that you did!" She hugged me tighter, and I wondered if she would ever let go. I was not going to be the first to pull away.

"Lilly's here," I mumbled into her scrubs.

"Lilly?" Aunt Syl exclaimed, pulling away to make sure I was serious. "How? Where? How?" She repeated, the tears pooling in her eyes all over again.

"I just picked her up, she's sleeping on the couch," I gestured towards the living room, sharing Aunt Syl's joy.

"Ok, tell me everything!" She patted my shoulder and started moving around the kitchen, getting the coffee pot ready. "I want to know it all!" She pushed me towards the tall chairs at the island and I sat down heavily. This was going to take a while.

Aunt Syl poured coffee and I shared everything with her from start to finish. I told her about Silas, how he had agreed to help and then sent me to Gabriel. I told her all of the details about getting

Jericho back and flying in Gabriel's tiny plane to France. I told her about finding Avalon's team and that they were using Mr. Lambert's apartment as a safe-house, which was weird. I told her about Sebastian and how I started to think he wasn't such a bad guy. I opened up completely, telling her about the deal we made and that my part of it was to kill him at the end of all of this. I told her about his mother and how she begged me to keep him safe, and how it broke my heart even though she was my enemy. I shared what it was like seeing Kiran for the first time, and what it was like to have to look at him while he was dying, and how that broke my heart. And because it broke my heart, I felt even worse because I thought I should have absolutely no feelings for him. I told her how I failed that mission and just barely escaped, and then about India and how I found Avalon and healed him, but then lost him again in the explosion. I told her about all of the accumulated magic that was making me go crazy and then about Kiran again and the tent in Morocco and how I just barely got Lilly and I out of there.

I opened up to her more than I could have with anyone else, giving her every detail, every emotion and every tear that I had. She cried with me, laughed with me, and cried with me again. She listened carefully, only asking questions when she absolutely had to, and held my hand during the most difficult parts. She was therapy. She was everything I needed to heal.

"Oh, Eden, I am so sorry you had to go through any of that," she sighed at the end of my story. "It doesn't seem fair."

I smiled my bravest smile, knowing that it wasn't fair. I should never have lost my grandfather and my brother and then been propelled into a war I wanted nothing to do with for so long. I should never have had to figure out leading an entire Rebellion in only a few weeks, failing at every turn and losing my brother all over again.

Nevertheless this was life. I could wish that life was fair and that things were different, but this is what it was and I was determined to make the best of it. I needed to move forward, and fight the battles put in front of me and cherish the friendships that surrounded me.

"What about Kiran? What are you going to do about him?" She asked carefully, her brow furrowed the deepest with stories about him and I could see the concern etched in her eyes even now.

"I don't know," I mumbled, gloomily. "I'll probably have to kill him. I hate him, I really do. I hate what he did to my family and to me, how he took away my choice, and how even now selfishness consumes him. But, what I hate the most is this feeling I have whenever we're together! This whole thing isn't even about us, or him.... I mean, it doesn't have anything to do with him, but those are the thoughts I spend my time thinking about. I want to know how I can get away from him, when I should be trying to figure out how to kill him for the good of my people. Which, by the way, I feel like I shouldn't ever have to see him, we're on completely different sides of the war and I keep threatening to kill him, but then I keep running into him and forgetting my purpose!" I whined, folding my arms with frustration.

"Oh, Eden," Aunt Syl breathed, pulling me into another hug. "Dearest, your feelings for Kiran aren't just going to disappear overnight, no matter how he betrayed you and especially just because you're not fighting a war that revolves around your relationship. What you shared with him was something deeper than just a crush; really it was deeper than how most people love each other. And you loved each other despite everything that was against you. That builds something that establishes a pattern so that even still, everything is against you and your love is still fighting."

I sniffled in her arms, realizing she was right. "So what do I do about it?"

"I don't know, dear," she said thoughtfully, "but I don't think doing nothing about it is working. Maybe you have to choose to accept those feelings, but also decide to move forward, as you said. Don't forget about him, maybe don't even hate him, just know that *that* part of your life is over and it's time to move on."

"I can do that, I think," I agreed, sitting up straighter. I felt better just telling the story, just saying how I felt aloud; so maybe Aunt Syl was right. Instead of running from Kiran and my fears, I would face them, confront them and then conquer them.

"And for right now, just focus on getting Avalon back, hmmm? Everything else will fall into place when the time is right." She patted my knee and stood up to stretch. The sun was starting to rise outside and the coffee was wearing off. I stretched too, yawning widely.

"I am so ready for my own bed!" I sighed, and we walked up the stairs together. Lilly was still conked out on the couch.

Eventually, I would have to face my real parents. They were here, just across town. I came home to devise a strategy with them, at some point I would have to meet them. But for right now, I wanted to go to bed, knowing Aunt Syl was just down the hallway, and to breathe in deeply the house I grew up in, my real home, with the woman who raised me.

----

I reached out in sleep, my hands coming away with fistfuls of sand. I sat up quickly, searching out my blankets, my bed, my pillows, anything. But they were all gone. I was in the middle of the desert, surrounded by sand dunes that rolled across countries.

The sun just rose in the east, the horizon painted orange and yellow blending together with the golden sand. The stars still twinkled in the lightened sky and the dry, desert air was still cool and crisp.

I panicked, afraid that I was left behind, afraid that I would have to traverse the desert alone to safety. I searched the landscape for anything that would remind me of how I got back to the desert, how I ended up here alone. Then I saw it.

The black and ivory, striped tent lay out over the sand. The silk, fabric folds flapped in the breeze and the inside glowed warmly with the light of the lanterns. In the breeze, I could smell the exotic spices and freshly baked bread.

I breathed slowly, realizing I awoke in a Dream-Walk. The tent was there, across the sand, inviting me in. The warm glow and pretty fabric beckoned me to enter, to explore more deeply what the tent had to offer.

He called me here. He called me to a place that would stir my better emotions and tug at my tired resolve.

I folded my legs and crossed my arms, staring at the tent and breathing deeply. There was part of me that was hungry to go inside, the part of me that remembered the passion of a forbidden kiss and what my magic felt like wrapped up in its other half. But, there was another side to me that remembered everything else, remembered the cause I fought and sacrificed for.

I sighed, almost wanting to give in to the emotional part of me. Nobody was here in the desert or inside of my head. Nobody was pressuring me, pushing me in any one direction, reasoning with my logic or appealing to my emotions. I had a choice for the first time.

There was no one here to influence my decision. I knew that whatever happened in this dream world would remain a secret that would be mine forever. I admitted to myself that I wanted to go into that tent. I wanted to connect to him, to let our magics run wild.

With that admission, I knew I could walk away. Because I could admit what I genuinely wanted, I could also realize what I wanted would have consequences. And, I had goals and desires that went beyond the present, far beyond this dream and this moment.

I stared for a few more minutes at the tent, knowing I was in no danger of moving toward it. I was in no danger of him.

He came then, after the moments of stillness. He stood in the open entrance, shirtless and god-like. We stared at each other across the desert expanse. He didn't move toward me, or call my name.

Then I knew it was time to go. I took another step away from him, his hold diminishing before I could even open my eyes back in the real world.

## Chapter Thirty-One

"Are you sure you want to do this?" Aunt Syl asked, during the drive to Amory's. "I mean, I want you to of course, but I just want to make sure you're ready. You've been through so much in a very short amount of time."

"I have to, I've stalled long enough," I mumbled, glancing at Lilly in the backseat of Aunt Syl's red convertible. Her vibrant, unrestrained red hair whipped in the wind. She smiled encouragingly at me, her bee-stung lips forming the happiest expression. She was perfection today, she looked infinitely better than she had two days ago and I was so happy to see her look healthy.

"I know, I know, I just worry about you, that's all." Aunt Syl turned to me; I could see the anxiety in her eyes even through her overly large sunglasses.

"Besides, Jericho is going crazy," I laughed. Thinking of Jericho made this journey easier somehow. He was my rock; he made impossible situations possible and offered hope where there was none. If the time had come to meet my parents, my real parents, at least I could rest in the knowledge that he would be by my side.

Aunt Syl pulled into Amory's driveway and shut off the engine. We all stepped out of the car and glanced around. I knew, somehow, somewhere someone followed us, but I couldn't worry about that for now. I hoped that at least they weren't cognizant of everyone in the house, but there was no way to be sure of that either.

I unlocked the front door, and walked inside to a darkened sitting room. All the blinds in the house were pulled, but the basement door was open and the staircase down had the light on. I led the way over to the door, feeling the pull of magic and hearing the excited chatter of almost two dozen Immortals.

I took a breath, closing my eyes for a second and finding courage. I didn't know what to expect in a situation like this, there was no experience to draw from and my Titan intuition did nothing for the good kind of confrontations. I decided to move; obsessing over my fears was not going to accomplish anything.

I took each step with calculated intent, deciding I had faced worse things than awkward moments. At the bottom of the staircase, I turned a corner to meet the gathered Immortals. Another big breath and I entered the Rec room that Jericho turned into makeshift housing. Lilly and Aunt Syl stayed right by my side and that helped ease my tension.

The room fell silent when I walked in, all eyes turning to me. I tried to take in the crowd, to find my mother's face, but I was too nervous. Familiar faces blended with new ones and I didn't know whether to wait for them to approach me or be the first one to make the move. A small debilitating fear began to grow and spread inside my veins, convincing me I wouldn't recognize them, whispering that I wouldn't know them at all when they introduced themselves.

Then unexpectedly, they walked out of a downstairs bedroom with Jericho. I caught my mother's eyes first, as black as mine and brimming with tears. Her long, wild hair encompassed her small frame and she stood shaking with anticipation.

The moment felt surreal. It reminded me of the first night Amory had told me about my magic, and how I invaded his thoughts and memories to find an image of her. It felt like that now, like I was looking at a distant, beautiful picture that I would never be able to touch. Only, unlike in the memory, she was looking back at me, her eyes held mine and there were no words to express how amazing that felt.

"Go to her," my father whispered to her and she did. She took the length of the room in a few short strides, engulfing me in her arms before I had a chance to protest. She held me to her like a small child, kissing the side of my head and whispering promises and apologies too fast for me to understand.

I just smiled, letting the relief wash over me. I was with my mother, my real mother. I started laughing , then crying, and then laughing again. I was an emotional rollercoaster, but since my emotions echoed in my mother, I had to forgive myself.

"Delia, darling, I would like to see her too," my father said gently and my mother laughed; letting go of me and depositing me into my father's arms.

He didn't immediately hug me. He looked at me deeply in the eyes, memorizing my face and making sure that I was real. He felt like Avalon and that made me instantly trust him. His eyes were the same piercing green, his hair unruly and wild and his smile the absolute most genuine thing I had ever seen.

When he finally brought me into a hug, it was as though he were bearing his soul. He was a quiet leader, gentle but commanding, and I felt the traces of Titan upbringing in his careful reservations. He was good and wise, and I was so grateful that he had come, that he could take over leadership.

"I'm proud of you," he whispered and the breath caught in my throat. I wanted to protest, to remind him that I had done nothing to be proud of, but I couldn't voice my disagreement, so I let his words float over me and I tried to believe that I was worthy of them.

Justice did not hold me for as long as my mother did, and when he let go, all I could do was stare at them. Our embraces conveyed every word that might be spoken between us. My heart swelled with happiness, I overlooked my frantic magic, and the hopelessness of this war lessened.

Nobody could replace Amory, but they were not supposed to. They held a different place in my life, a different role that I could treasure equally as much and hold equally as close to my heart. They were my parents and I was finally with them.

I thought of Avalon, how he was missing this, how his opportunity to be reunited with his parents was stolen from him and my purpose was renewed. I would do whatever it took to rescue him. He deserved to be here too, he deserved to hug his mother and feel loved. He deserved to look into his father's eyes and find pride and respect. I finally found the place where I could easily lay myself on the altar and be sacrificed for him.

"How about we go upstairs and talk?" Justice offered and I nodded my agreement, too emotional yet to speak.

I tipped my head at Jericho to join us, and he moved from across the crowd immediately. We were away from each other for days; the need to touch him, to be embraced by him was making my blood tingle.

Sometimes I was so confused and hysterical that I reached out to Jericho for life support, forgetting the attachment growing between us. We kissed once and there hadn't been a moment since to even talk about it, let alone analyze what it meant for us. The days apart from each other made me crave his nearness now and I couldn't make myself wait much longer.

Lilly knew half the crowd from her short days as part of the Amory and Avalon run Resistance and so she had already dragged Aunt Syl into the gathering to mix and mingle. I followed my parents back up the staircase and to the dining room table.

The house was painfully marked with the memory of Amory. His furnishings, all made from dark, expensive wood were freshly polished and dusted. One of a kind antiques and tasteful, priceless art decorated the rooms and an extensive bar, with crystal glasses of every size and shape took up one entire wall of the dining room. The house even smelled like him and so although it was mine, I didn't know if I would ever be able to call it home. Maybe when Avalon got back, he could take it over.

I sat next to Delia and she immediately put her arm around me, rubbed my shoulder and leaned her head against mine sweetly. Justice sat on the other side of her at the head of the table and Jericho sat down directly across from Delia.

This felt like an actual meeting of the minds and I couldn't help but feel more confident with my parents near. I watched them silently for a moment. They were adorably in sync; always aware of exactly what the other one was doing, always watching each other out of the corner of their eyes affectionately and always touching. My father reached one hand out to my mother and she took it instinctively without even looking.

Theirs was a love that was worth risking everything for. They had sacrificed community, friends and family; they left everything they had ever known or cared about behind, just to be together. Their magic moved as one entity, their bodies in perfect harmony; they were the definition of soul mates. Being in their presence almost felt like a religious experience, such was the capacity of their love for each other.

I looked up at Jericho from under my eyelashes, wondering if we would ever love each other like that. Whatever feelings were between us felt utterly immature and childish next to the centuries-old, sacrificial love my parents shared. Still, there was something to look forward to, watching a romance that survived all odds; it gave me something to hope for.

"Eden, there is so much I want to say to you," Delia turned to me and smiled. Her lips were cherry red and perfect, her smile changed the temperature of the room and her eyes danced with expressiveness. She was exquisite.

"I know," I blushed, feeling the same way and knowing what I needed to say next, "I'm so sorry about Avalon. I had no idea what would happen, I was selfish and blind and if I had known how Kiran would betray me, I would have never trusted him. I would have never let that happen to Avalon, or to Amory, and please believe I did everything in my power to stop it," my voice broke from a torrent of emotions. I had been looking for someone to apologize to for months now. I was told repeatedly what happened was not my fault, but my parents were people that would actually be able to forgive me. I was the sole reason for the death of my mother's father and their son's captivity. They had to blame me for at least part of it.

"Oh darling," Delia gushed, taking my face in her hands, "it's not your fault, it's not your fault at all!" She pulled my face forward, kissing me on the forehead.

"Eden, listen to me," my father commanded and I looked up at him immediately, "Lucan is a tyrant; he is an evil man and you cannot blame yourself. You simply cannot. I don't believe there was anything you could have done. If it weren't Avalon, then it would have been you. And Amory, well, they have been trying to kill him since this whole thing started. It's not your fault Eden. We would never blame you."

"If anything, we blame ourselves!" Delia glanced at her husband who nodded his head solemnly and then turned to stare at the closed blinds. "We have been selfish and foolish. I should have known from the beginning how determined Lucan was, even after all of these years.... It's not your fault, darling; it's his. That is why we're here; we can stop him together. The time has finally come to end this abomination."

I exhaled in relief; their forgiveness meant more to me than anything else. I always knew the truth about Lucan and his oppression, but it was too easy to blame myself. With the confirmation from my parents that Lucan and his bloodline were as bad as I experienced them to be, I could move forward in a different way than before.

There was still some self-blame, I wondered if I would ever escape the guilt of that night, but it lessened. I was not the only one that loved the victims wholeheartedly, and I was not the only one that could blame the king and his son for the events that unfolded.

"Eden, I need to tell you that we will have to leave again," Delia was suddenly grave, her onyx eyes conveying the worst kind of heartbreak. "It doesn't seem fair, after we've just found each other again. But in order to keep you as safe as possible, we have to keep moving."

"Safe? I'm not safe, there's a detail on Aunt Syl right now anyway; they know exactly where I am," I protested, not ready to say goodbye after just finding them. My heart felt crushed, I thought we were going to work together, that I wouldn't have to carry this Resistance alone. I needed guidance, someone that was a better leader, someone that people would listen to; I thought I had found that in them.

"That is exactly why we have to go," Justice jumped in, reaching across the table and taking my hand in his. "By now they've figured out we are here. We've stayed too long already. But we had to see you; we couldn't leave until did. Still, they are coming for us. In hours, Omaha will be swarming with Titans looking for us."

"Kiran will protect you, Eden. I believe that he will, but his father will hunt us until the day he has us in his possession and so we have to keep moving to keep you safe." A single tear slipped from Delia's eyes and I could feel it in her magic how desperate she was to stay with me. "You have a place here; you're the leader of the Rebellion, for goodness sakes. We will meet you soon; we will attack the Romanian Citadel with you."

Delia looked back at Justice and he smiled. His green eyes sparkled with intensity and the idea of battle and the room was quickly flooded with his warrior-like magic, hungry for conflict, ready for blood, "We are only leaving until your teams are ready to move. We will meet you there and we can rescue your brother together. We've contacted with many more that are willing to fight. I'd say, at last count, we had about two hundred that have promised to go with us."

"Wow!" I marveled at those kinds of numbers. In the same amount of time, I was able to recruit.... Gabriel. In all that time, I was able to recruit one. Well, and if you counted Silas, that made two. The rest were all just a re-gathering of the people already enlisted by my brother or grandfather. "So when? When are we doing this?" I could hardly contain my excitement to go.

"Well," Jericho spoke up from across the table, "we were thinking, as long as you agree, how about we add ourselves to the guest list for the royal wedding?"

# Chapter Thirty-Two

"What I am worried about is Lucan's showmanship," Delia continued, as if she needed to convince me that destroying any hope of happiness Kiran had was a good thing. "I am worried for your brother. Lucan loves these big moments where he can display his power and authority. If he has been waiting for the right moment to hurt your brother anymore, it would be during his son's wedding, as either a gift or a promise."

"You had me at royal wedding." I smiled. I wondered at my mother's deep knowledge of Lucan. I knew they spent time together when they were young and that is how Lucan fell in love with her, but I always just assumed she only had eyes for my father. Something was revealed though, when she spoke about Lucan, it wasn't with contempt or hatred, it was with deep sadness, the earth-shattering kind that broke a heart in two.

"It will be tricky getting all of our side into the Citadel without alarming the Titan Guard far in advance. We are thankful for our numbers, but there is no way to smuggle that many Immortals into a heightened security situation without setting off some bells and whistles," Justice explained and his accent was so similar to Talbott's that I found it slightly off-putting.

"Well, do we need all two-hundred?" I asked, and everyone's eyes turned to me. "I mean, what is our goal here? Personally, I would prefer to focus only on extracting Avalon, and then regroup and decide how to take down the Monarchy later. Avalon is my first concern."

"Ours, too," Justice agreed, sitting up straighter and talking to me differently, like I was an equal and not a child.

"All right, so, my thought is, save the other two-hundred, train them to fight and then use them in a greater battle in the future. A battle where maybe our target is Lucan or at least aimed more towards the royal family," I suggested, suddenly nervous with everyone staring so intently at me.

"So, use a smaller base and like a get in, get out kind of scenario," Jericho jumped on board, nodding his head enthusiastically.

"Unless you think we need all of those people to get Avalon?" I asked, second-guessing my ability to decide anything.

"No, I think you're right," Justice pressed his fingertips together and rested his chin on top of them. "Security will, of course, be heightened, but they will also be distracted with the entire royal family present. It could be the perfect opportunity for a small ops kind of scenario. We could even slip in before the wedding starts, grab Avalon, and escape. Simple as that." He returned my smile, the proud kind of grin that only a father could offer their children and I beamed with admiration for him.

"Will it be possible though? I mean to move around the castle undetected?" I asked, trying to improve at thinking entire plans through. There was no way I was ever going to get sucked into another Morocco situation by being unprepared and naive.

"If worse comes to worst, then I can step in," Delia announced confidently. "I haven't seen Lucan in a hundred and sixty three years, it's time I met the man face to face," her eyes saddened and Justice reached out his hand instinctively to comfort his wife. I was almost unbearably curious about their history with Lucan, but I kept my questions to myself, saving them for a different day, a day when Avalon would be here to listen to the answers too.

"Besides, the whole Kingdom both adores Delia and absolutely despises her at the same time," Justice gazed at his wife as if he wanted to take whatever burden this meant on himself and carry it for her. "At the very least, she will be a distraction."

"What do you mean?" I asked.

"They love her because Lucan loves her and because she escaped and found life outside of the Kingdom. They hate her for the exact same reasons," Justice answered seriously.

"Do they feel the same way about you?" I asked him and his face lit up in a smile.

"Oh, no, they pretty much all hate me," he laughed and Delia turned to him, laughing too.

"The wedding, do we have a date?" I asked, working out a time line in my mind.

"Our sources tell us everything is being prepared for the first of May," Jericho spoke up again and both Delia and Justice nodded their agreement.

"Kendrick unions are always held on the first of May; it's sacred tradition," Delia practically whispered her response.

"All right, then that only leaves one small detail," I grinned, happy to have a plan in motion that was only three weeks away from being carried out, "How do we get inside?"

"Eden, is it true that last fall, you escaped through the underground river?" Justice asked, his eyes proud again and his expectation confident.

"Yes, Amory took me," I swallowed, finding it almost impossible not to weep at the memory.

"Without magic?" Justice pressed, his eyes growing ever more excited.

"Yes, the entire way," I couldn't help perk up with pride.

"That is incredible!" he exclaimed, and then turned to his wife, "Lia, isn't that incredible?"

"Yes, it is." She gazed intently at me, her eyes brimming with tears again.

"Then, that is how we will go back," Justice declared. I could tell Lucan had an amazing bodyguard in him at one time. "Delia, Eden and I will sneak in to the Citadel that way without magic. If we can operate without magic through the castle, we can theoretically stay undetected until Avalon is out and safe. Jericho, how many are there of you?"

"Almost two dozen," Jericho replied, he was buzzing with excited energy, ready for battle and ready to rescue his best friend.

"Fantastic! Lucan will be expecting something, some kind of display or protest from you. Jericho and his people can draw out the Guard from the Citadel, leaving the castle nearly empty. When we have Avalon, Eden can call Jericho, who can retreat into the forest and disappear. I do not believe the Guard will follow you far into the mountains, because they will assume it is a trick to get inside the Citadel!" Justice half-shouted, leaning back in his chair and bringing his fist to his chin. "This just might work!"

"It has to work, I have to get Avalon back," I whispered seriously, as excited as everyone else was, but not able to drop sight of the real goal: my brother.

"Yes, we know you do," Delia agreed seriously and I felt her words to my very bones. She stood up abruptly and Justice followed.

The mood in the room changed quickly; it was obvious that they needed to move on. The feeling that the conversation was at an end was almost bizarre; the whole climate of our communion changed as if time itself warned my parents that this visit was over.

Delia pulled me into another embrace, holding me to her and rocking back and forth gently. "It gets easier," she whispered into my ear.

"Being without Avalon?" I asked, clarifying. I hoped she was wrong, I desperately hoped she didn't mean my brother. I didn't want it to get easier; I didn't want *not* to push every second of every day to get him back.

"No," she shook her head in my tangles of hair, "to be without Kiran."

I stood speechless, letting her arms comfort me against the harsh reality of her words. I wondered again at her relationship with Lucan and if my life was a mere echo of hers. She kissed me on the cheek, not wanting to let go, but when Justice tapped her on the shoulder, she immediately consented.

Justice was next, hugging me with fatherly satisfaction and reminded me that I was the leader of the Rebellion whether I wanted to be or not. "Train hard, be ready for May first," he instructed slowly. "Do you know where the cave opens to the split river?" When I nodded, he continued, "Meet us there at five o'clock on the first and we will take the river together," he pulled away, grinning at me. I felt premature victory with every fiber in my being. I had my parents now and we would conquer this together.

"Eden, we love you, darling, and I will look forward to meeting you every moment until that day," Delia promised passionately; and even my magic believed her.

"I love you too," I insisted, looking at them both. They were not parents that gave up their children in order to have a better life; they were parents that sacrificed their family in order for their children to live. Delia was not running from a scorned love; she was running to a life in which she could openly love her family. Somehow, along the way, I joined their flight. I held my own past to chase me, and my own promise of freedom relentlessly to pursue.

"I love you, Eden, see you soon," Justice echoed and then they were gone. They slipped out the backyard into the spring twilight and across the yard. I watched them disappear into the wooded area that backed up to Amory's house and wondered where they would go. What would life be like as a couple on the road?

But, when I looked at Jericho, I knew. If we didn't defeat the Monarchy and find victory, it would be our future together for as long as we lived.

Then I realized that I was already referring to him and me as "us" and "our."

----

"Well, that was wild," Jericho turned to me in the kitchen, after my parents disappeared in the freshly budding trees.

"Yeah," I agreed, turning to him and desperately wanting his touch.

"Are you Ok?" he asked, taking a tentative step forward.

"Yes, I think I am," I decided, watching him with hungry eyes and wondering if he could feel how badly I wanted him to put his arms around me.

"What about Morocco? Did things go smoothly with the exchange?" He smiled nervously, uncomfortable with my intense gaze.

"Honestly," I sighed, "as smoothly as could be expected."

"What is with you?" he asked, an anxious laugh escaping him.

"What do you mean?" I played naive, feeling like I had an idea of what he was talking about, but I wanted to make him squirm a little.

"You came back.... I don't know.... different somehow." He was moving towards me, but I was confident he wasn't even conscious of the gravitational pull between us. My magic didn't immediately search him out like it did with Kiran, but my body did. I was used to letting Jericho hold me, so when I needed to be held, I couldn't help but selfishly long for him.

"I don't know what you mean," I laughed, taking a step forward and then closing the distance between us. I pushed him against the kitchen counter and laid my head against his chest, listening to his heart beat wildly inside the fragile protectiveness of his body. I wrapped my arms around his waist and decided for the next three weeks I would never let him leave my presence and then after that, I might never be without him again.

I wanted what my parents had. I wanted an all-consuming love that encapsulated complete self-sacrifice and offered only an equal amount of love in return. I wanted to be held without an agenda and without a desperate man's motives. I wanted to be respected and have my opinions heard. I knew that Jericho was a man that would offer me all those things and more.

I lifted my head, tipping my chin to him. "I missed you," I sighed, the tears glossing over my eyes.

"I missed you too," he whispered, searching for something in my expression that couldn't be defined with words.

"Please, don't ever make me leave you again, unless it is absolutely necessary!" I begged, enthusiastically.

"I think I can agree to that," he answered playfully.

He stared into my eyes for a few, silent moments more before dipping me back, holding me securely in his arms and kissing me. Our magics met each other in tantamount excitement, mine surprising me by its willingness to find Jericho's.

He lifted me closer to him, pressing firmly into the small of my back and I remembered why I found him sexy the moment I met him. His mouth caressed mine in a sweet, gentle way that promised to behave, but also threatened to push some boundaries.

It was the first time that *he* kissed me and I got lost in the heady, suffocating sensation of his magic trying to encompass mine. A sigh escaped my lips without conscious awareness, giving him permission to kiss me longer.

I could have stayed wrapped in his arms, thinking only of him for the next three weeks, but someone opening the basement door interrupted our moment and reminded me of the wedding I was going to crash in only three short weeks. A part of me couldn't wait to prevent this wedding from happening, and the other part wanted desperately for Kiran to commit to someone else. Either way, the plan was set in motion and Avalon only had to hold on until that day.

## Chapter Thirty-Three

I stared intently at Sebastian, deciding there was something I was missing. We worked on his magic for over an hour but accomplished nothing except one black eye and a bump on the head.

He was reluctant to keep working at it for obvious reasons, but I was determined to give him back his magic. Not only did I have to figure out the process so I could give Avalon his the moment I saw him, but the electricity still buzzed frenetically inside of me. Uncomfortable and exhausted, I needed to get rid myself of even just one magic. I was confident it would make me feel better.

"Maybe it's just not possible," Sebastian suggested. Appearing utterly defeated, even sighing in exhaustion took concerted effort on his part.

"No, it's possible. It has to be possible!" I argued, trying to figure out a different approach.

Sebastian walked over to the broken porch and sat down heavily. We were back at the old farm. The teams needed a place to spread out and work on combat skills and this place provided the proper isolation and accommodations. Because most of the structures were at least partially destroyed, we didn't worry about breaking anything.

A cool breeze blew across the greening grass, and the sun warmed my face on this perfect spring day. Birds chirped, the leftovers of Angelica's garden bloomed and the farmers on neighboring farms worked hard to prepare the land for planting.

I was happy to be back here, if it weren't for the bloodstained concrete barn floor, and body-sized openings in the center of buildings, that left broken, gaping windows that reminded me of the pain of that night. The devastated farm stood as a constant reminder of what we were working for and motivated the teams to work as hard as possible.

I walked over to Sebastian and sat down next to him. The porch creaked under my added weight and if it weren't for the huge chunk of wood missing from one entire end of it, I would have felt self-conscious.

"You're not planning on killing me anymore, are you?" Sebastian asked quietly, staring out across the farm at Caden Halstead and his team working through combat training.

"Are you kidding me? I'm pretty sure I just tried to kill you," I joked, remembering the nasty bump on his head when I had grown frustrated and impatient.

"Seriously, Eden, I just need to know," Sebastian looked at me. His eyes were as sunken in as ever. He had lost weight and was sleeping more and more. I saw how miserable he was, but I didn't know how to reconcile that without giving his magic back. Murder had been out of the question for a long time now.

"I don't think I have it in me," I mumbled, hating that I wasn't the warrior I started out as or the leader this Rebellion needed me to be.

"I don't think you do either," he agreed, a smile playing at his lips. "All right, then you'd better get back to work. I can't stay like this much longer!" He playfully pushed me into standing and I walked a few feet away from him.

There must be a different way than trying physically to force his magic back into him. His electricity stood ready though; accustomed to the tireless trials, it sat on top of my blood wanting to go home and willing to try anything.

Sebastian stood up and walked over to me, following the call of his primed magic. Even though he and his magic were disconnected, Sebastian still reacted to his energy; he could still feel the faint calling that made him move, whether he was conscious of it or not.

I watched the small spark of life that lit his face when I brought his magic full force in my veins and wondered if there was any magic left inside of him. I took all of it, I thought, but he still lived, he still felt magic; he was just impossibly weak. Maybe there wasn't a way to take someone's magic entirely unless you killed him at the end of it. Since Sebastian was still living, part of him was still Immortal and maybe that was the key to giving him back his life's-blood.

"Sebastian, can you feel any magic inside of you? Is there anything left?" I asked, crossing my arms in determination.

"I don't know," he sighed, "I guess, I'm not dead. So maybe there's still something there."

"Ok, so let's try something new, the other way is obviously not working," I motioned for him to walk over to me.

"Really?" He rolled his eyes, his tired voice finding a strong amount of sarcasm.

"Don't be a smart-ass," I reprimanded then smiled at his spunk. "Ok, instead of me trying to give you your magic, why don't you try to take it from me," I suggested but he only squinted in return. "I'm serious, there has to be something there, something for you to pull at. I can't make you take your magic, but you might be able to!"

He cracked his neck and stood up straighter, taking the challenge. I gave him my hands, remembering that most other Immortal's needed to touch someone else in order to take their magic. His skin performed like a magnet to his imprisoned energy. His electricity came alive in my skin, pulsing with the hope for freedom and I said a silent prayer that this would work.

"Ok, so when I take someone's magic, I find it first and then I just kind of like pull at it with my own, like a rope...." I tried to explain, assuming he had never stolen anyone's magic before. "Does that make sense?"

"Kind of," he mumbled, concentrating hard on the task.

We stood silently for several moments. To me it felt like absolutely nothing was happening, but Sebastian's forehead lined with small beads of sweat and his shoulders started to shake.

I wanted to encourage him to try harder, to shout at him not to give up, but I could see that this was taking everything out of him. So, instead of verbalizing my encouragement, I closed my eyes and became as docile as possible.

I reigned in my own magic, and my carnal need to protect the stolen energies. I could feel how weak he was, how hard of a struggle it was for him to stand and fight, but he was determined. He wouldn't give up.

His fingertips began to buzz with the tiniest pull of electricity from me to him. Immediately my magic fought impulsively back without my consent. My hands sent off an explosion of energy that threw him backwards twenty feet. My eyes popped open and I sprinted over to him, afraid I killed him after all.

He moaned, struggling to sit up and I opened my mouth to apologize.

"Ok, let's try it again," he cut me off. I helped him stand up and we moved into position, taking each other's hands with hard concentration. I thought about offering to quit for the day, and suggest we try again tomorrow, but his expression had a spark in it that was missing before and I couldn't argue with the life that suddenly gave his chocolate brown eyes spirit.

With his fingers tightly intertwined with mine, his magic surfaced once again; the determination and the desire to go home were there. I closed my eyes again, forcing my aggressively defensive electricity into control and pushing his magic forward.

I breathed deeply, pulling from my yoga training and relaxing into a meditative stance. I had to reign in the energy; I couldn't be blasting him across the field every time he made a little progress.

Sebastian's fingers pulsated with vibration and transferred electricity. He squeezed my hands tighter, working at getting his hands under control. Slowly, tirelessly, he extracted more magic. He worked miniscule amounts at a time, and every time he was able to claim more of what was originally his, I fought desperately against my own magic to let it go.

I often thought of my magic as a separate entity than me. It didn't have what you would call emotions, but it did have connections and habits that dictated its behavior. In the struggle to give Sebastian back his magic, I felt how different my magic could be from me; it was greedy and hungry to keep what did not belong to it. Inside my blood, it melted together with all of the other stolen magics and now restrained that connection with dangerous desire.

My slow, relaxed breathing was getting harder to control. I squeezed my eyes shut tightly, fighting against every internal instinct I possessed. Sebastian reclaimed the tiniest bit more and I felt his energy grow stronger. The more he pulled, the easier it got for him in the smallest of increments. I hoped it would get easier for me to let go also, but I was wrong.

I had to force my magic back with every bit of electricity I lost. I felt that I held the leash to a hundred enraged dogs that dragged me behind them as they chased down an intruder that was threatening their livelihood.

Sweat started to appear on my own forehead, trickling down my temples and reminding me of how much work this was. I was thrilled in the success that Sebastian and I finally figured out. But the discouraging factor remained how incredibly long it was taking.

I knew that time felt magnified with the intense effort we both put forward, but even objectively, I knew slow and laborious how the process was. I repressed my fears concerning the length of the process, choosing to remain excited that we figured it out.

Sebastian's strength increased; I could feel him stand up tall and pull at his magic with confidence. I worried for a few moments that neither one of us would know when he was finished, but I rested in the belief that my magic would never let that happen.

Finally, after a long, grueling process, Sebastian hit a turning point and a channel opened between us. It must have been the halfway point because suddenly Sebastian was in control. The rest of the magic took only seconds for him to drain. When I opened my eyes, his face confirmed his joy; he grinned from ear to ear. His face held life again, his eyes no longer sunken and hollow, instead they sparkled with mischief. His skin had color, his hair was shining, he looked like himself and I was relieved.

"Would you be mad if I kept going?" he asked playfully.

"You can try," I laughed, releasing my magic that had been arduously detained. The rushing energy cracked loudly like thunder, breaking us apart and sending Sebastian up into the air and far away from me. At least this time, now that he had some extent of his magic back, I didn't feel bad about his possible injuries.

He jumped to his feet, the smile never leaving his face, and jogged back to me. The change in him was incredible and I couldn't help but laugh and grin with him.

"Eden, I cannot believe you did it!" he shouted, drawing the attention of the rest of the Resistance.

"Thanks for the vote of confidence," I joked, sitting down on the porch again and recovering from the effort the process demanded.

"I feel amazing! I completely forgot what it felt like to be normal!" He tested out his magic, picking up heavy objects and moving them about in the air.

Jericho sat down next to me, concern written obviously across his face. "It worked, huh?" he asked, clearly not trusting Sebastian now that he was not weak and incapacitated.

"Yes, it did. I know exactly what to do now when we get to Avalon," I smiled, leaning over and resting my head on his shoulder.

"You seem tired," Jericho commented, more misgivings affecting his tone.

"I'll be Ok," I mumbled, closing my eyes. I *was* tired, exhausted in fact, but I also felt better. I had taken an entire magic out of my blood and my energy was more relaxed because of it.

"So what are you going to do with him now? Should we restrain him?" Jericho asked. I was happy someone didn't trust him. I knew that my attachment to Sebastian was completely out of place and irrational, especially now that he possessed magic again.

"I was thinking about another prisoner exchange," I sat up and opened my eyes, gauging Jericho's reaction. My guilt was still thick from the last exchange that I forgot Jericho didn't know the specifics.

"That's a good idea," Jericho agreed. "Who did you have in mind?"

"I suppose a Prince should be worth something, hmmm?" Jericho nodded his agreement. "Worth maybe four, tired, magic-less Immortal's?"

Jericho's eyes lit up with revelation; he smiled at Sebastian who was having a contest with Titus over who could lift the heaviest object, Sebastian with his magic, Titus with his brute strength. "Clever, Eden. Very clever."

"We'll see if it works, I am learning the hard way that Lucan is not an idiot," I mumbled.

"But his favorite nephew might be good enough incentive," Jericho countered and I hoped he was right.

"This time, let's just make sure Lucan is the one on the other end of the phone." I stood up, angry at the memory of Morocco.

Jericho stared after me with a hundred questions, but I never wanted to have that conversation. I walked over to Sebastian, hoping he still wanted to go home.

## Chapter Thirty-Four

"Ok, do you remember what you're going to say?" I asked Sebastian. With a sour look on his face, he held Gabriel's cell phone, flipping it over and over in his hands.

"Are you sure you want to trade me?" he asked and I took a step back in disbelief.

Sebastian was sitting in the living room, on the over-stuffed couch at Aunt Syl's, full of magic and attitude. I wondered if I would have problems with him once he was feeling better, but it was the contrary. He was more involved with the Resistance, helping others train, offering to assist with meals and cleaning up after everyone. At first, I chalked it up to all of the energy he had with his magic back, but now I was starting to worry that he felt like he was one of us.

"Yes, Sebastian! I'm sorry if you don't want to go home, but I can't trust you for one, and second, I need to get those guys back their magic, and not even for their sakes! Physically, I need to get rid of more magic!" Exhausted mentally, physically and emotionally I held on to the hope that once I gave Avalon's old team back their magic, I would feel a hundred times better.

"Eden, of course I want to go home. I mean, obviously.... I mean, clearly, you are the bad guys, it's just that, aren't you worried I know too much?" he questioned, squinting his eyes at me.

"What? What do you know?" I demanded, wondering if he did know something but then dismissed the idea immediately. The only thing that could possibly hurt us was our plan for the first of May, but Jericho and I hadn't even told the rest of the Resistance yet so I was sure that it was impossible for him to know any of those details.

"Well," he started, searching deeply for information that would grant him stay, "I saw your parents, that's something."

"Ok, but your uncle knew they were here, he sent Guards after them," I answered, remembering the team of Titans that swept through Omaha without even paying the rest of us a visit. They pursued my parents and only my parents.

"All right, well what about this? I know how you can give magic back, that kind of information cannot fall into the wrong hands, and you never know what they might do with it!" He had yet to be even slightly convincing.

"Sebastian, what? What would they do with it?" I asked,

genuinely curious how that kind of information could hurt me. I struggled to picture Lucan working as hard as I did to quell my magic and set it free.

"What about your relationship with Jericho?" His eyes lit up as if that was the most brilliant idea he had ever had and he pointed his finger between the two of us rapidly.

"I would actually prefer it if you let that be known," I rolled my eyes, "now call Lucan!"

"Fine," he huffed, turning on the phone and dialing the number.

"Make sure you talk to Lucan, Sebastian," I quickly reminded him, dreading another Morocco fiasco. "I'm serious; make sure you get Lucan on the phone. You know what; just put it on speaker phone, that will make it easier." I tried to grab the phone from him to do it myself, but he brushed my hands away, working swiftly to obey.

Now Jericho and I could hear the dial tone, while Sebastian held it away from his face. The phone rang for a while before Talbott answered the other end.

"Talbott, it's Sebastian, can I speak with Kiran?" Sebastian asked politely. I immediately started waving my arms in the air to get Sebastian's attention quietly, cutting my finger across my throat and reminding him non-verbally, that I wanted to speak with Lucan.

"What are you doing? Stop it! There are proper channels one must use! Just relax," Sebastian covered the mouth piece of the phone with his hand and whispered to me harshly. "Sorry about that," he said, tuning back into the conversation Kiran was trying to have on the other end of the phone. "Hello, Cousin."

"Bastian? How are you? Are you all right?" Kiran was overly surprised, and happy to hear from his cousin. I was equally surprised to find that the sound of Kiran's voice didn't bother me tonight. No flood of emotion or torrent of memories troubled me; it was just my enemy on the other end of the phone and I was fine with that.

"Yes, I'm all right. How are you doing? I was glad to hear you're better," Sebastian said sincerely and I couldn't stop from rolling my eyes again, while the two of them caught up. I kicked Sebastian in the shin aggressively to remind him there was a point to this phone call. "Ow!" he shouted, and glared up at me. "Hey, Kiran, sorry to move along so quickly, but I need to speak with your father, is he available?"

"He is around, but he won't get on the telephone, can I pass along a message?" Kiran asked, sounding severely curious.

"Actually, the leader of the Rebellion would like to have a word with him; it's rather important I'm afraid," Sebastian sighed, and *I* didn't even believe his sincerity.

"Really? The leader of the Rebellion? Will she speak to me?" Suddenly Kiran's interest was piqued and I couldn't stop the blush from finding my cheeks.

"Just give me the phone," I snapped, not wanting anything else said over speaker phone.

I fumbled with the cell phone until it was no longer a conversation that the room could hear, and then I left the living room and went into the garage, feeling very self-conscious with Jericho and Sebastian listening in.

I cleared my throat and took a breath before speaking, "Kiran, if I want to discuss something with your father, is there someone else I could talk with? The head Titan, or a human resources director or something?" I started out politely, although I was seconds away from threatening my way to what I wanted.

"Eden," he started with the same measured civility, "you're talking to him."

"Because that worked so well last time," I accused.

"I thought it did," he laughed gently into the phone. This was not the way I wanted the phone call to go.

"I have a prisoner that I would like to return if you are interested," I ignored his comment and got straight to business.

"I hope you mean Sebastian," Kiran said and there was suddenly a very hard edge to his voice.

"I do," I agreed, taken back by his anger.

"It's about bloody time," he growled into the phone and then found his composure again, "And what do you want in return? Don't bother asking for Avalon."

"I want the four prisoners without magic," I decided not to play games this time. Sebastian was worth a lot more than Talbott as far as political prisoners went, and because he wasn't in any hurry to go anywhere, it wasn't as if I absolutely had to get rid of him.

"Really? Why?" Kiran asked, almost mocking my request.

"Do we have a deal?" I refused to let him derail the conversation.

"How long do I have to consider this deal?" Kiran inquired and I didn't know if I could take him seriously or not. I regretted not making Jericho take the call.

"Do you want to discuss this with your father?" I pushed. I really wanted Lucan to be aware of what was going on this time. I wanted him to know that I was in control and that I had my own bargaining chips.

"My father would never negotiate with you," Kiran sighed.

"You do realize I could easily keep Sebastian and kill him, don't you?" I grew frustrated.

"In my father's eyes, Sebastian is already dead," Kiran said with a hint of contempt thickening his tone. "You have a deal. I'll make things easy and come to you."

"No, there's absolutely no need for you to come all the way here," I stomped my foot in the empty garage.

"Would you rather meet in the desert?" his voice got low and husky and I rushed to answer him.

"That is not what I meant," I defended myself. "I mean, you personally do not have to come, you could just send Talbott if you're not going to involve your father." I breathed deeply, searching for my patience, "And Kiran, what happened in the desert will never happen again. Not ever."

"We'll meet you at the private club tomorrow night at eight," he ignored my promise, changing the subject.

"Absolutely not," I argued, picturing his underground club as the perfect place for him to set a trap. "We can meet tomorrow night at Kingsley, the center courtyard."

"Fine," he agreed. "I take it you won't be coming alone?"

I hung up the phone, not even dignifying him with an answer.

----

I stood in the moonlit bathed courtyard of Kingsley feeling severely out of place. I never considered myself a high school dropout until now, waiting for Kiran and his Guard to arrive. I looked up at the brick, academic buildings surrounding me and realized I felt more at home at Kingsley than anywhere else, and yet I would never return.

With Amory gone, and until I could claim leadership over the entire Kingdom, a high school education was last on my long to-do-list. Besides, I made it almost all the way through my junior year; that was probably as good of an education as I needed.

Then it dawned on me that I never finished a full year my entire high school career. Magic always got in the way.

I wondered for a moment what it would have been like to live a normal human life. Would I have had lots of friends? Or gone to prom? Or had a normal, non-royalty, non-rebellious boyfriend? Then the hairs on the back of my neck stood up and my blood began to prickle with warning that the Titans had arrived.

I breathed in slowly, wanting to find complete control before I was face to face with my enemies. I turned around to address the entire team gathered with me but my eyes met Sebastian's and I realized that I wanted to talk to him the most.

"Sebastian," I whispered in the darkness, "I'm sorry, I'm using you again. I'm sorry; I didn't keep my end of our deal."

Surprisingly, he pulled me into a hug, squeezing me tightly and lifting me off the ground, "I should have known better than to expect you to, but that's all right, you made up for it!" He set me down and smiled at me. "Thank you for my magic, I think I've learned a valuable lesson through all of this," his smile turned roguish and I couldn't help but laugh.

"As long as you've given up your spy days, you're always welcome back with us," I offered, surprising myself.

"You could just keep kidnapping me," he joked, "you might be able to get a few more prisoners out of me before they catch on."

"I think you have Stockholm Syndrome," Titus interrupted playfully, and I left Sebastian to say goodbye to his new best friend.

"He does kind of grow on you, doesn't he?" Jericho grumbled, still not really sold on Sebastian.

"Like a rash," I agreed.

"Hey, are you going to be Ok tonight?" Jericho looked down at me with smoldering eyes and a clenched jaw. I knew he was anticipating meeting Kiran face to face with a current of silent rage pumping wildly through his blood. His magic radiated off him in waves of hatred and I suddenly felt like I needed to comfort him.

I felt the Titans surround the courtyard, offering as much protection for their Crown Prince as they could. There were not more than our numbers, maybe twenty-five. I felt Kiran's magic in the distance, watching us, waiting for the right moment. I could feel his eyes on me, even from far away; his movements filled my consciousness.

I stayed gazing into Jericho's eyes, worried about him, and now finding my resolve shrinking. I reached up to his collar, pulling it towards me and I met his mouth with frenzied desperation.

I kissed him aggressively, forcefully pushing my magic into his, allowing myself to wrap completely up in him. I had to find courage and strength and remember that even if I still felt hated feelings for Kiran, there was life after him. There was love after him.

A throat cleared from across the stone path and I relinquished my hold on a bewildered Jericho. I didn't completely pull away though, I held his gaze, smiling encouragingly. We could do this.... together we could do this.

I glanced back at Sebastian, to make sure Titus and Gabriel grabbed hold of him to make him appear more like a prisoner than a reluctant martyr. Sebastian hung his head as if standing in the midst of us was a struggle all of its own. I shook my head, trying to wipe away the smile and then walked forward to meet Kiran and Talbott, Jericho at my side.

"I will not conduct business with anyone but you," Kiran growled standing underneath the bell tower. He stared Jericho down with equal contempt and disgust; I couldn't help but find that a little bit satisfying.

"Then we have no deal," I replied casually, and turned to walk away.

"Eden, it's fine, really," Jericho offered before I could leave completely.

I turned to him quickly, hating that he trusted me so much. He gave me an inspiring nod of the head and I wanted to run into his arms again and never leave them.

"Fine," I cleared my throat, forcing courage forward, "but then Talbott has to go too."

"Fine," Kiran echoed and tipped his head for Talbott to obey.

We were suddenly very alone in the shadows of the bell tower. Our individual backup felt worlds away. This was better than Morocco; we were not actually alone. There was nothing to seduce my senses, but still a palpable tension between our magics made business awkward to conduct.

"You gave Sebastian his magic back?" Kiran looked down at me, his eyes the deepest, intense blue.

"Yes," I sighed.

"Why?" he asked, almost taunting me.

"I have my reasons," I snapped, growing impatient. "Where are the prisoners?"

"They're here, but first we need to talk." He chewed on the inside of his cheek. He was completely serious; there was no smirk, no sarcasm, not even a hint of amusement, so I narrowed my eyes and listened. "Have you thought any more about my offer?"

"What offer?" I stalled, not wanting to answer the question.

"To take your brother's place?" he asked flatly.

"No, I haven't thought about it and my answer remains the same," I insisted strongly.

"There has been an amendment," he continued slowly, and for the first time I noticed that he was holding his magic back from mine. "My father wishes you to know that if you would rather be sacrificed, that can be arranged."

"Do you mean instead of marrying you and producing your hundreds of children?" I mocked.

"Yes, an heir isn't really necessary now with my father's elevated circumstances and if I had your magic then that would be that," he explained quietly, but every syllable was crisply clipped as if the words were hard to say.

"I'll have to think about that one," I laughed, sarcasm thick in my tone.

"You have until the wedding," Kiran threatened. "May first my father will sacrifice your brother, magic or no, you have until then." He gestured to his Guards, and they produced the four prisoner's, pushing them forward roughly.

I motioned the same way and then tried to ignore the snickers from Titus and Sebastian as Titus tried to treat Sebastian with equaled cruelty. The Guards from either side moved forward and worked out the details to simultaneously exchange while Kiran and I observed.

"Eden, it's time to start taking my offer seriously, you are running out of time," he whispered fiercely.

"Like I said, I'll think about it," I vowed back, the new offer striking a reluctant chord in my mind.

"You could do better than him," Kiran accused, with just a slightly louder, angrier tone, staring across the dark courtyard at Jericho.

"Well, I've certainly done worse," I mumbled and then the prisoners were deposited on their respective sides of the war and everyone backed away slowly, carefully disappearing into the night, vanishing back to the opposite corners of our world.

## Chapter Thirty-Five

I sat down, utterly exhausted. I dismissed Ronan Hannigan, too tired even to hear him say thank you. He happily walked to his teammates, who were all marveling at their restored magic. The four of them had been without magic the longest of anyone that I stole from and were weak, tired shells of people when they came back from Romania.

So far, they had thanked me at least a million times, but I assured them that I was the one who was grateful. The process of giving their magic back took everything out of me, but I couldn't believe how much better my magic felt. My blood, finally, had room to stretch out and move around, and it felt wonderful.

The moon, a perfect orb of illumination tonight, at its fullest and brightest, shined down on the broken farm. The sky sparkled with millions of stars, perfectly visible this far from city lights. I breathed in the crisp spring air, and sighed. These moments made me perfectly happy never to leave Omaha again.

Gabriel walked over from cleaning up the meal of roasted hotdogs and s'mores. Our community now consisted of almost thirty, and Aunt Syl took over planning meals and assigning chores, which I found a bit ironic since it was nothing like how she ran her own household.

She took a leave of absence from work to spend as much time with me as possible before we left again. I hadn't told her about the mission yet, but she knew we wouldn't stay in Omaha for long. I decided that when I got back from Romania, she would need to quit her job altogether. I couldn't be leaving her alone, unprotected and vulnerable, while I was off trying to save the world. Whether Lucan respected Angelica or not, he would not stay his rage once I brought Avalon home; and then, Aunt Syl would be in serious danger.

For now though, I was simply thankful for her, thankful for this time we could spend together, for her love and understanding, and her listening ear, an ability that very few people grasped with such grace.

I didn't know what the other end of this mission held for me. If I was honest with myself, I admitted that there was a greater chance that I was not coming back than rescuing Avalon and escaping alive. But, I repressed the doubt; there wasn't any substantial reason to believe it. We had a good plan, a capable team and vengeance was on our side.

Gabriel sat down slowly next to me, always in his priest's outfit.

He was characteristically moving his fingers sequentially over his rosary beads, as if perpetually in prayer. He had been reluctant to leave my side at all after he saved me in India and so I was used to his quiet presence, his worn prayer beads and his fiery eyes.

"I think it's time to call Silas," I whispered, hesitantly, not wanting to interrupt the perfection of the night with talk about missions and death.

"Should he leave tonight?" Gabriel asked, not questioning my motives.

"Yes, if he can," I answered, hoping he was ready for what I was going to ask him to do. I hoped everybody was ready for what I was going to ask them to do. I swallowed the oppressive guilt and premature anguish; people would die on both sides for this cause, and for Avalon. It was a heavy cross to bear. Even if they were Titans, they were still my people and I struggled with sacrificing even one life.

"And then will you tell us our mission?" Gabriel the wise warrior could feel the task ahead even if there were no specific orders yet.

"Yes, Jericho will hold a briefing," I replied.

"It should come from you. You are the leader, and we are all here to follow you," he whispered with the strength of a thousand men.

"You're right," I sighed, reminding myself of the resonating truth of his words. I was the reluctant leader, hungry for vengeance, blinded by erratic emotions. Avalon was the real leader, he built the Resistance, he was wise and discerning, and he never questioned his cause or doubted his intuition. My heart fluttered wildly in my chest, and my blood flared with determination. I had to get him out, no matter the price; the Rebellion needed him if we wanted a hope of winning this war, more than they needed me with my tragic past and ties to their enemies.

Gabriel stood up to call Silas. And I stood up to find Aunt Syl and Lilly. They were sitting together on some of the gathered debris picked up from around the farm. Lilly leaned against Aunt Syl, they were laughing quietly and enjoying the night. I slowed down for a moment, taking in the sight of them. They were my best friends, and Aunt Syl was the only mother I had ever known. I wanted to remember them like that forever, happy, healthy, and laughing.

"Hey!" Lilly called, sitting up when she saw me approach. "What are you up to?" she patted the seat next to her, inviting me to join them.

I took it gratefully, treasuring the moments of peace we had tonight. "I should probably gather everyone together and have a meeting," I mumbled, dreading every upcoming minute.

"Oh, are we going on a mission?" Lilly asked, trying to act surprised.

Jericho and I decided to keep the exact specifics of the mission quiet until closer to departure, so few details about my parent's whereabouts and plans were floating around. We trusted the Resistance completely, but certainty in our situation was never a guarantee. Titans could sweep in at any moment to start conflict and if someone were kidnapped, Lucan would stop at nothing to get what he wanted.

It was actually a miracle that the Titan Guard hadn't hunted us down by now. We weren't exactly hiding. Jericho thought they were too busy preparing for the wedding and now that the entire royal family was safe behind the walled Citadel, we hoped they felt isolated and protected.

Besides, we were yet to be much of a threat. Lucan had Avalon, the date was set, and I was warned. An obnoxious nagging feeling sat at the base my neck that Lucan expected me, and he stayed his Guard for that reason. Why waste resources when in a few days I would be coming to him?

And he would be right. I would be coming to him. Only I wouldn't be coming alone.

Even though Jericho and I kept the details of the mission secret, the mission itself wouldn't be much of a surprise. Everyone knew about the wedding date and about Avalon. It wasn't hard for them to put two and two together.

"Oh yes, we are going on a mission!" I tried to be excited, but it came out sarcastically.

Lilly laughed at me, throwing her arm around my shoulders, "Do you know that I never doubted you?" she turned serious, her emerald eyes shining with sincerity, "I always trusted you would come for me. After they took us that night, we weren't allowed to talk of course, but if something was said, if anyone dared to speak up, it was to promise the others that you would come for them. Everyone believes in you, Eden, everyone. The Titans are scared of you and even Lucan will not tolerate your name spoken in his presence."

"That cannot be true," I whispered, trying to find some reason I had given people to fear me.

"It is true, you frighten them. Whatever this mission is about, you have the upper hand just by being you!" She was so sweet, so honest that I had no choice but to believe her.

"Well, that's a start, I guess," I agreed, deciding that it was great that people were afraid of me, but right now I needed them to want to follow me and that was an entirely different matter.

"I'll get everyone together," Lilly offered. Her out-going manner surprised me. She had become a completely different person than when we met, not even a year ago. She used to be shy and timid, suffering in a life that demanded she hide her identity. Even if she was still a little bashful now, she had grown to be assertive, brave and decisive. Her parents were imprisoned, her life just as much ripped from her as it had been from me. Yet revenge did not engulf her, she simply believed in her convictions and stepped forward with determined action.

I watched in awe as she flitted from group to group, giving them instructions and holding short conversations with almost everybody. She knew the team members infinitely better than I did. I wondered if I would always be a loner.

"What are you thinking about?" Aunt Syl asked, offering another voice in my head. She scooted closer to me, replacing Lilly's arm with her own.

"Oh, I don't know," I smiled, not wanting to get into my real thoughts; they were not nearly as deep as Aunt Syl expected them to be.

"When will you leave?" she pressed, her voice husky and strained.

"Two days," I suddenly had a hard time finding my voice as well.

"Well, Jericho has claimed you tomorrow night, but tomorrow, during the day, I want you all to myself, Ok?" When I nodded, not completely understanding her meaning, and fighting back the tears, she continued, "We are definitely going to need pedi's, right? You cannot go into battle with unpainted toes!"

I laughed at her, wondering when the last time we had actually really laughed together was. It had been a very long time and I couldn't help but hope that tomorrow would be full of it. If things didn't work out in Romania, I wondered if I would ever get the chance to laugh again.

The teams gathered around one lone barn light, the only one still working, shining down like a spotlight. Jericho walked to the front, pulling me aside and out of the light.

"Before we get started, I just wanted to ask you.... I mean, do you have plans tomorrow night?" He asked softly, blushing from the collar of his shirt to the top of his forehead.

"Nope, no plans," I replied. This must be what Aunt Syl was talking about and if he was going to ask me on a date, I was going to make him actually ask me.

He smiled at me for a moment, as if searching for the right words, "Then, would you like to go on a date with me? I mean, I know it might seem kind of pointless the night before we leave for a mission and maybe even a little silly, but I just thought it would-"

I cut him off with a finger to his lips. "I would love to go on a date with you."

"Good." His hazel eyes smoldered and the color from his blush enhanced his perfect skin. He was absolutely charming and I was thankful for the opportunity to look forward to something. "Well, then, I'd better start this meeting."

"Actually, would you mind if I explained everything?" I mumbled self-consciously, hoping he would, but he turned and smiled, backing out of the light and giving me complete authority.

I cleared my throat nervously and then began, "So, most of you have probably figured out by now that we are planning something for the royal wedding. Lucan has decided the perfect wedding gift for his son would be the meaningless murder of my brother," I spoke up loudly, finding strength in the anger of my sizzling blood. "Avalon doesn't even have any magic right now, so the whole thing is obviously a ploy to get us to react. Well, ask and you shall receive, because we are sure as hell going to give him a reaction."

I paused for a few moments, surprised by the clapping and whistling from the crowd. I glanced at Jericho nervously, but he just smiled encouragingly and nodded for me to go on.

"Our plan is simple and straightforward. We are going to rely some on the reaction from our enemies, but mostly we are trusting in your skill and experience. Getting into the Citadel unnoticed will be the trickiest part, the entire Guard will be there, or what's left of them," more cheering from the crowd and I had to laugh at that. "They will have every exit and entrance watched. I will meet my parents hours before the rest of you arrive, we will break into the Citadel without magic before the ceremony starts and find Avalon. The Citadel will no doubt be crawling with Titans from every direction. Jericho is going to lead the rest of you into the wilderness outside the walls and create a diversion. Your goal is to draw out as many Titans as possible, distract them to the outside, while we take what is ours, from inside. Let me remind you that we are not there to enjoy the party or stick around. This is simply a get in, get out situation. Our goal is Avalon, not anything else. Once, we have him out safely, you have to get out of there just as fast. The Titans will not be playing around; but don't worry about them, just get yourselves out of there as safely and as quickly as possible. Any questions?"

"What if the diversion doesn't work? What if they are expecting that?" Te Che asked, his hand around his wife's waist and his eyes more worried than the rest of the groups.

"Delia, Justice and I will still be able to move around the castle without magic. Our tunnel into the Citadel will take us directly into the castle completely undetected. Worst-case scenario, my mother has decided to go directly to Lucan and beg for her son's life. Now, we all know that will not get us anywhere, but while that is happening it will act as a backup decoy. The only thing that would change at that point is that our rescue mission would include two of my family members instead of just one," I answered, authoritatively. I wondered if I was getting the hang of this whole leadership thing.

"What happens if Avalon dies? Will they get any of his magic?" Caden Halstead asked, looking completely disgusted.

"I cannot be sure, but I want to say no. I possess all of Avalon's magic; he doesn't have anything except maybe the most miniscule amount." I insisted, putting more than just Caden's fears to rest. "But they won't kill Avalon, I will never let that happen," I spat defensively, "Next question?"

"When do we leave?" Titus shouted, full of energy and excitement.

"The day after tomorrow. Everyone will stagger commercial flights and then meet at a safe-house in Timisoara before moving towards the Citadel. Gabriel and I will take a smaller plane directly to Sibiu." I explained, absolutely dreading the idea of riding in another airplane with Gabriel, but he insisted on taking me; Jericho would be busy organizing everyone else.

"So what are the plans for the diversion?" Naima asked, her pink eyes flashing fuchsia with excitement.

"I'll let Jericho explain those details," I handed over the floor to Jericho who took command with practiced charm.

I sat back down next to Aunt Syl who had not moved from the pile of debris. She looked at me for a moment, her face completely unreadable. She was afraid, almost terrified, but calm at the same time as if she was expecting this moment. As I snuggled closely to her, and I looked back out into the crowd I realized I felt the same way. Fear nearly paralyzed me; something was not right, something was out of place in our plan and that terrified me. But, at the same time it was like I was expecting these feelings, I knew they were long in the making.

## Chapter Thirty-Six

I felt pretty. Aunt Syl pampered me the whole day. She took me to get my hair and nails done, a much needed deep tissue massage, and then shopping for dresses that I had absolutely no need for. The day was completely extravagant and most certainly unnecessary, but it was what Aunt Syl had always loved to do with me and I didn't have the heart to tell her that I preferred split ends and chipped fingernails when storming a castle.

I did have use for at least one of the dresses though. I changed into a lavender halter-top summery dress that had a full skirt ending a couple inches above my knees. I let my hair down, pulling it over my shoulder and tying it loosely with a hair-tie. I did my best to hide the glowing tattoo that I noticed distracted most people during conversations. My black tangles were freshly cut and styled so the curls had more construction than normal, and the frizz was well under control.

I worked at my make-up for the first time in months. More than just eyeliner I used powder and shadows, mascara and even blush, reminding myself that I was a girl and capable of being pretty.

Jericho was already downstairs, making dinner. We would not even leave the house for our date, but for me, tonight, it was the perfect way to celebrate the evening.

I took off the necklace that hadn't left my chest in months and laid it on my dresser. The emerald engagement ring sparkled next to the dull, obsidian stone and I looked away quickly, not able to listen to its silent accusations.

I slipped on some silver, six-inch pumps for good measure and mostly because I knew that it would be a very long time before I would get another chance to wear heels again and walked downstairs.

The house was empty except for Jericho. Aunt Syl had taken Lilly out for the night and I assumed she was reenacting her day with me on poor, unsuspecting Lilly.

I could smell Jericho's cooking from upstairs, and whatever it was smelled amazing. When I walked into the kitchen, he was busy stirring something on the stove and adding spices from different glass containers. I leaned against the doorframe watching his expert precision as he tasted and re-tasted everything to make sure it was to his liking.

He had gotten a haircut today too, and the stray curls at the bottom of his collar had disappeared. He was wearing a white collared shirt with the sleeves pushed up to his elbow and a brown vest that screamed his style. I expected an apron tied around his waist, but decided he was probably too advanced and skilled to need any kind of protective garment.

"Don't be shy, come on in," he announced coyly, with his back still to me.

"Oh, I'm not shy, I was just watching the master in his domain," I replied.

"It's almost done; we're just waiting on the rice...." He turned his burners down and then checked the oven before turning around to greet me properly.

Jericho stood across the kitchen gazing at me and the faintest hint of a smile turned the corners of his lips. He let his eyes sweep over me appreciatively in the gentlest of ways and then slowly walked over to me, pulling me into his arms.

He kissed me with his soft, warm lips, carefully moving them against mine. "Is this Ok?" he pulled away for a moment, until I could answer him with an "Uh, huh," and a kiss of my own.

Our magics, now accustomed to finding each other, moved around us in connected bliss. I pressed my body against his, fully valuing who he was and how he made me feel. He was a great leader and could command armies, but when he was with me, he didn't always have the perfect words. He was passionate and courageous in battle, but with me, he was gentle and careful. He was honest with me always, not even allowing a hint of manipulation between us and he was like that from the beginning, from the first time I asked about Lilly in prison. He let me fight, without the desperation to protect me. There were times when he wanted to defend me, wanted to go with me and fight at my side, but he gave me the room I needed to become the warrior that the Rebellion needed. He respected me, he pushed me to be a better leader and what I loved most about him was that he put my brother, this mission, and our cause all before our relationship.

I knew that he loved me. I had known for a long time. But, Jericho did not pursue the relationship in these last several months; he dedicated himself to our mission and to rescuing Avalon. That is what I needed in a man.

I didn't want him swept away with me and forget everything else, or fight only to save me. Life held consequences and real responsibility, and Jericho understood that. Our personal relationship played second to a cause that would come first in my life until I could destroy every opposition. Jericho not only respected that but fought side by side with me believing in the same purpose.

Even with all of that, all of the reasons to love him and to wait for him until after everything was decided, still his kiss sent butterflies fluttering in my stomach and my magic tingling from excitement. This wasn't the all-consuming love that I had for Kiran, but it was the healthy, rational love that I needed, the only kind of love that I wanted.

"I think something's boiling over," I mumbled, breaking our kiss and moving my eyes to the stove where a pot of something yellow was spilling onto the stove.

Jericho jumped back, stopping the spill with his magic and sprinting back to the boiling pot. I watched him clean up the mess with practiced skill and turn off the stove completely. When he finished he spun around to me.

"Dinner is ready." He smiled sheepishly, gesturing at the dining room table that was set for two.

A beautiful bouquet of spring tulips and lit candles decorated the center of the table; my aunt let him borrow her fine china. The chairs sat closer together, one at the head of the table and one on the side.

"Can I help you set the table?" I offered, feeling useless.

"No, I've got it, just sit down." He waved me away, walking to the table with a big pot of yellowish stew and another pot of rice. He returned to the oven and pulled out delicious smelling bread that reminded me of India.

"Did you make Indian?" I gasped, my mouth suddenly drooling.

"Well, Avalon mentioned how much you loved the food over there, I mean before.... so anyway, I thought that I would make you something I knew that you liked." He sat down next to me, dishing up for the two of us.

"This is absolutely amazing," I gushed, floored by his kitchen accomplishments and willingness to serve.

We ate in silence for a few minutes; I was too busy devouring his food to bother with conversation. I couldn't believe how authentic his curry was and how delicious everything tasted.

"Wow, Jericho, this is really.... it's so good! I'm just so impressed!" I set my fork down for a minute, afraid I would eat my weight in Indian food.

"Well, good." He blushed at my compliments.

"So, are you ready for tomorrow?" I asked, pushing my plate forward and turning the conversation more serious.

"Sure, I'm ready," he said passively, but I could hear the confidence resound in his voice. "What about you? Are you ready?"

"I'm most scared about the trip over there! Do you think Gabriel will mind if we take the Cessna?" I asked, hoping Jericho would take me seriously.

"You know, I could fly over with you, you don't have to go with Gabriel," Jericho offered, his serious eyes reflecting his concern about our separation.

"I know you could, and I've thought about it.... but I think everyone needs you to greet them at the safe-house. I mean, you're really the one running this show...." I trailed off, not knowing how to explain to Jericho that I needed space from him before the mission. I needed to focus and forget about love and relationships and get ready to lay it all down for Avalon.

"You're probably right, I just.... I can't help but feel like.... I'm just worried about you, that's all," he found his words, reaching forward and pulling me towards him. I kissed him sweetly, pressing my mouth against his in wordless promises that there was nothing to worry about. "Come on, let's leave this for later and go someplace more comfortable."

He held my hand, leading me into the living room and onto the couch. He lit the fire with his magic and I cuddled close to him, sinking down into the soft cushions. He radiated warm and happy magic. I couldn't imagine leaving his arms for the coldness of a mission tomorrow, or wanting to belong anywhere else than next to him for the rest of my life.

"This is nice," I sighed, breathing deeply and setting my magic free. I didn't realize I was holding it back, a natural reaction from old habits. When my magic met Jericho's it was like taking a full breath, breathing in deeply just to let it out slowly again. He supplied safety and happiness, everything I wanted.

"We've been through a lot together, huh?" he commented quietly, resting his lips against my hair.

"Yes we have," I agreed and then sat up to stare him in the eyes, "like the first time we met and you threw me off the rooftop!" I gasped, surprised that I still remembered how to flirt.

"I didn't throw you!" he defended himself. "You fell off!"

"No way! You totally pushed me!" I laughed, settling back down into the nook of his arm.

"Well, in my defense, I didn't think you would really get hurt, you are Immortal after all," he mumbled, still laughing at me.

"Do you really think that? Do you really think I'm Immortal?" I asked, and the tone of the conversation was suddenly sober.

"I do think that," Jericho answered, his tone matching my own. "I mean, I thought the same thing about Amory and eventually the world outlived him, but when you look at a life as long as his, it's hard not to say that he was anything but."

"You're right," I agreed, remembering my grandfather before he died. Death offered peace for him, like going home. I had watched him slip away into the other side of eternity with a smile on his face and eyes that looked towards heaven and I envied him.

"Why do you ask?" he whispered, his voice hoarse and thoughtful.

"I don't know, it's just that I haven't known about magic for even an entire year yet, but these last few months have already felt like a life time. I can't imagine fighting battles like this forever. I can't imagine Lucan as my enemy for the rest of time. And if I'm Immortal, surely, after Amory's death Lucan is too. And the King's goal is to make his son just as allergic to death as we are. If it's going to be the three of us fighting for all of eternity, I think I will just give Kiran my magic and call it quits! Doesn't that sound awful?" I whined, truly afraid of the words I was speaking.

"It won't just be the three of you, though, we are going to get Avalon back. You might as well consider his company guaranteed, and then your parents. They will at least live for a very, very long time. And then your husband, whoever you choose for that role; I mean, he'll share your magic so.... I mean, he will also be Immortal," Jericho finished his point slowly, as if he hadn't meant to bring the last part of it up.

"Oh, right! My husband. I forgot about him! I wonder what he will be like?" I tried to remain serious, and get under Jericho's skin, but I couldn't keep a straight face.

"He's going to have to be a patient man," Jericho teased, "a very patient man."

"Hey now! That's not very nice!" I acted offended, but, secretly, I agreed with him.

"Eden," his tone changed back to serious, and I could sense the direction he was going before he said anything else. Butterflies attacked my stomach and I could feel my cheeks blush with anticipation. "I'm a patient man," he whispered and I breathed in deeply with confirmation that he still loved me.

Logically, I knew that he did, but emotionally, I needed to hear him verbalize his feelings. He said the words before, but I wasn't ready to hear them. And now that my heart was ready, now that I was subconsciously planning our future and not having a single thought that didn't include him, now that Kiran was an embarrassing memory and my magic had moved on, now I would hear those words and say them back. I would believe them and hope that he believed me.

"I know that you are," I admitted, turning my face to his. "You were patient all this time. I had to find myself first; I had to remember who I was and become the person I was meant to be. You have been there for me patiently while I searched for you, even when I didn't know I was looking for you, you were there."

"And, did you find me?" he asked, nuzzling his nose against mine.

"Mmmm... hmm.... I did, I found you," I closed my eyes, relishing every moment of our togetherness.

"I love you, Eden, I always have," he whispered sweetly and I almost cried at his sincerity.

"I love you, too," I answered honestly, and with all that was left of me.

He kissed me then, sealing our commitment to each other with a kiss. Our magics pressed against each other, refusing to leave one another and my lips mimicked the sentiment. I loved Jericho in the way two people are supposed to love each other, with trust, commitment and honesty.

We settled down, nestling into each other and falling asleep on the couch. We had eternity before us, there was no need to hurry, no need to rush things. Part of me felt like we had been together for a long time, and that he was always my intended destiny once life had turned upside down. And the other part of me felt like for the first time, tonight, with our words and purpose for each other we were finally together and I had been waiting forever to be with him.

I curled up, even closer to him, offering him my future and

trusting him with what was left of my heart. I struggled to get closer, finding it hard to get comfortable and relax. I argued with myself that I was just panicking, that I had been hurt before and so I wasn't willing to trust happiness that felt too good to be true. But these moments on the couch, with my soul bared and promises whispered felt more like goodbye than the start of something.

I eventually shook the feeling, and fell asleep to his peaceful, measured breathing. I promised myself that all I needed to do was get through Romania, I just needed to get Avalon back and then every night thereafter, could be spent like this with Jericho. I just needed to rescue Avalon first.

# Chapter Thirty-Seven

"Please, Lilly, I'll never forgive myself if something happens to her!" I pleaded, begged and almost cried out to my friend.

"Eden, of course I will stay with her! Of course I will," she said quickly, soothing my desperation. "As long as you're sure you would rather have me stay with Syl, then go?" I could tell that Lilly was disappointed she wouldn't get to go on the mission, but I awoke this morning with the urgent need to protect Aunt Syl and Lilly. I started thinking about the mission and how Lilly was already in prison twice and I decided I couldn't let Lilly risk her life again or leave Aunt Syl alone again, for even a moment. So, because they loved each other so much, and because I couldn't bear it if something happened to either of them, I turned them to each other and forced them to promise me they would take care of the other one.

"Thank you!" I threw my arms around her neck, holding her tightly to me, "You have no idea how much that means to me! I owe you big!"

"Yes, you do," she agreed seriously, pulling away to look at me sternly in the face. "And if you really want to repay me, you'd better come home with Avalon and completely unharmed!" She pointed her finger sternly as if she was already disappointed with me; I hugged her closely again, silently promising that I would.

I eventually let go of my chokehold on her and moved over to Aunt Syl. She reached for me before I could even say a word, holding me as if I was the most loved thing in the entire world. "I love you so much, Eden," she whispered fiercely in my ear, "and I am so very proud of you."

I couldn't say anything back to her, I couldn't even breathe normally; I was too emotional to even express my feelings aloud.

I loved her more than anything, and it killed me to leave her here, while I flew half way around the world. I was so thankful that Lilly agreed to stay. I hoped Lilly would keep them both out of trouble, and instantly I was overjoyed to know that, no matter what happened, they had each other. I promised myself they would be fine here, out of danger. I was the one putting my life at risk and that was infinitely more reassuring for some reason.

After a long time just hugging Aunt Syl, she reluctantly set me free and deposited me into Gabriel's care. I already said goodbye to

Jericho earlier in the morning because he needed to spend the rest of the day organizing all of the teams and their departure times.

Saying goodbye to Jericho proved harder this morning than when I picked up Lilly, even though I knew he would be with me in Romania, and even though I knew that as soon as Avalon was in my possession I would find him and be with him again.

Letting him go this morning was awful. I decided that after this mission, I would find a way to wake up next to him every day for the rest of my life. We loved each other now; we voiced it aloud and we committed ourselves to each other. Leaving for our separate missions meant gambling with higher stakes.

Stakes I wasn't ready to risk yet.

Gabriel was waiting patiently in the cockpit for me to say my goodbyes and climb aboard. I kissed Aunt Syl and Lilly one more time, promising them that I would bring Avalon back safely and with equal magic, I then turned to the Cessna.

Gabriel was more than willing to take my luxury jet over his pitiful, little plane after I suggested it as a possibility. Now, sitting down next to him, I wondered if I was too trusting.

I looked back at the hangar that housed his small deathtrap of a plane and decided that I would risk it anyway. I needed to prepare for a mission, not die of a heart attack before it even started. Besides, he pushed all the right buttons and got the engine started so I determined he couldn't be all bad.... even if his plane did look like a heavy-combat left over from World War II.

"Ok, are you ready?" I asked, as he moved the plane to the runway.

"Of course, why wouldn't I be?" he mumbled, solemnly. He recently re-shaved his head and as usual, he was wearing his dark, aviator sunglasses. I was convinced they were more to shield the world from his burning, orange eyes than protect his vision from the glaring sun that they seemed to made out of. His burgundy, beaded rosary hung around his neck, the perfect accessory to his priestly robe.

We remained silent for a long time. I watched the Nebraska farmland shrink under the rising plane. The landscape turned into small, perfectly shaped squares of green, like a quilted blanket lying comfortably across the earth. The Cessna shot through the full billowy clouds scattering wisps across the wide, blue sky.

"Did Silas get to Omaha Ok?" I asked, breaking the silence and reaching for conversation.

"Yes, late last night," Gabriel responded, his thick Latin accent making even the simplest of phrases sound musical. He was silent again for several minutes before he continued, "He brought his people."

"His people?" I gasped, wondering what prompted him to do that after he made it clear to me they would be no part of my Rebellion.

"Yes, he said that if he was going to follow you, then he would have to take your example and give them a choice. So, when he asked them what they wanted to do, they wanted to come." He shrugged his shoulder casually, as if it were not a big deal.

I sat back against the chair trying to understand the extra numbers and the willingness of Silas's people to help. Even harder to comprehend was that I was an example, that Silas, who was centuries old, looked to me for leadership, and instead of feeling encouraged; I was suddenly heavy with the weight of what that meant. I was not a good leader, but even worse, I was a terrible example. I was emotional, and vindictive and indecisive. Again I was reminded how desperately our cause needed Avalon.

"We need to get Avalon back," I whispered, echoing my anxiety aloud.

"You think he will be a better leader than you?" Gabriel asked, his intuitions hitting the nail on the head.

"I know he will," I promised. "Well, really at this point, anyone would be a better leader than me." I tried to joke, but Gabriel stared ahead, his lips not even hinting at a smile.

"You are not a bad leader, Eden. If there were only success in your life, you would not learn anything. Leadership is experience and you are still young. You still have much to learn about our people and war; it should not come easy to you. If it did, you would be robbed of life's most valuable teacher." He tilted his head as if to agree with himself and I marveled at the anomaly that was Gabriel: part priest, part therapist, part warrior.

"But I cannot afford to learn at the expense of our people," I argued, "I cannot continue to fail when there are lives at stake."

"Do you think you will fail this time?" he asked, his tone never changing.

"I am determined not to," I replied, avoiding a direct answer. I couldn't allow myself to think the question all the way through, I would fight with my life to save Avalon, but if experience was my best teacher then experience would tell me that I was doomed to fail.

"So, you do think you will fail," Gabriel mumbled, coming to his own conclusion.

"I don't know.... I don't want to think that, and it's not that I don't believe in us or in our plan. It's just me; I think. I can't believe in myself. I have no idea what I'm doing, or what is going on half the time. All I have is this weight, this consuming desire for vengeance for my family; that is all that is pushing me. Sometimes I wonder if it's enough.... Other times I think about my parents and how they were forced to live this life of fear away from everyone they love. Then I think of how Amory's life was taken from him and Avalon's situation and how unfair it is for him to be imprisoned without magic. I know there is no other choice but to avenge them, but I hate dragging other innocent people into my fight." I liked the way Gabriel helped me get to the root of my thoughts and down to the very core of what I had never put into words.

"Then you *will* fail," Gabriel stated simply and I looked at him in disbelief. "You are fighting for lies and false truths that you have convinced yourself mean something. None of those things are true, and none of them are worth fighting for." I continued to stare at him, silently willing him to explain. "Your parents are not away from everyone they love, they are where they are because they have each other and it is that love that keeps them away. And Amory's life was not cut short, he lived a full life, and fought a good fight, but he wished for death. He did not struggle against the opportunity, but walked fearlessly forward into the peaceful beyond. And your brother is not there against his will, he is only alive against his will. He knew what the Resistance would mean for him, what the price was, and he offered his life to the cause. Yes, save him, give him back his magic so that he can fight again, fully restored; but do not feel pity for him. He, as any of us would be, is happy to martyr his life for the pursuit of freedom."

I sat silently for a few minutes, letting his words rattle my beliefs and ring true in my ears. He was right.

"You can doubt yourself, you can even doubt your cause, but do not let your fears diminish the hope that your people have in you," he continued, turning his head to look directly at me. His orange eyes flared behind his sunglasses like dime-sized flames dancing against his mahogany skin. "You have called us all to your cause, and demanded that we answer. You, who were raised apart, but born with a spirit that will unite this Kingdom, you are the one that leads this kingdom. It is not just our side that listens to you, but when you stand tall in front of the enemy and bravely petition that they answer for their prejudice, you call into question what they believe and you shake them to their core. This Kingdom is clueless, satisfied with injustice and fattened by wealth, yet you look even the highest Prince in the eye, and challenge his basic instincts and then stay ungratified until they align with yours. This Monarchy must be overturned if our people hope to survive, and you are the wind of change that blows through this Kingdom demanding that not just a few, not just the outcasts and rebels, but that every Immortal stands up and follow you."

My mouth dropped open and I sat floored by his words. At best, I assumed Gabriel felt like he was babysitting me most of the time. Now, with the weight of his words, something began to stir inside me, something I couldn't define yet. But, I started to see how my cause, my individual purpose, had to reach beyond the Rebellion. Change needed to exist in more than people that already saw truth; the Kingdom itself must think differently, to believe in something more and to demand that Lucan and his family step down. I needed a stronger platform.

"There is something else that you need to know," Gabriel called me out of my reflection.

"What is that?" I asked, and when I spoke, my voice was hoarse with conviction.

"Lucan will never let your mother go," Gabriel declared and I realized instantly that he was right. "If she steps foot into that castle or on the side of those walls, she will never leave again."

"What will he do to her?" I whispered, afraid of the answer.

"What would your Prince do to you after centuries of searching for you?" His words hung in the air, threatening me with their dangerous foreboding. "What would he do to Jericho?"

The most chilling thought of all was that I did not know. I did not know what would be my fate or how Kiran would react if this game continued for hundreds of years. And worst of all was what I imagined would happen to Jericho if Kiran got his hands on him at the end. Paralyzed with fear, I thought about how they would treat Jericho in a similar circumstance. I could lay my own fears aside for what fate would await me, but if Jericho were in my father's place, I would not be able to bear it.

"Why did they suggest this? Don't they know how dangerous it is for them?" I demanded, suddenly sick with fear.

"Of course, they know," Gabriel snapped as if he were angry at how I doubted my parents. "The one man they hate most in this world holds their child; what would you sacrifice to bring your own child home?"

Then I saw the mission clearly. There was no plan of escape for them, they never intended to come home or make it back safely to freedom. They would sacrifice themselves to give Avalon a chance at survival.

I was naive and inexperienced. Whether it was Kiran, or Lucan or even my own parents for what they thought would be the good of their children, people manipulated me and moved me around the chessboard of this war. I was too easily influenced.

I was silent for the rest of the trip. I thought about the task ahead of me and completely through the mission, as if I were seeing it anew, with wiser eyes. I couldn't let my parents victimize themselves; it wasn't going to accomplish anything. Instead of one person to save, there would now be three and instead of a stronger Rebellion, two more of its greatest assets would be taken out of the equation. I could even look at our circumstances objectively, without taking into account the love I felt for my parents, and realize their captivity would be a giant step backwards for my cause.

And then, I thought about the diversion tactic in the woods and all of the willing Rebellion forces whose lives were being risked. I knew that the majority of them would survive and that they would execute their plan to victory. Not all of them would make it. This mission sacrificed lives and I could not move forward with a plan in which my parents offered themselves as a trade anyway.

Gabriel was right. What if Jericho did not escape? He would be the first one in and the last one to leave, because of his commitment to leadership. Now that I looked through the mission with new eyes, I knew he had no hope of surviving. If he was captured.... If Kiran hurt him....

My mind was inarguably made up. Maybe I suddenly made up my mind because Gabriel's words finally opened my eyes, helping me see things clearly. Or, maybe I was going forward with the decision already in my subconscious, moving with the innate intuition that my life would always be sacrificed for Avalon.

Fate tasked me with protecting my people, and that included my parents, Avalon and Jericho. I was the only one with the power to stop the bloodshed before it started. I was the only one with the opportunity to save everyone I loved.

Kiran was right all along. I was lying to myself for months. But, now that the wheels of the mission had started to turn and with time running out, I was finally ready to accept his offer.

I was finally ready to forfeit myself for the hope of my people.

## Chapter Thirty-Eight

Gabriel and I said goodbye at the edge of the wilderness just outside of Sighisoara, Romania. A handshake and an intense flare from his orange eyes was all I needed to turn my back on him and courageously walk forward with my individual mission he unknowingly burdened me with.

I didn't bother repressing my magic, I needed it to guide me to the castle and fuel my intention with hot electricity purposed for sacrifice. Afraid, and nervous I walked forward, across the path that Amory and I traversed months before; I continually reminded myself that what I was doing was necessary.

My parents and I determined a meeting time three weeks ago, so I picked up my pace, knowing I would have to be much earlier than them in order to save them. My magic sizzled underneath my skin, rushing wildly with nervous energy and so I let it push me forward as I ran through the wilderness.

I worried that Lucan would send his Titans once they felt my frenetic energy outside their castle and I needed to get to the river before my parents to stop them from breaking into the Citadel. If they arrived at the river and I didn't show, they would assume that both of their children had been taken and their resolve would be strengthened. I needed to leave them a sign. I needed to send them a message to find Jericho and wait for Avalon. And I needed to be long gone before they arrived.

The mountainous forest enclosed me with an eerie quietness. The wildlife seemed stilled by my presence and the distant call of birds lessened as I moved deeper into the mountains. The only audible sounds came from my pounding feet, crunching against the woodland floor and my heavy breathing that echoed in my ears.

When I came with Amory, the darkness of the night had hidden the beauty of this part of the Romanian wilderness. But now, while I ran up mountains and in between budding trees, I breathed in happily the crisp air and let myself enjoy creation. I knew that these were my last moments before death and it felt suddenly surreal to be among such exquisiteness.

By the time I reached the cave mouth, where the river split in two, I was ready. I swallowed my fears and replaced them with courage.

I was doing what was right. I was doing what was necessary. The

Resistance had no chance of success with me as their leader and the rest of my family dead. So, I was not just saving the three lives that I cherished most, but the whole of our people.

I held that truth against my heart, close to the core of my soul so that I would not lose focus or tremble in uncertainty. Whatever happened, my campaign would continue.

The small, two-person rowboat was tied in the same spot that Amory left it months ago and I thought of him with happiness. Gabriel was right; Amory knew exactly what he was doing and he was ready for death.

I could go forward with the same hope, the same peaceful joy. His lifelong goal was to return freedom to his people and he did not breathe his last breath on earth until he felt his cause was in capable hands. I did not realize the truth in his actions until this moment, until I held the rope of a boat he helped me escape in, his granddaughter, his hope of victory for his people.

And now, I would pass the torch of salvation on to my brother. And he would actually know what to do with it.

I stood for a moment on the riverbank, deciding how to send my parents a clear message. I took off my backpack, throwing it on the soggy riverbank and scrawled a quick message on an old receipt from my wallet.

*Find Jericho. He will have Avalon. I love you both.*

I turned the rowboat around with magic, so that it faced downstream and stepped inside, using my electricity to stabilize it. I paused for a moment searching the wilderness for signs of my parents but found nothing. I was still early and they would wait for the exact moment we discussed.

I untied the small boat and let the current carry me inside the cave. The river moved quickly downstream, the frozen water from high in the mountains melting with the warmth of spring and sending the lower rivers rushing with life. I only had a moment to act.

Once inside, I turned towards the cave mouth and held the boat still with magic, in the middle of the rushing current. At the same time, I built the energy inside of me, setting my blood on fire in a hot boil of aggressive electricity.

I released the magic against the cave ceiling, careful to protect myself, and the boat that I needed to travel the remaining distance. Large boulders crashed into the riverbed, while the water fought to move through the heavy rocks and continue downstream. Not satisfied with the obstruction, I pulled from trees and nearby shrubbery building a wall that would be almost impenetrable without concerted effort. I pulled at the stone walls, crashing them to the earth and reinforcing the message that this passage was sealed. Not only did it keep my parents out, but I would soon be reminded that I could not exit this way either. I would be a true prisoner until the moment my fate was decided.

The water rushed forward from the force of the collapse, sending me forward with intensified vigor. The remainder of the current, propelled forward by the tidal wave of leftover river, rushed the little boat forward and to the cavernous docking space in minutes. I steadied the small vessel with my magic and reached for the rusted, iron ladder with the same energy I used to destroy the cave mouth.

What took hours to travel with Amory, only wasted minutes since going the opposite direction and with the intensified current. I tied the boat to the ladder, but the river already started to drain now that the source was cut off.

I scrambled over the ledge and to the surface in complete darkness. Using magic to heighten my senses, most of all my vision, I found the second iron ladder that led to the bowels of the castle. I jumped, using magic for the extra effort and held tightly to the bottom rung of the shaky ladder.

I struggled to the top. There wasn't enough magic in the world to slow my racing heart and quell the fears that the ladder would snap in half at any moment. It rocked back and forth violently with my speedy effort to get to the top. The bolts that held it precariously in place against the rock ceiling creaked in protest at my urgency.

At the top, my hands pushed against the heavy ceiling, searching for the handles Amory used to close it months before. Moving it was impossible without magic and so I pushed upwards with super strength, fueled by my ever-increasing nervous energy.

I reached back down to the ladder, pulling it magically from its place and letting it crash loudly against the cave floor, the sound echoing noisily off the walls. Now anyone with magic could easily escape or enter with or without a ladder. But, for someone trying to sneak in or out undetected and without magic, the secret passageway would now be impossible.

I stood up and closed the floor with the camouflaged stone, sealing it with more magic and putting yet another obstacle in the way of someone trying to remain discreet. My breathing became uneven and the fear settled over me, as I remembered that these precautions were not just for my parents, but to keep me inside the walled Citadel.

In the darkened corridor, I felt along the walls, trying to repress the memories of Amory that came flooding back; our escape, his secret knowledge of the castle, and his fierce determination to get me as far from here as possible. Now, not even a year later, I willingly walked the same path with the purpose to never leave these walls again.

I let magic lead the way, guiding me through the darkness and underground maze of tunnels. I felt myself incline towards the surface. The air grew less musty and suffocating. I forced myself to breathe evenly, to remain strong and I used magic to stop my hands from trembling. I was almost there, they surely felt me coming and soon it would be over. These fears would only last a few minutes more.

Finally, I found the passage that opened to the inside of the castle. I leaned back against the cool stone for a moment, feeling violently ill and losing courage. I clasped my shaking hands that even magic was useless to stabilize and pressed them against my wildly beating heart.

I thought for a moment about the first time I came here and my determination to save Lilly and how I burst through the courtroom doors. To hell with the consequences, I needed that resolve now. I needed to get Avalon out of the Citadel before my parents made other plans and Jericho descended on the castle walls.

I decided to use the same tactics now; so when I emphatically pushed through the final door that led into the internal walls of the castle, I stumbled into a stone corridor already filled with Titan Guard.

I stared at them for a moment, reminding myself that I wasn't exactly restrained in my efforts to get inside and this was what I should have anticipated. But the glaring eyes and menacing faces of thirty thick, towering Titans confused me; panic took over immediately, whispering in my ear to run, igniting my blood with the thirst of battle.

I shut the door politely behind me and cleared my throat nervously, "Um, can I talk to Lucan?"

Every instinct inside me screamed to fight, to run away or to struggle, but I repressed the magic. I searched for submissiveness, wondering if I even possessed the skill.

One of the Guards inclined his head and I followed him. The rest of the Titans closed in around me and I found myself in the middle of a wall of armed men. When they walked, their decorative swords clinked at their belts and I found the sound to be both intimidating and an inviting call to conflict.

We walked into parts of the castle that my short visit before had not revealed to me. The castle evoked medieval, with colorful tapestries hanging from cold stone walls and ancient antiques decorating the passageways. The only windows were narrow slits just below the vaulted ceilings, but even they disappeared the farther we walked into the castle.

The lead Guard opened a door and I was suddenly handled by two Titans half pushing, half dragging me into a throne room. The room was large, and exactly how I pictured King Arthur's court to look. Ample open space spanned the area between the door and three thrones almost identical to the thrones in the courtroom, only these royal seats dwarfed the room with their grander size and opulent embellishments.

They were all made out of gold, the one in the middle the largest. What I assumed to be Lucan's throne, was massive, with a tall, straight back and plush, red upholstery on the seat and back to allow for some comfort. The armrests were wide and adorned tastefully with every kind of precious stone. The top of the throne was ornately detailed with more stones and the symbol I remembered seeing on a note that Kiran had sent me once, a snake wrapped around eating its own tail, intricately interwoven with a crown and dainty lilies. I realized then that it was the Kendrick royal crest.

The same symbol repeated on the two surrounding thrones, one delicate and obviously made for a woman and the one to the right of the king's chair, sturdy but plain and simple. I imagined that was Kiran's place but wondered why it was bare and uncomplicated. Compared to the other two royal seats it looked painfully rugged and out of place.

I stood in the Guard's grasp, still and silent. They clutched my arms as if I were going to run away at any moment, and since they were only doing their job, I didn't have the heart to tell them I wasn't going anywhere.

A door behind the thrones opened and Lucan entered the room in all of his pomp and circumstance. A long crimson robe draped around his neck, flowed out from behind him as he walked and his thick golden crown sat crooked on his head as usual. An extensive entourage of Guards followed him and filled in along the walls, surrounding the throne room.

He walked around the throne and took his seat, tipping his goateed chin and eying me with practiced benevolence. The guards pushed me into a bowing position and this time they really did have to force me. I would sacrifice my life, but I was not about to bow to Lucan in a sign of respect that I didn't even pretend to possess. After a bit of a struggle, they seemed satisfied and let me stand up again.

"So you've come to bargain your brother's life? How valiant of you," Lucan spoke and the arrogance of victory quilted his tone. My magic flared with disgust causing the Guards to tighten their grips. "It's too late," he finished flatly, his gaze turned to pure hatred.

"Is he dead?" I questioned, positive that this was only part of the game.

"Not yet," Lucan laughed, the sound of evil filling the room.

"Is Kiran married?" I demanded, wondering if that would change the outcome of this bargain.

"Not yet." Lucan grew more somber, sitting forward in his chair.

"Then, it is not too late," I insisted quietly, firmly confident that I was right.

"What if I have changed my mind?" he asked, his eyes narrowing and his smile turning cruel.

"Then kill my brother and gain nothing. I will take my magic and return to what I was doing," I answered simply, severely wishing I could cross my arms; instead, I jutted my chin in defiance.

"You're here now, surrounded. How do you expect to escape?" Lucan inquired, half laughing. His eyes turned to stone with the challenge.

My anger got the best of me; I needed to get Avalon to safety, not waste time chatting with Lucan when we both knew what he wanted. I built the magic in my blood, turning it to a fast boil in moments, not even dignifying Lucan with a verbal response and drained the two Guards holding me equally as fast.

I hadn't drained someone so quickly since the night at the farm, and I was happy to know I still had it in me, at least for a little bit longer. The two Guards let go of my arms and crumpled instantly to the floor, unconscious and mortal.

"That's how," I mumbled, crossing my arms and stepping forward, away from the two victims of my magic.

"How unfortunate," Lucan looked at his Guards with the mildest appearance of disgust and then gestured to his entourage to have them removed. "It's not entirely up to me, my dear Eden. You have made more than one enemy in this castle. Get my son," he demanded and a guard disappeared into the corridor.

# Chapter Thirty-Nine

I stood in the throne room, nervously waiting for Kiran. Anxiety unexpectedly surfaced in an entirely different way than fear for my life or getting Avalon to safety in time.

If my fate truly rested in Kiran's hands, I did not know what to expect. I wanted to believe that he was pushing for this and that he would take the trade without question. I remembered the last time we met, how he kept his magic from me; the hard look in his eyes and made me wonder if he was as tired of this game as I was.

I felt completely alone in the room, unguarded and pleading my own case, and I couldn't help but regret the two Titans that were dragged from my feet. They at least put a physical barrier between the royalty and me. But no other guards attempted to grab hold of me or detain me physically and Lucan simply sat in his golden chair, staring me down with the perfect mixture of amusement and disgust.

Soon a Guard reappeared, opening the door for his Prince. Kiran walked into the room in full wedding attire. His hair was slicked back stylishly and his crisply perfect tux was double breasted with a smart tie that rose off his chest, pinned with the royal crest. He even wore white gloves.

He was not surprised to see me or at least didn't act like it, his eyes flitted over me, as if I were an irritation, before he sat down next to his father and sighed. I annoyingly felt under-dressed in my regular mission attire, a black long-sleeved shirt and gray cargo pants.

"She has come to bargain her brother's life," Lucan explained to his son. The delight on his face grew with every minute.

"And what have you decided?" Kiran asked, his turquoise eyes turning to deep blue with hardness.

"Isn't this the deal you made with her?" Lucan glowered at his son, almost as shocked by his reaction as I was.

"Yes, I suppose it is." His crisp English accent was clipped and short and I wondered for a moment if I should have made a Plan C.

"All right, Eden," Lucan looked at me, his eyes narrowing again to small slits of distrust. "You are here to offer yourself for your brother. How can I trust you?"

"I came to you. This was my decision. I will uphold my end of the bargain as long as you uphold yours," I promised, hoping to get the whole thing over with soon. "I just have one small request."

"A request?" Kiran mocked, loudly, and even his father turned in surprise. "And what would that be?"

"I want to be able to say goodbye to Avalon, and I want to walk him out; I want to make sure he reaches safety," I requested quietly and with more humility.

"I will agree to that," Lucan countered, "as long as you retain the magic. If you give Avalon back even the smallest hint of what you possess our deal is off and I will murder him on the spot. Is that understood?"

"Yes, I understand," I nodded my head, realizing I hadn't exactly thought my plan through all the way. How would I give Avalon the magic back now?

"Eden, swear it," Kiran stood up, pointing his finger angrily at me.

I paused for a moment, breathing deeply and searching for a loophole to the impossible scenario, "I swear it; I will not give anything back to Avalon."

"Not good enough," Lucan said calmly from his chair. "I want a blood oath; I want our deal signed in magic."

"Absolutely not," I argued, afraid of the very words.

"Then our deal is off," Kiran spat, angrily.

"Fine," I shook my head, frustrated and irritated with the next question I had no choice but to ask, "What exactly is a blood oath?"

"Is she serious?" Lucan asked his son and couldn't hold back his laughter any longer.

"That's not fair," I stomped my foot, "I was raised-"

"Human," Lucan and Kiran growled together, in obvious vexation.

"A blood oath," Lucan continued, "is a contract written for us and signed with our blood. It is magically binding and if either end is broken, the law-breaker dies. It's very simple, but binding and I have found it to be the most effective way to assure trust between two sides." He grimaced at me with the cruelest of expressions, but I had already agreed. There was no turning back now. "Send for the Witch," Lucan ordered and another Guard disappeared into the hallway.

When the door opened a few minutes later, a handsome but expressionless middle-eastern man, wearing a turban and long ivory robes walked through the door. He carried parchment paper and a long, feathered quill. He stared at me with dead eyes and unmoving lips; his presence disturbed me in a way I could not explain.

A Guard brought a small, wooden, writing table and a stool for him to sit on into the middle of the room. He unrolled his parchment, and tilted his feathered quill that needed no ink and waited patiently for instructions on what to write.

"Write this," Lucan instructed but then looked to me, "What is your full name?"

"Eden Diana Matthews," I replied solemnly, feeling as though I were handing over more than my freedom.

"Diana? After your grandmother, how sweet," Lucan mocked, although that was information that I did not know. I wondered for a moment if they named me after my maternal or paternal grandmother. "And don't put Matthews, that's not her real last name. Eden Diana St. Andrews is bound to the Crown Prince with full possession of her magical powers. If she releases her magic to anyone magical or not, in even the most miniscule of ways that will be considered a breach of contract. Likewise, the King, Lucan Henry Sevim Kendrick is bound to the contract,"

"And Kiran," I interrupted, finding it necessary to include him.

"Fine," Lucan conceded easily, "Likewise, the King, Lucan Henry Sevim Kendrick and his son, the Crown Prince, Kiran Cedric Dupont Kendrick are bound to the contract in that if they harm or prevent the girl's brother in any way from successfully reaching safety today, May first, that will be considered a breach of contract. Consequences are as follows: death to either side of the contracted if said stipulations are broken."

Lucan finished abruptly, holding his hand out to the Witch with an exasperated sigh. The scribe stood and handed the parchment to him carefully. He read it over finding the simplicity of the arrangement agreeable.

"Are you satisfied with our terms?" Lucan asked, as if I had a choice.

The careful wording was not lost on me, not on Lucan's part, although I was hardly naive to his conscientious dictation, and that Avalon's safety was only to be honored today. The exact phrasing of the contract also worked in my favor. If Avalon wanted his magic back I wouldn't be the one to give it to him. If there were any way for him to get it back, he would have to do what all of the others did and take it from me himself.

The Witch took the parchment back to the writing table and

produced a knife from underneath his robes. The eight-inch, crescent-shaped blade glinted in the light, shining dangerously in the dim lighting of the room. The ivory hilt of the knife carefully carved with the royal crest would not be considered beautiful. Its sinister blade sharpened in Immortal blood was used with greedy intent.

Lucan walked forward, a sign of good faith, and held his hand open over the paper. The scribe slid the knife across his palm and his blood dripped instantly from his hand across the words of our contract.

Kiran was next, walking forward and removing one of his gloves, tucking it firmly under his arm. He pulled back his sleeve, to prevent ruining his tuxedo, and held open his palm. The Witch used the same swift movement against Kiran's hand and his crimson blood mixed with Lucan's on the contract.

I took a short breath and moved forward, feigning courage, but out of options. I held open my palm, using magic to steady it over the paper and fought against flinching from the size of the blade. The Witch moved quickly against my skin, and I barely felt the incision of the sharp knife.

Hot blood flowed from my hand, mixing together with the other on the paper. When I looked down to make sure my blood found its target on the contract, I was mesmerized to see that when all three bloods joined they disappeared along with the ink into the paper itself and all that was left was blank parchment that held my life in its balance.

I wanted to comment on the mystery, but I felt that too much awe would be a sign of weakness. So instead, I healed my hand with magic and pretended to be unimpressed.

"It would appear we have a deal," Lucan stood up with his son and put a strong hand on his shoulder, "I will leave it up to you then, will she be your bride or your sacrifice?"

I pleaded silently with Kiran, willing him to pick sacrifice. In that moment, I knew that if I died Avalon would not get his magic back, but selfishly, and momentarily, I hoped that the misery of my choice would end in the quick events of death, instead of the endless suffering that would accompany the role of Queen.

He stared at me, his hard blue eyes searching mine, his expression ominous and unreadable.

"She will be my bride," he decided quietly and then tore his eyes from mine. He clenched his jaw and his hands balled into fists, tugging at his black jacket impatiently.

"Fine," Lucan agreed, almost disappointed. "Then we have work to do;" he turned to his Guards, "find her something suitable to wear."

"No, not today," Kiran turned to his father, almost begging him to agree. "This is Seraphina's day; please do not humiliate her by replacing her with another. Send the guests away quietly, and in a few months we can arrange a simple ceremony."

"Absolutely not," Lucan snapped with rage, "royal weddings are only held on this day alone, if you are not wed today, then you will have to wait an entire year and I cannot trust her to comply."

"Father, it is only a year then," Kiran appealed, reasonably. "She is here now, we have her magic, her brother possesses none of it and if we have to, we can keep her in the dungeons until that day. Think with reason, there is a blood oath. And what of Seraphina's father? He will be upset again and you cannot afford the complete loss of his allegiance. You have won; let us not be hasty and cause the Kingdom reason for animosity."

Lucan sat silently brooding for several minutes before conceding, "Fine." He breathed deeply, struggling for restraint. "She is your prisoner, keep her wherever you want. But be reminded, young Prince, that she is the key to your magic, I am not the one that needs her in order to survive."

And with that, Lucan left the room in a swirl, of stolen, arrogant magic. It was not until he was gone that I realized how suffocating his aura was; aggressive energy that attacked almost every other magic in the room filled him.

Only Kiran, the Guard and I remained. I did not move or utter a sound. Kiran ran his hands through his hair as if he didn't know what to do now. He glanced at me for a brief moment and I didn't know what I expected, but contempt and irritation was not it.

I was about to demand to be taken to my brother when the door behind the thrones blasted open and folds of white silk came crashing through. Immediately I recognized Seraphina's beautiful face contorted with rage, blonde hair flowing elegantly behind her, underneath a delicate lace veil. I was suddenly thrown backwards into the stone wall, hitting my head and sliding to the ground in misery.

## Chapter Forty

I felt the sticky, hot blood run down my neck and I struggled to my feet. I didn't know what to do, I didn't know if the Guards would attack me should I fight back, or if Kiran would intervene and remove the jilted bride from the room. I didn't have time to think it over before she lifted me off the ground again, dropping me violently onto the stone floor. This time I smashed my face against the cold stone, breaking my nose and scraping my forehead painfully.

I was instantly to my feet, holding my nose and trying to stop the gushing blood. "Damn it, Seraphina!" I yelled, spraying and spitting the crimson blood that dripped into my mouth like a faucet. I picked her up with my own magic, furious and ready for revenge. She screamed at me with words I couldn't even understand, accusations that I probably deserved and eyes that would kill me if they could.

Even in the air, her magic was a savage force that I could not control. All I wanted to do was hold her away from me and keep her from smashing my head against something else. Even with my magic holding her aloft she still managed to shove me ferociously against the wall, my feet sliding across the floor as if they would slow me down. I hit the stone wall hard, losing my breath and my concentration and dropping her to the floor.

She landed on her feet, taking the length of the room in a second and lifting me off the ground with her hands tightly wrapped around my neck. I struggled for breath and clawed at her clenched fingers. I started to panic as her hands pressed together, threatening to snap my neck in two.

In a moment of pure self-defense, I lashed out with my magic, sending her across the room and away from my delicate throat. I caught her, generously, before she hit anything substantial and held her in the air again, this time creating more of a magical force field than I had the first time.

I felt some pity for her, since I stole her day and her crown.... again. But, most of all I hated the thought of ruining her gorgeous gown. As much as I despised Seraphina and as frustrated as I was that this was the second time she was trying to kill me, I had to admit that she really did have impeccable taste.

"Eden, put her down!" Kiran shouted at me, and when I moved to fulfill the request, he held up his hand and yelled louder, "Gently!"

I obeyed, regretfully. I could not risk losing the chance to see Avalon and for the moment, if that meant a marriage to Kiran was the ultimate revenge for a concussion and broken nose, I would swallow the disgust and behave.

I sent magic to the back of my head and then to my nose, repairing the damage. Kiran pulled Seraphina aside and talked to her quietly in soothing, careful tones. Even as angry as she was, she was stunning. With a train at least ten yards long, her silk gown flowed around her as if she were coated in liquid. Her waist was cinched impossibly small and her bust the perfection of bridal elegance. Her face was flawless; even scrunched in rage and animosity she was still the most beautiful girl I had ever seen.

"Clean her up and take her to her brother," Kiran snapped, turning on his Guard with frustration. "Wait for me to move them."

The Guards walked me into the hallway and down a long corridor. Someone jogged up from behind after a minute and handed me a wet towel that I used to wipe at my face and neck. I followed the Guards up a staircase, wrapping around one of the castle towers.

At the top of the tower stood a heavy, wooden door that led into an almost empty room, with only a bed off to one side. Avalon sat on the bed, moving his foot idly across the floor in silent meditation. He looked up reluctantly at the opening of the door, obviously waiting to be taken to his death.

When I walked into the room, something like hope vanished from his expression. Our eyes met and it was as if they murdered me in front of him. His shoulders sagged and his face became a canvas of despair.

"Eden, what are you doing here?" he groaned, standing up, alarmed by my presence.

"I had to.... I couldn't let them...." And then I burst into tears, breaking through the Guards and running to him. I sobbed against his chest, knowing this was goodbye and not knowing how to explain to him how to get his magic back without voicing it in front of the Guards.

"You shouldn't have come, you shouldn't have done this," he whispered, crying unashamed tears and holding me close to him.

"It's time for him to go," Kiran's crisp voice, ordered from the doorway.

I pulled away from Avalon, nodding my consent and then slipped my hand into his and pulled him along with me. He was reluctant to go, he stood firm, refusing to let me sacrifice myself.

"No, you will have to kill me instead." His eyes searched mine for understanding and silently accused me of betraying him.

"You don't mean anything to us," Kiran snarled, gesturing at the Guards to use force.

"Please, Avalon, please go," I begged, trying to convey through furtive, emotional glances that I had a plan.

Still he refused until the Guards surrounded us, pushing us through the door and down the staircase. Eventually, Avalon moved on his own, holding my hand in his and whispering his disapproval whenever he had the chance.

Kiran walked in front of us, leading the way through the castle that had grown deathly quiet and through the seemingly empty Citadel. The courtyard in front of the castle was set up for a wedding. Decorated chairs sat in neat rows, separated by a long aisle and extravagant floral arrangements hung from posts and adorned every open space. A stage was set up to the side of the venue for a band, stringed instruments abandoned, music scattering across the cobblestone plaza with the movement of the soft wind.

My hand began to tremble inside Avalon's and I was fighting a fear that threatened to overcome me. I couldn't be without him; I didn't want to let him go again, even to safety.

There were times in the past when I felt lonely, when my task, my position, even fate asked me to stand apart from everyone else. But, on the other side of the gates I would say goodbye to Avalon and then truly be alone for the rest of my life. I would be isolated from everyone I loved indefinitely and depending on Kiran's whims or wishes, I could be separated from even those that I hated, too, which, unless I figured out a way to explain to Avalon how to get his magic back, might be for the rest of eternity.

A Titan opened the wide, heavy gate to the outside and I turned to Avalon to say goodbye. I wrapped my arms around his neck and felt the Immortal presence over the hill, watching us silently. By now, my parents had reached Jericho, by now they stood waiting for whatever outcome I decided for them.

I hugged Avalon, knowing I wasn't just saying goodbye to him, I was saying goodbye to whatever happiness, whatever life I had imagined, and whatever hope remained on the outside of these walls.

"I love you," Avalon whispered fiercely in my ear.

"I love you too," I whispered back, not willing ever to let go of him. "Jericho is waiting for you, just over the hill."

A Guard started to pull Avalon away, to force him through the gate and I clung to him as if he were my last lifeline.

"Eden, it's time," Kiran reprimanded callously, reminding me that I was a prisoner now, devoid of any will.

"Avalon," I said louder, grasping at a way to convey instructions to him. "Find your first team, find them immediately and they will tell you what to do!"

He stared after me in confusion, but the Guard kept pushing him out of the city. He eventually turned around and walked forward, taking deliberate but painful steps away from me.

Jericho appeared then, on the hillside, a lone figure against the backdrop of the Romanian mountains. He stared at me with an intensity that was more than human, watching me as if I had betrayed even him. He looked to Avalon and the look in his eyes was a struggle against understanding. He loved Avalon like a brother, but my choice was so obviously incomprehensible to him that it felt like treason.

It was better this way, better that Jericho looked at me as if I betrayed him, as if I abandoned him for selfish gain. His life would be better if he could move on, if he could think of me as a traitor and enemy.

I looked at him for a moment longer, meeting his eyes and saying my own eternal goodbye. I sent a thousand, silent thoughts to him, reminding him that I loved him, and that only hours ago I dreamed of a time when we would wake up next to each other every day for the rest of our lives. He couldn't hear my thoughts, or read my mind, but the desperate look in his eyes turned from confusion to acceptance and I decided I could live with acceptance.

A Guard tapped me on the shoulder and I reluctantly turned around and let the Citadel gates close behind me. My heart jumped with the finalized click of the lock and I breathed in the painful loneliness of captivity.

I followed Kiran back into the castle. He didn't verbalize instructions, but I didn't need any. I was his prisoner, his father made that clear and I would obey completely until Avalon had his magic back and then I would willingly let them kill me.

Kiran took the stairs up a different castle tower. This one was larger, with different levels of what seemed to be residences. In the middle of the turret, was a single door that opened into his room. He held the door for me, allowing me to walk through first.

"Thank you, I won't be needing you any longer," Kiran addressed his Guards before closing the door behind him.

It was the first time we were completely alone today and it felt strange and threatening. Our magics stayed respectively far away from each other; there was no more attraction between them, no more feral desire to find each other.

"You are to stay here, with me," Kiran instructed, his words harshly reserved. "My father insists that you are my prisoner and therefore my responsibility."

"What are you going to do with me?" I asked with a small voice, suddenly afraid of what his words meant.

"I'm not going to rape and pillage you if that's what you're worried about," he mumbled, tugging at his bow tie and the buttons of his high tuxedo collar.

"I wasn't worried, I-" I started, but he cut me off.

"Eden, this is nothing more than a business transaction. You get to save your precious family and I get to have access to your magic. Whatever happened.... before.... whatever there was between us is over," his steely eyes held my gaze and I felt the sincerity of his words. "Obviously, we have both moved on and you would be a fool to assume otherwise. Now, I have business to attend to elsewhere, there will be Guards posted outside the door so please do not try anything ridiculous."

"No, I wouldn't.... I gave you my word," I gushed, finding some relief in his words.

He looked at me one more time and the expression on his face was indecipherable, except that whatever it meant was hard and full of hatred. I gulped silently and then bravely turned away towards the picture windows that took up most of one wall. I heard the door close behind him and then I couldn't take it anymore.

I fell to the stone floor in a mess of emotions, covering my face with my hands and trying my hardest to sob quietly. I cried for what felt like hours, until the sun dipped beyond the horizon and the room grew dark and cold. Then I slipped into a dreamless sleep, exhausted from the events of the day and the oppressive loneliness that would, from here on out, be my constant companion.

## Chapter Forty-One

I awoke well into the night. Something was nagging at me, an irritation that pulled at my senses and shook my blood roughly. I sat up in the darkness, flaring my magic and finding myself defensive.

It took a moment for my eyes to adjust. I rubbed at them, feeling as though I could have slept for days straight. I stood up, and found a comfortable chair near the window.

I sat down in it and let my eyes focus on the darkness. The clear, unclouded moonlight flooded the room with soft light through the large picture windows and when my eyes decided to obey I could see the room clearly.

Kiran's bedroom was more modern than the rest of the castle. His windows, glassed instead of open, faced the back of the castle, towards the Carpathian Mountains and the unending Romanian wilderness.

He had all of the gadgets one would never expect to find in a medieval castle, like a huge flat-screen TV, gaming systems and computer. His bathroom was ginormous, housing a massive stone-walled shower, an equally large ivory bathtub and a double set of sinks.

I realized then, that his room was also set up for the honeymoon night. Fresh arrangements of flowers filled the room with fragrant smells; a bottle of champagne grew warm in a bucket of water, that at one time was ice. Two silken bathrobes hung from the bathroom door, one charcoal gray, the other a soft pink.

"Oops," I mumbled aloud.

Kiran's bed was empty. Whatever business he needed to attend to was apparently lengthy. Or he just didn't want to be around me, which I was perfectly Ok with.

Suddenly my magic flared again, defensive and angry. I sat up straighter, trying to find the source of alarm, but the room remained still. Something tugged at the back of my neck. It was more a feeling than anything physical, but the irritation was there all the same.

I stood up and paced the length of the room, trying to find the source of the pain. When my magic flared for a third time and nothing in the room moved out of place, the thought dawned on me that Avalon was trying to get his magic back.

I sat back down on the edge of Kiran's bed and tried to relax. I couldn't physically give Avalon anything, the blood oath prevented me from helping at all and I could feel my promise with every attempt Avalon made.

My magic, pulsing defensively inside my blood refused by oath to be taken away. I reminded myself that if Avalon was capable of taking my magic that I was helpless to stop him. I worked to relax, worked to calm my frantic nerves and fighting magic.

I was on edge; everything about me was desperately working to keep what was mine. I leaned over, pulling my knees to my chest and rested my head on one of Kiran's pillows. I closed my eyes and focused on falling asleep instead of holding on to my magic.

Avalon pulled again, from an unknown distance and a small, almost unnoticeable amount of magic disappeared from my blood. I could not even fathom how hard Avalon was working to get even the most miniscule amount and claim it as his. He couldn't touch me, he didn't even know exactly where I was or what I was doing, and now with the oath, there was an extra set of protection.

I could not help Avalon, but I did not have to stop him either.

He worked further into the night, occasionally a little more would disappear from my blood and then my magic would struggle that much more to keep the rest. But, with every small amount Avalon claimed, the next amount would be just a tiny bit bigger.

Beads of sweat poured from my forehead, soaking Kiran's pillow and reminding me how difficult it was to do nothing. My shoulders shook with the concentrated effort for stillness and my neck ached from straining.

At some point, late into the night I started to feel Avalon again, I felt our connection and the bond that flowed between us as twins. Part of me was happy just for that, for the feeling that I wasn't completely isolated and that I could communicate with the outside. Part of me wanted to argue he had taken enough, that once the magic was divided; there was no need to drain the rest of me. Part of me argued that if I had magic, I could find a way to kill Lucan.

But the other side of me demanded reason, demanded that all of the magic be taken completely for the sake of my people and the downfall of the Monarchy. The wiser side of me argued that even half of my magic would be enough to give Kiran true Immortality and it would never be enough to destroy Lucan. And both of those scenarios were unacceptable. Either, Avalon would kill him alone, or together we would face him and together we would destroy him, but Kiran would have no share in our magic.

Eventually, through the darkest hours of the night, Avalon reached the halfway point of our transaction. I was a weak shell of buzzing energy and wavered near the brink of unconsciousness with the strained effort relaxing my magic took on my body.

*Eden?* Avalon spoke through our shared connection and his voice was soothing to my system.

*Avalon.* I sighed, whispering his name, even inside of my head.

*You should have let me die.* He accused, and I had to laugh at him.

*Never.* I breathed slowly, fighting now to stay awake. *You are the better leader; the Resistance needs you, not me. Have you met our parents yet?*

*Yes.* He mumbled shyly, trying to hide the joy at his reunion with them. I knew that he felt it was unfair, but all I could do was sigh with joy at the completeness of my family.

*Avalon, you have to take it all. Just like I did for you, now it's your turn to take all of mine.* I ordered, finding the urgency of the moment.

*I can't.* He argued. *I can't leave you like that.*

*What? I'll be fine.* I said confidently, knowing I would welcome death with open arms. *I've lived without magic before. Besides you will come for me. Just like I came for you, only you will do a better job.*

*Will he take care of you?* Avalon asked, and I knew that he was talking about Kiran.

*Did he take care of you like he promised?* I asked, deflecting the question.

*Yes, he did.* Avalon admitted seriously.

*Then, you have nothing to worry about, do you?* I lied, and I knew Avalon could tell that I lied but there was an unmistakable hope in his spirit that Kiran would protect me. I wished desperately that I shared it.

*I love you, Ede, I will come for you soon.* He promised and I held his words in the depths of my soul as if they were a sweet memory I would carry into eternity with me.

*I love you, too.* I whispered and then he pulled at the magic again.

This time I did not have to fight my own magic for him to take it, it flowed out of me with ease and openness. Avalon was the one that controlled the magic now; it belonged to him.

At the end of it, when there was nothing left I was surprised to be still breathing. Before I knew about magic, I believed I lived without it, but it had always been there, circulating in my blood, but imprisoned and repressed like I was tonight. Now there was nothing, no energy, no electrical charge to my blood. I was completely mortal and utterly exhausted.

The early morning light began to fill the room with rays of gentle sun. I made it through the night, Avalon successfully saved our magic. He was safe for now. My parents were safe. Jericho, Lilly, Aunt Syl and all the others that I fell in love with over the last couple months were safe for now.

They wouldn't always be. I trusted that they would continue to wage this war with better leadership and more victories. But, for tonight they were safe and they were together. My fight was paused, but, from my actions a stronger battle could be waged. And I could finally slip into the deep abyss of uninterrupted sleep.

The door opened and Kiran walked in. I stayed awake for just a moment longer to acknowledge his presence. He stood, unmoving, in the doorframe watching me and I wondered if I would have to wait for death much longer.

"Eden, what have you done?" he gasped, moving towards me in anger.

But I was already slipping away, into the black unconsciousness that promised respite from this world. I breathed evenly, trusting that when I woke up judgment would be decided and a verdict passed and I could finally say my fearless goodbye to this never-ending struggle.

List of Resistance Teams
* Denotes the Team Leader

**Brazil Team (Also known as the Rescued Team)**

Ebanks Camera
Oscar Rodriguez
Ronan Hannigan
Jett Fisher

**Omaha Team**

*Avalon St. Andrews
Jericho Bentley
Titus Kelly
Xander Akin
Xavier Akin

**Czech Republic Team**

*Ryder Thompson
Fiona Thompson
Roxie Powers
Baxter Smith
Felipe Gonzalas
Trenton Chase

**Australia Team**

*Hamant Kumar
Christi Rogobete
Priya Fahir
Eshe Iyare
An Tang

**Swiss Team**

*Alina Pascut
Alexandre Ballamont

Hale Oliver
Ben Hamilton
Evie Santoz

**Morocco Team**

*Caden Halstead
Bex Costello
Kya Hasting
Lucy Barello

**India Team**

*Te Che
Pan Che
Grace Lewis
Naima Desai
Sunny Magar

**South Africa Team**

*Abraham Patel
Henrik Van de Merwe
Jess Zuma
Mamello Mensah
Mandisa Mensah
Lenka Bello

# Acknowledgements

I am so grateful to get to write an acknowledgement section that I just might start back as far as I can remember and start thanking everyone I've ever met! Ok, maybe I won't. But there are so many people that have helped bring me to where I am today that I should probably start naming them!

First of all, this gift of writing that sometimes feels more like a miracle at the end of the day came from God alone and to Him I give the glory. He has had a plan since the beginning and I am so blessed to be invited along on this wild ride.

Thanks to my loving family, who have put up with my sleepless nights, and all of my "Not right nows…" and "In a little bits…." You've put up with a dirty house, dirty laundry and let's face it a dirty mommy, but you have supported me through it all and I thank you for that.

Thanks to my parents, who promised me from childhood I could do and be anything that I wanted. To my dad, who although might be disappointed I'm not a missionary in the jungles of Africa, would be proud to know I followed my dream. And to my mom who has spent endless hours babysitting, encouraging me, spreading the word about my books and even done my dishes and laundry a few times! Thank you for your support.

Thanks to Kylee who sat by me for hours and hours while I bounced ideas and thoughts off her. To Pat who let us exchange yard work for cover art. And to Carolynn for going through the first, very, very rough versions and donating her editing eye.

Thanks to Jenn Nunez who took me under her wing and walked me through this whole crazy process step by step, holding my hand and answering all of my millions and millions of questions!!

Finally, thanks to my amazing husband, Zach. Without him, I would never have taken the plunge and published, or continued to publish, or maybe even continued to write. He has been a constant source of encouragement, always helping me be better and pushing me to do more. Love you Zachary.

# About the Author

Rachel Higginson was born and raised in Nebraska, but spent her college years traveling the world. She married her high school sweetheart and spends her days raising their growing family. She is obsessed with bad reality TV and any and all Young Adult Fiction.

Fearless Magic is the third book in The Star-Crossed Series.

Look for the Relentless Warrior, the sixth book in The Star-Crossed Series, coming early 2013

Other books coming in 2013 are Sunburst, the second book in the Starbright Series and The Rush, a new and more contemporary series.

Other Books by Rachel Higginson:
Reckless Magic (The Star-Crossed Series, Book 1)
Hopeless Magic (The Star-Crossed Series, Book 2)
Endless Magic (The Star-Crossed Series, Book 4)
The Relentless Warrior (The Star-Crossed Series, Book 5)
Starbright (The Starbright Series, Book 1)

Follow Rachel on her blog at:
www.rachelhigginson.blogspot.com

Or on Twitter:
@mywritesdntbite

Or on her Facebook pages:
Rachel Higginson
Or
Reckless Magic